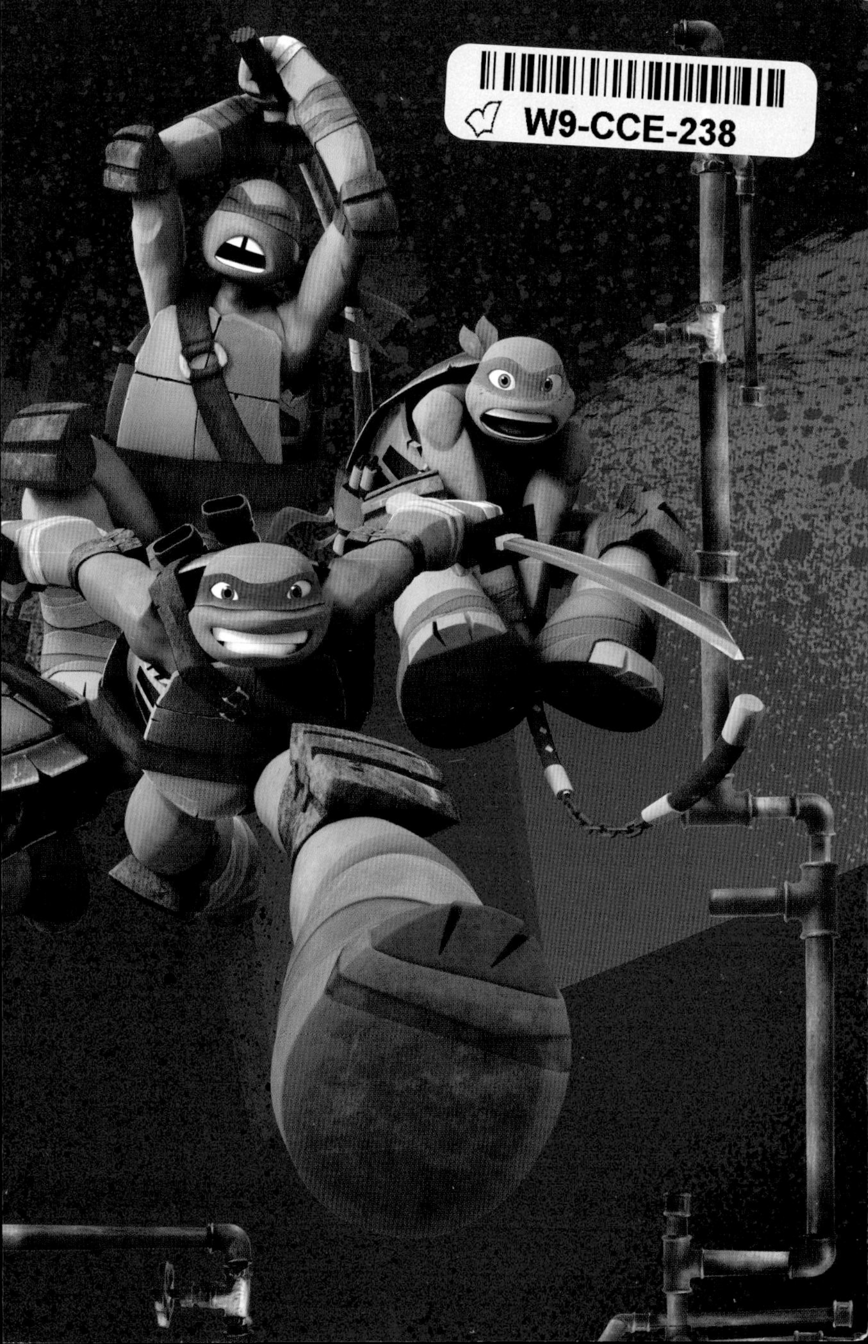

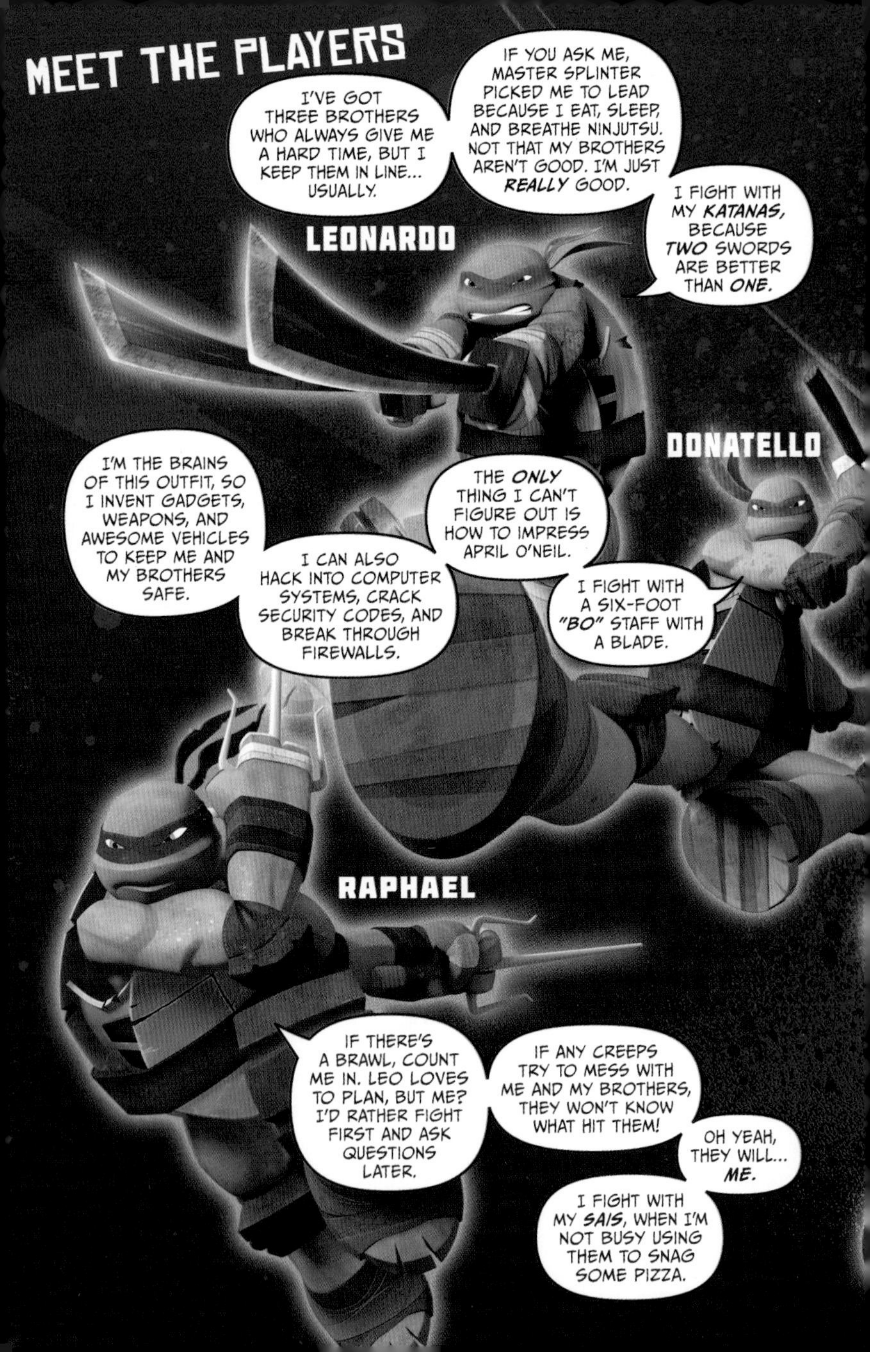
MEET THE PLAYERS
LEONARDO
I'VE GOT THREE BROTHERS WHO ALWAYS GIVE ME A HARD TIME, BUT I KEEP THEM IN LINE... USUALLY.
IF YOU ASK ME, MASTER SPLINTER PICKED ME TO LEAD BECAUSE I EAT, SLEEP, AND BREATHE NINJUTSU. NOT THAT MY BROTHERS AREN'T GOOD. I'M JUST *REALLY* GOOD.
I FIGHT WITH MY *KATANAS,* BECAUSE *TWO* SWORDS ARE BETTER THAN *ONE.*
DONATELLO
I'M THE BRAINS OF THIS OUTFIT, SO I INVENT GADGETS, WEAPONS, AND AWESOME VEHICLES TO KEEP ME AND MY BROTHERS SAFE.
I CAN ALSO HACK INTO COMPUTER SYSTEMS, CRACK SECURITY CODES, AND BREAK THROUGH FIREWALLS.
THE *ONLY* THING I CAN'T FIGURE OUT IS HOW TO IMPRESS APRIL O'NEIL.
I FIGHT WITH A SIX-FOOT *"BO"* STAFF WITH A BLADE.
RAPHAEL
IF THERE'S A BRAWL, COUNT ME IN. LEO LOVES TO PLAN, BUT ME? I'D RATHER FIGHT FIRST AND ASK QUESTIONS LATER.
IF ANY CREEPS TRY TO MESS WITH ME AND MY BROTHERS, THEY WON'T KNOW WHAT HIT THEM!
OH YEAH, THEY WILL... *ME.*
I FIGHT WITH MY *SAIS,* WHEN I'M NOT BUSY USING THEM TO SNAG SOME PIZZA.

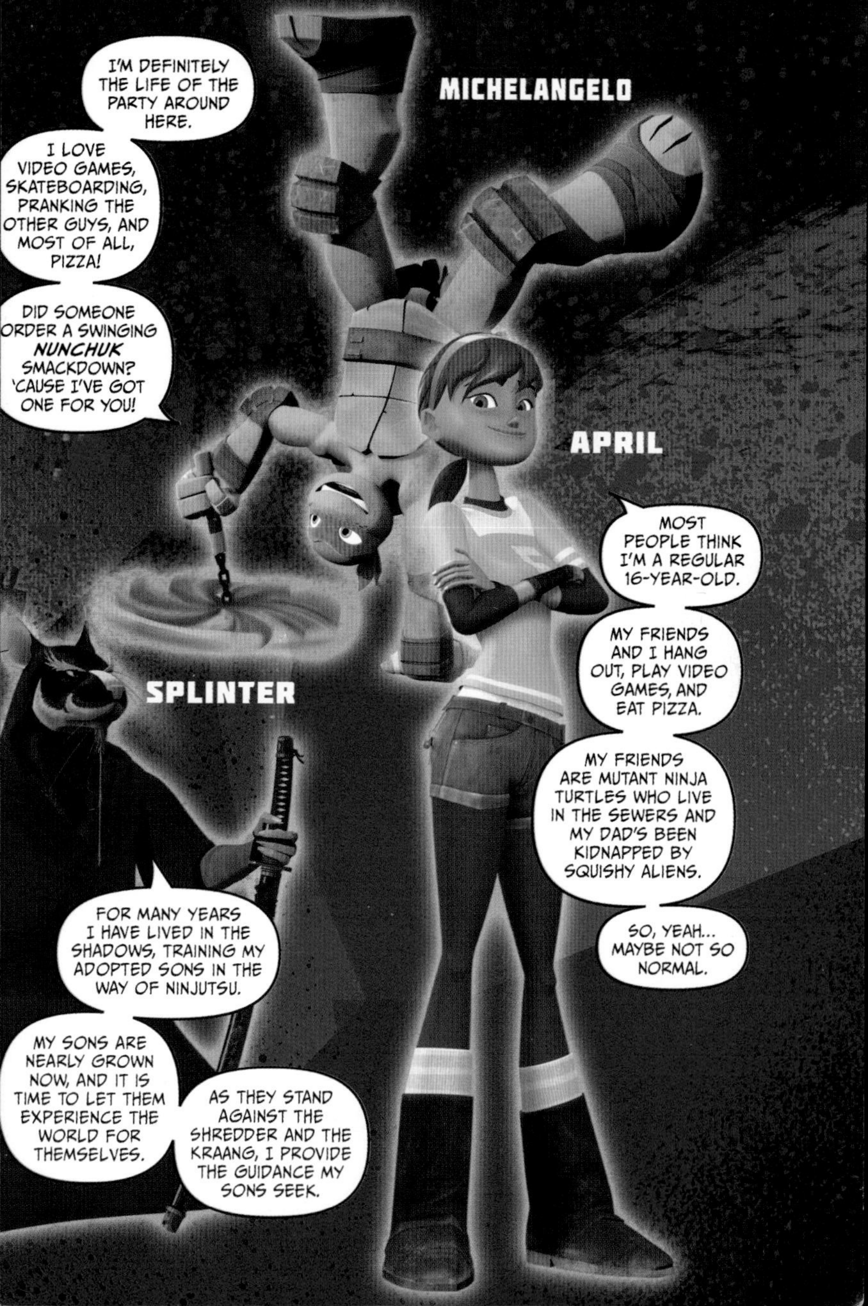
MICHELANGELO
I'M DEFINITELY THE LIFE OF THE PARTY AROUND HERE.
I LOVE VIDEO GAMES, SKATEBOARDING, PRANKING THE OTHER GUYS, AND MOST OF ALL, PIZZA!
DID SOMEONE ORDER A SWINGING NUNCHUK SMACKDOWN? 'CAUSE I'VE GOT ONE FOR YOU!
APRIL
MOST PEOPLE THINK I'M A REGULAR 16-YEAR-OLD.
MY FRIENDS AND I HANG OUT, PLAY VIDEO GAMES, AND EAT PIZZA.
MY FRIENDS ARE MUTANT NINJA TURTLES WHO LIVE IN THE SEWERS AND MY DAD'S BEEN KIDNAPPED BY SQUISHY ALIENS.
SO, YEAH... MAYBE NOT SO NORMAL.
SPLINTER
FOR MANY YEARS I HAVE LIVED IN THE SHADOWS, TRAINING MY ADOPTED SONS IN THE WAY OF NINJUTSU.
MY SONS ARE NEARLY GROWN NOW, AND IT IS TIME TO LET THEM EXPERIENCE THE WORLD FOR THEMSELVES.
AS THEY STAND AGAINST THE SHREDDER AND THE KRAANG, I PROVIDE THE GUIDANCE MY SONS SEEK.

THE KRAANG

The Kraang could not be reached for comment. So far, all that's known of their background is that they are a race of multi-tentacled brain-like creatures, who are very far from home and up to no good. After recent events, they are determined to destroy the ones known as the Turtles.

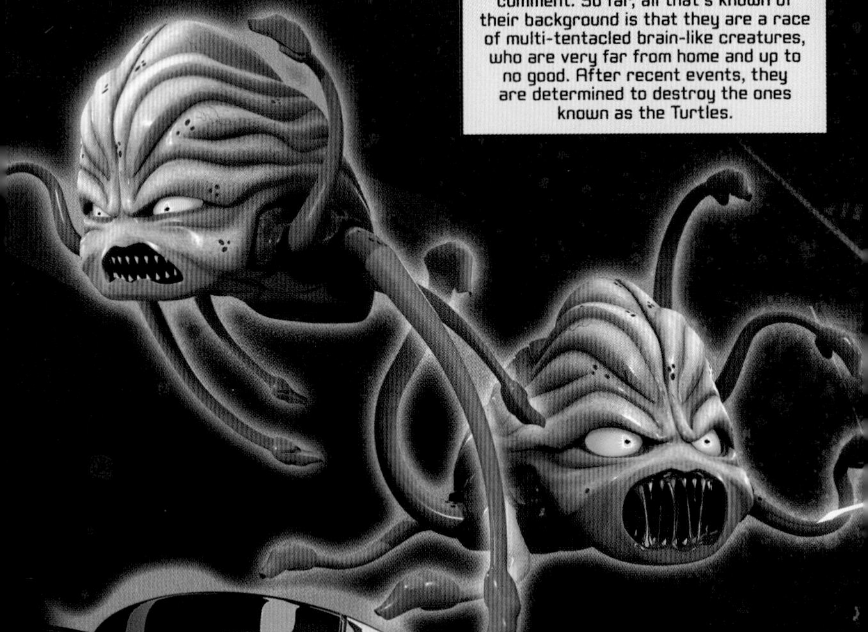

MUTAGEN MAN

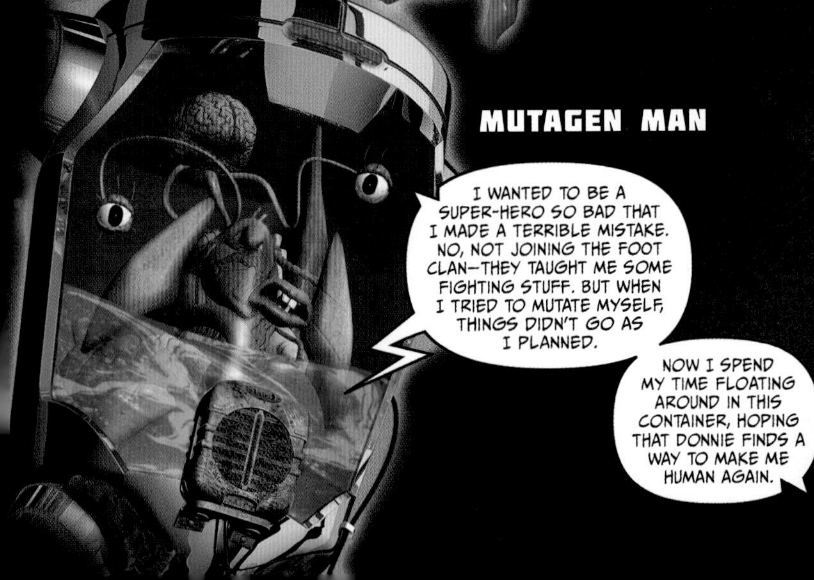
I WANTED TO BE A SUPER-HERO SO BAD THAT I MADE A TERRIBLE MISTAKE. NO, NOT JOINING THE FOOT CLAN—THEY TAUGHT ME SOME FIGHTING STUFF. BUT WHEN I TRIED TO MUTATE MYSELF, THINGS DIDN'T GO AS I PLANNED.
NOW I SPEND MY TIME FLOATING AROUND IN THIS CONTAINER, HOPING THAT DONNIE FINDS A WAY TO MAKE ME HUMAN AGAIN.

SHREDDER
CALL ME MASTER SHREDDER. I HAVE TRAINED IN THE WAYS OF NINJUTSU MY ENTIRE LIFE AND I'VE SHARPENED MY SKILLS TO THE HIGHEST LEVEL.
I'VE COME TO NEW YORK CITY SEEKING REVENGE ON MY OLD ENEMY, HAMATO YOSHI.
I WILL STOP AT NOTHING TO CAPTURE HIM AND HIS NINJA TURTLES!
KARAI
THE MASTER IS HARD TO PLEASE, EVEN WHEN YOU'RE HIS DAUGHTER. BUT WITHOUT ME, HE WOULDN'T HAVE KNOWN ABOUT THE KRAANG.
SO HE CAN THANK ME LATER—AFTER I HELP HIM WIPE OUT THE TURTLES!

THE MUTATION SITUATION

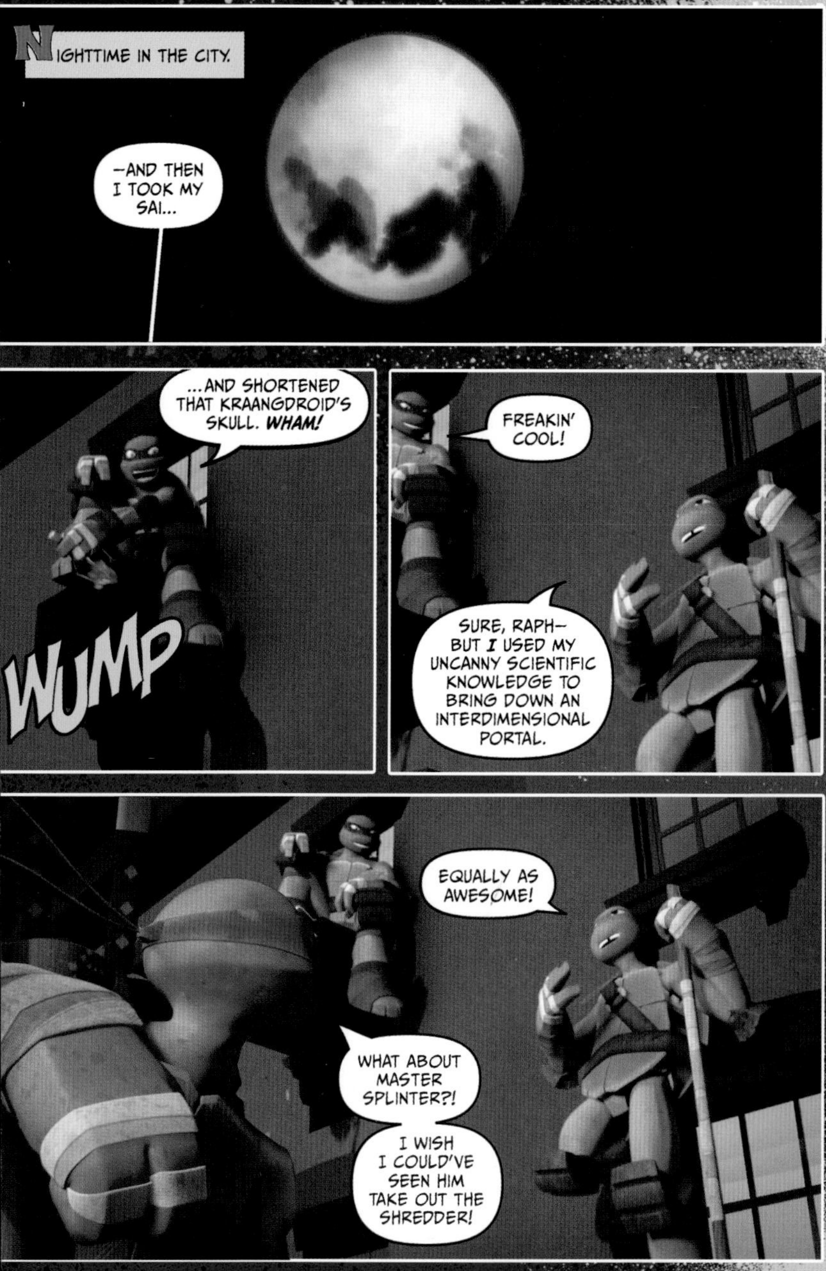
NIGHTTIME IN THE CITY.
—AND THEN I TOOK MY SAI...
...AND SHORTENED THAT KRAANGDROID'S SKULL. *WHAM!*
WUMP
FREAKIN' COOL!
SURE, RAPH— BUT *I* USED MY UNCANNY SCIENTIFIC KNOWLEDGE TO BRING DOWN AN INTERDIMENSIONAL PORTAL.
EQUALLY AS AWESOME!
WHAT ABOUT MASTER SPLINTER?!
I WISH I COULD'VE SEEN HIM TAKE OUT THE SHREDDER!

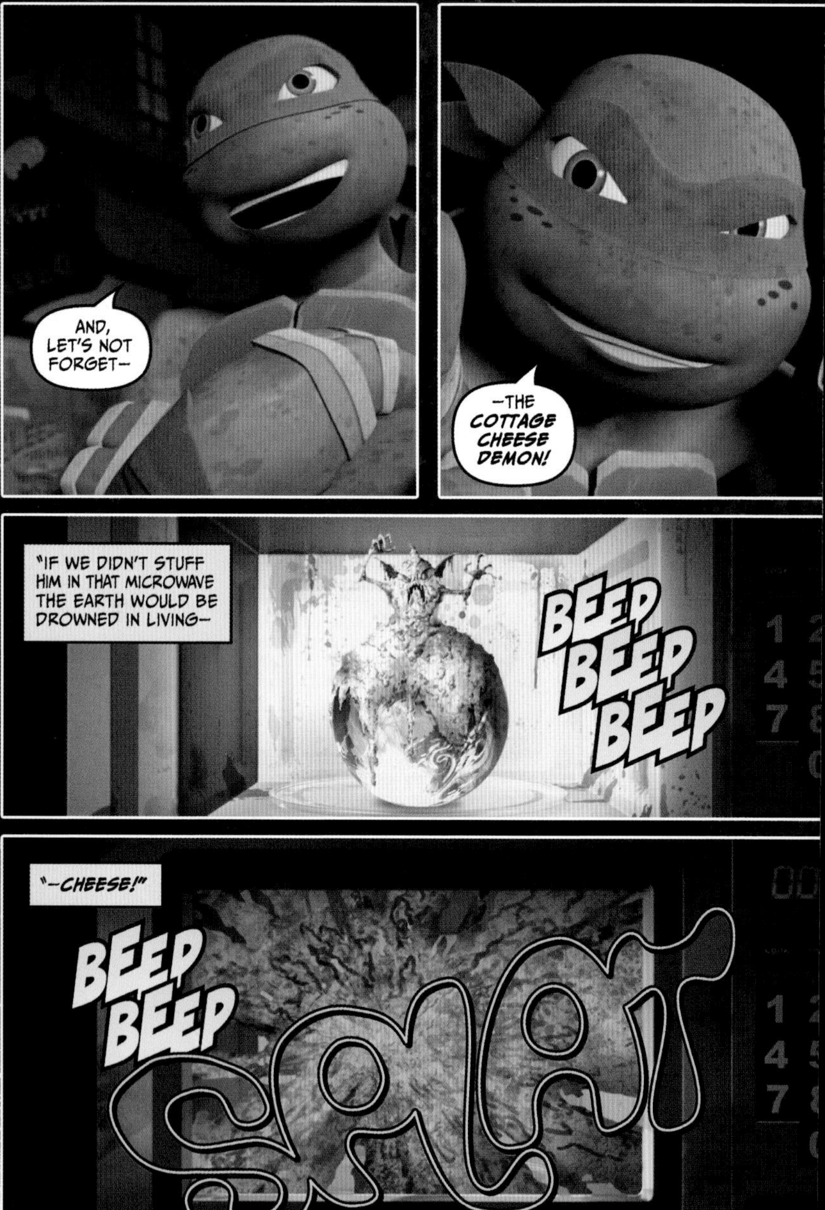
AND, LET'S NOT FORGET—
—THE COTTAGE CHEESE DEMON!
"IF WE DIDN'T STUFF HIM IN THAT MICROWAVE THE EARTH WOULD BE DROWNED IN LIVING—
BEEP BEEP BEEP
"—CHEESE!"
BEEP BEEP
SPLAT

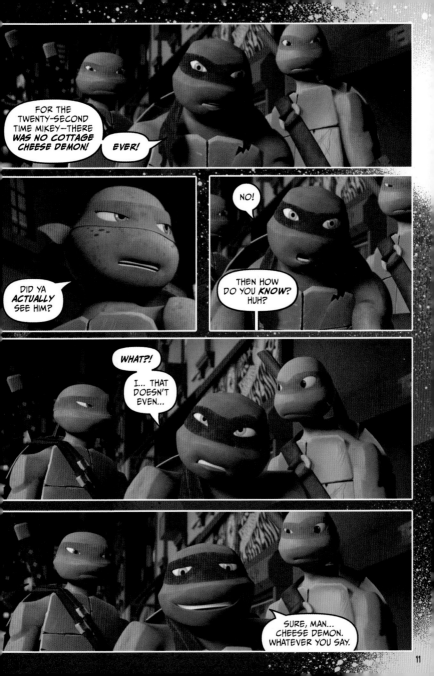

FOR THE TWENTY-SECOND TIME MIKEY—THERE **WAS NO COTTAGE CHEESE DEMON!**

EVER!

DID YA **ACTUALLY** SEE HIM?

NO!

THEN HOW DO YOU **KNOW?** HUH?

WHAT?!

I... THAT DOESN'T EVEN...

SURE, MAN... CHEESE DEMON. WHATEVER YOU SAY.

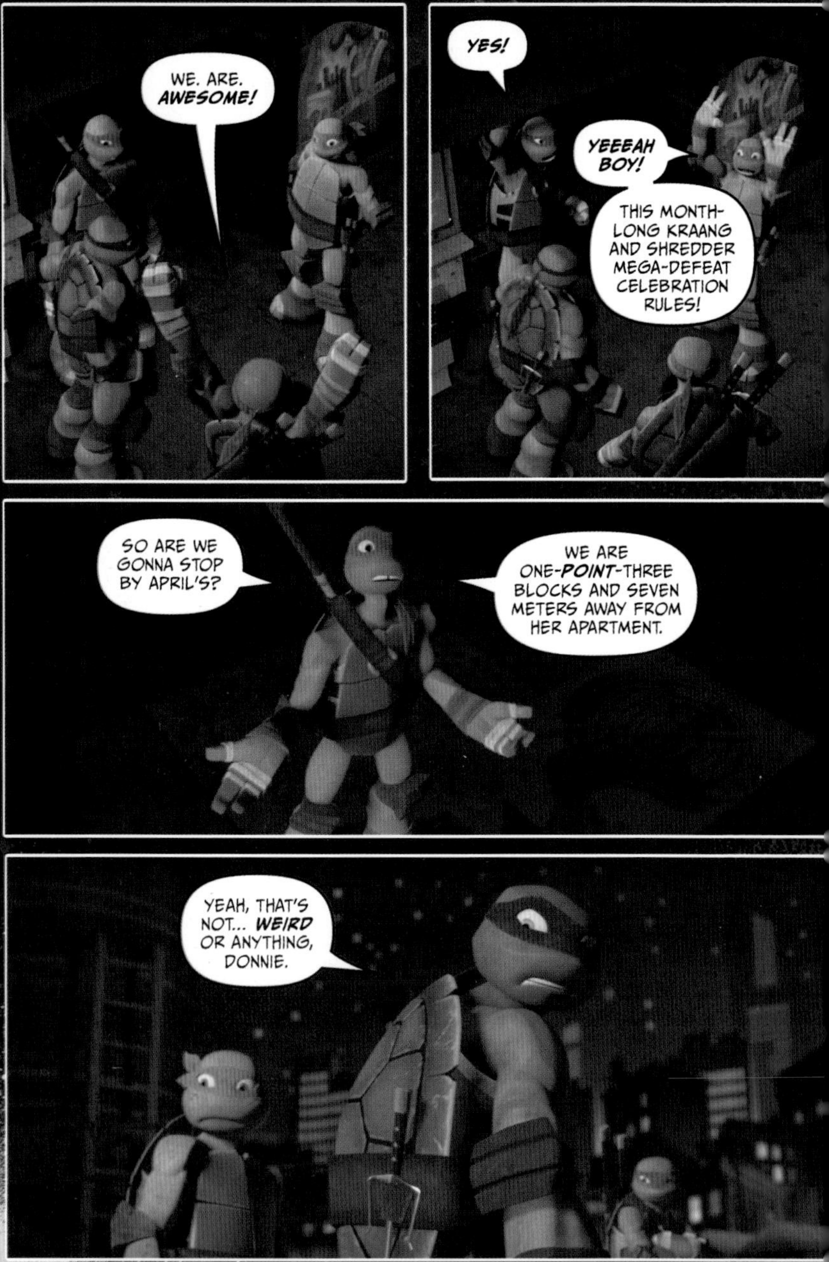
WE. ARE. AWESOME!
YES!
YEEEAH BOY!
THIS MONTH-LONG KRAANG AND SHREDDER MEGA-DEFEAT CELEBRATION RULES!
SO ARE WE GONNA STOP BY APRIL'S?
WE ARE ONE-POINT-THREE BLOCKS AND SEVEN METERS AWAY FROM HER APARTMENT.
YEAH, THAT'S NOT... WEIRD OR ANYTHING, DONNIE.

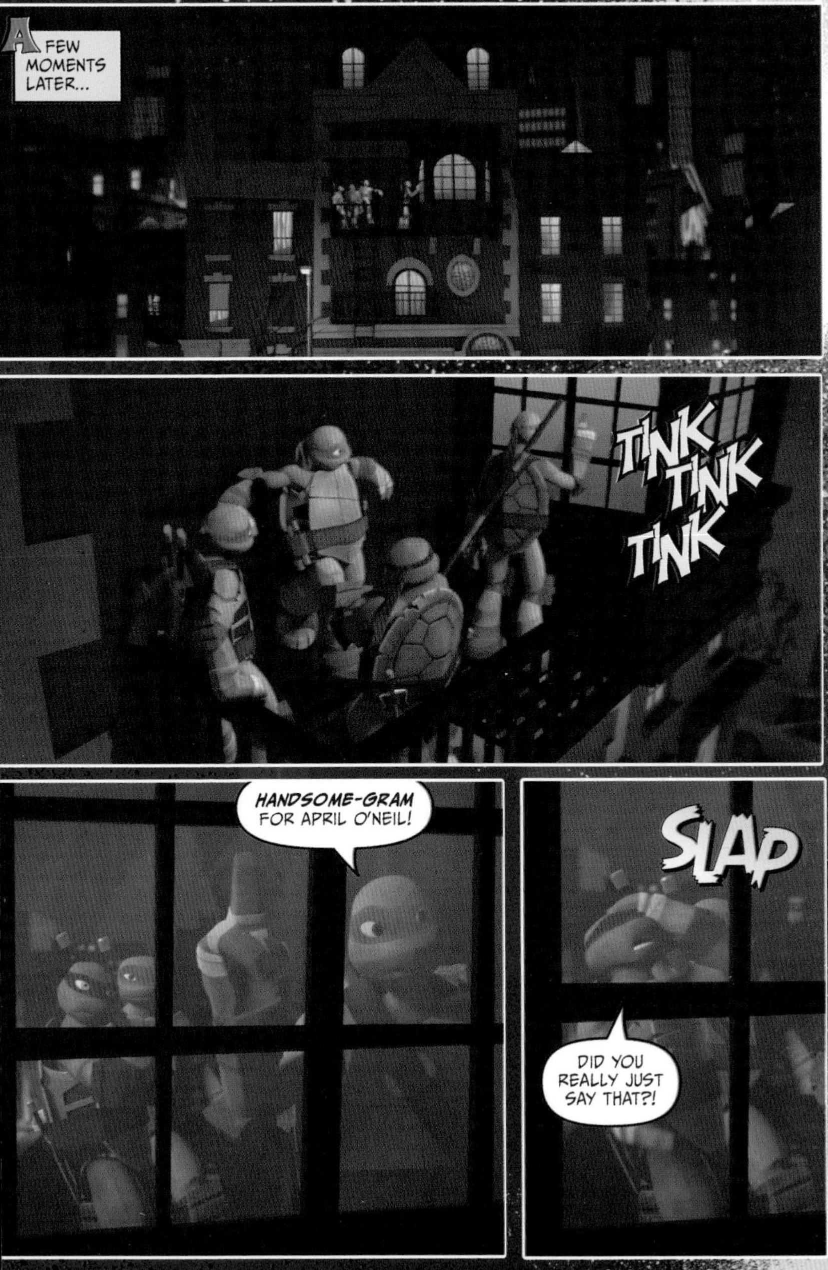
A FEW MOMENTS LATER...
TINK TINK TINK
HANDSOME-GRAM FOR APRIL O'NEIL!
SLAP
DID YOU REALLY JUST SAY THAT?!

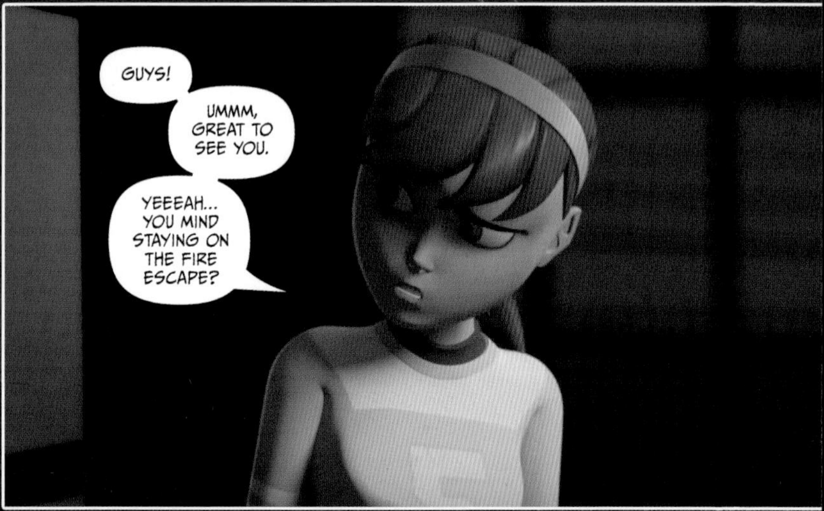
GUYS!
UMMM, GREAT TO SEE YOU.
YEEEAH... YOU MIND STAYING ON THE FIRE ESCAPE?

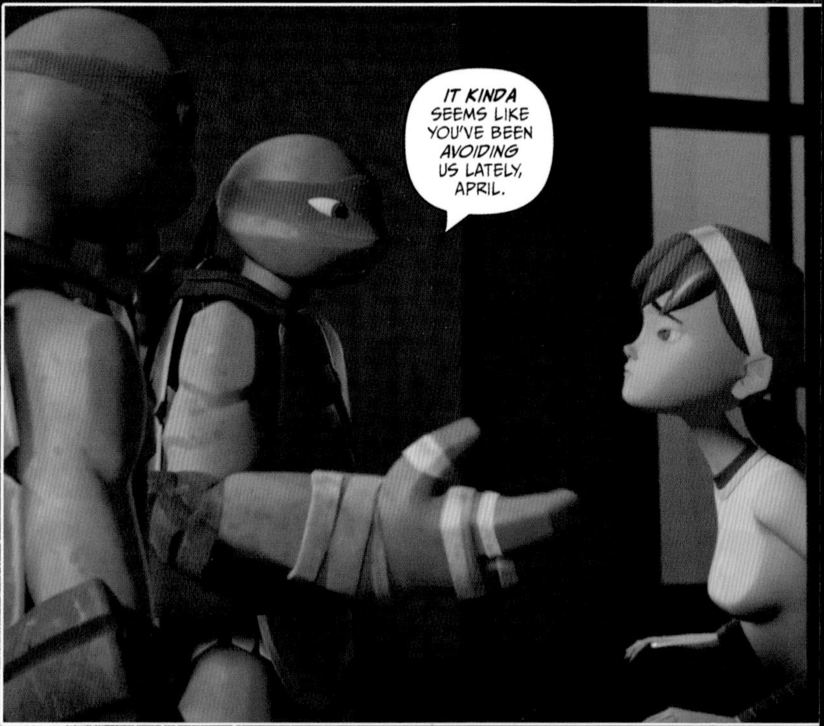
IT KINDA SEEMS LIKE YOU'VE BEEN *AVOIDING* US LATELY, APRIL.

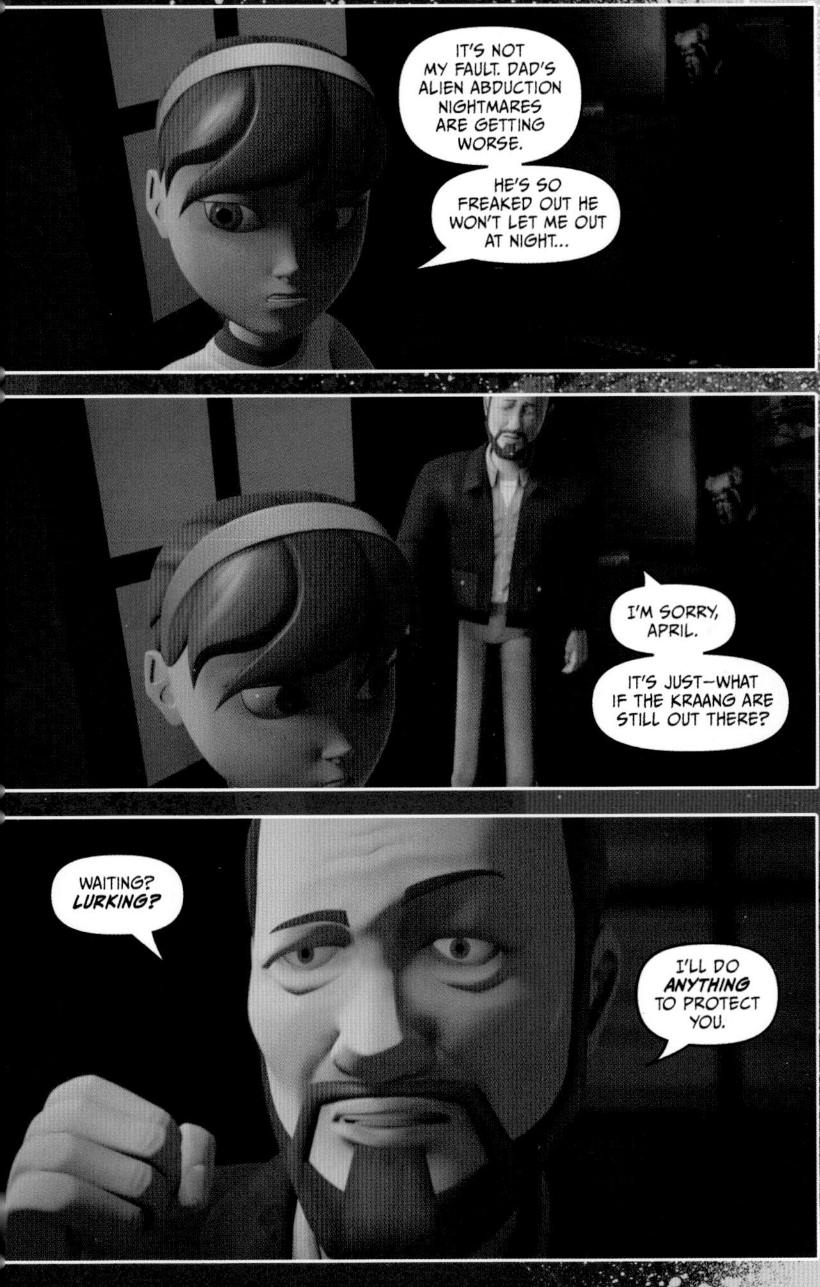
IT'S NOT MY FAULT. DAD'S ALIEN ABDUCTION NIGHTMARES ARE GETTING WORSE.
HE'S SO FREAKED OUT HE WON'T LET ME OUT AT NIGHT...
I'M SORRY, APRIL.
IT'S JUST—WHAT IF THE KRAANG ARE STILL OUT THERE?
WAITING? *LURKING?*
I'LL DO *ANYTHING* TO PROTECT YOU.

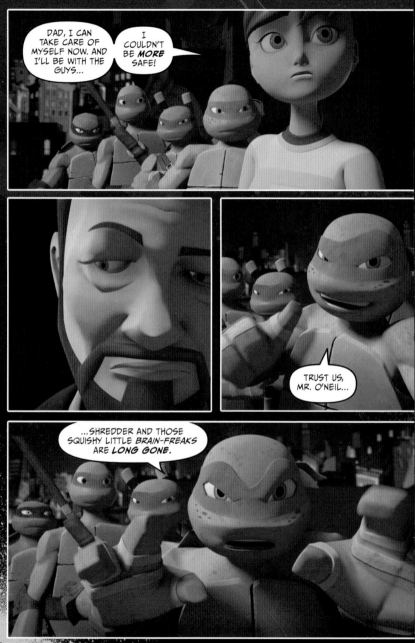

DAD, I CAN TAKE CARE OF MYSELF NOW. AND I'LL BE WITH THE GUYS...

I COULDN'T BE *MORE* SAFE!

TRUST US, MR. O'NEIL...

...SHREDDER AND THOSE SQUISHY LITTLE *BRAIN-FREAKS* ARE *LONG GONE.*

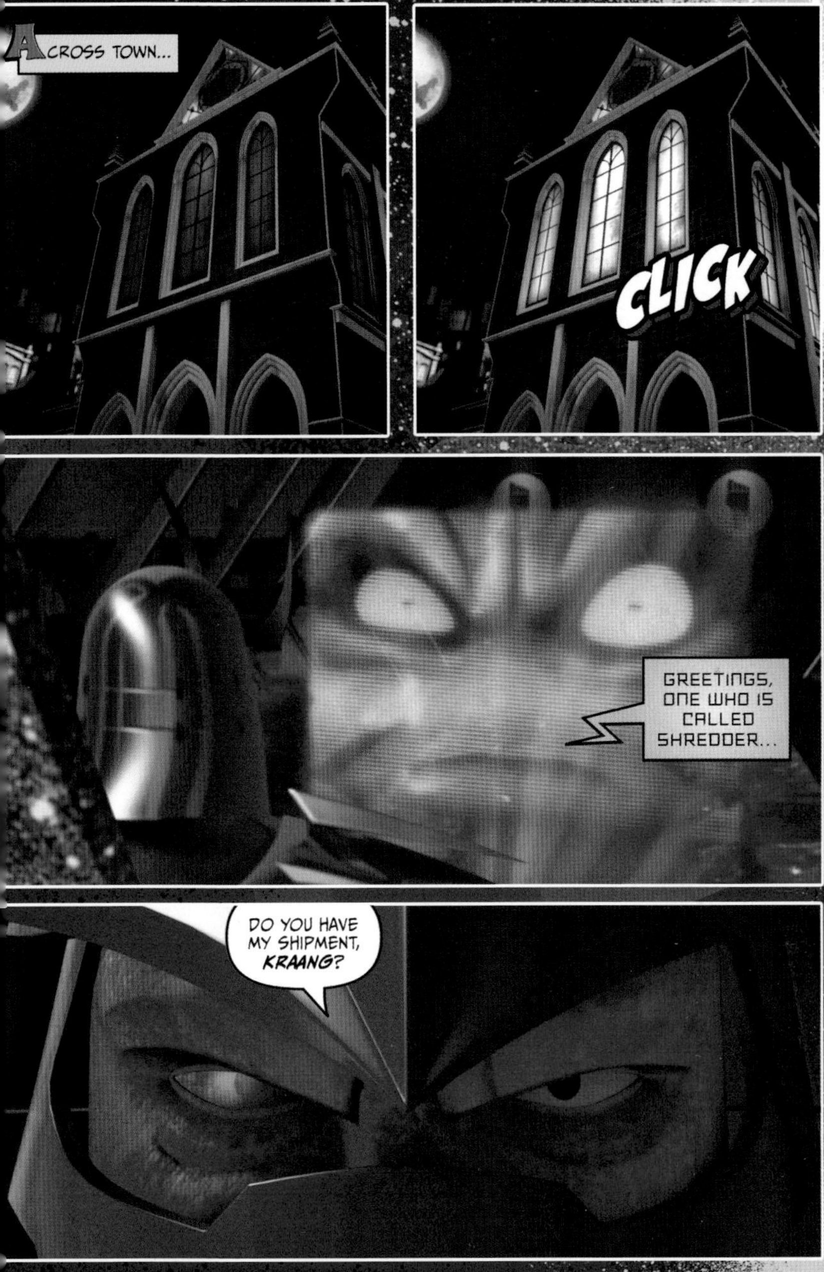
ACROSS TOWN...
CLICK
GREETINGS, ONE WHO IS CALLED SHREDDER...
DO YOU HAVE MY SHIPMENT, *KRAANG*?

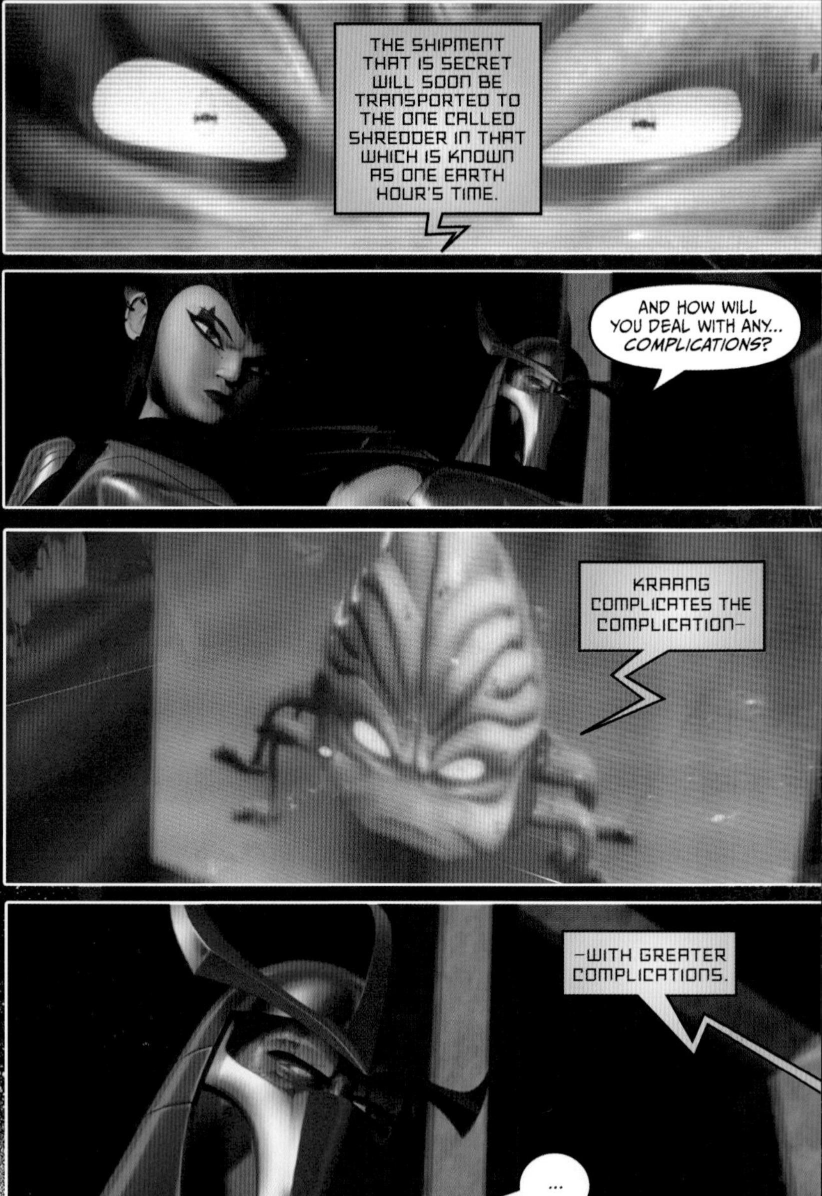

THE SHIPMENT THAT IS SECRET WILL SOON BE TRANSPORTED TO THE ONE CALLED SHREDDER IN THAT WHICH IS KNOWN AS ONE EARTH HOUR'S TIME.
AND HOW WILL YOU DEAL WITH ANY... *COMPLICATIONS?*
KRAANG COMPLICATES THE COMPLICATION—
—WITH GREATER COMPLICATIONS.
...

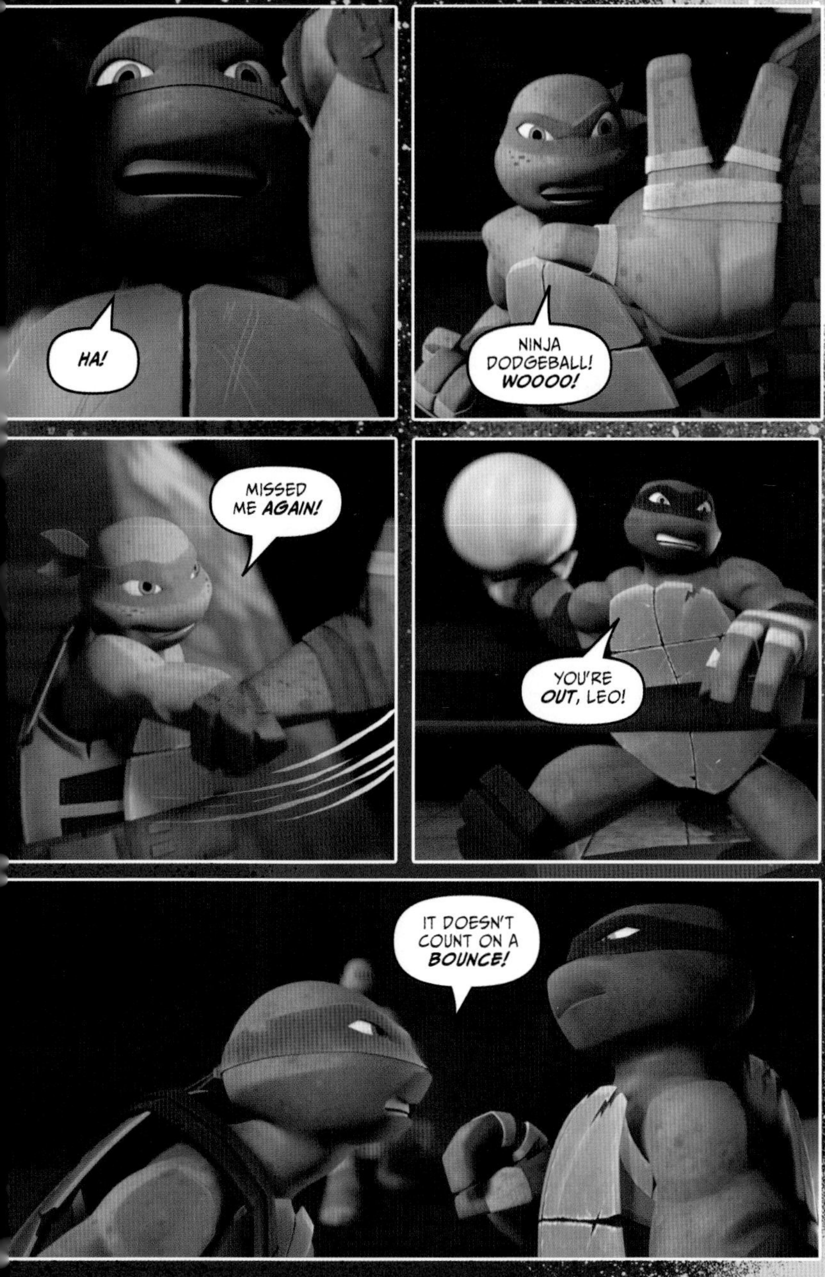
HA!
NINJA DODGEBALL! WOOOO!
MISSED ME AGAIN!
YOU'RE OUT, LEO!
IT DOESN'T COUNT ON A BOUNCE!

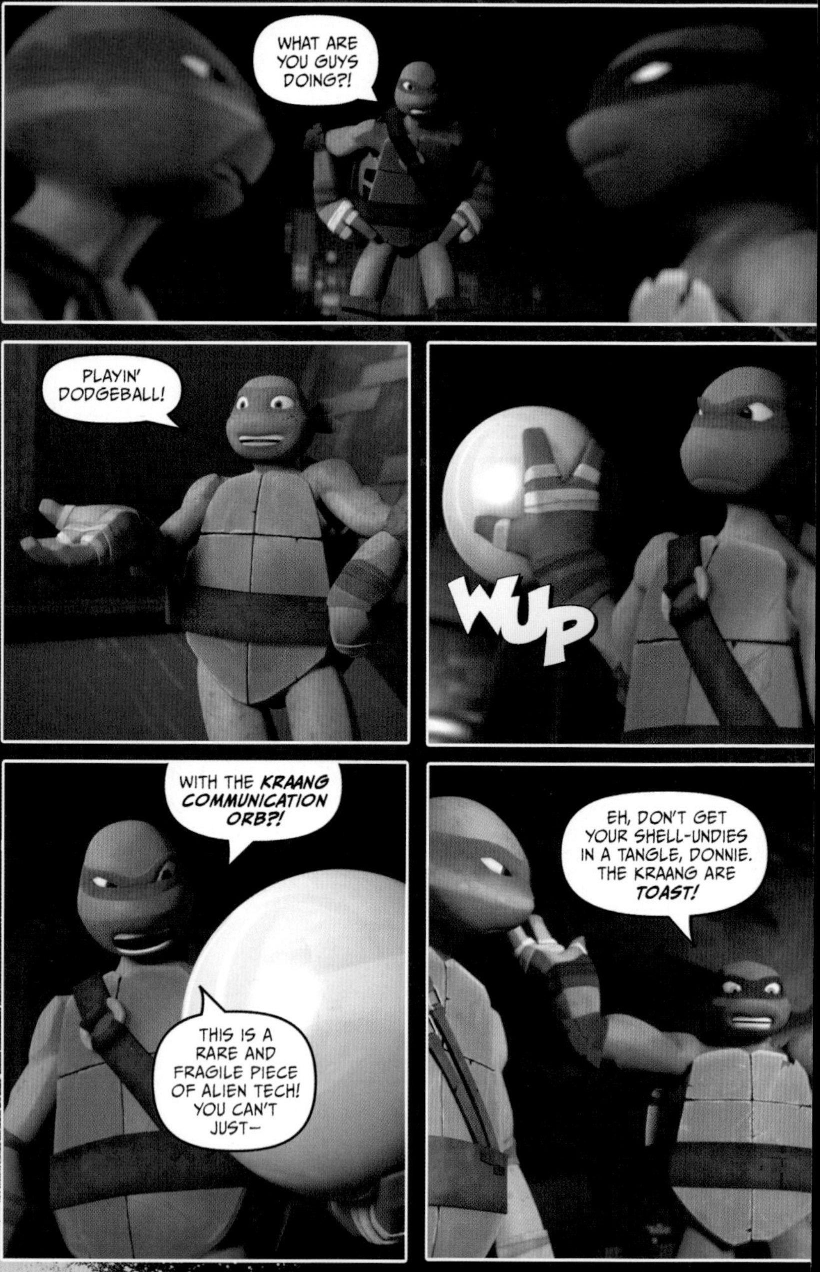

WHAT ARE YOU GUYS DOING?!
PLAYIN' DODGEBALL!
WUP
WITH THE *KRAANG COMMUNICATION ORB?!*
THIS IS A RARE AND FRAGILE PIECE OF ALIEN TECH! YOU CAN'T JUST–
EH, DON'T GET YOUR SHELL-UNDIES IN A TANGLE, DONNIE. THE KRAANG ARE *TOAST!*

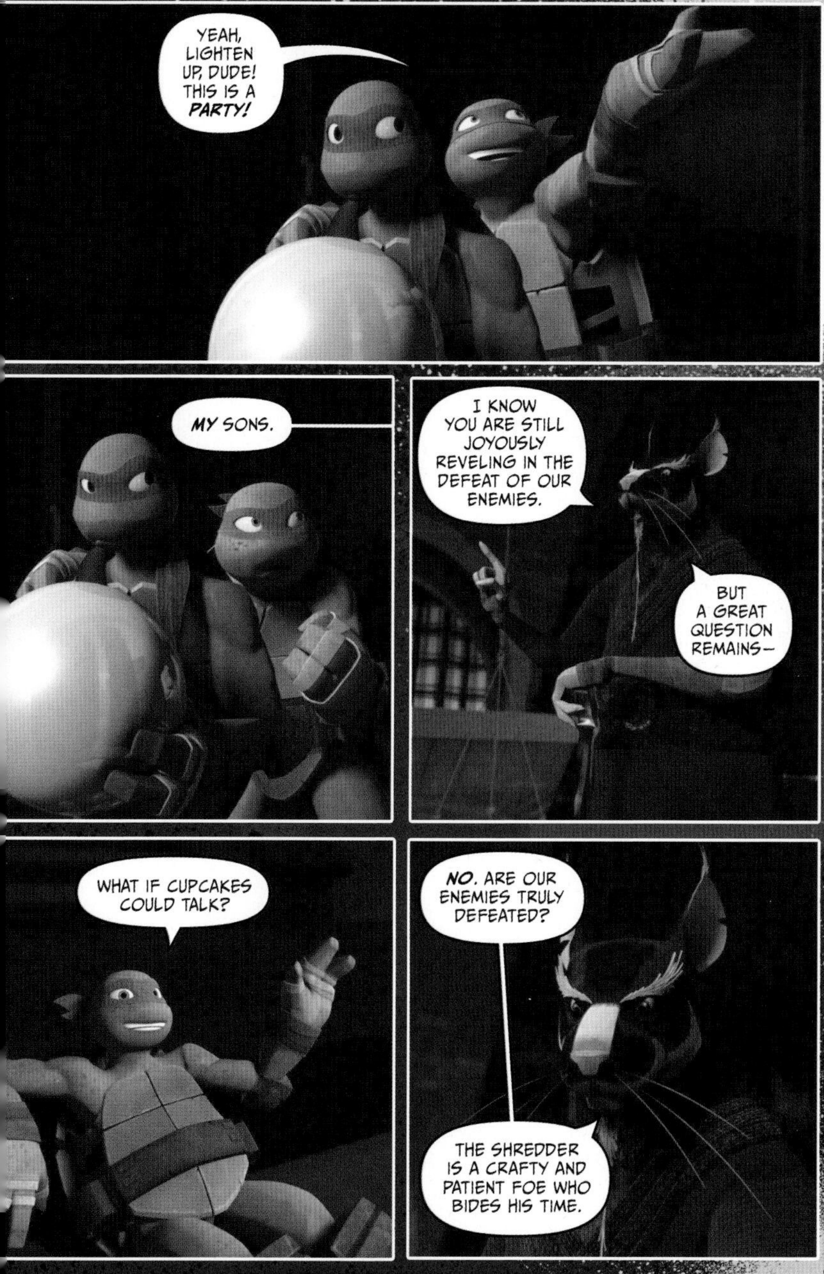
YEAH, LIGHTEN UP, DUDE! THIS IS A *PARTY!*
MY SONS.
I KNOW YOU ARE STILL JOYOUSLY REVELING IN THE DEFEAT OF OUR ENEMIES.
BUT A GREAT QUESTION REMAINS—
WHAT IF CUPCAKES COULD TALK?
NO. ARE OUR ENEMIES TRULY DEFEATED?
THE SHREDDER IS A CRAFTY AND PATIENT FOE WHO BIDES HIS TIME.

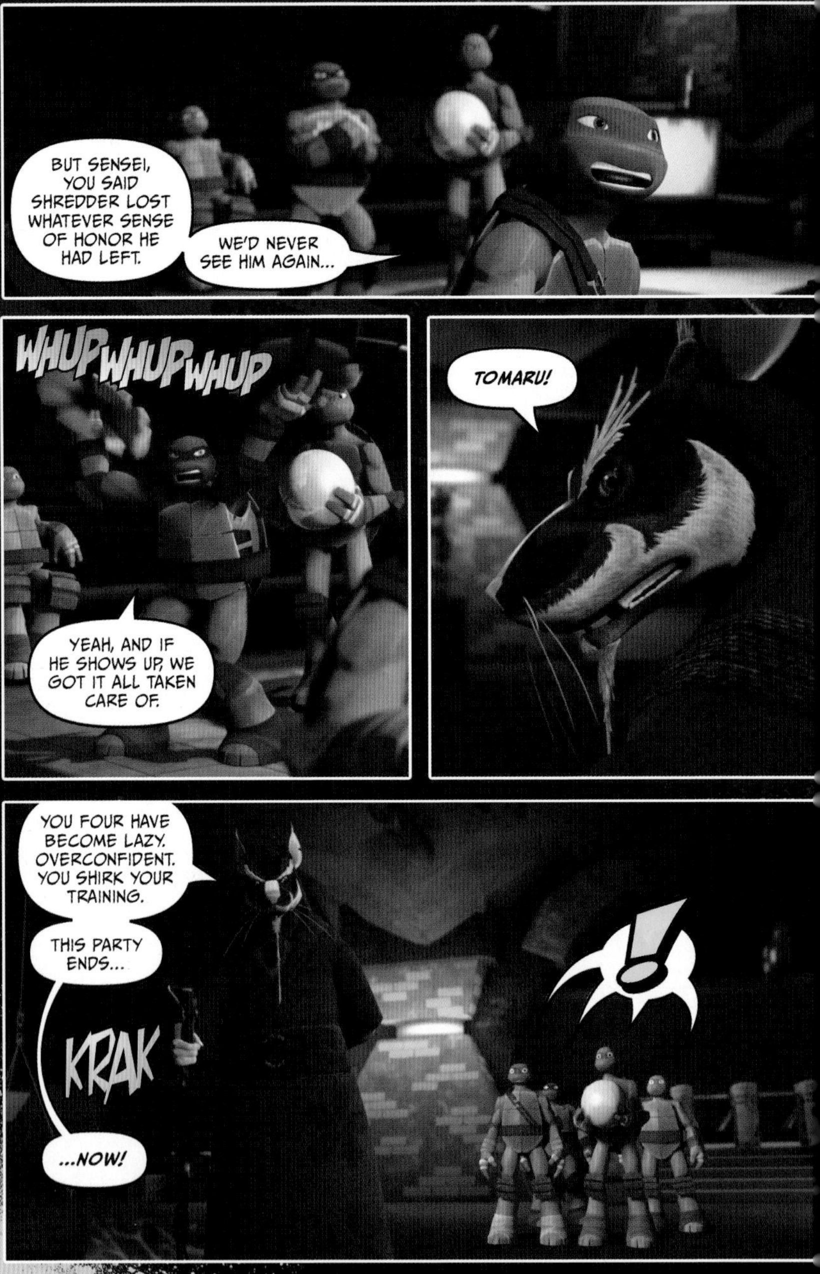
BUT SENSEI, YOU SAID SHREDDER LOST WHATEVER SENSE OF HONOR HE HAD LEFT.
WE'D NEVER SEE HIM AGAIN...
WHUP WHUP WHUP
YEAH, AND IF HE SHOWS UP, WE GOT IT ALL TAKEN CARE OF.
TOMARU!
YOU FOUR HAVE BECOME LAZY. OVERCONFIDENT. YOU SHIRK YOUR TRAINING.
THIS PARTY ENDS...
KRAK
...NOW!
!

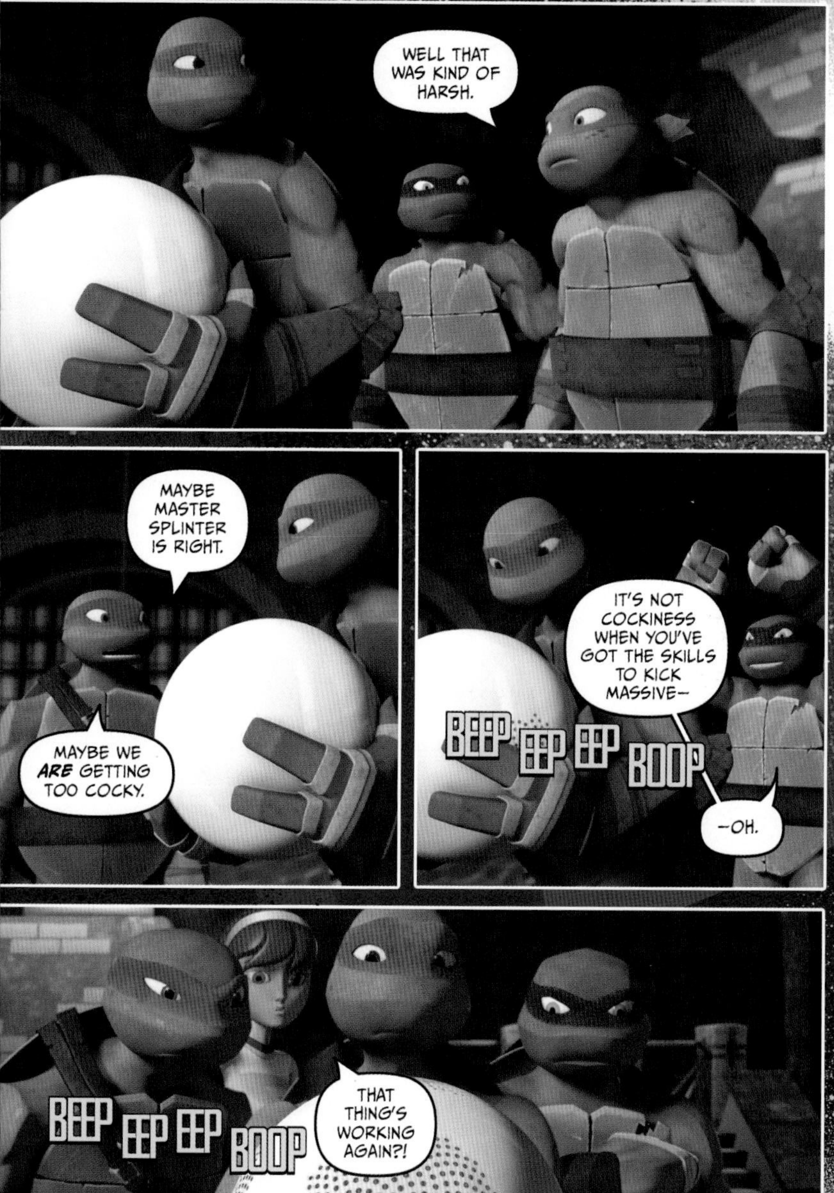
WELL THAT WAS KIND OF HARSH.
MAYBE MASTER SPLINTER IS RIGHT.
MAYBE WE **ARE** GETTING TOO COCKY.
IT'S NOT COCKINESS WHEN YOU'VE GOT THE SKILLS TO KICK MASSIVE—
BEEP EEP EEP BOOP
—OH.
BEEP EEP EEP BOOP
THAT THING'S WORKING AGAIN?!

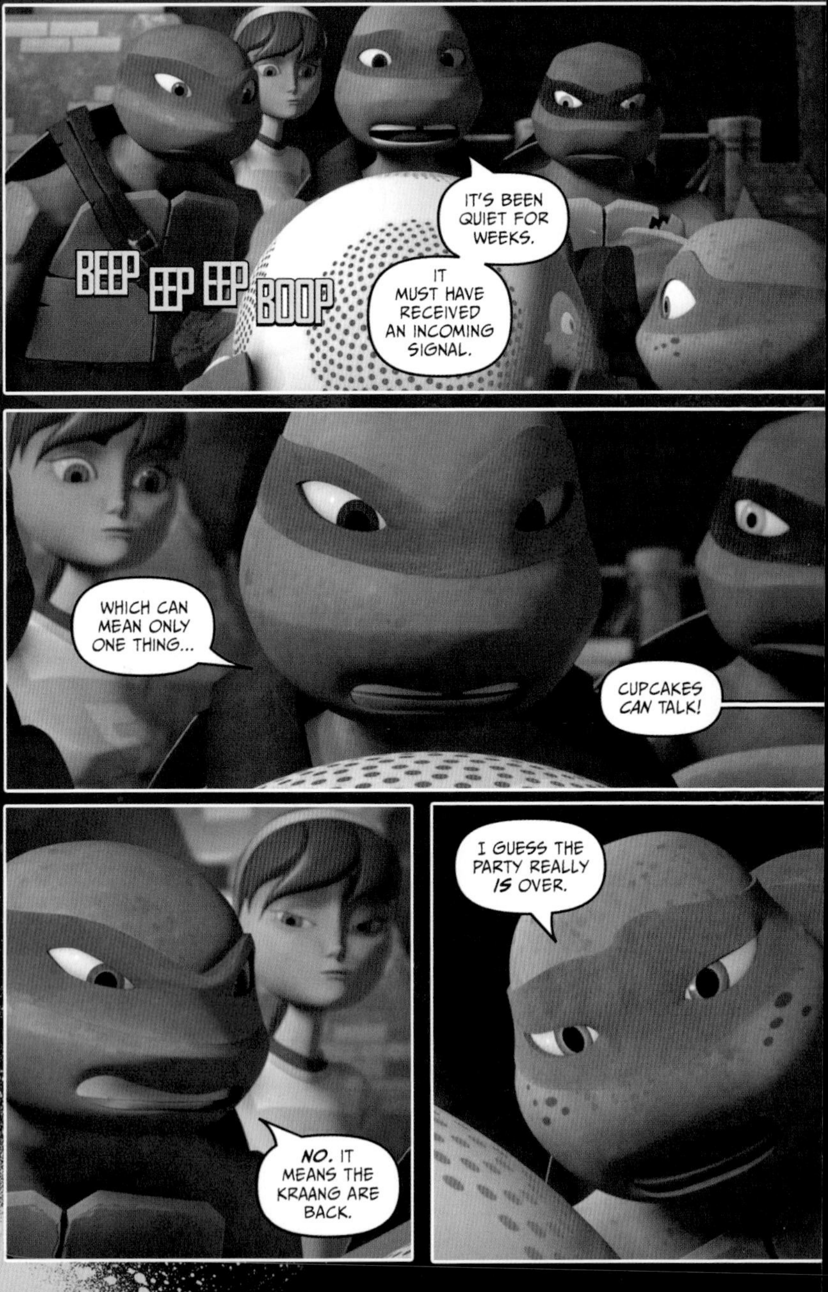

IT'S BEEN QUIET FOR WEEKS.
BEEP EEP EEP BOOP
IT MUST HAVE RECEIVED AN INCOMING SIGNAL.
WHICH CAN MEAN ONLY ONE THING...
CUPCAKES CAN TALK!
NO. IT MEANS THE KRAANG ARE BACK.
I GUESS THE PARTY REALLY IS OVER.

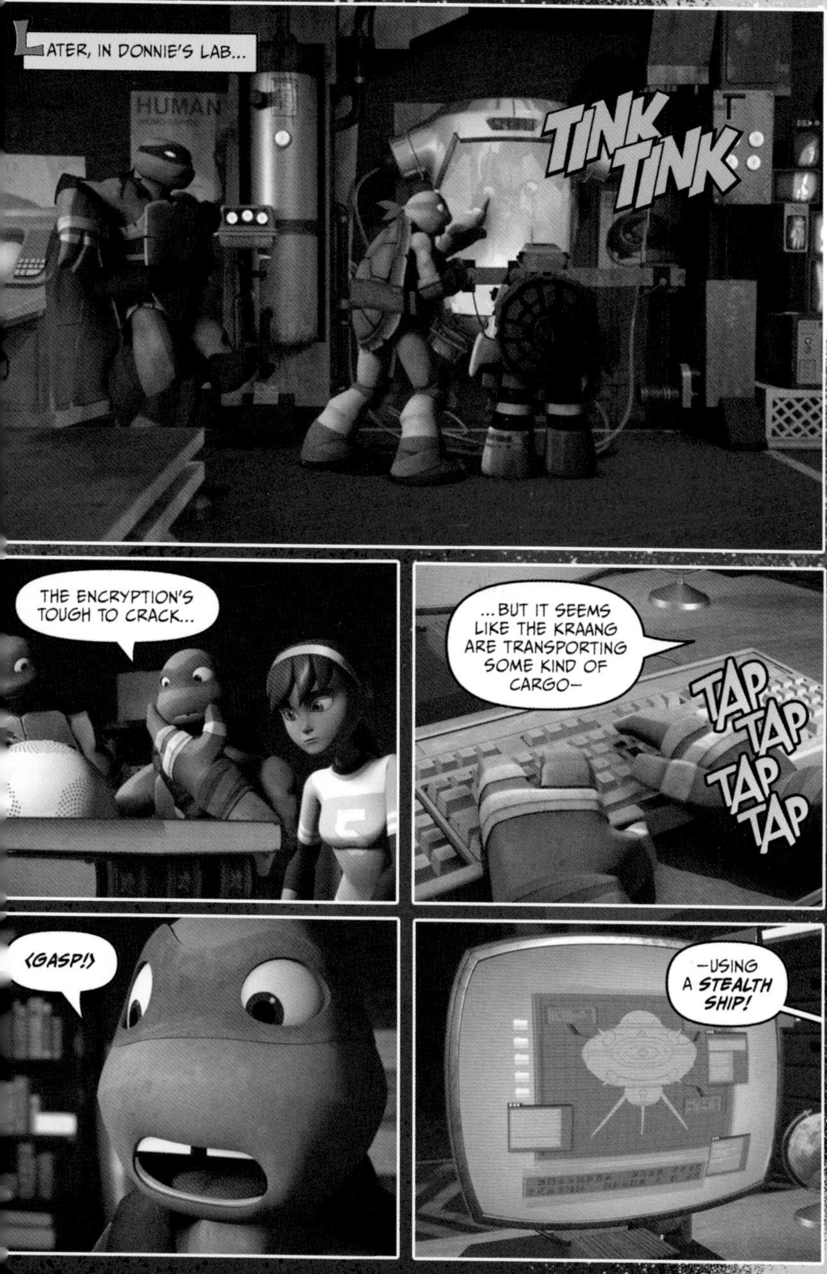
LATER, IN DONNIE'S LAB...
HUMAN
TINK TINK
THE ENCRYPTION'S TOUGH TO CRACK...
...BUT IT SEEMS LIKE THE KRAANG ARE TRANSPORTING SOME KIND OF CARGO—
TAP TAP TAP TAP
<GASP!>
—USING A STEALTH SHIP!

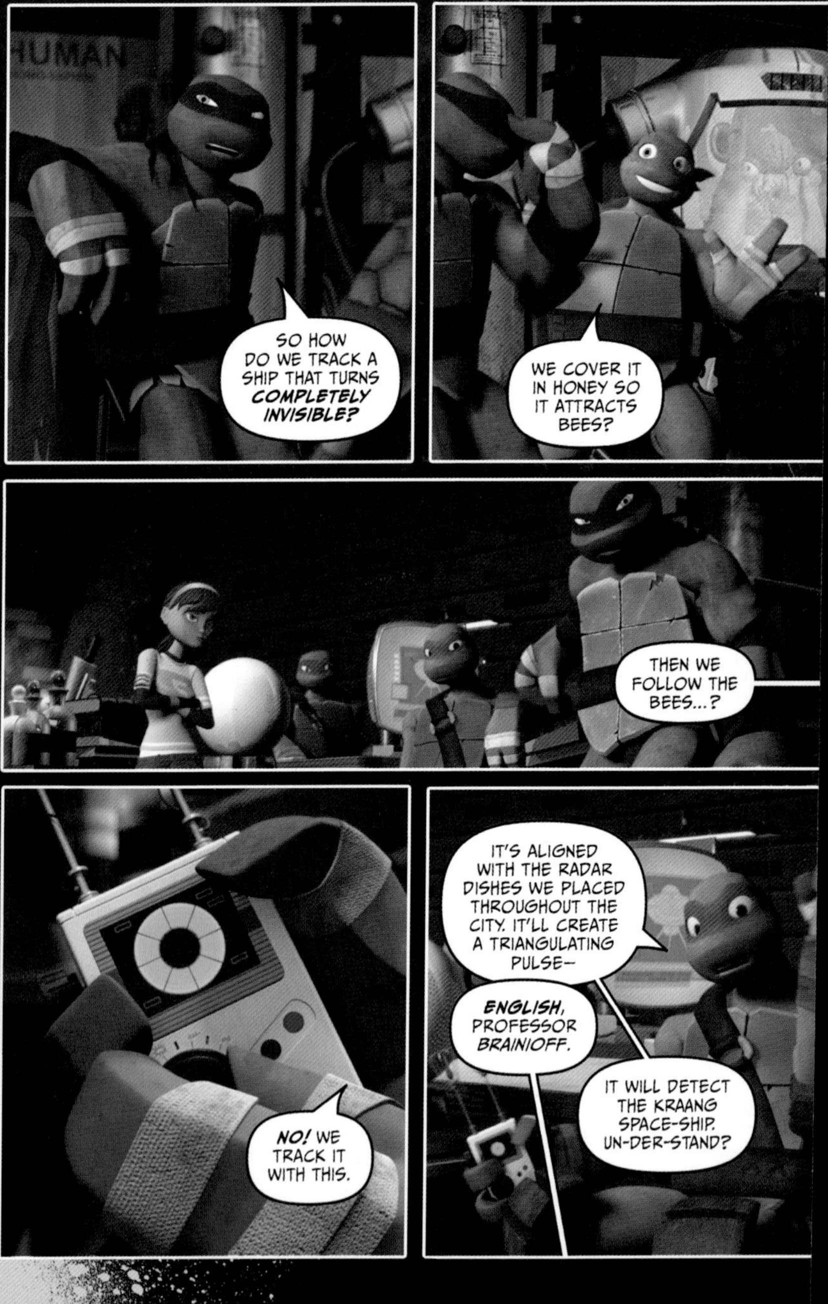
HUMAN
SO HOW DO WE TRACK A SHIP THAT TURNS ***COMPLETELY INVISIBLE?***
WE COVER IT IN HONEY SO IT ATTRACTS BEES?
THEN WE FOLLOW THE BEES...?
NO! WE TRACK IT WITH THIS.
IT'S ALIGNED WITH THE RADAR DISHES WE PLACED THROUGHOUT THE CITY. IT'LL CREATE A TRIANGULATING PULSE--
ENGLISH, PROFESSOR *BRAINIOFF.*
IT WILL DETECT THE KRAANG SPACE-SHIP. UN-DER-STAND?

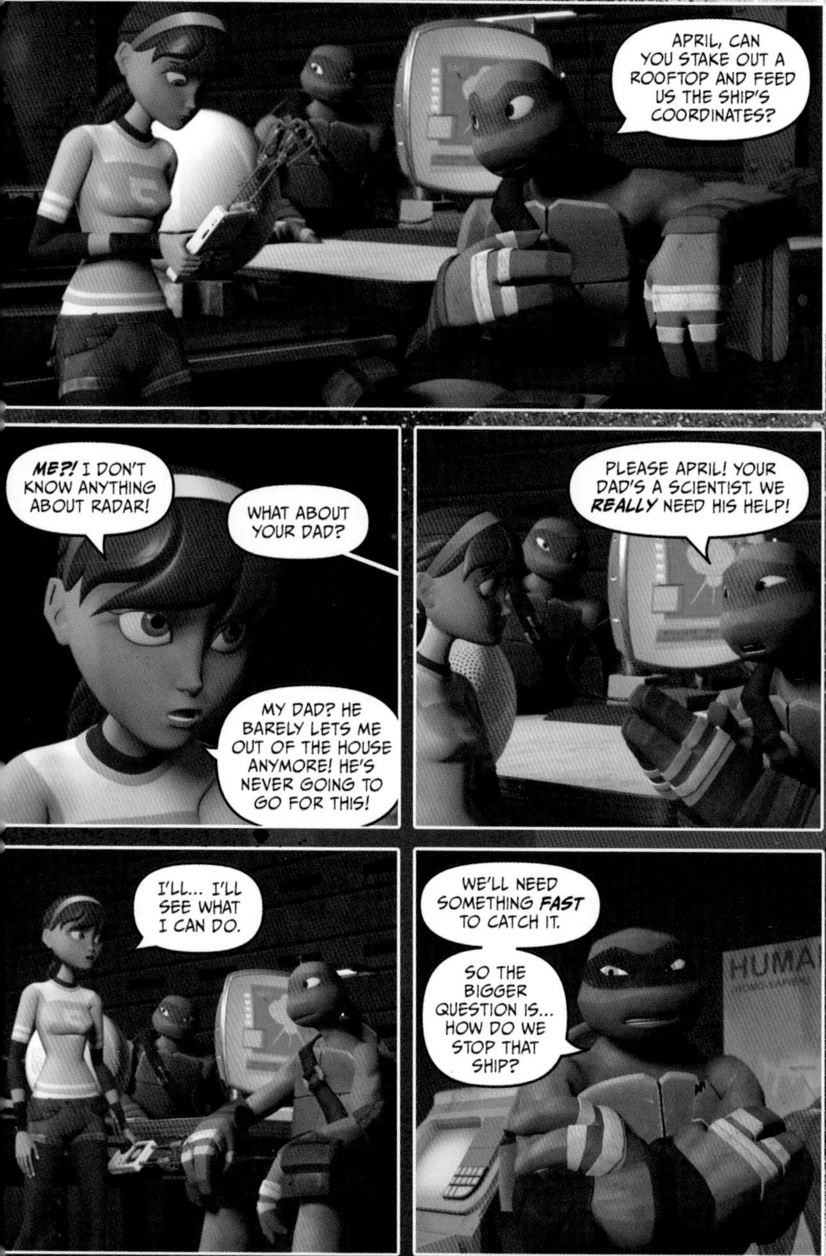
APRIL, CAN YOU STAKE OUT A ROOFTOP AND FEED US THE SHIP'S COORDINATES?
ME?! I DON'T KNOW ANYTHING ABOUT RADAR!
WHAT ABOUT YOUR DAD?
MY DAD? HE BARELY LETS ME OUT OF THE HOUSE ANYMORE! HE'S NEVER GOING TO GO FOR THIS!
PLEASE APRIL! YOUR DAD'S A SCIENTIST. WE REALLY NEED HIS HELP!
I'LL... I'LL SEE WHAT I CAN DO.
WE'LL NEED SOMETHING FAST TO CATCH IT.
SO THE BIGGER QUESTION IS... HOW DO WE STOP THAT SHIP?
HUMA

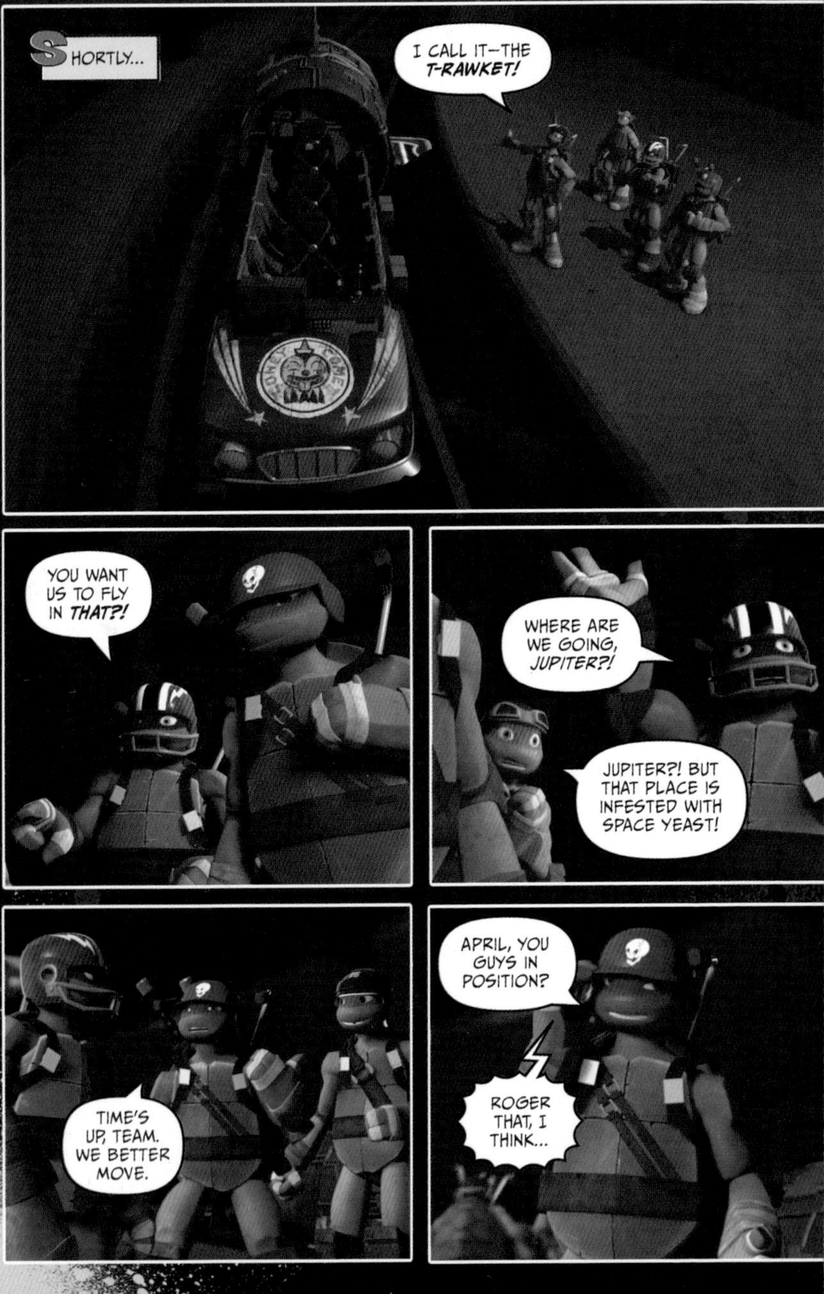
SHORTLY...
I CALL IT—THE T-RAWKET!
COWEY COMET
YOU WANT US TO FLY IN THAT?!
WHERE ARE WE GOING, JUPITER?!
JUPITER?! BUT THAT PLACE IS INFESTED WITH SPACE YEAST!
TIME'S UP, TEAM. WE BETTER MOVE.
APRIL, YOU GUYS IN POSITION?
ROGER THAT, I THINK...

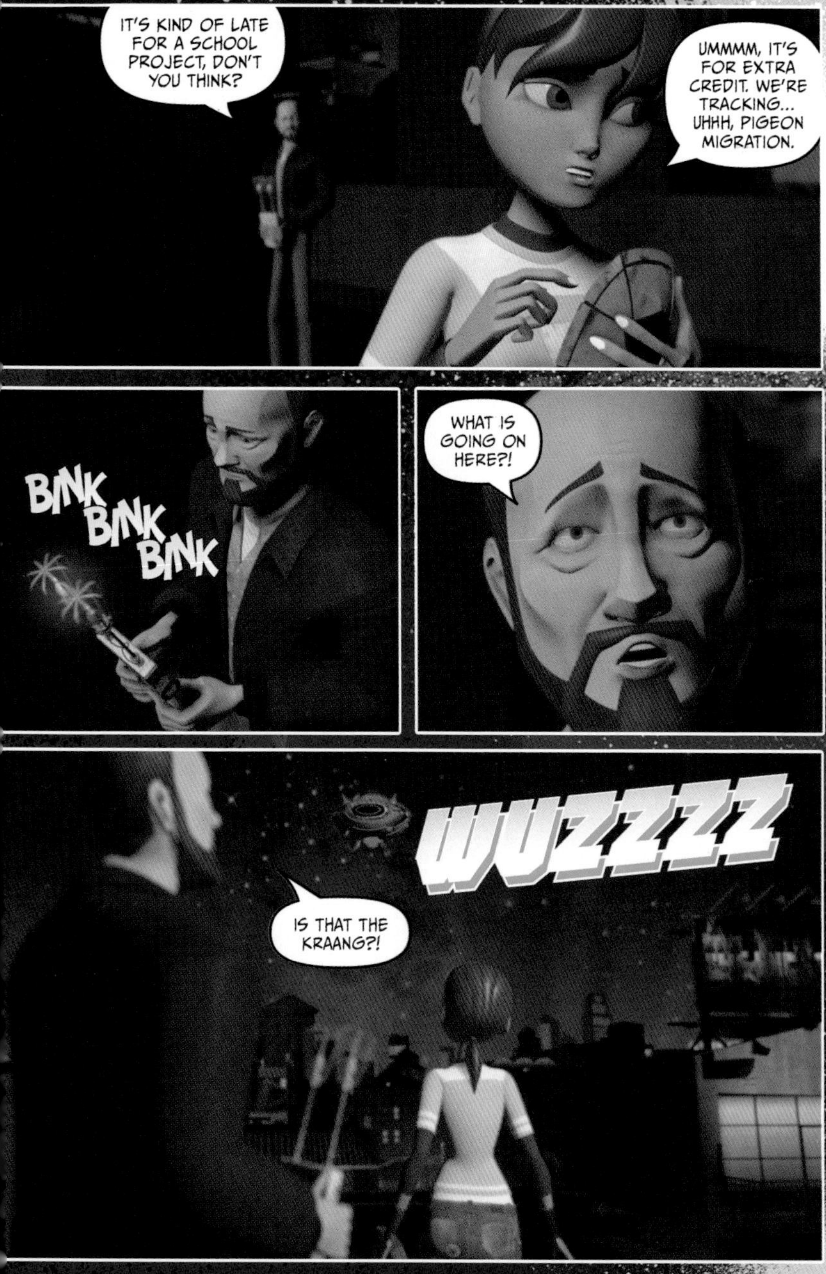
IT'S KIND OF LATE FOR A SCHOOL PROJECT, DON'T YOU THINK?
UMMMM, IT'S FOR EXTRA CREDIT. WE'RE TRACKING... UHHH, PIGEON MIGRATION.
BINK BINK BINK
WHAT IS GOING ON HERE?!
WUZZZZ
IS THAT THE KRAANG?!

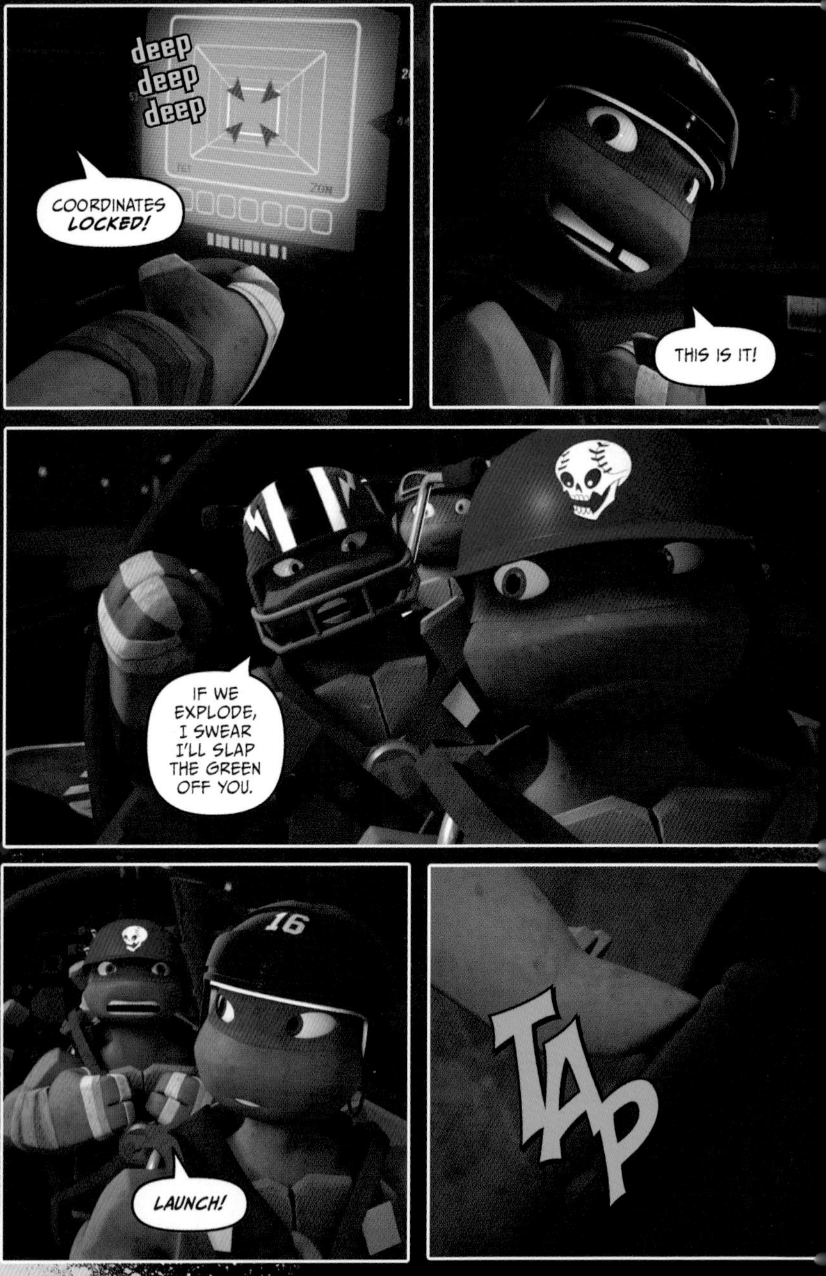
deep
deep
deep
COORDINATES LOCKED!
THIS IS IT!
IF WE EXPLODE, I SWEAR I'LL SLAP THE GREEN OFF YOU.
LAUNCH!
TAP

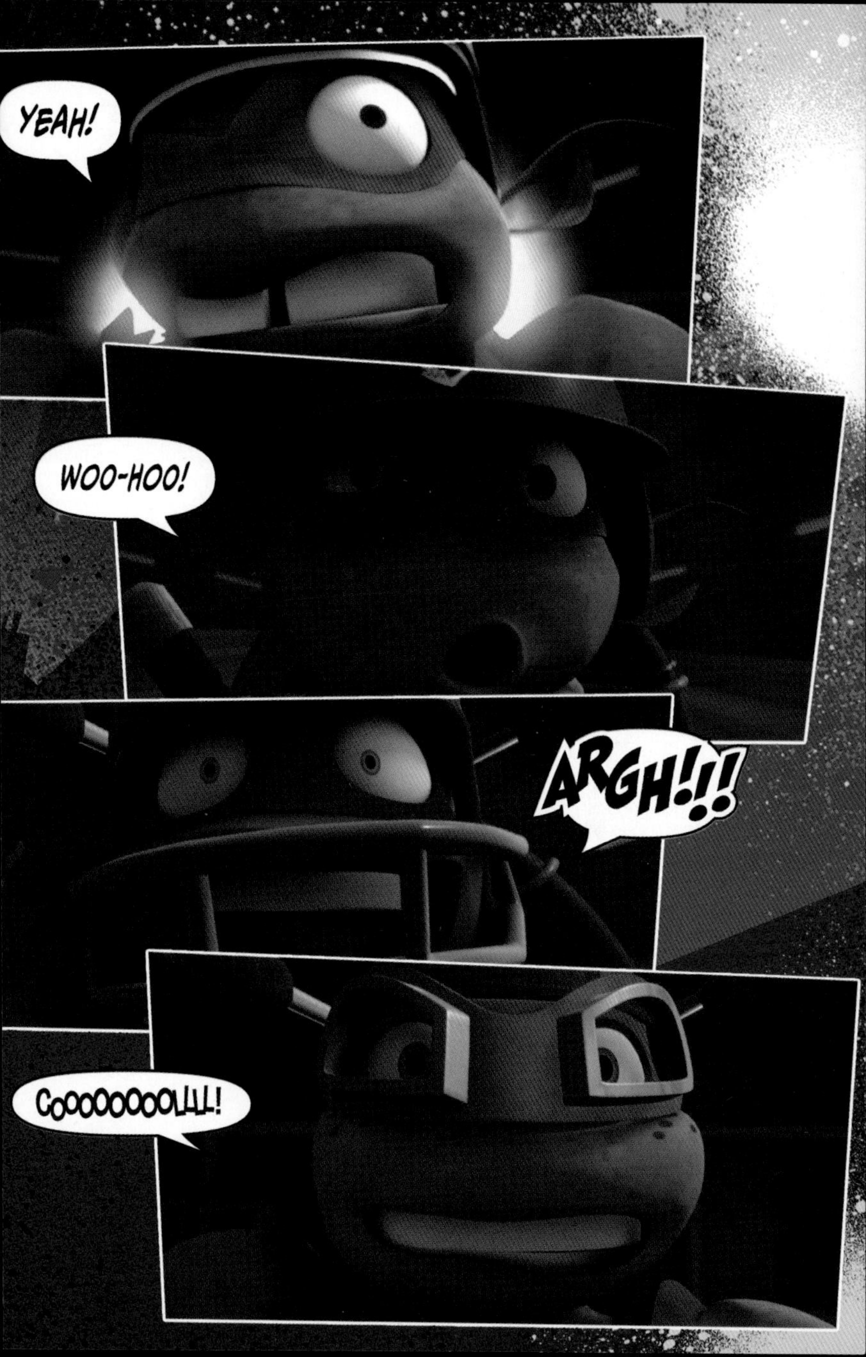
YEAH!
WOO-HOO!
ARGH!!!
COOOOOOOOLLLL!

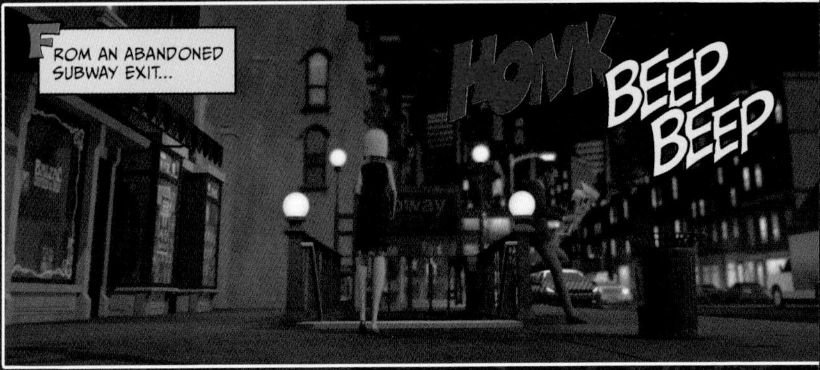
FROM AN ABANDONED SUBWAY EXIT...
HONK
BEEP BEEP

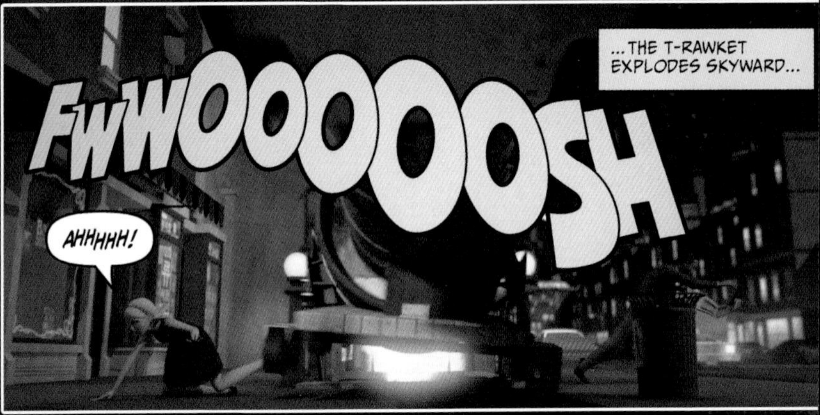
...THE T-RAWKET EXPLODES SKYWARD...
FWWOOOOOOSH
AHHHHH!

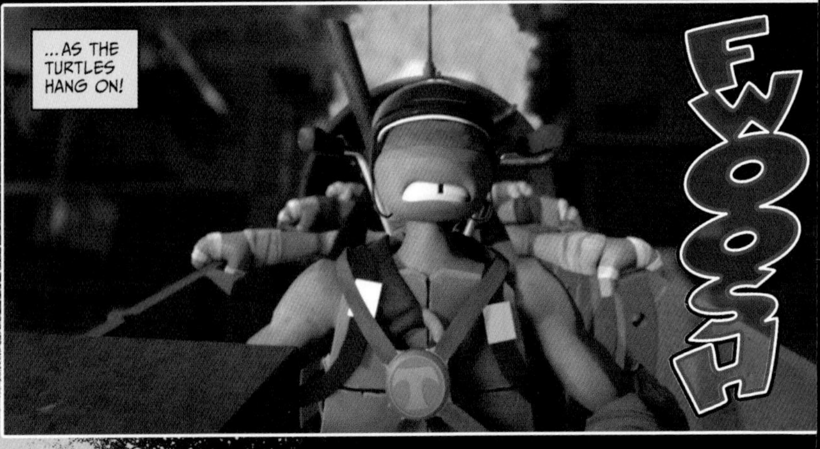
...AS THE TURTLES HANG ON!
FWOOOSH

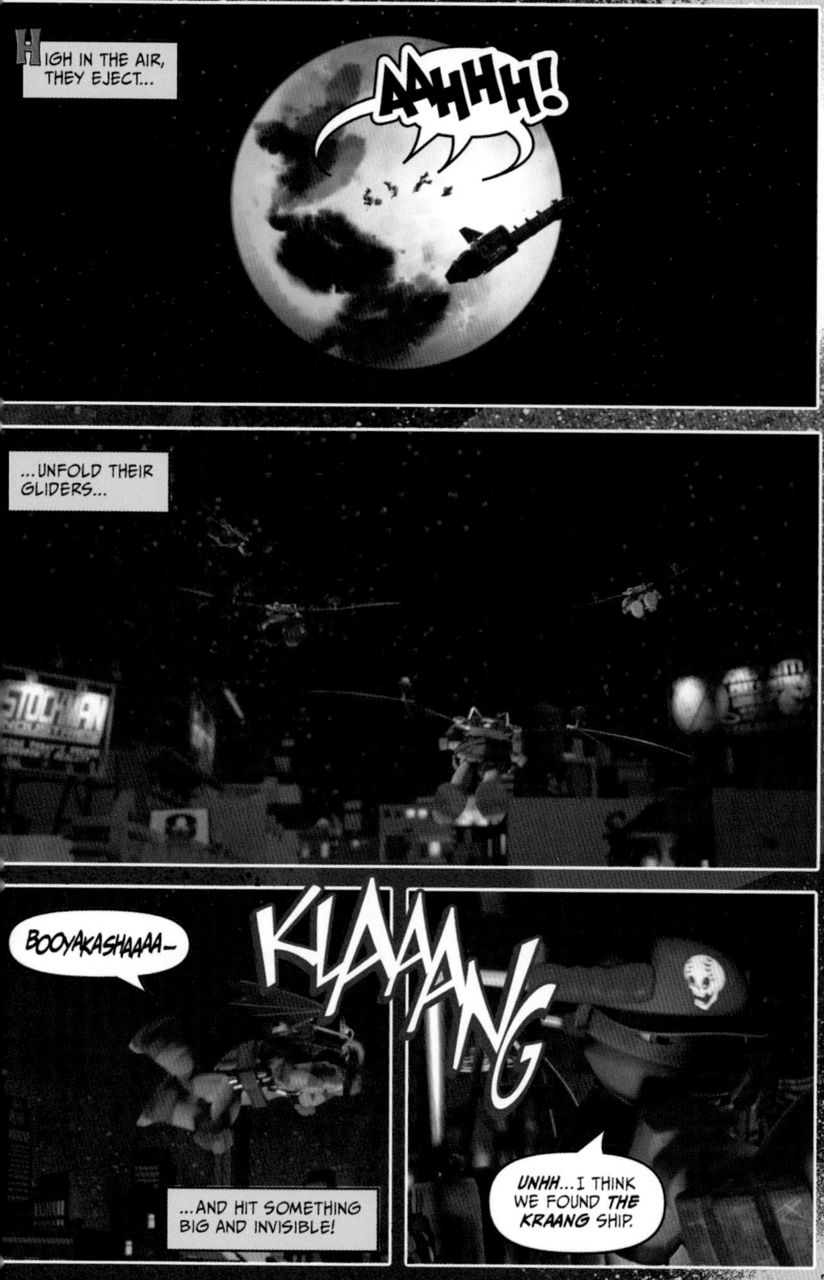
HIGH IN THE AIR, THEY EJECT...
AAHHH!
...UNFOLD THEIR GLIDERS...
BOOYAKASHAAAA—
KLAAANG
...AND HIT SOMETHING BIG AND INVISIBLE!
UNHH...I THINK WE FOUND THE KRAANG SHIP.

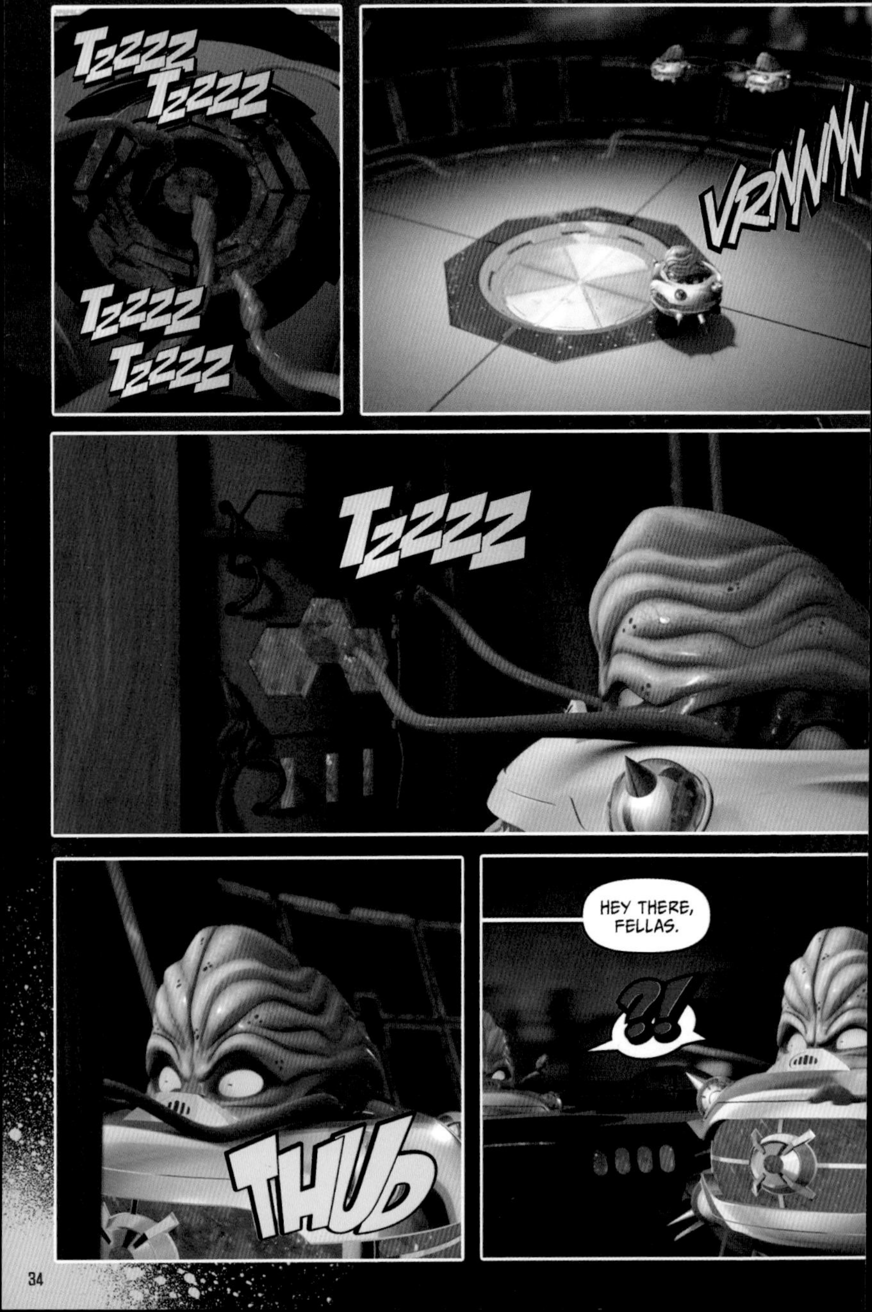
TZZZZ
TZZZZ
TZZZZ
TZZZZ
VRNNNN
TZZZZ
THUD
HEY THERE, FELLAS.
?!

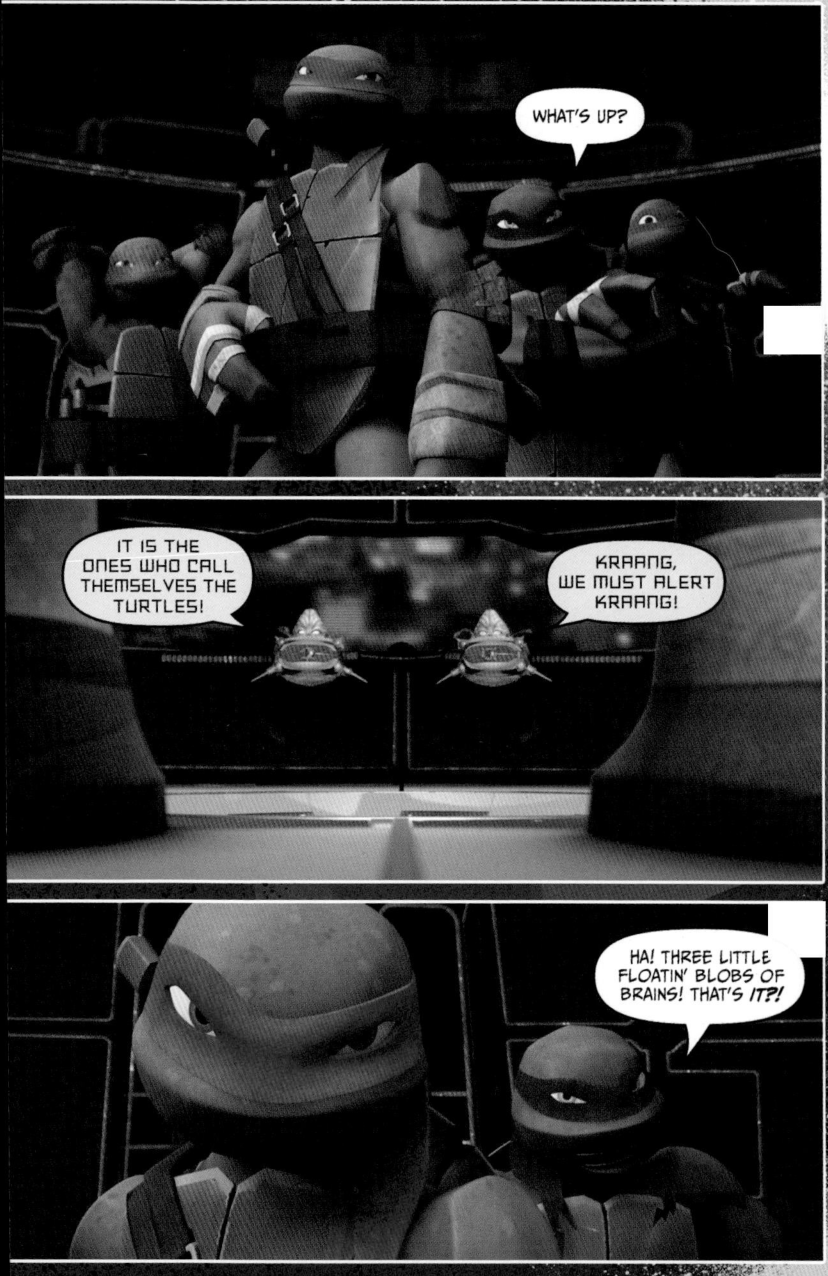
WHAT'S UP?
IT IS THE ONES WHO CALL THEMSELVES THE TURTLES!
KRAANG, WE MUST ALERT KRAANG!
HA! THREE LITTLE FLOATIN' BLOBS OF BRAINS! THAT'S *IT?!*

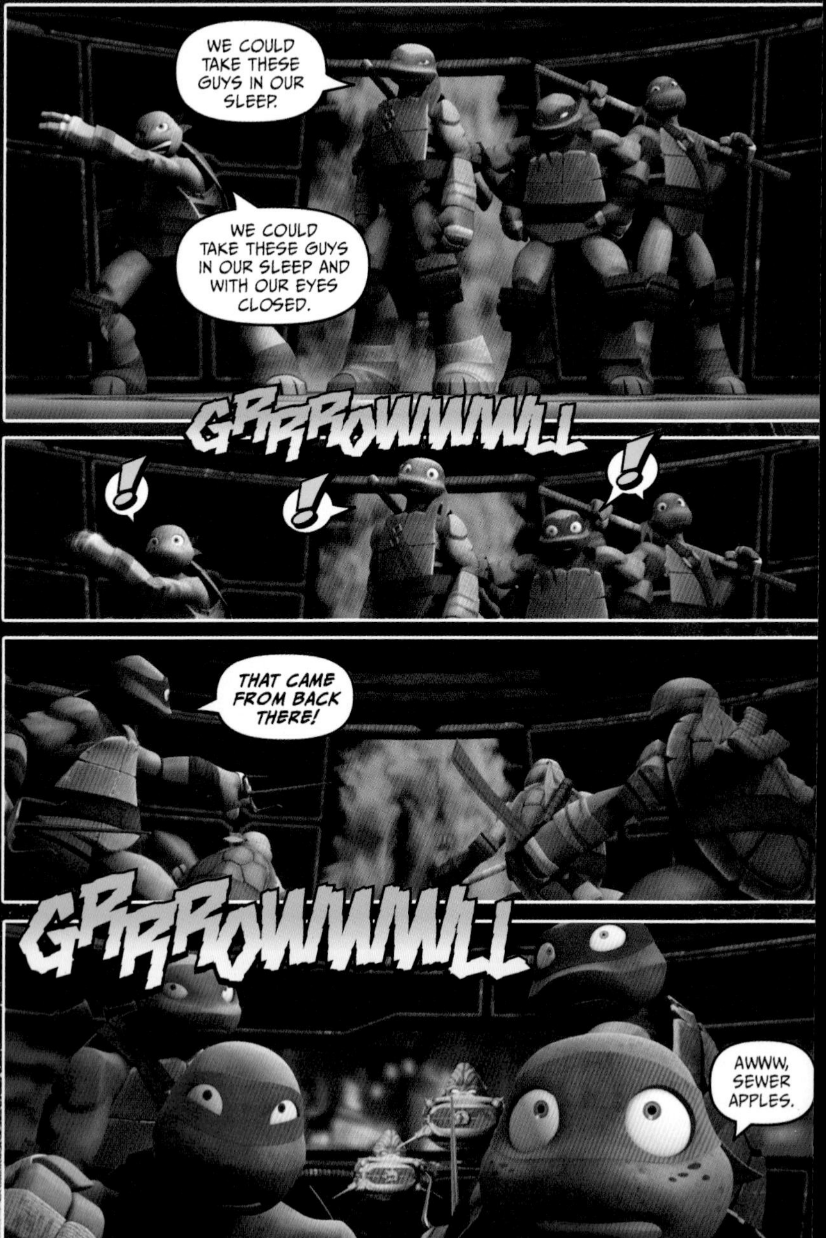

WE COULD TAKE THESE GUYS IN OUR SLEEP.
WE COULD TAKE THESE GUYS IN OUR SLEEP AND WITH OUR EYES CLOSED.
GRRROWWWLL
!
!
!
THAT CAME FROM BACK THERE!
GRRROWWWLL
AWWW, SEWER APPLES.

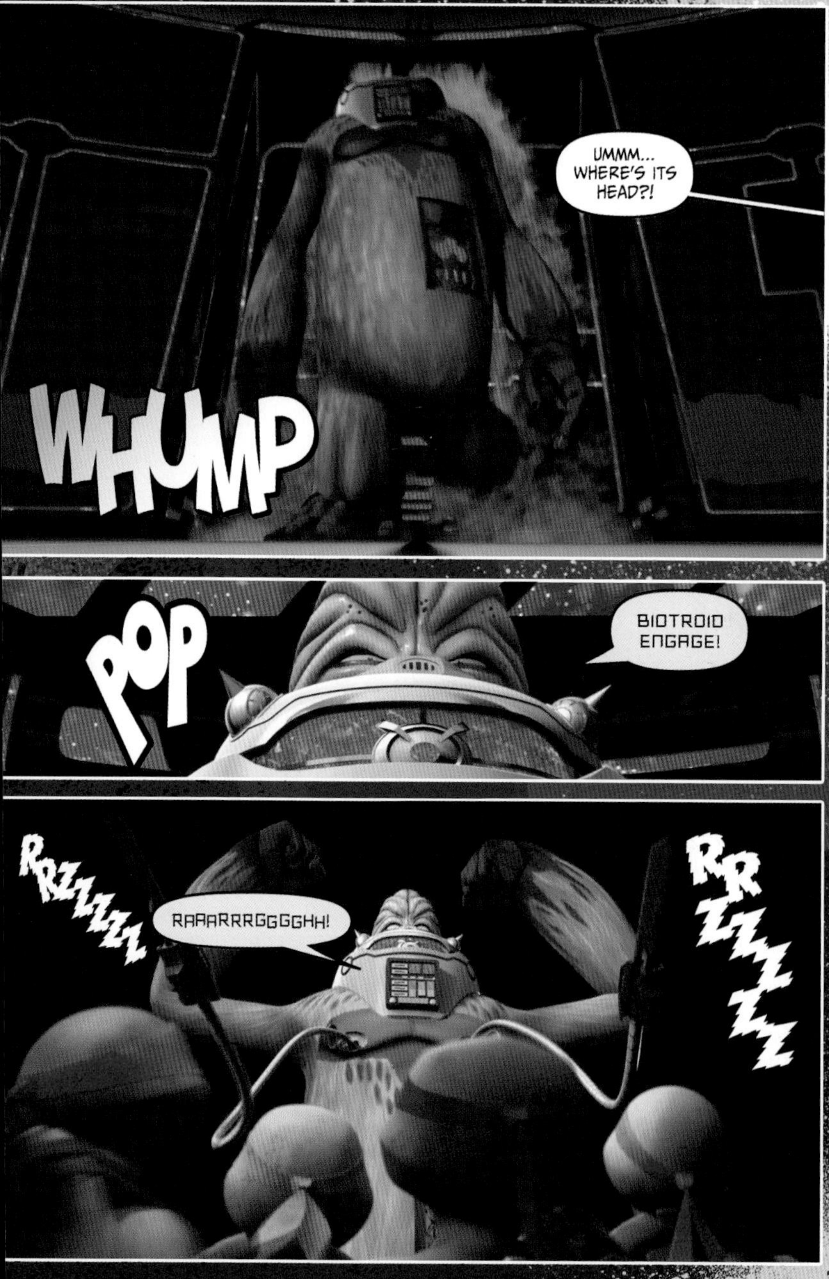
UMMM... WHERE'S ITS HEAD?!
WHUMP
POP
BIOTROID ENGAGE!
RRZZZZZZ
RAAARRRGGGGHH!
RRZZZZZZ

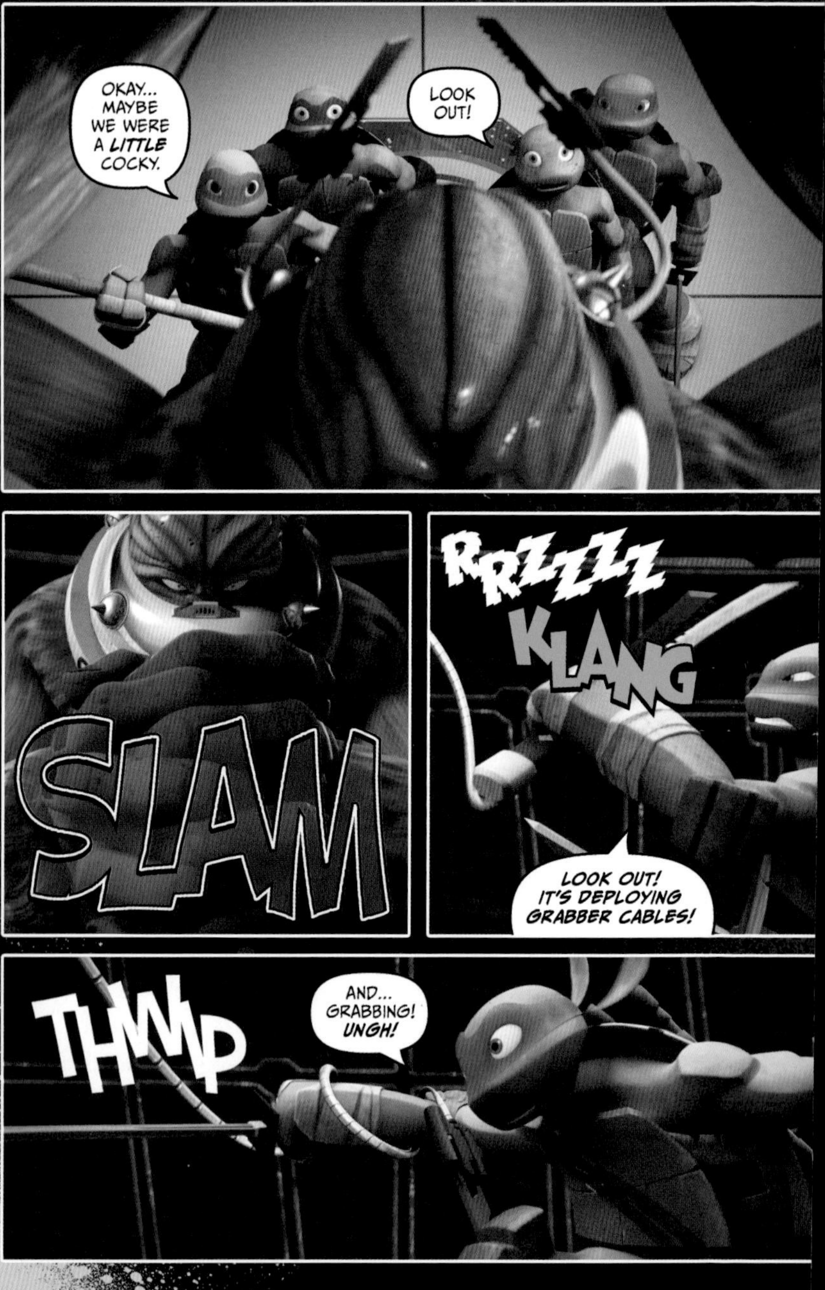
OKAY... MAYBE WE WERE A *LITTLE* COCKY.
LOOK OUT!
SLAM
RRZZZZ
KLANG
LOOK OUT! IT'S DEPLOYING GRABBER CABLES!
THWMP
AND... GRABBING! *UNGH!*

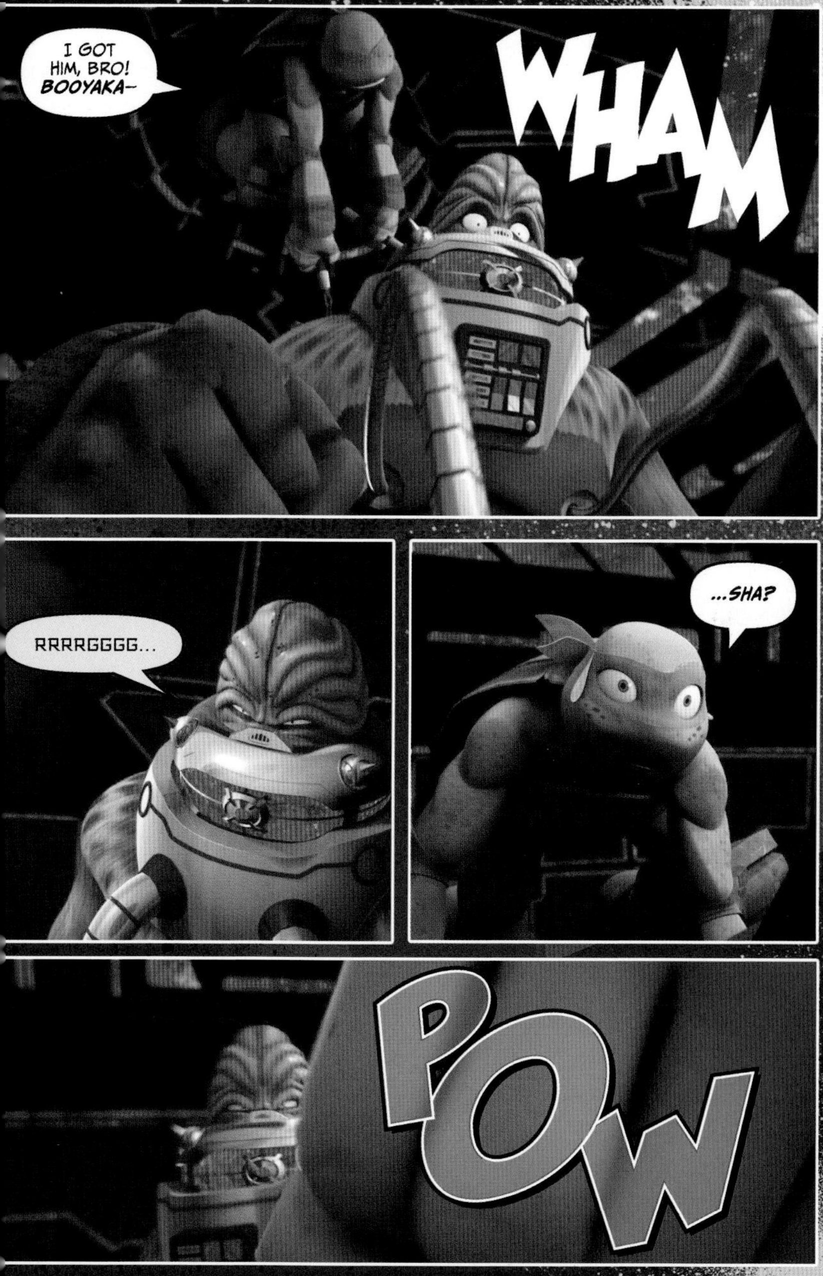
I GOT HIM, BRO! BOOYAKA-
WHAM
RRRRGGGG...
...SHA?
POW

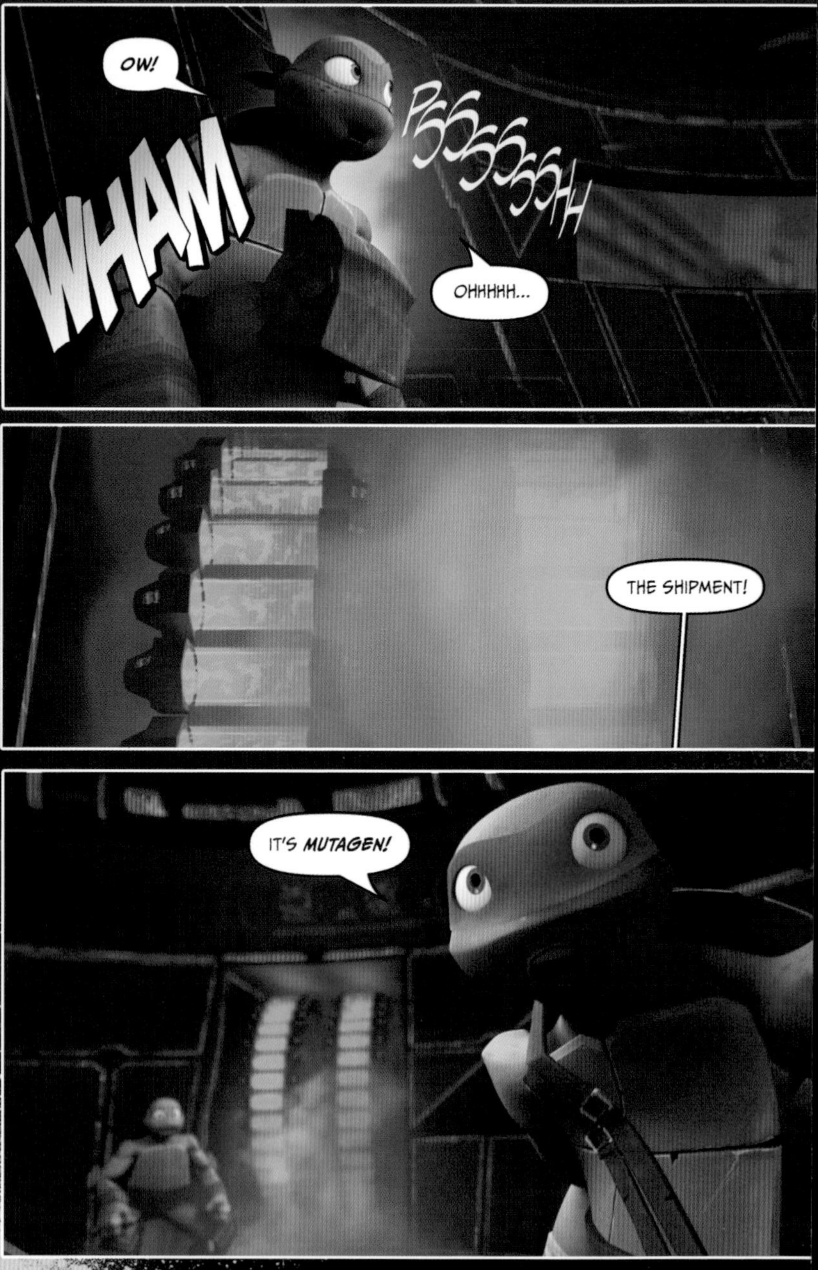
OW!
WHAM
PSSSSSSHH
OHHHHH...
THE SHIPMENT!
IT'S MUTAGEN!

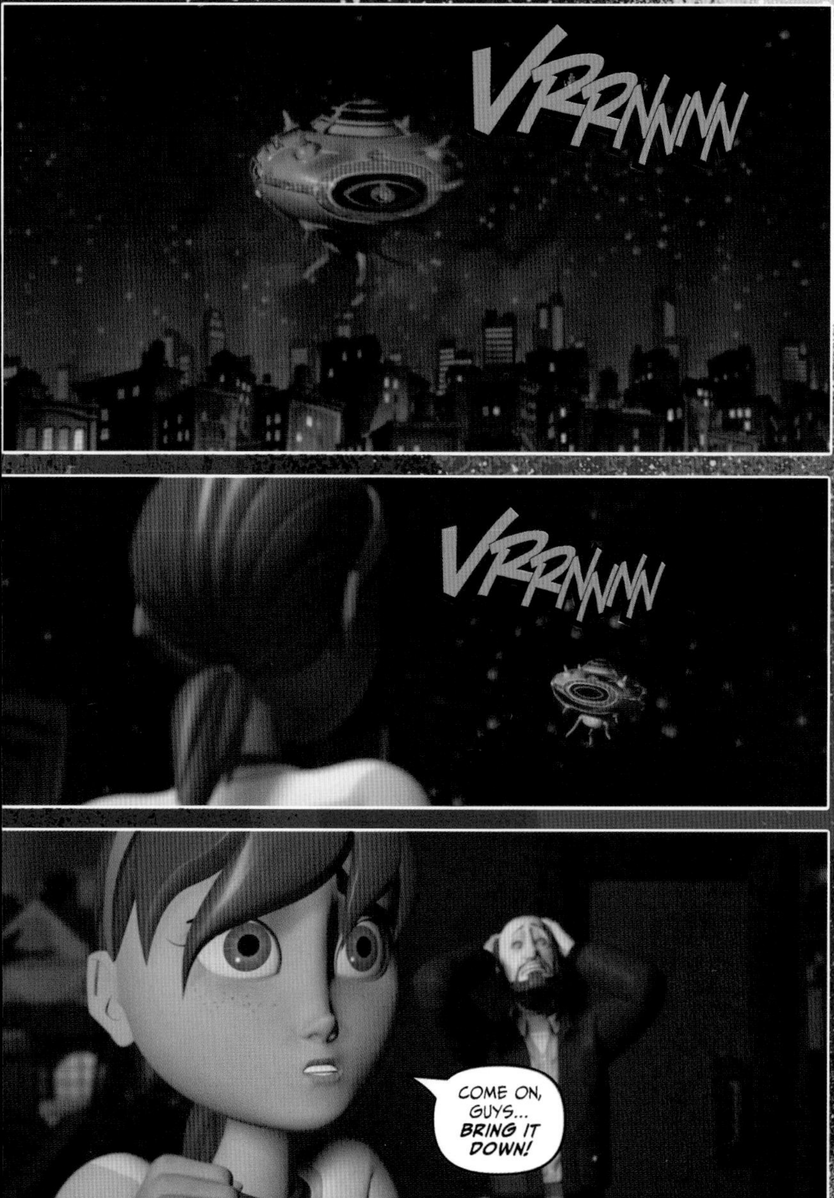
VRRNNNN
VRRNNNN
COME ON, GUYS... **BRING IT DOWN!**

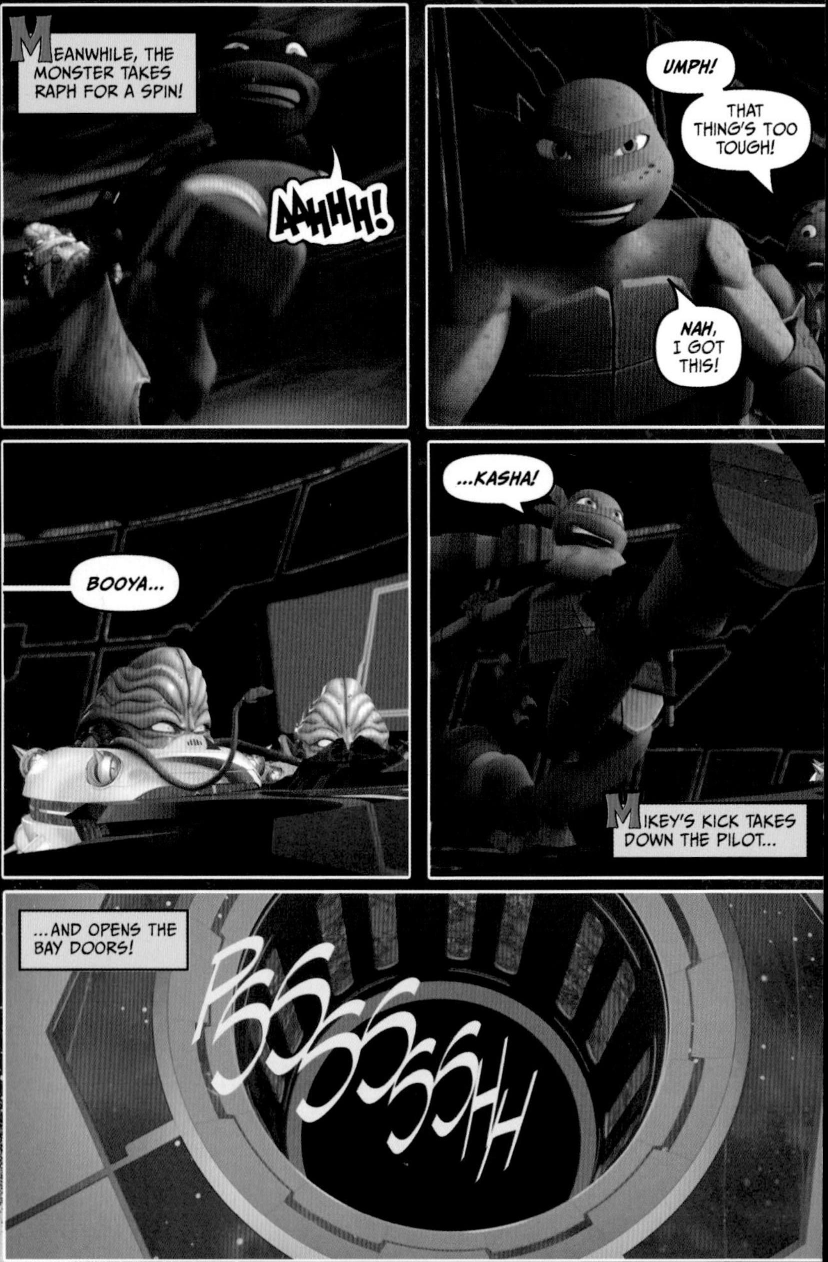
MEANWHILE, THE MONSTER TAKES RAPH FOR A SPIN!
AAHHH!
UMPH!
THAT THING'S TOO TOUGH!
NAH, I GOT THIS!
BOOYA...
...KASHA!
MIKEY'S KICK TAKES DOWN THE PILOT...
...AND OPENS THE BAY DOORS!
PSSSSSSHH

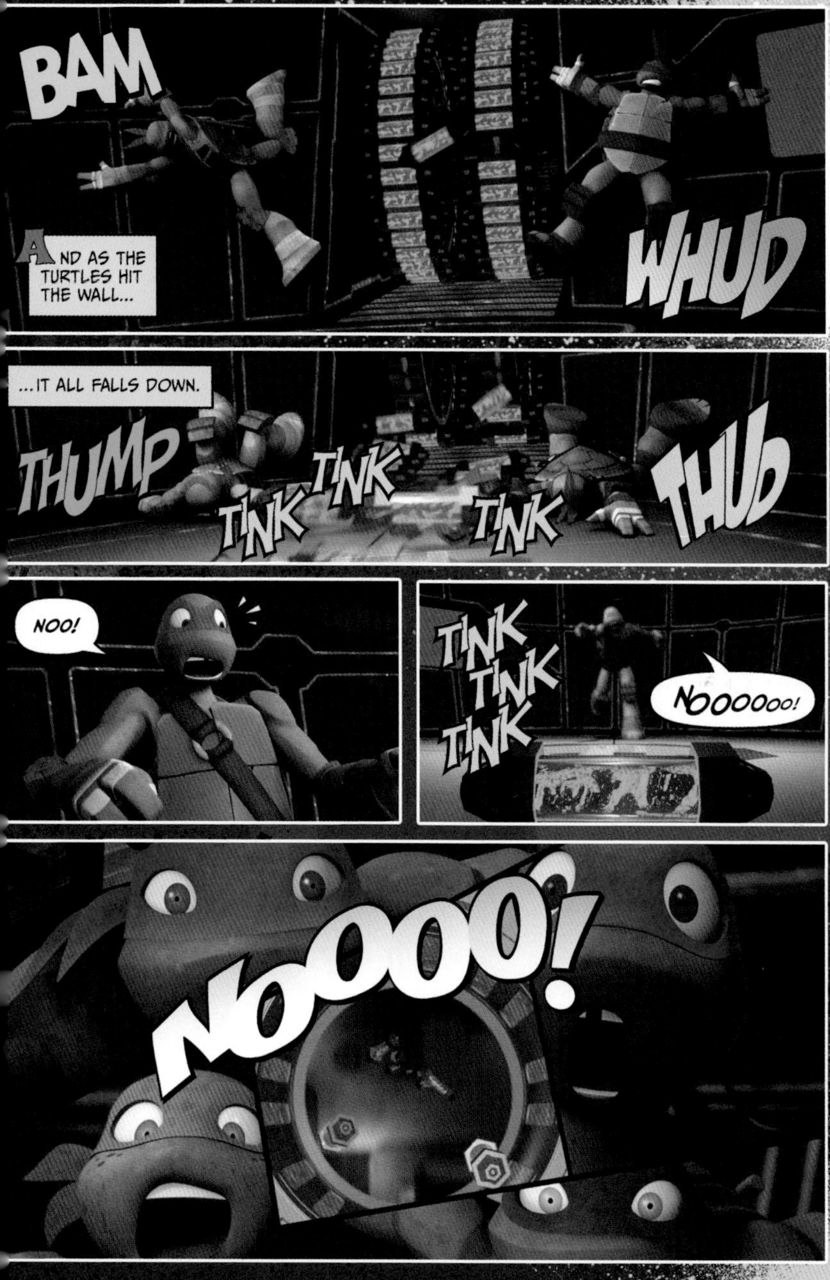
BAM
AND AS THE TURTLES HIT THE WALL...
WHUD
...IT ALL FALLS DOWN.
THUMP
TINK
TINK
TINK
THUD
NOO!
TINK
TINK
TINK
NOOOOOO!
NOOOO!

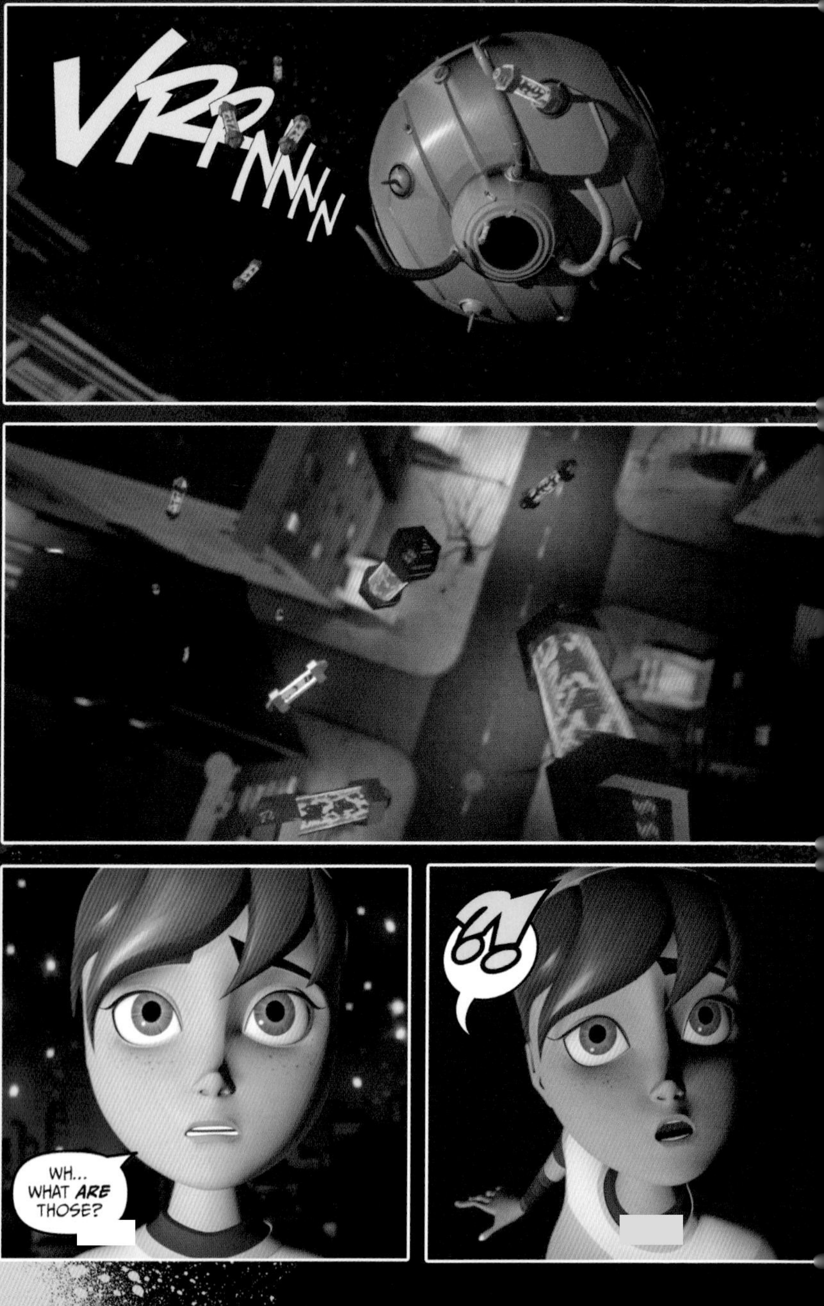
VRRRNNNNN
WH... WHAT **ARE** THOSE?
??

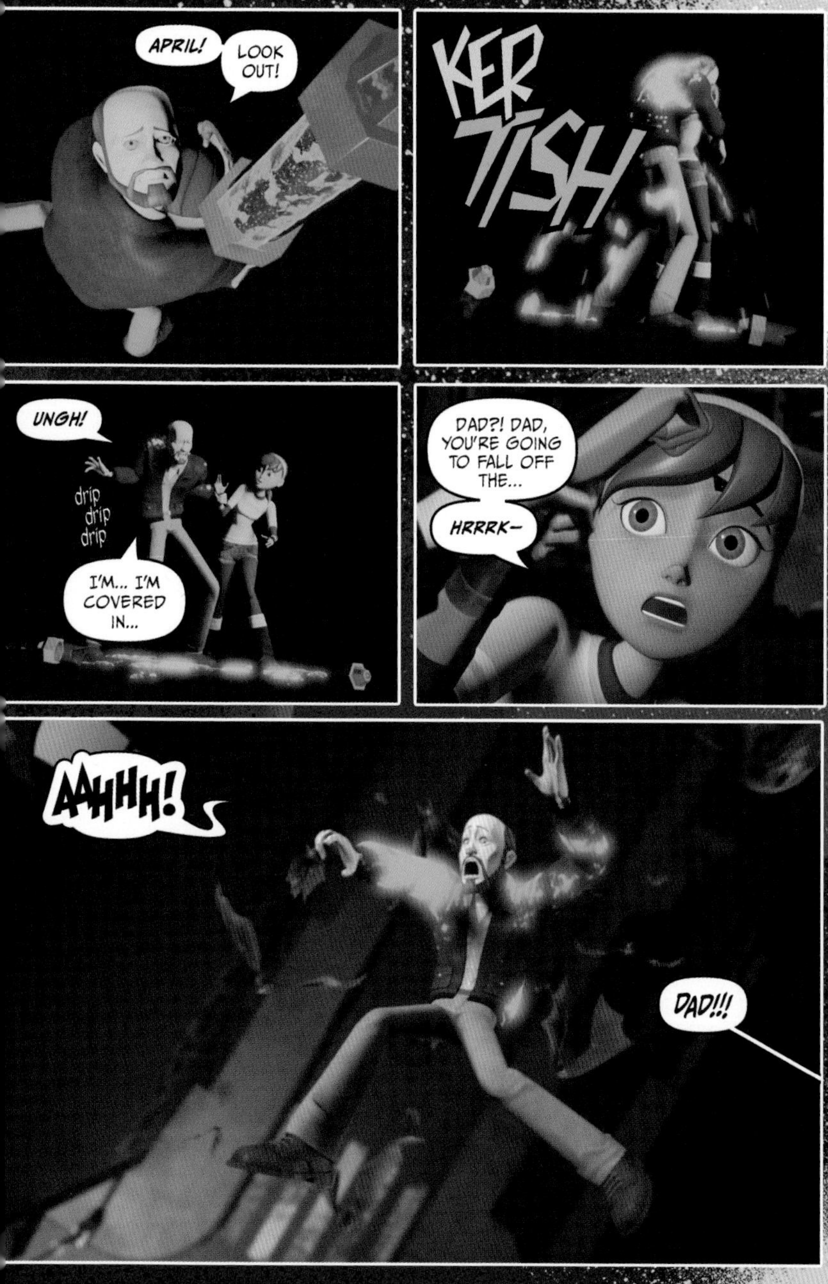
APRIL!
LOOK OUT!
KER TISH
UNGH!
drip drip drip
I'M... I'M COVERED IN...
DAD?! DAD, YOU'RE GOING TO FALL OFF THE...
HRRRK—
AAHHH!
DAD!!!

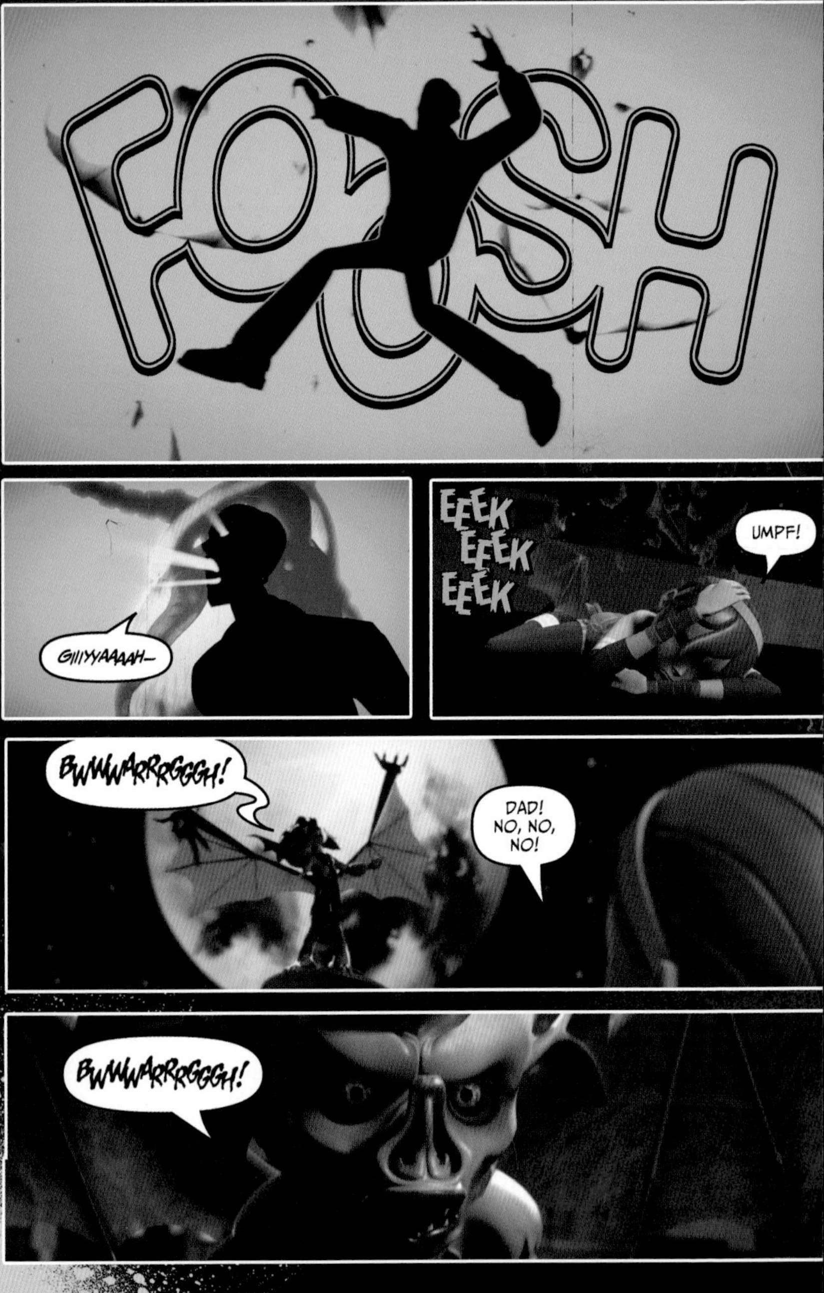
FOOSH
FOOSH
GIIIYYAAAAH—
EEEK
EEEK
EEEK
UMPF!
BWWWARRRGGGH!
DAD! NO, NO, NO!
BWWWARRRGGGH!

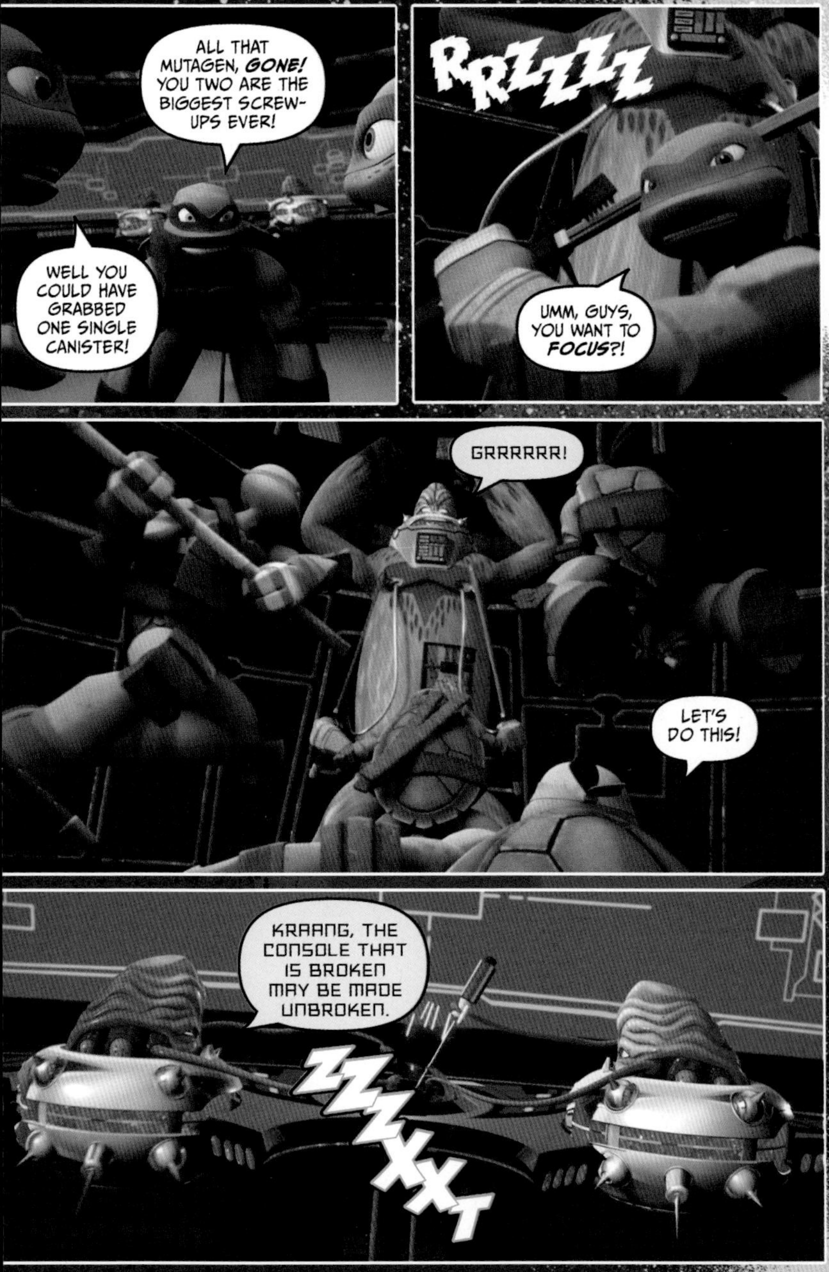
ALL THAT MUTAGEN, GONE! YOU TWO ARE THE BIGGEST SCREW-UPS EVER!
WELL YOU COULD HAVE GRABBED ONE SINGLE CANISTER!
RRZZZZZ
UMM, GUYS, YOU WANT TO FOCUS?!
GRRRRRR!
LET'S DO THIS!
KRAANG, THE CONSOLE THAT IS BROKEN MAY BE MADE UNBROKEN.
ZZZXXT

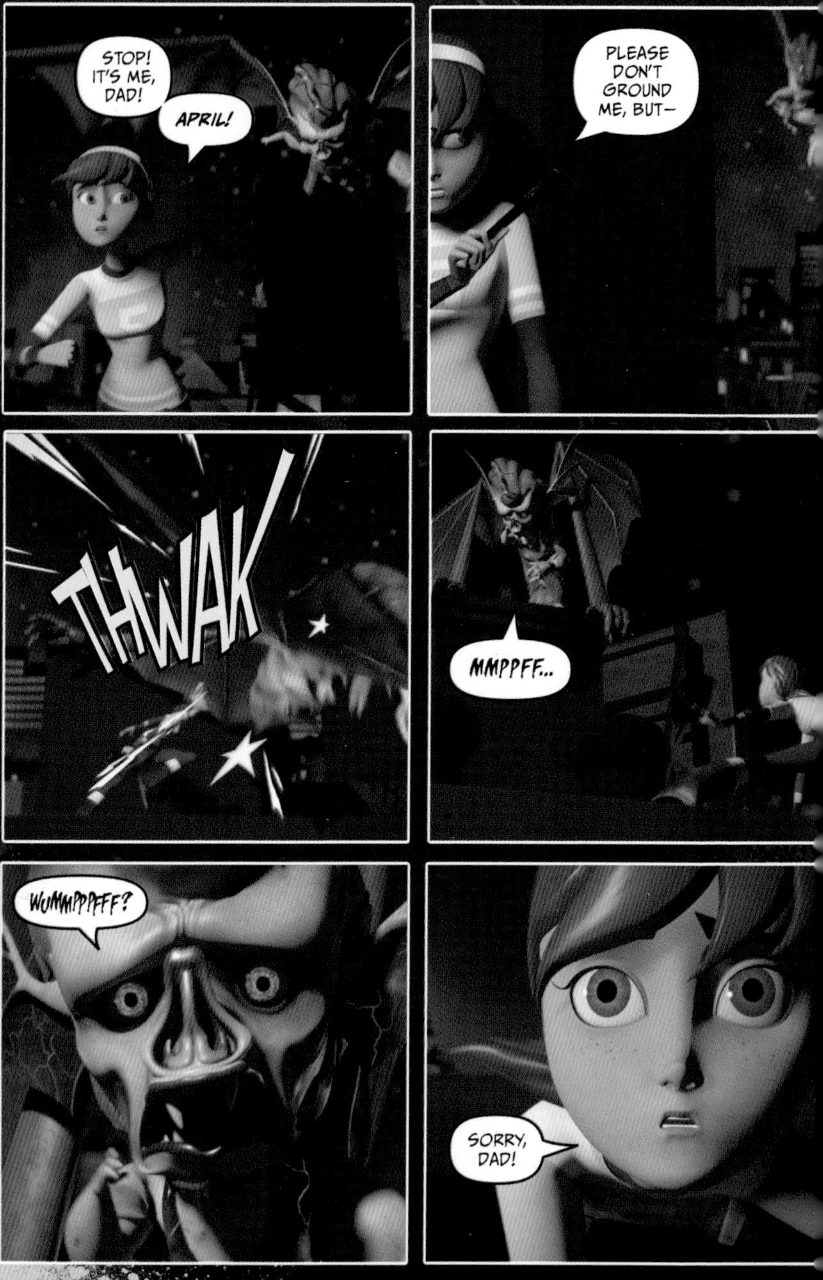
STOP! IT'S ME, DAD!
APRIL!
PLEASE DON'T GROUND ME, BUT–
THWAK
MMPPFF...
WUMMPPPFFF?
SORRY, DAD!

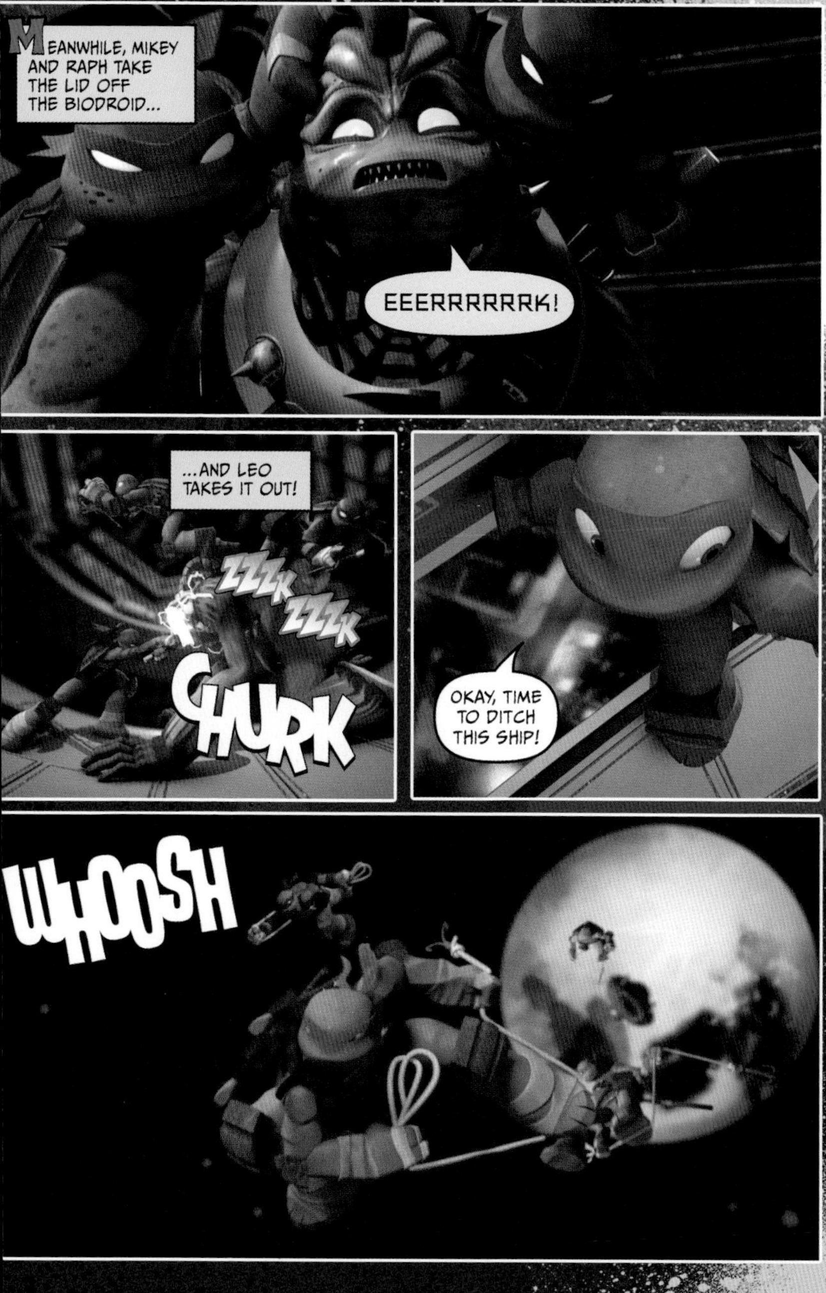
MEANWHILE, MIKEY AND RAPH TAKE THE LID OFF THE BIODROID...
EEERRRRRRRK!
...AND LEO TAKES IT OUT!
ZZZK
ZZZK
CHURK
OKAY, TIME TO DITCH THIS SHIP!
WHOOSH

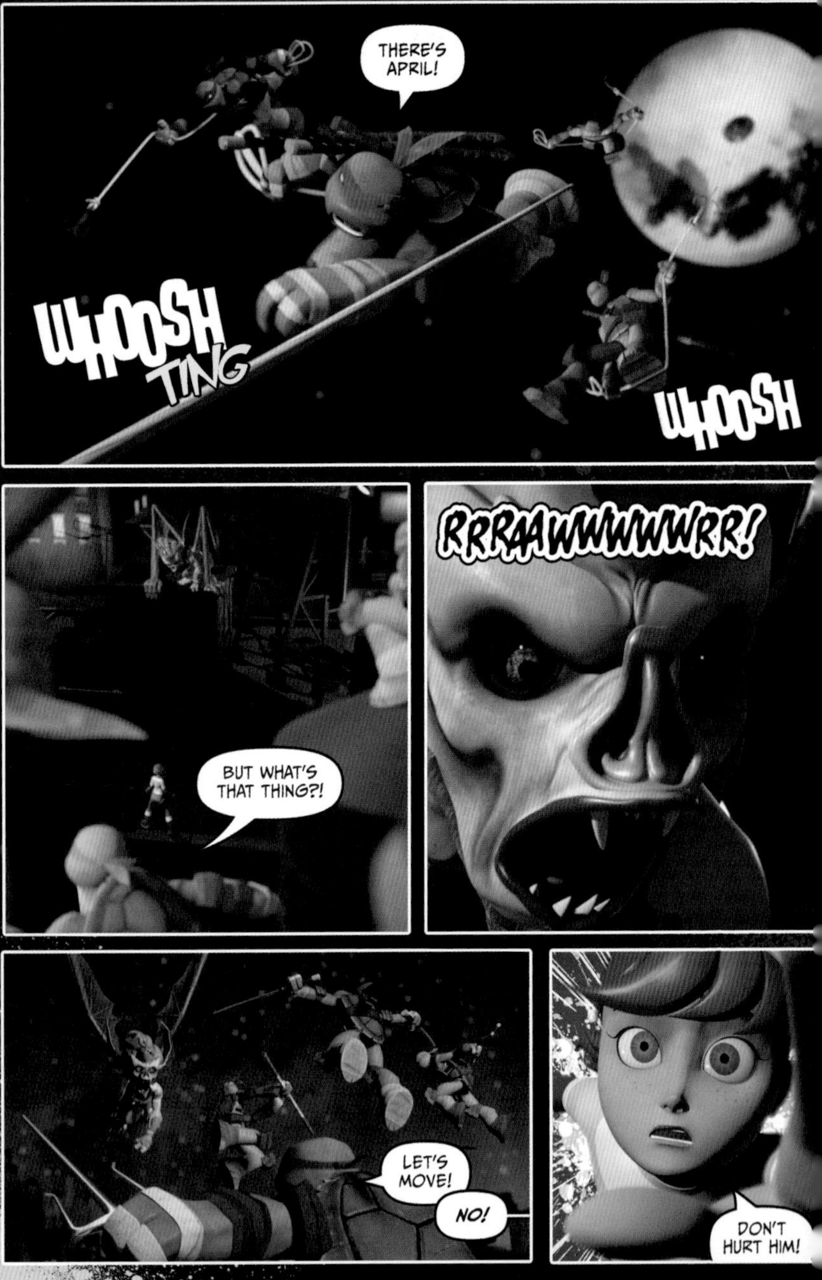
THERE'S APRIL!
WHOOSH
TING
WHOOSH
RRRAAWWWWWRR!
BUT WHAT'S THAT THING?!
LET'S MOVE!
NO!
DON'T HURT HIM!

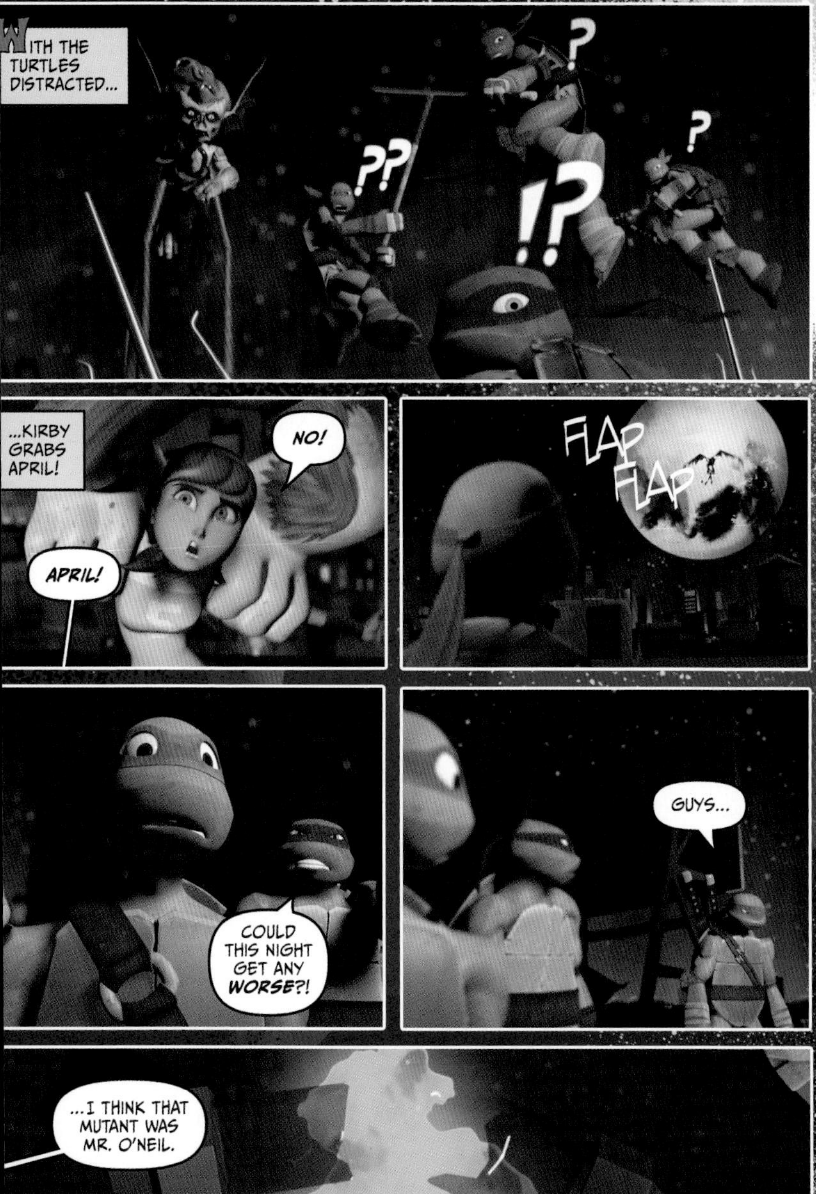
WITH THE TURTLES DISTRACTED...
??
?
!?
?
...KIRBY GRABS APRIL!
NO!
APRIL!
FLAP
FLAP
COULD THIS NIGHT GET ANY WORSE?!
GUYS...
...I THINK THAT MUTANT WAS MR. O'NEIL.

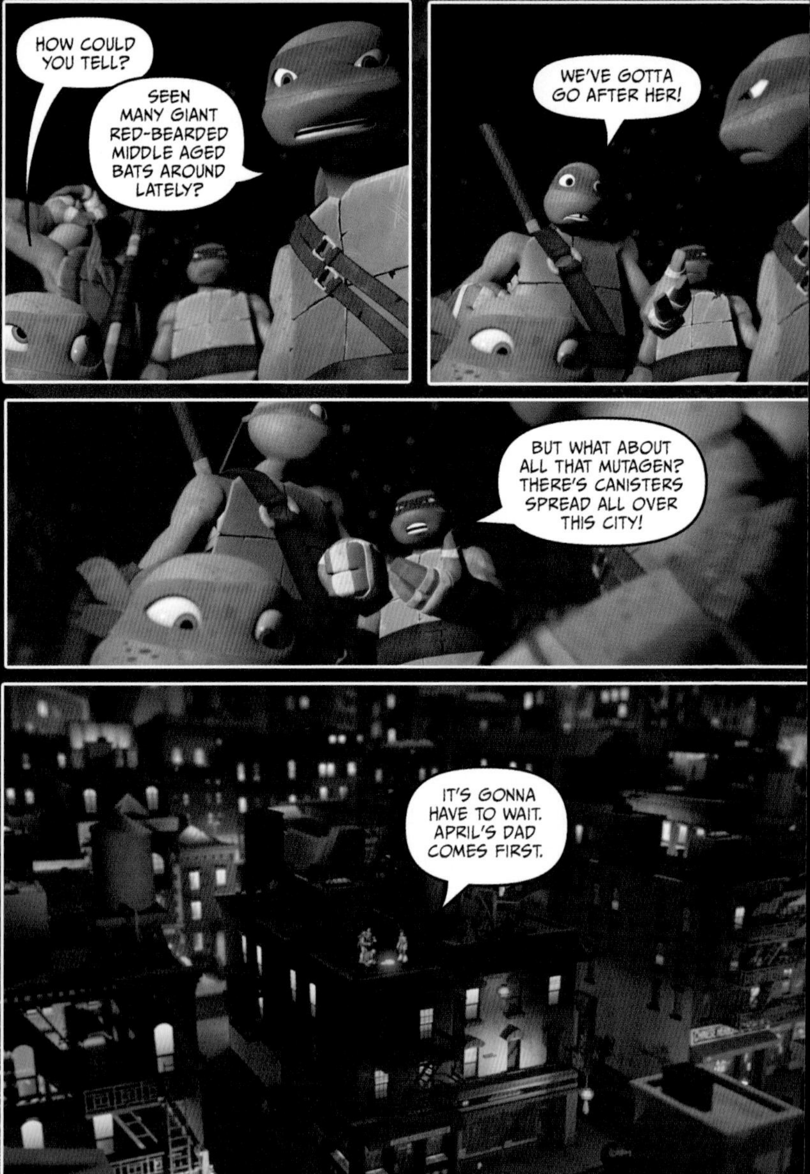
HOW COULD YOU TELL?
SEEN MANY GIANT RED-BEARDED MIDDLE AGED BATS AROUND LATELY?
WE'VE GOTTA GO AFTER HER!
BUT WHAT ABOUT ALL THAT MUTAGEN? THERE'S CANISTERS SPREAD ALL OVER THIS CITY!
IT'S GONNA HAVE TO WAIT. APRIL'S DAD COMES FIRST.

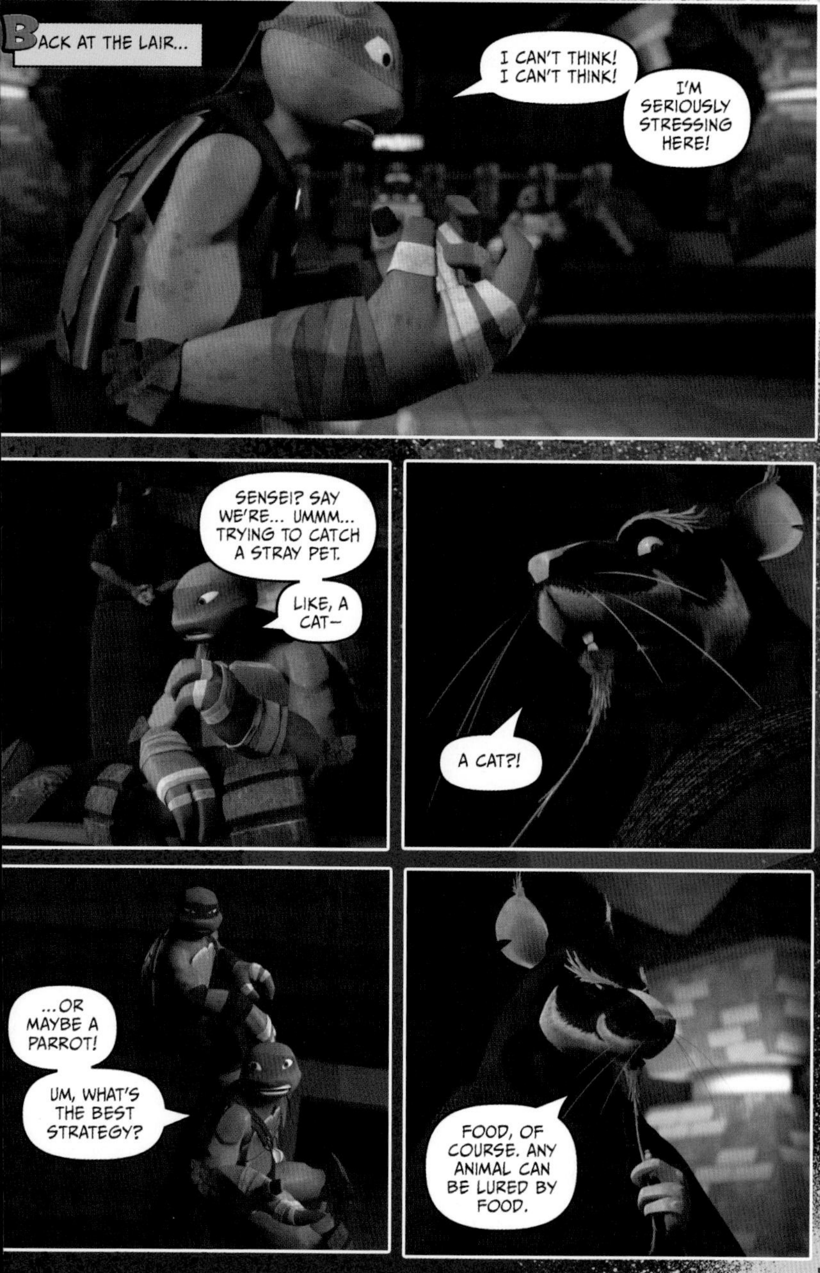
BACK AT THE LAIR...
I CAN'T THINK! I CAN'T THINK!
I'M SERIOUSLY STRESSING HERE!
SENSEI? SAY WE'RE... UMMM... TRYING TO CATCH A STRAY PET.
LIKE, A CAT—
A CAT?!
...OR MAYBE A PARROT!
UM, WHAT'S THE BEST STRATEGY?
FOOD, OF COURSE. ANY ANIMAL CAN BE LURED BY FOOD.

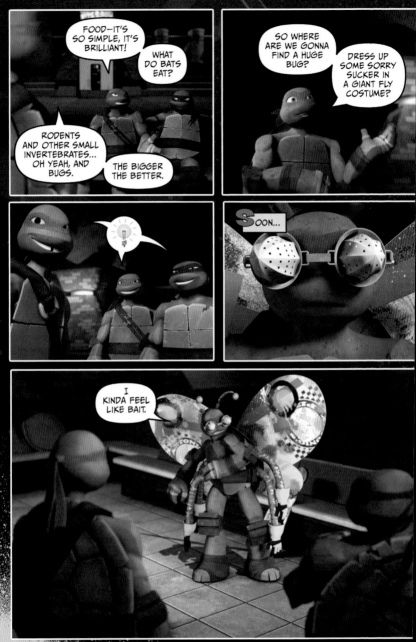

FOOD—IT'S SO SIMPLE, IT'S BRILLIANT!

WHAT DO BATS EAT?

RODENTS AND OTHER SMALL INVERTEBRATES... OH YEAH, AND BUGS.

THE BIGGER THE BETTER.

SO WHERE ARE WE GONNA FIND A HUGE BUG?

DRESS UP SOME SORRY SUCKER IN A GIANT FLY COSTUME?

SOON...

I KINDA FEEL LIKE BAIT.

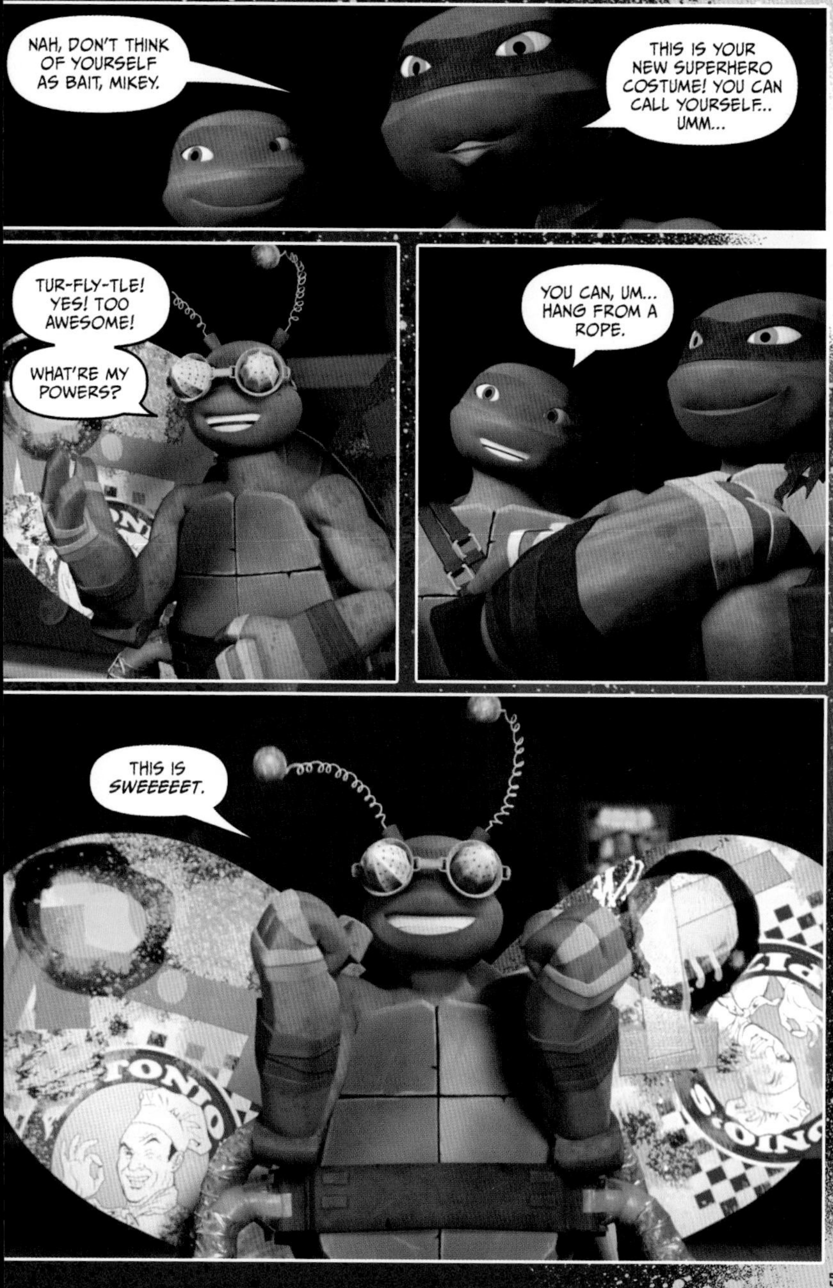
NAH, DON'T THINK OF YOURSELF AS BAIT, MIKEY.
THIS IS YOUR NEW SUPERHERO COSTUME! YOU CAN CALL YOURSELF.. UMM...
TUR-FLY-TLE! YES! TOO AWESOME!
WHAT'RE MY POWERS?
YOU CAN, UM... HANG FROM A ROPE.
THIS IS SWEEEEET.

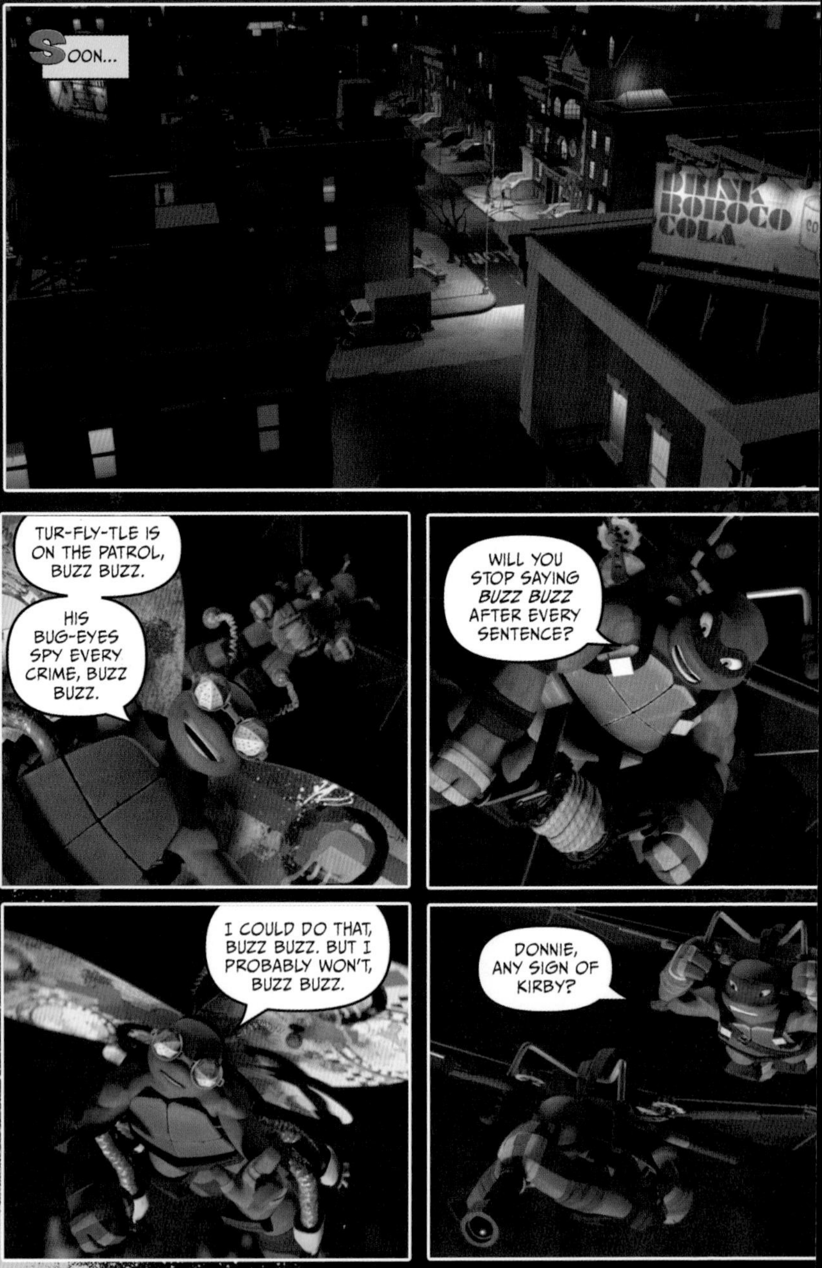
SOON...
DRINK BOBOCO COLA
TUR-FLY-TLE IS ON THE PATROL, BUZZ BUZZ.
HIS BUG-EYES SPY EVERY CRIME, BUZZ BUZZ.
WILL YOU STOP SAYING *BUZZ BUZZ* AFTER EVERY SENTENCE?
I COULD DO THAT, BUZZ BUZZ. BUT I PROBABLY WON'T, BUZZ BUZZ.
DONNIE, ANY SIGN OF KIRBY?

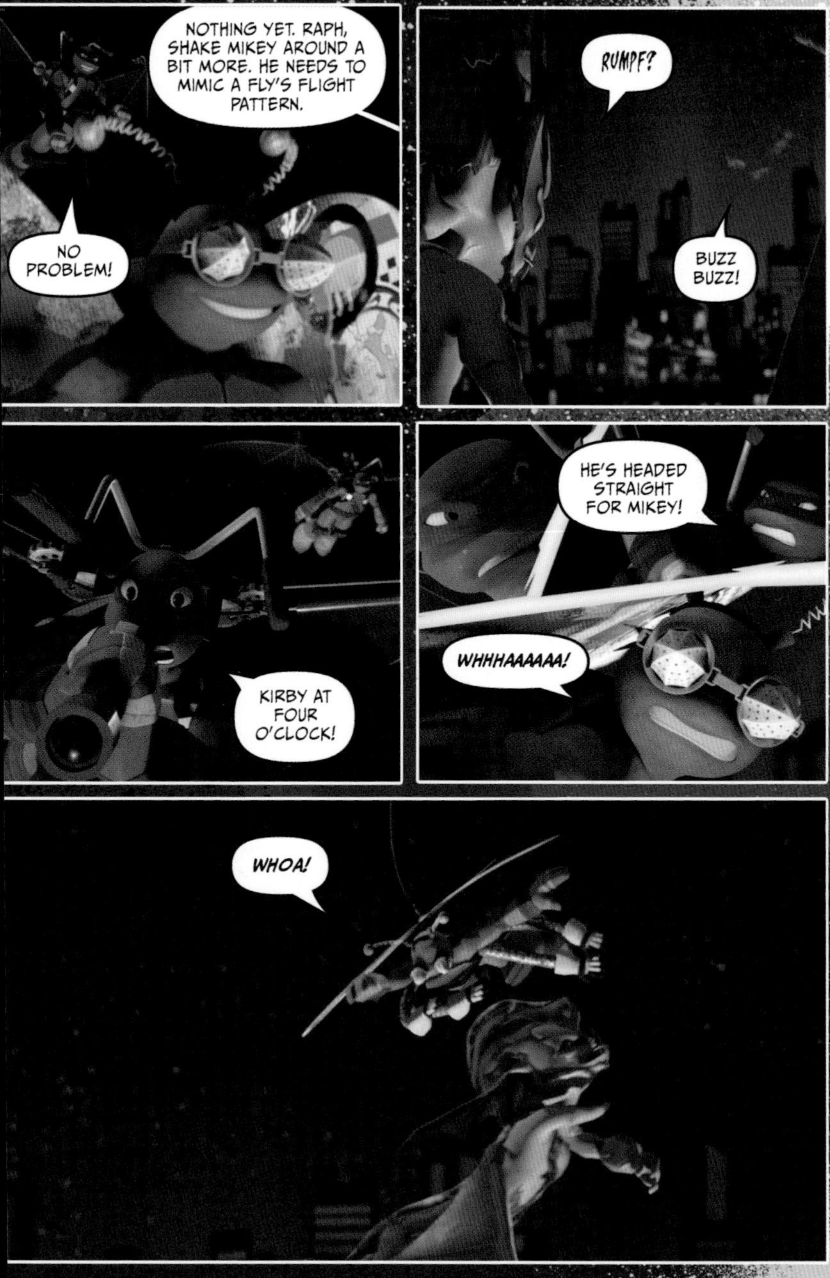
NOTHING YET. RAPH, SHAKE MIKEY AROUND A BIT MORE. HE NEEDS TO MIMIC A FLY'S FLIGHT PATTERN.
NO PROBLEM!
RUMPF?
BUZZ BUZZ!
KIRBY AT FOUR O'CLOCK!
HE'S HEADED STRAIGHT FOR MIKEY!
WHHHAAAAAA!
WHOA!

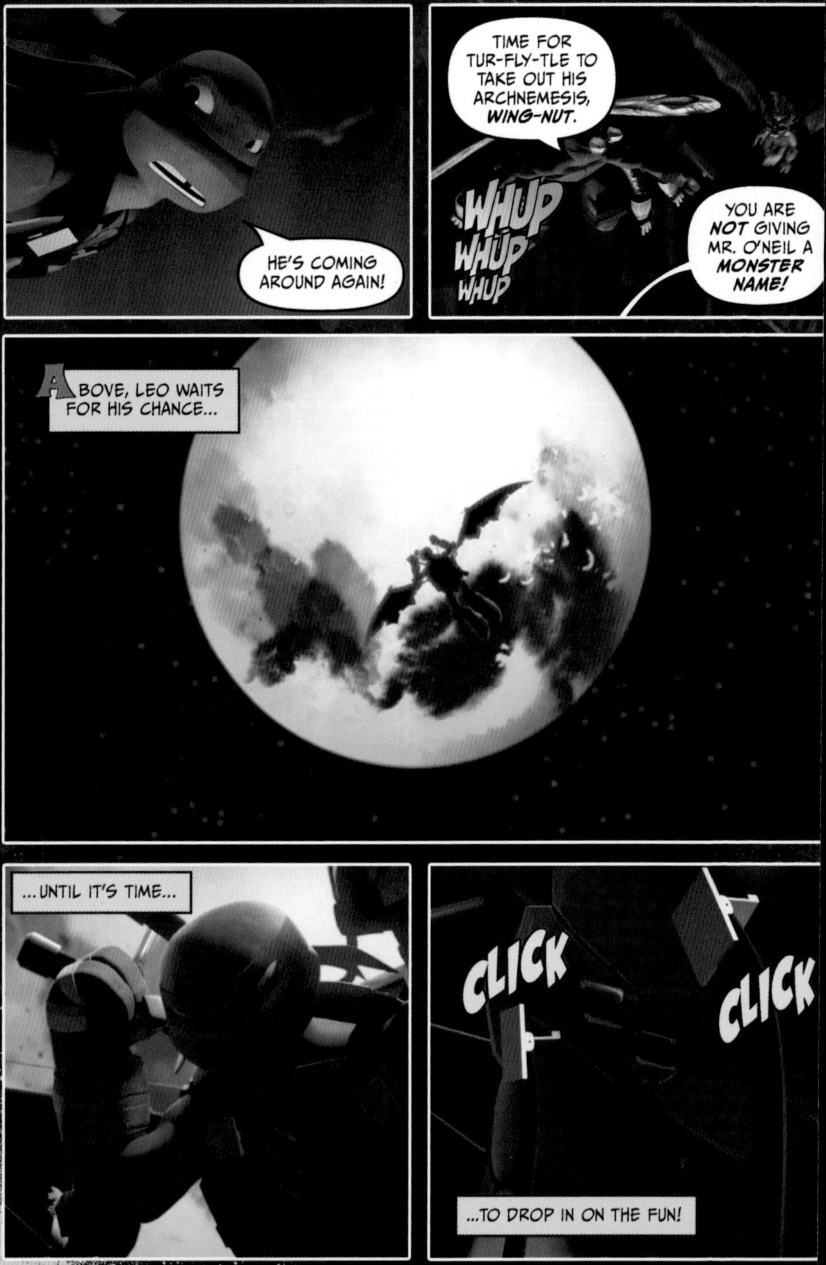
HE'S COMING AROUND AGAIN!
TIME FOR TUR-FLY-TLE TO TAKE OUT HIS ARCHNEMESIS, WING-NUT.
WHUP WHUP WHUP
YOU ARE NOT GIVING MR. O'NEIL A MONSTER NAME!
ABOVE, LEO WAITS FOR HIS CHANCE...
...UNTIL IT'S TIME...
CLICK
CLICK
...TO DROP IN ON THE FUN!

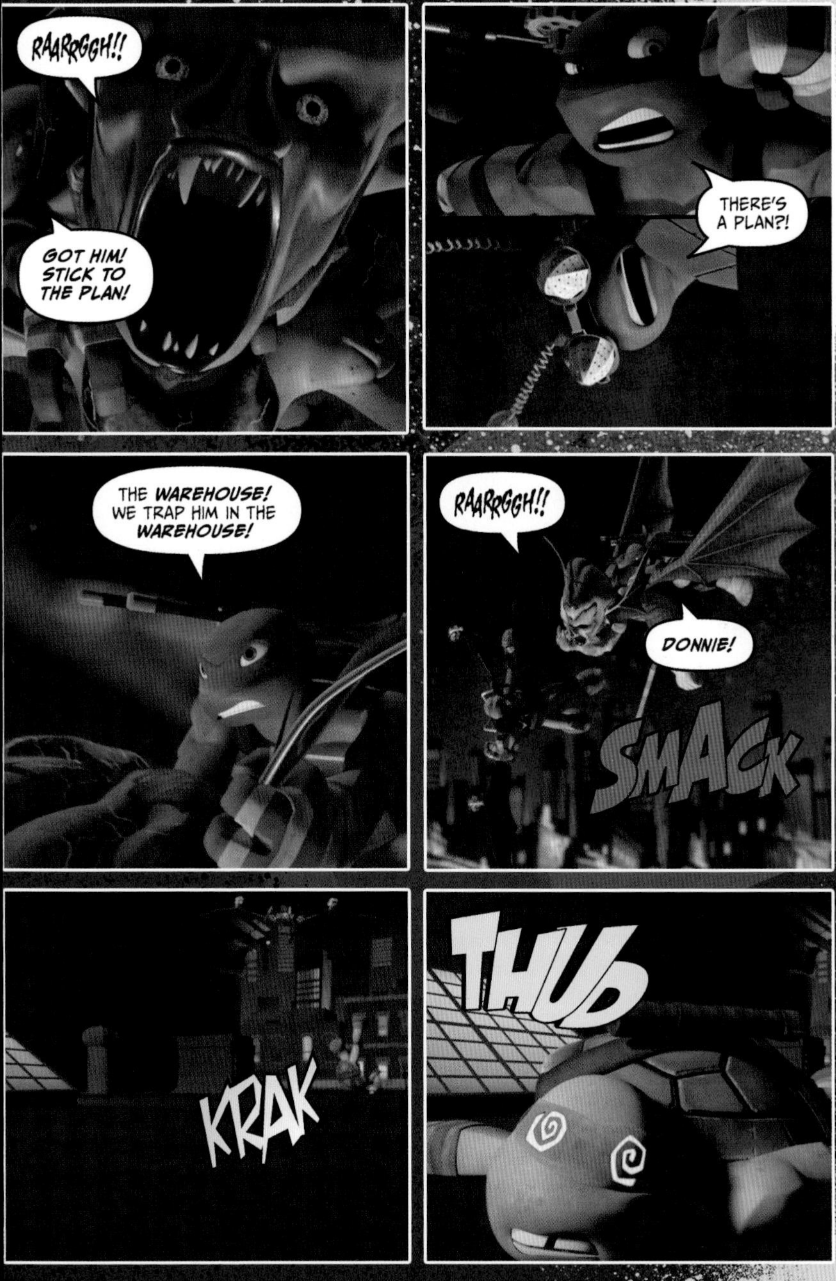
RAARRGGH!!
GOT HIM! STICK TO THE PLAN!
THERE'S A PLAN?!
THE WAREHOUSE! WE TRAP HIM IN THE WAREHOUSE!
RAARRGGH!!
DONNIE!
SMACK
KRAK
THUD

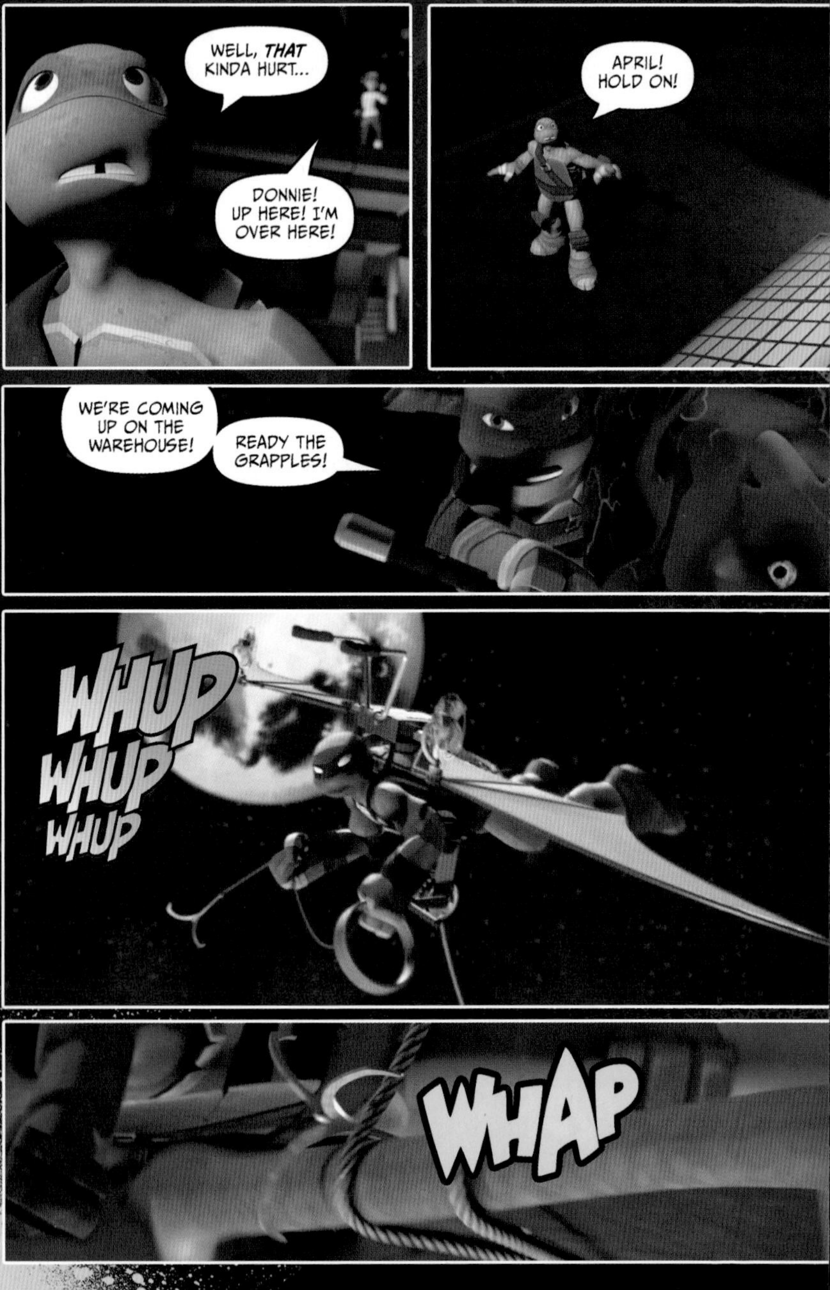
WELL, *THAT* KINDA HURT...
DONNIE! UP HERE! I'M OVER HERE!
APRIL! HOLD ON!
WE'RE COMING UP ON THE WAREHOUSE!
READY THE GRAPPLES!
WHUP WHUP WHUP
WHAP

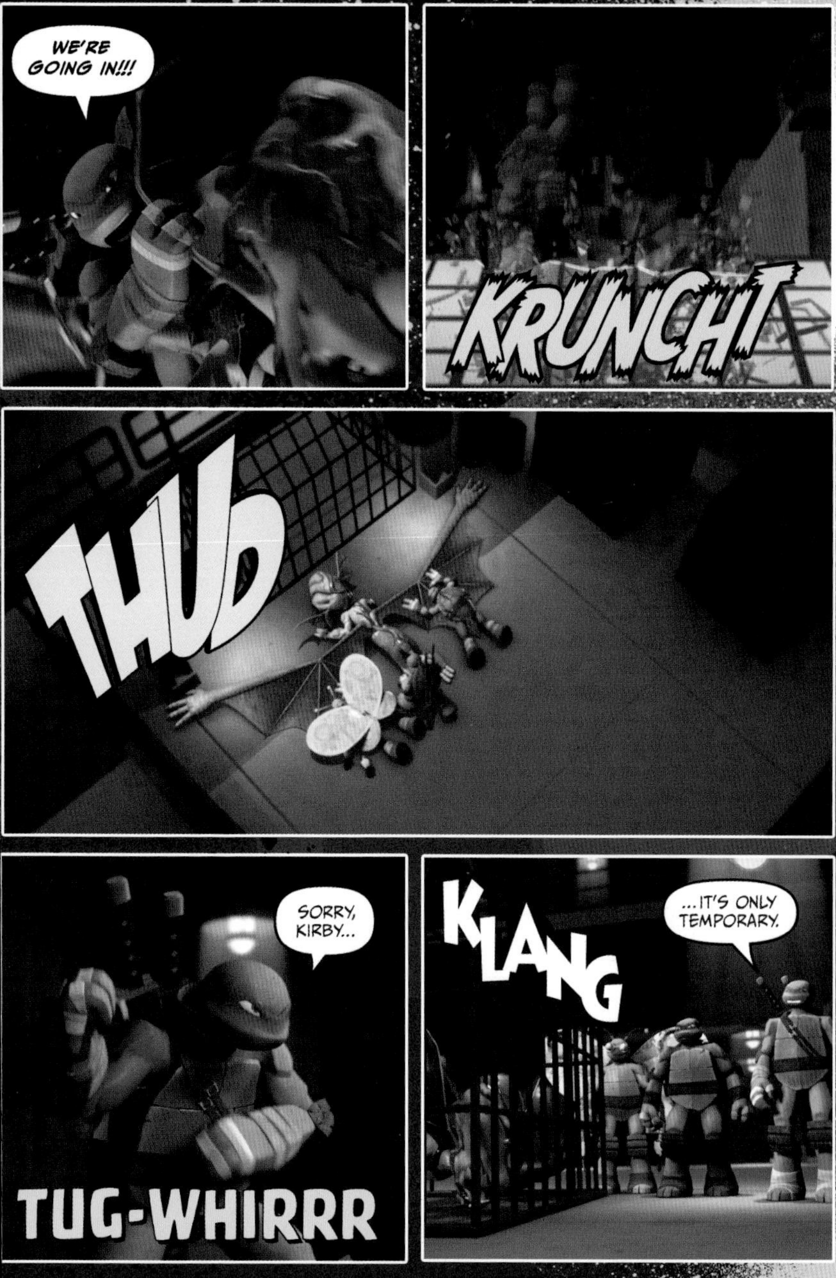
WE'RE GOING IN!!!
KRUNCH!
THUD
SORRY, KIRBY...
TUG-WHIRRR
KLANG
...IT'S ONLY TEMPORARY.

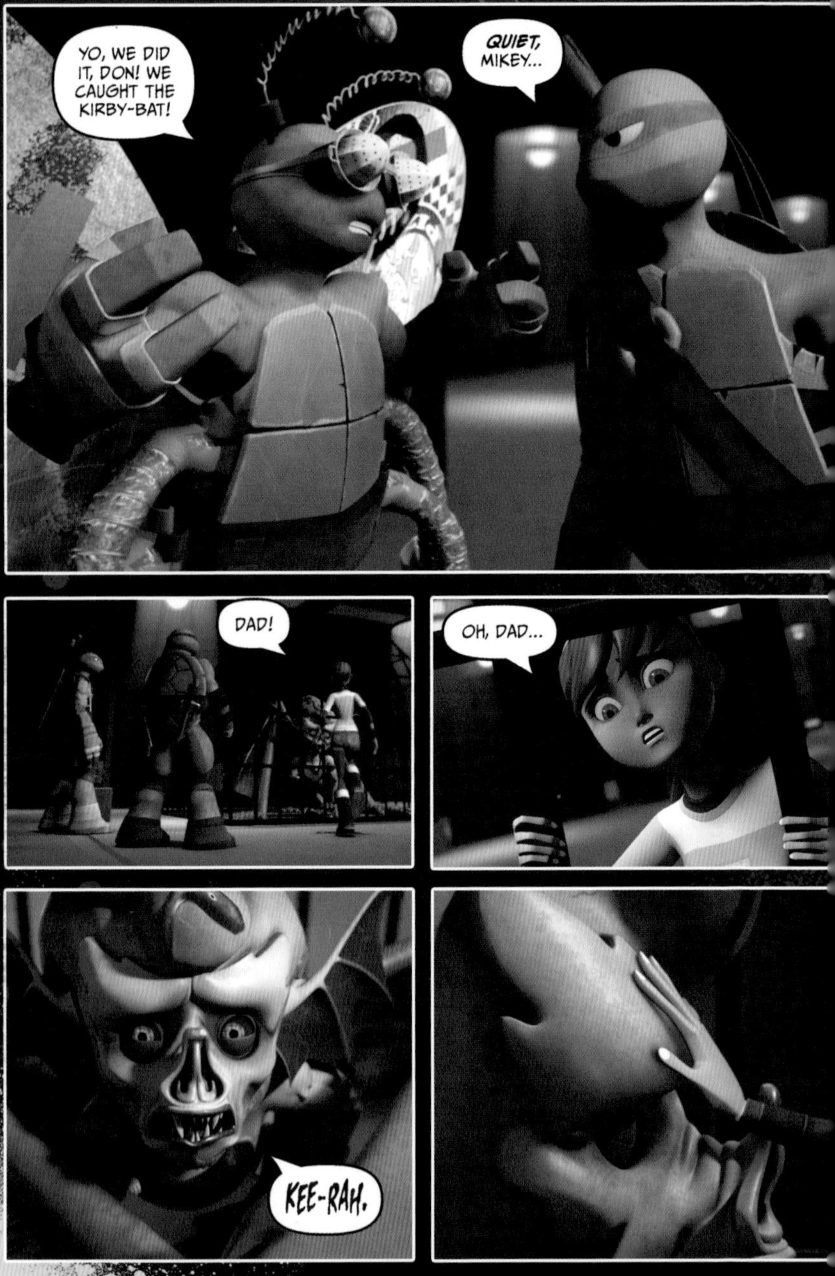
YO, WE DID IT, DON! WE CAUGHT THE KIRBY-BAT!
QUIET, MIKEY...
DAD!
OH, DAD...
KEE-RAH.

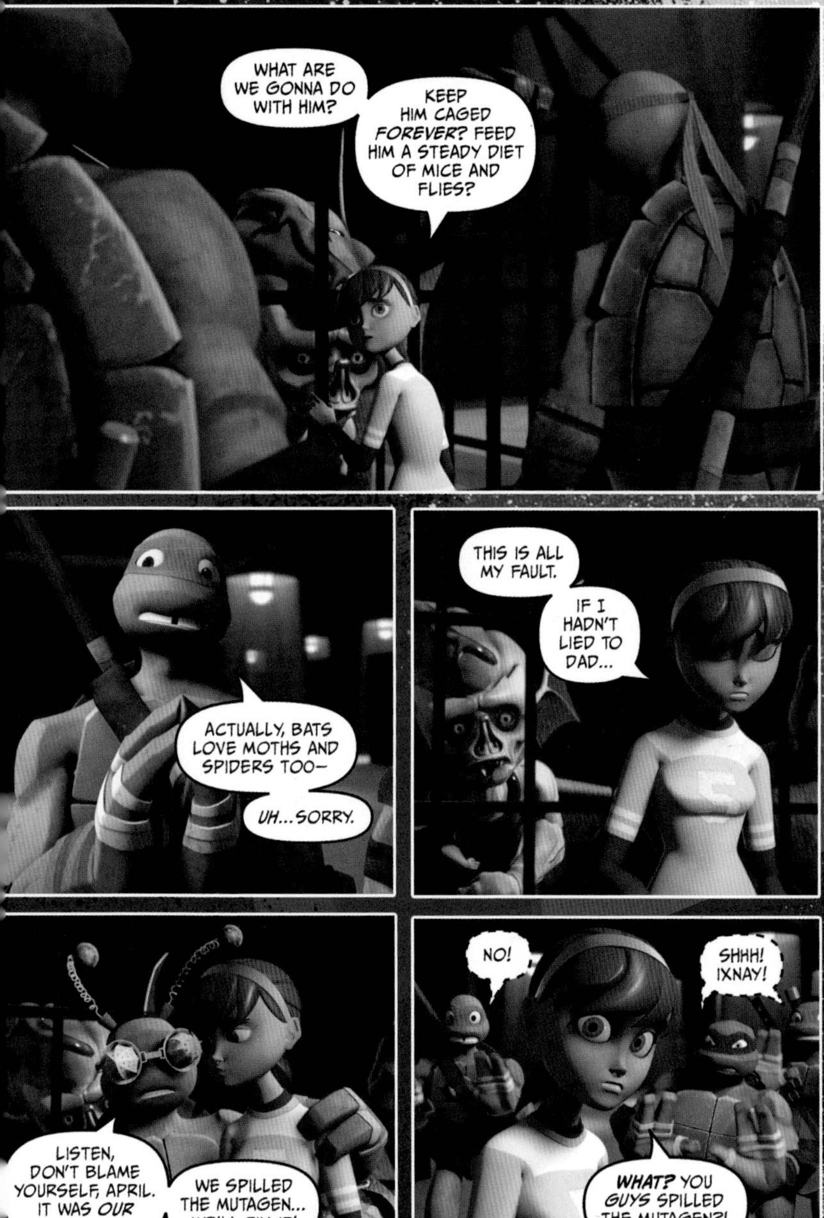
WHAT ARE WE GONNA DO WITH HIM?
KEEP HIM CAGED *FOREVER?* FEED HIM A STEADY DIET OF MICE AND FLIES?
ACTUALLY, BATS LOVE MOTHS AND SPIDERS TOO—
UH...SORRY.
THIS IS ALL MY FAULT.
IF I HADN'T LIED TO DAD...
LISTEN, DON'T BLAME YOURSELF, APRIL. IT WAS *OUR* FAULT.
WE SPILLED THE MUTAGEN... WE'LL FIX IT!
NO!
SHHH! IXNAY!
WHAT? YOU *GUYS* SPILLED THE MUTAGEN?!

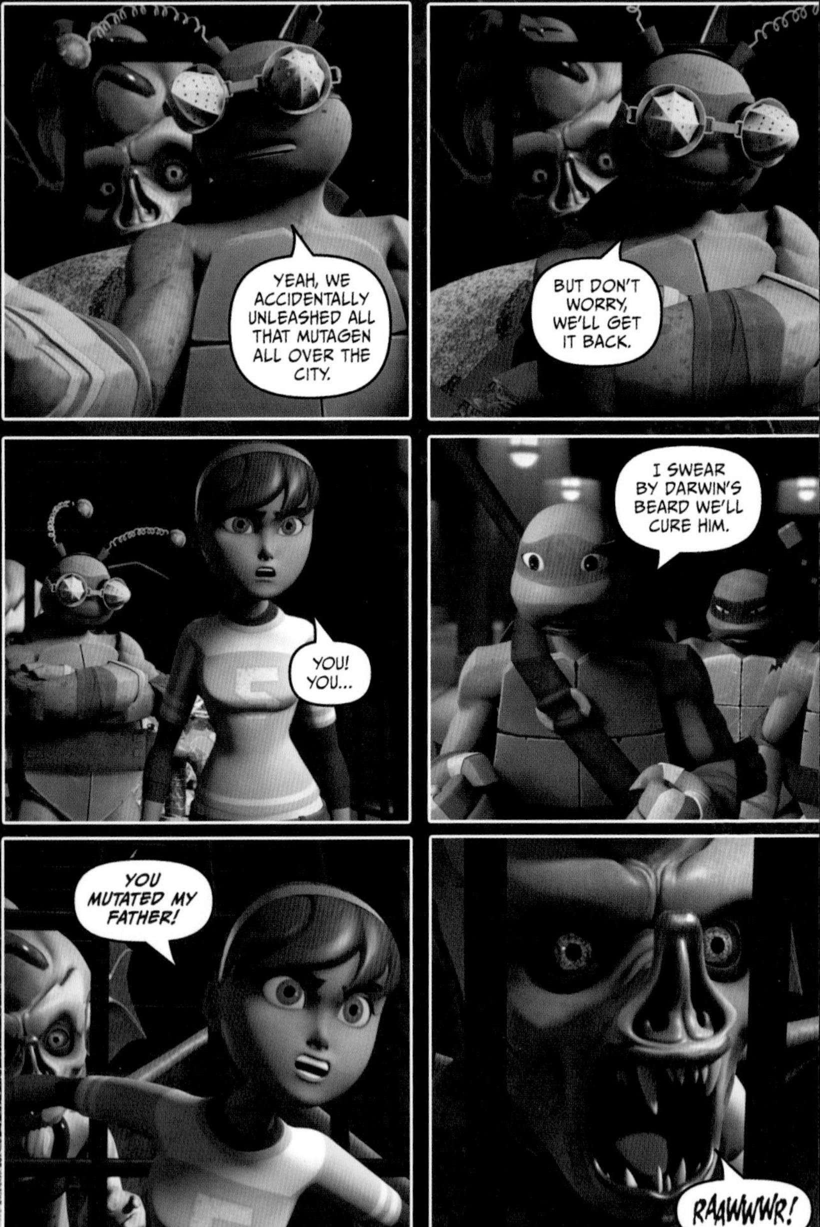
YEAH, WE ACCIDENTALLY UNLEASHED ALL THAT MUTAGEN ALL OVER THE CITY.
BUT DON'T WORRY, WE'LL GET IT BACK.
YOU! YOU...
I SWEAR BY DARWIN'S BEARD WE'LL CURE HIM.
YOU MUTATED MY FATHER!
RAAWWWR!

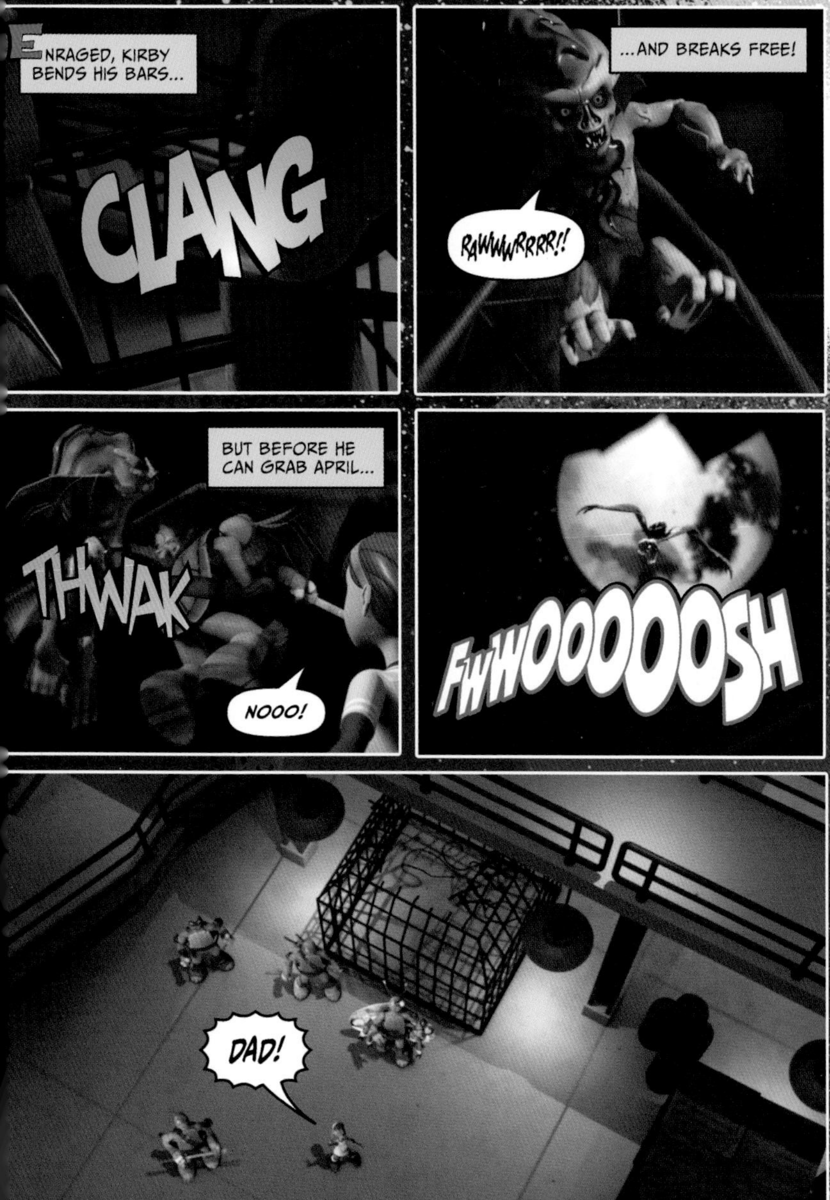
ENRAGED, KIRBY BENDS HIS BARS...
CLANG
...AND BREAKS FREE!
RAWWWRRRR!!
BUT BEFORE HE CAN GRAB APRIL...
THWAK
NOOO!
FWWOOOOOOSH
DAD!

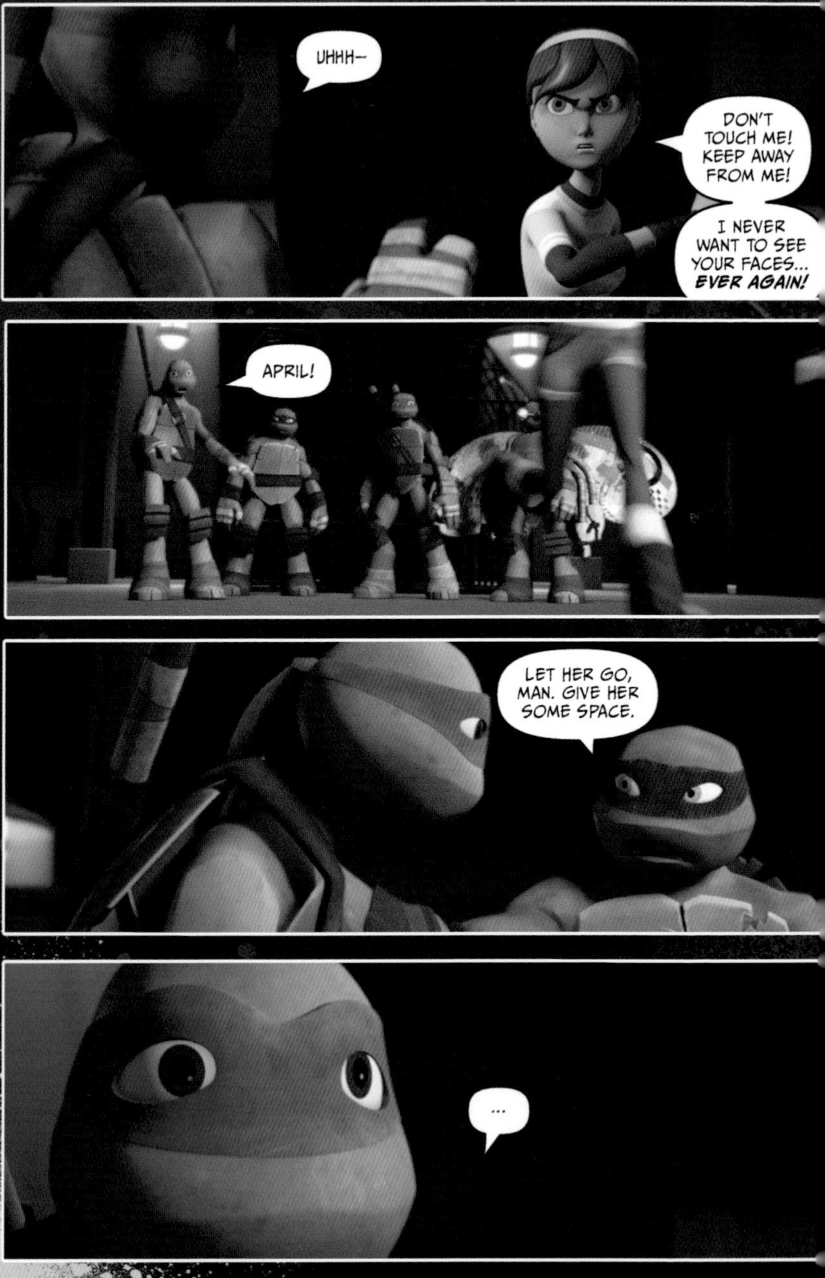
UHHH--
DON'T TOUCH ME! KEEP AWAY FROM ME!
I NEVER WANT TO SEE YOUR FACES... EVER AGAIN!
APRIL!
LET HER GO, MAN. GIVE HER SOME SPACE.
...

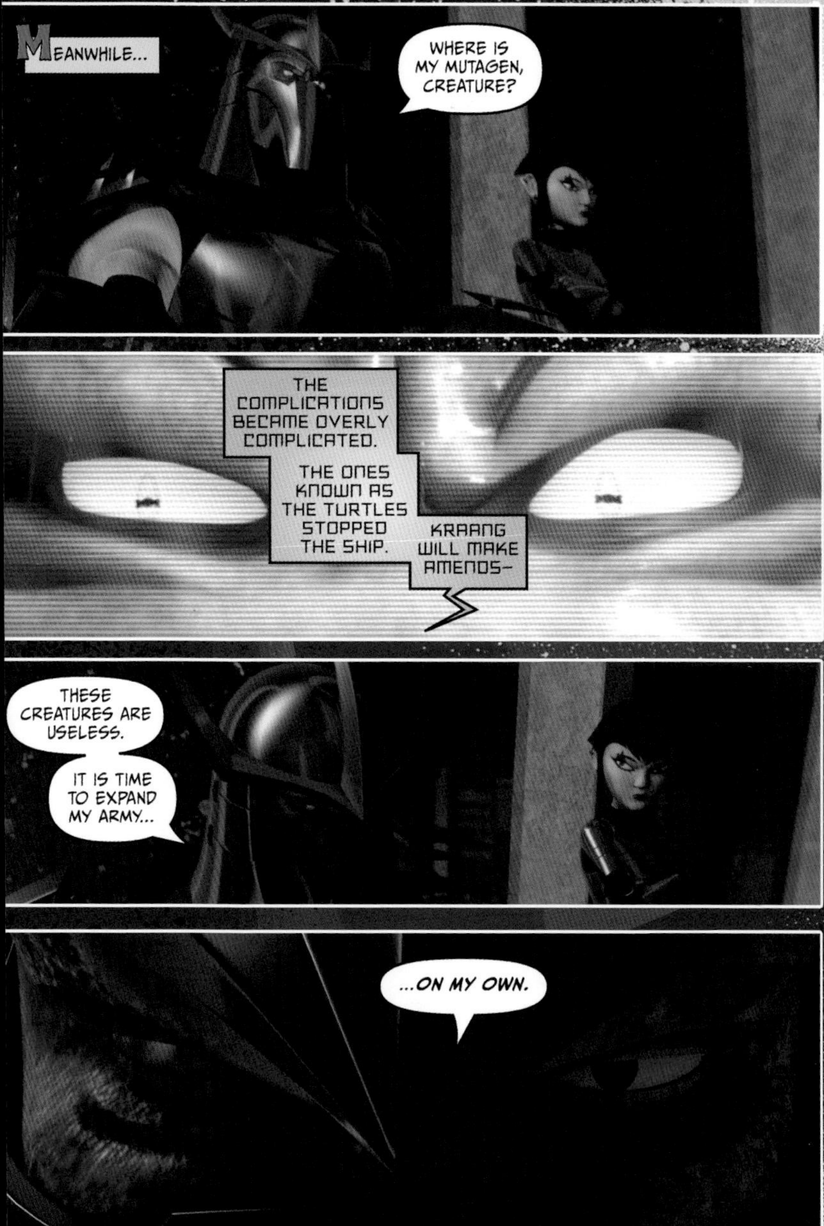
MEANWHILE...
WHERE IS MY MUTAGEN, CREATURE?
THE COMPLICATIONS BECAME OVERLY COMPLICATED.
THE ONES KNOWN AS THE TURTLES STOPPED THE SHIP.
KRAANG WILL MAKE AMENDS–
THESE CREATURES ARE USELESS.
IT IS TIME TO EXPAND MY ARMY...
...ON MY OWN.

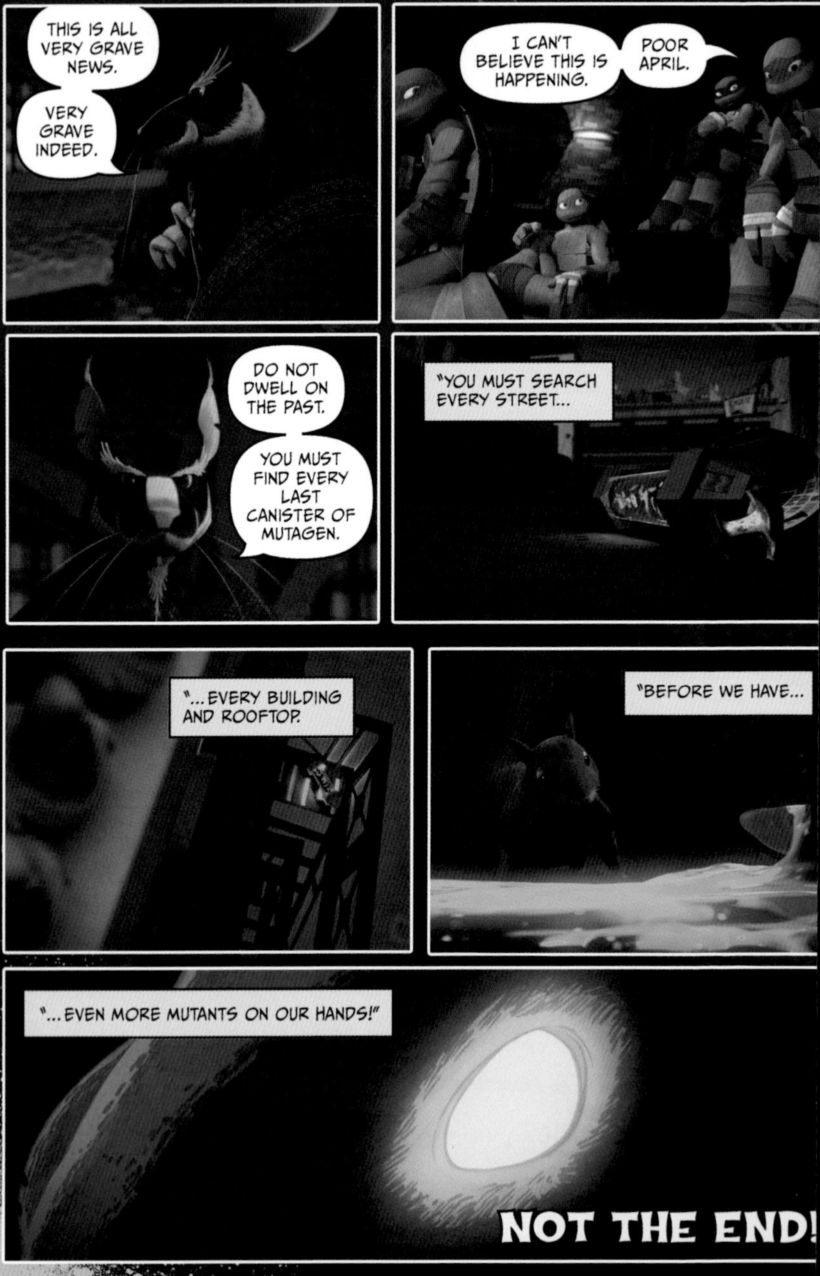
THIS IS ALL VERY GRAVE NEWS.
VERY GRAVE INDEED.
I CAN'T BELIEVE THIS IS HAPPENING.
POOR APRIL.
DO NOT DWELL ON THE PAST.
YOU MUST FIND EVERY LAST CANISTER OF MUTAGEN.
"YOU MUST SEARCH EVERY STREET...
"...EVERY BUILDING AND ROOFTOP.
"BEFORE WE HAVE...
"...EVEN MORE MUTANTS ON OUR HANDS!"
NOT THE END!

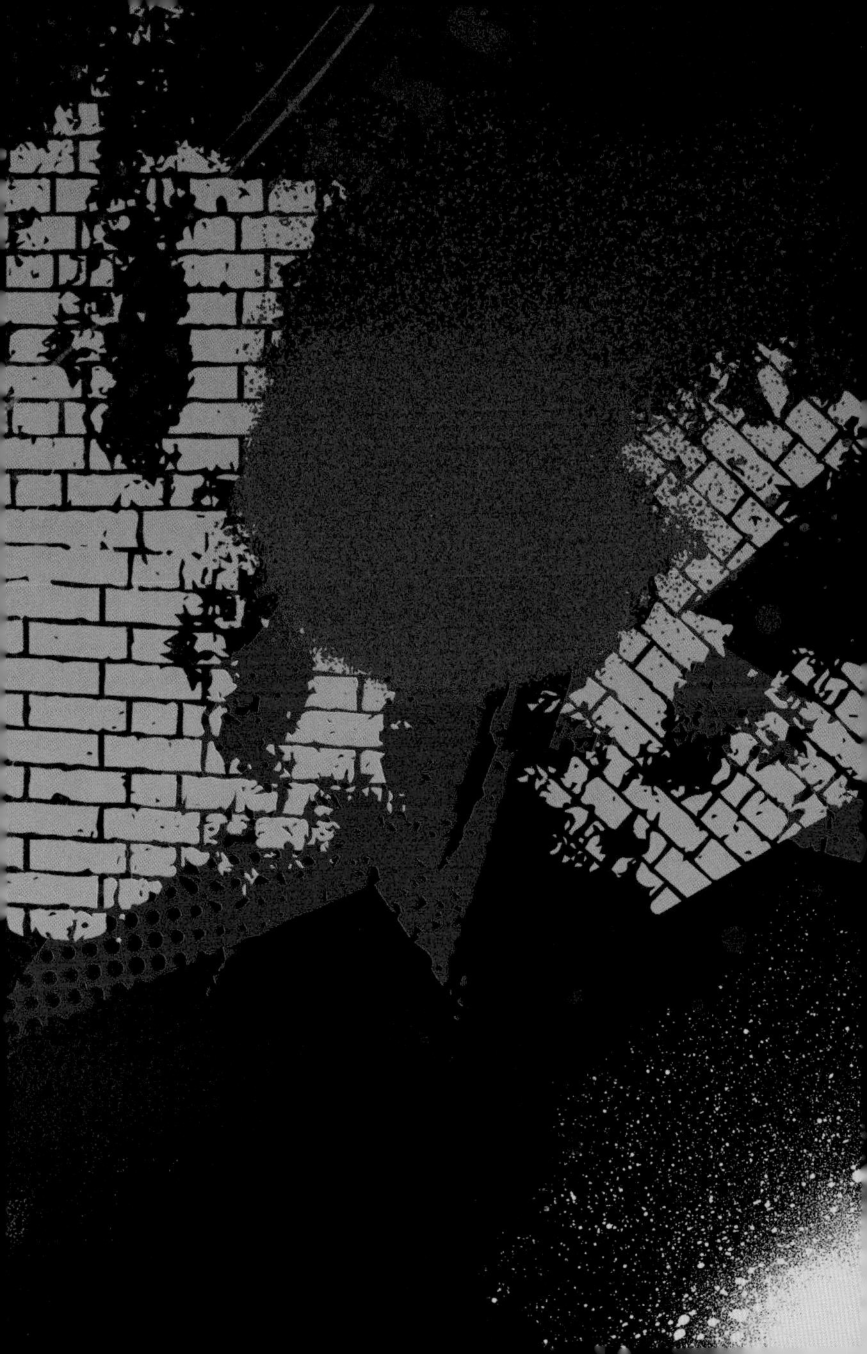

MUTAGEN MAN UNLEASHED

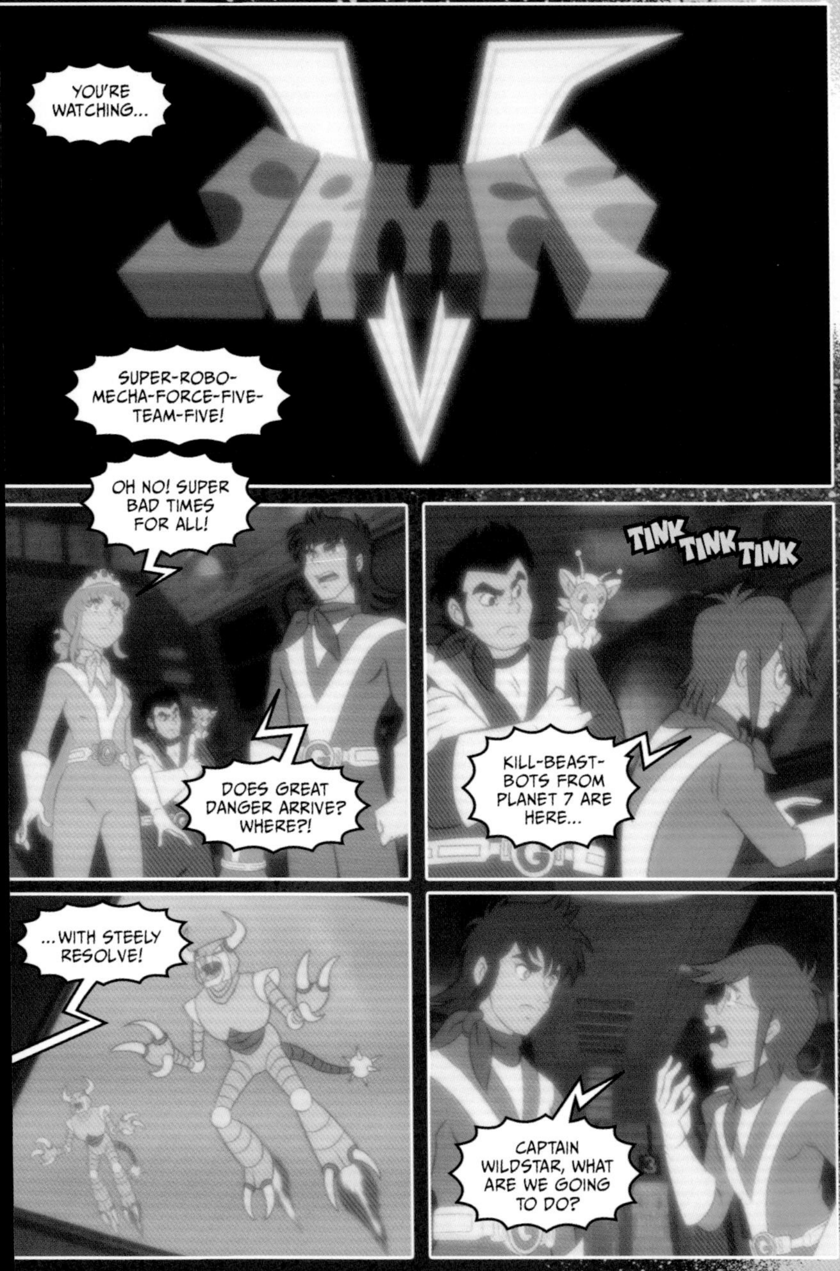
YOU'RE WATCHING...
SUPER-ROBO-MECHA-FORCE-FIVE-TEAM-FIVE!
OH NO! SUPER BAD TIMES FOR ALL!
DOES GREAT DANGER ARRIVE? WHERE?!
TINK TINK TINK
KILL-BEAST-BOTS FROM PLANET 7 ARE HERE...
...WITH STEELY RESOLVE!
CAPTAIN WILDSTAR, WHAT ARE WE GOING TO DO?

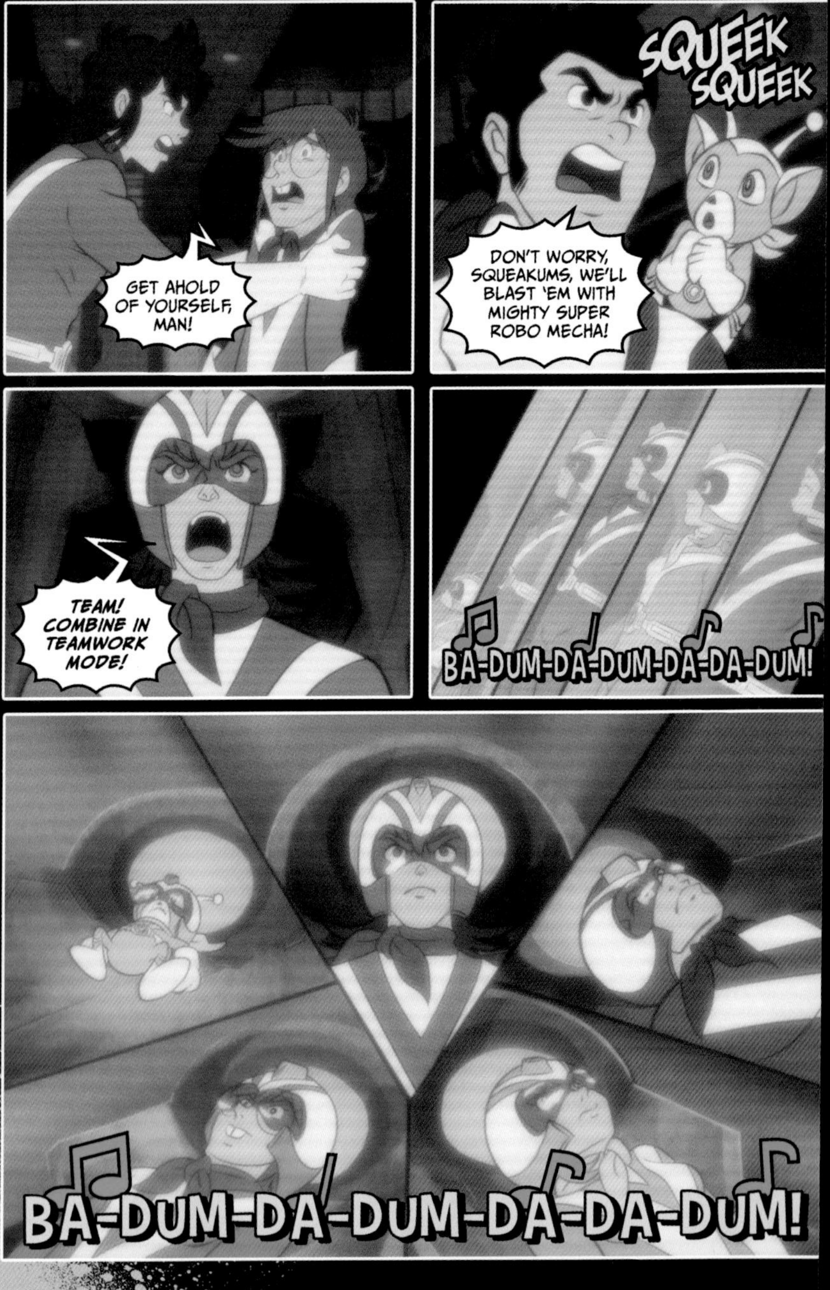

GET AHOLD OF YOURSELF, MAN!
SQUEEK SQUEEK
DON'T WORRY, SQUEAKUMS, WE'LL BLAST 'EM WITH MIGHTY SUPER ROBO MECHA!
TEAM! COMBINE IN TEAMWORK MODE!
BA-DUM-DA-DUM-DA-DA-DUM!
BA-DUM-DA-DUM-DA-DA-DUM!

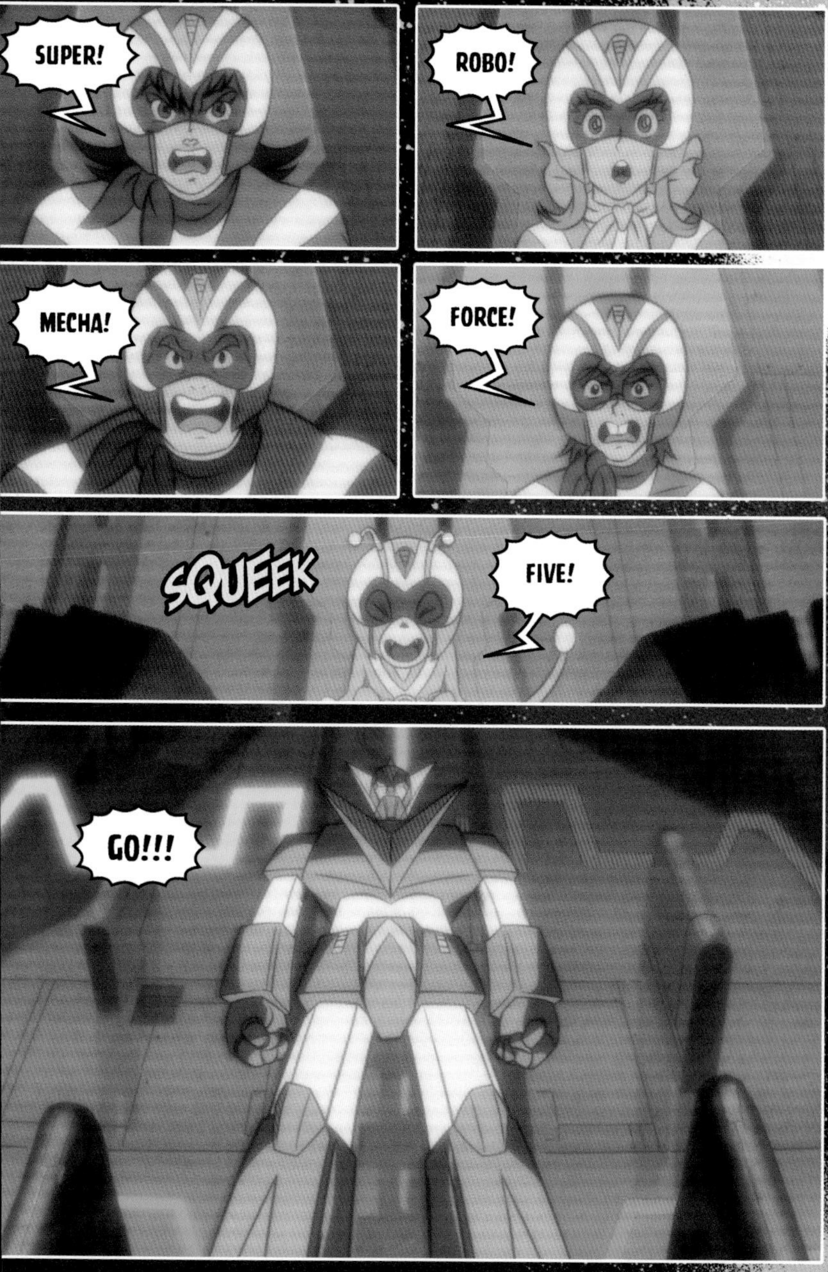
SUPER!
ROBO!
MECHA!
FORCE!
SQUEEK
FIVE!
GO!!!

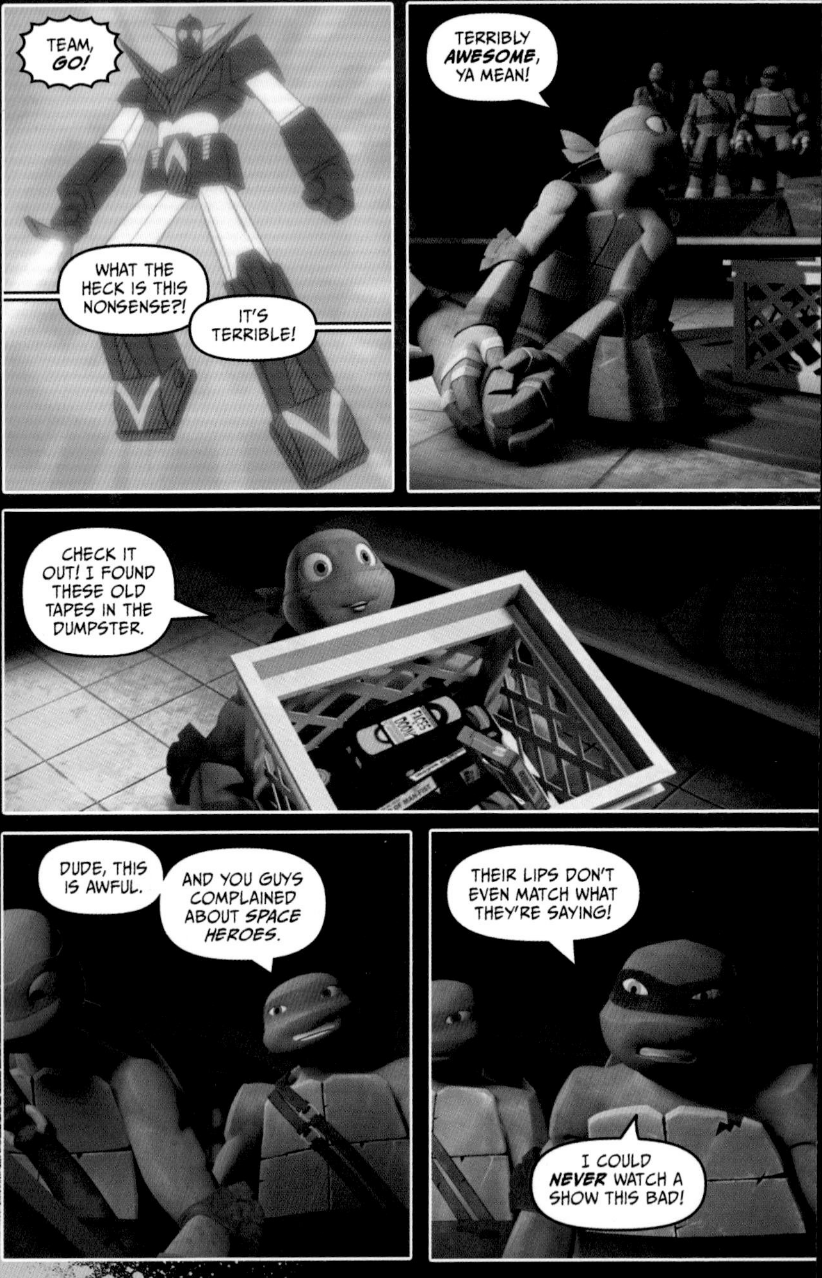
TEAM, GO!
WHAT THE HECK IS THIS NONSENSE?!
IT'S TERRIBLE!
TERRIBLY AWESOME, YA MEAN!
CHECK IT OUT! I FOUND THESE OLD TAPES IN THE DUMPSTER.
DUDE, THIS IS AWFUL.
AND YOU GUYS COMPLAINED ABOUT SPACE HEROES.
THEIR LIPS DON'T EVEN MATCH WHAT THEY'RE SAYING!
I COULD NEVER WATCH A SHOW THIS BAD!

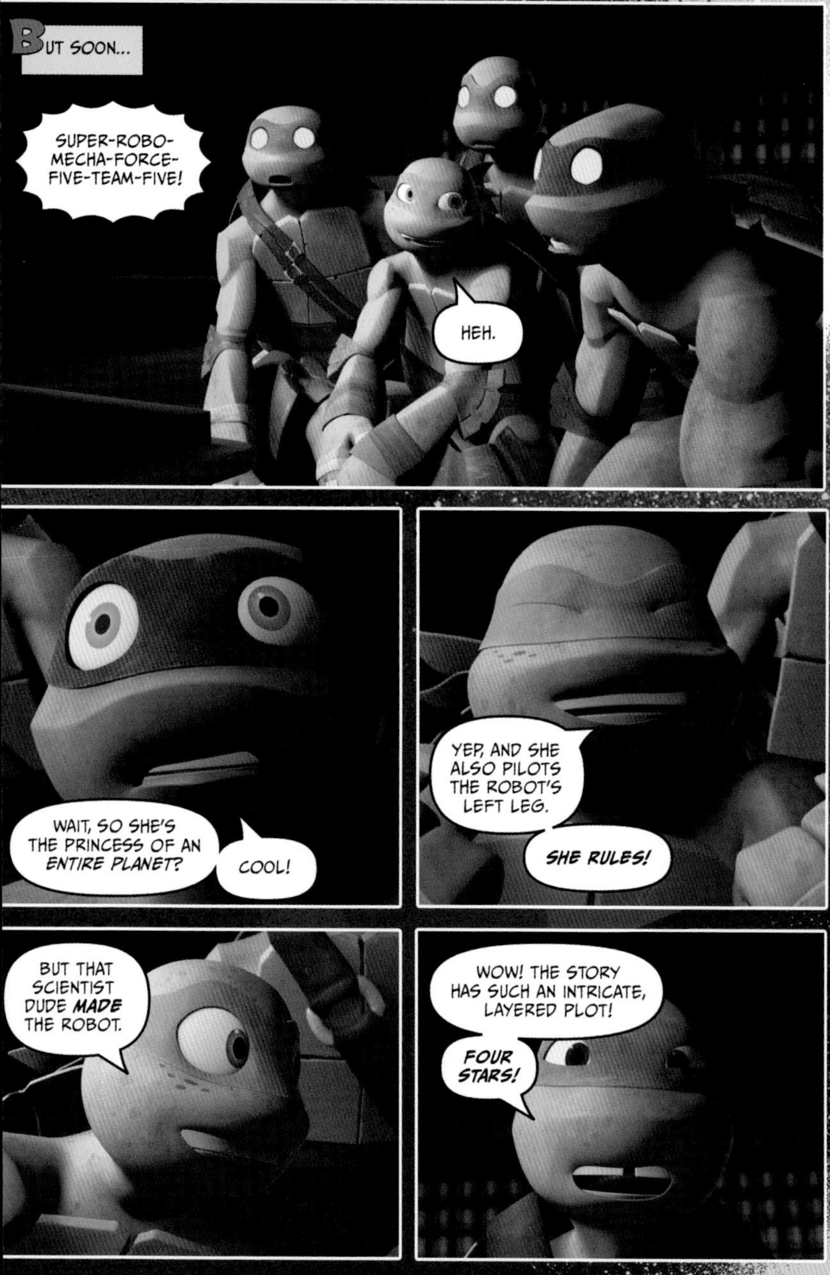
BUT SOON...
SUPER-ROBO-MECHA-FORCE-FIVE-TEAM-FIVE!
HEH.
WAIT, SO SHE'S THE PRINCESS OF AN ENTIRE PLANET?
COOL!
YEP, AND SHE ALSO PILOTS THE ROBOT'S LEFT LEG.
SHE RULES!
BUT THAT SCIENTIST DUDE MADE THE ROBOT.
WOW! THE STORY HAS SUCH AN INTRICATE, LAYERED PLOT!
FOUR STARS!

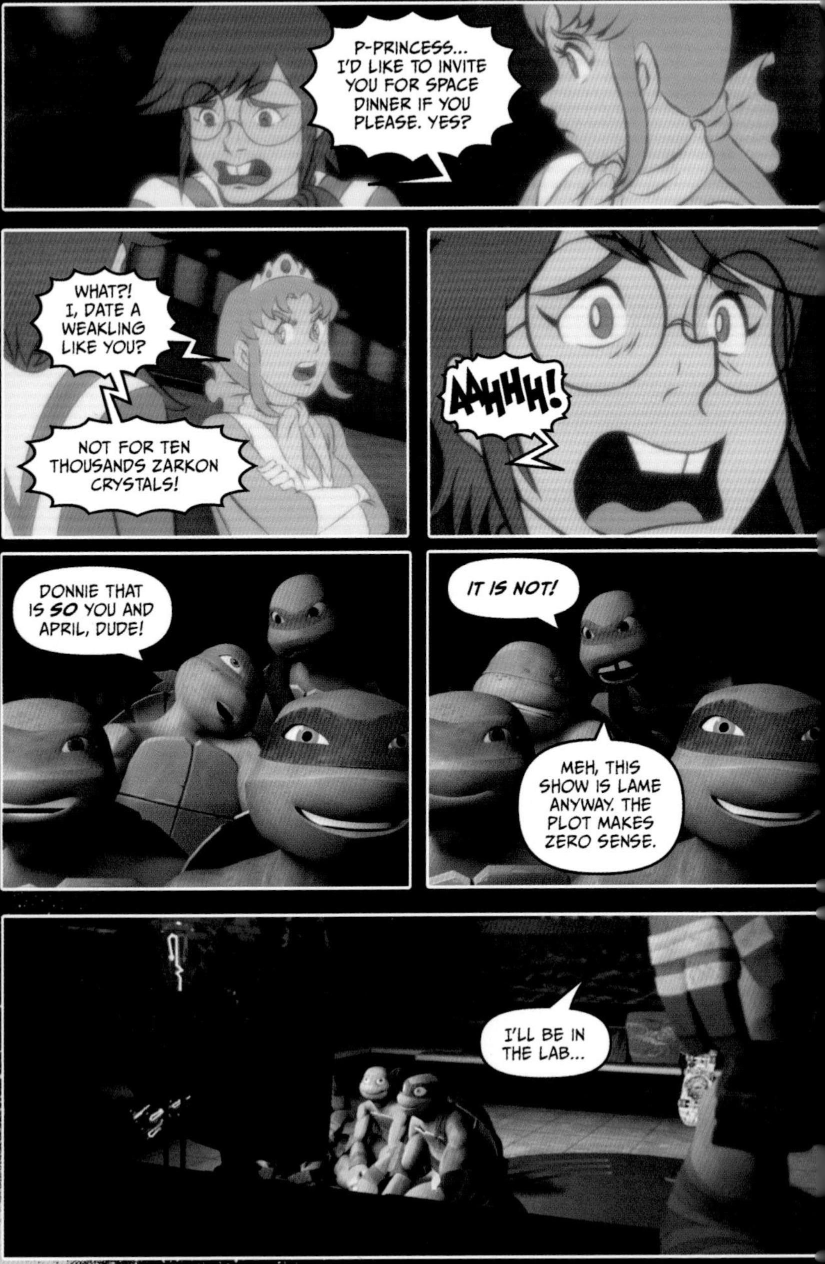
P-PRINCESS... I'D LIKE TO INVITE YOU FOR SPACE DINNER IF YOU PLEASE. YES?
WHAT?! I, DATE A WEAKLING LIKE YOU?
NOT FOR TEN THOUSANDS ZARKON CRYSTALS!
AAHHH!
DONNIE THAT IS *SO* YOU AND APRIL, DUDE!
IT IS NOT!
MEH, THIS SHOW IS LAME ANYWAY. THE PLOT MAKES ZERO SENSE.
I'LL BE IN THE LAB...

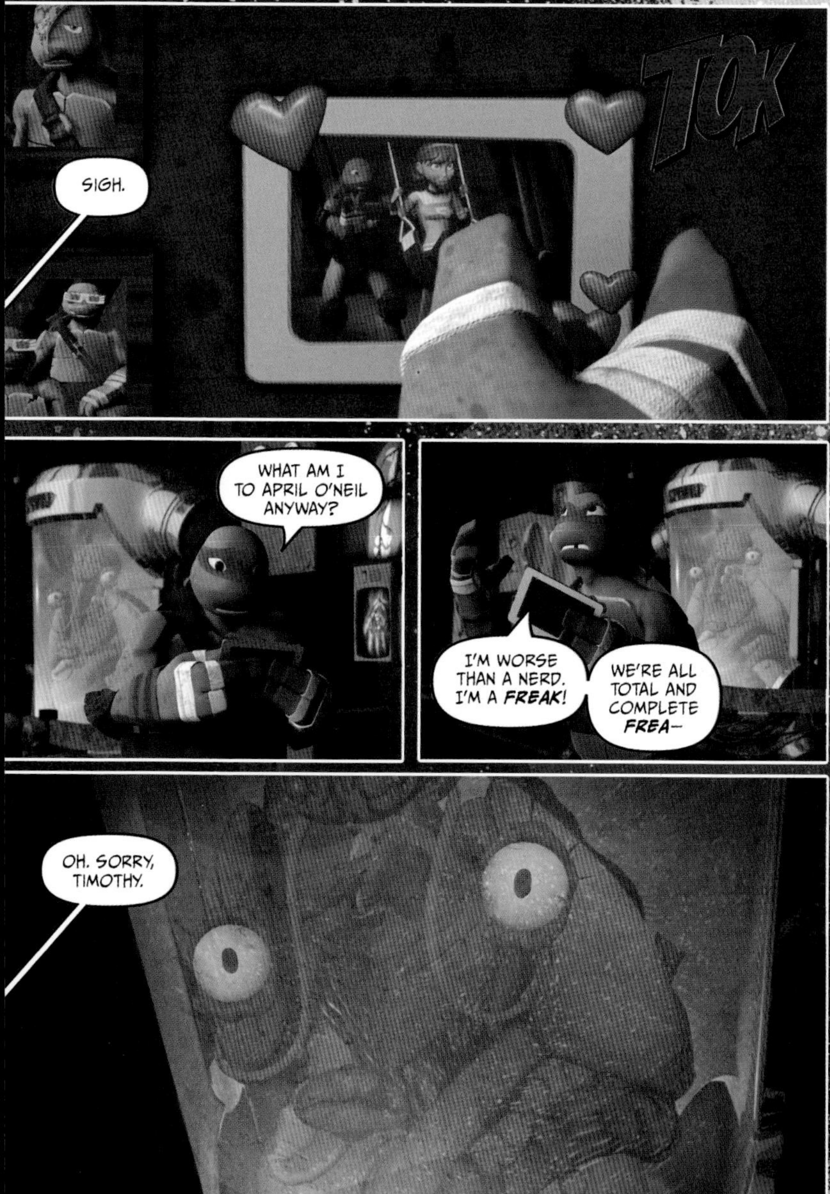
TOK
SIGH.
WHAT AM I TO APRIL O'NEIL ANYWAY?
I'M WORSE THAN A NERD. I'M A *FREAK*!
WE'RE ALL TOTAL AND COMPLETE *FREA*—
OH. SORRY, TIMOTHY.

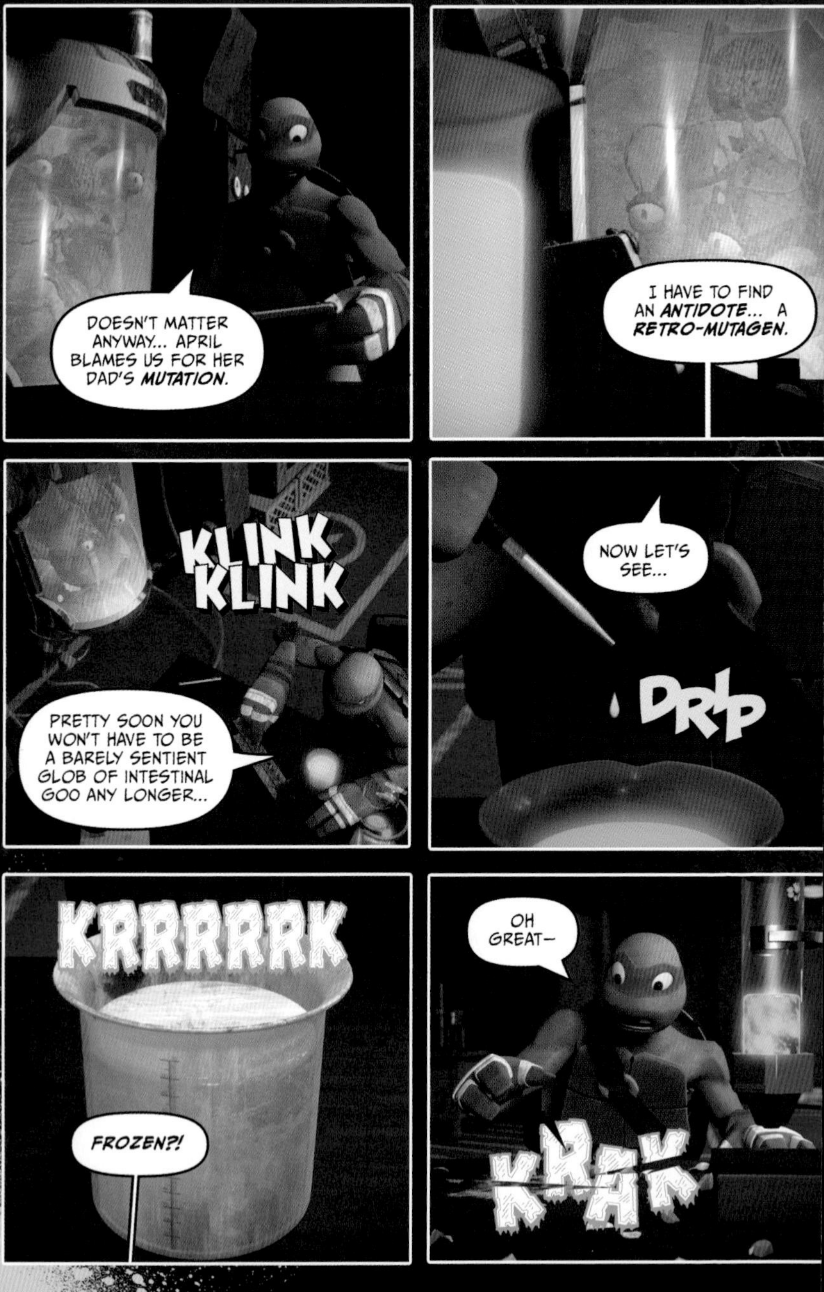
DOESN'T MATTER ANYWAY... APRIL BLAMES US FOR HER DAD'S MUTATION.
I HAVE TO FIND AN ANTIDOTE... A RETRO-MUTAGEN.
KLINK KLINK
PRETTY SOON YOU WON'T HAVE TO BE A BARELY SENTIENT GLOB OF INTESTINAL GOO ANY LONGER...
NOW LET'S SEE...
DRIP
KRRRRRK
FROZEN?!
OH GREAT—
KRAK

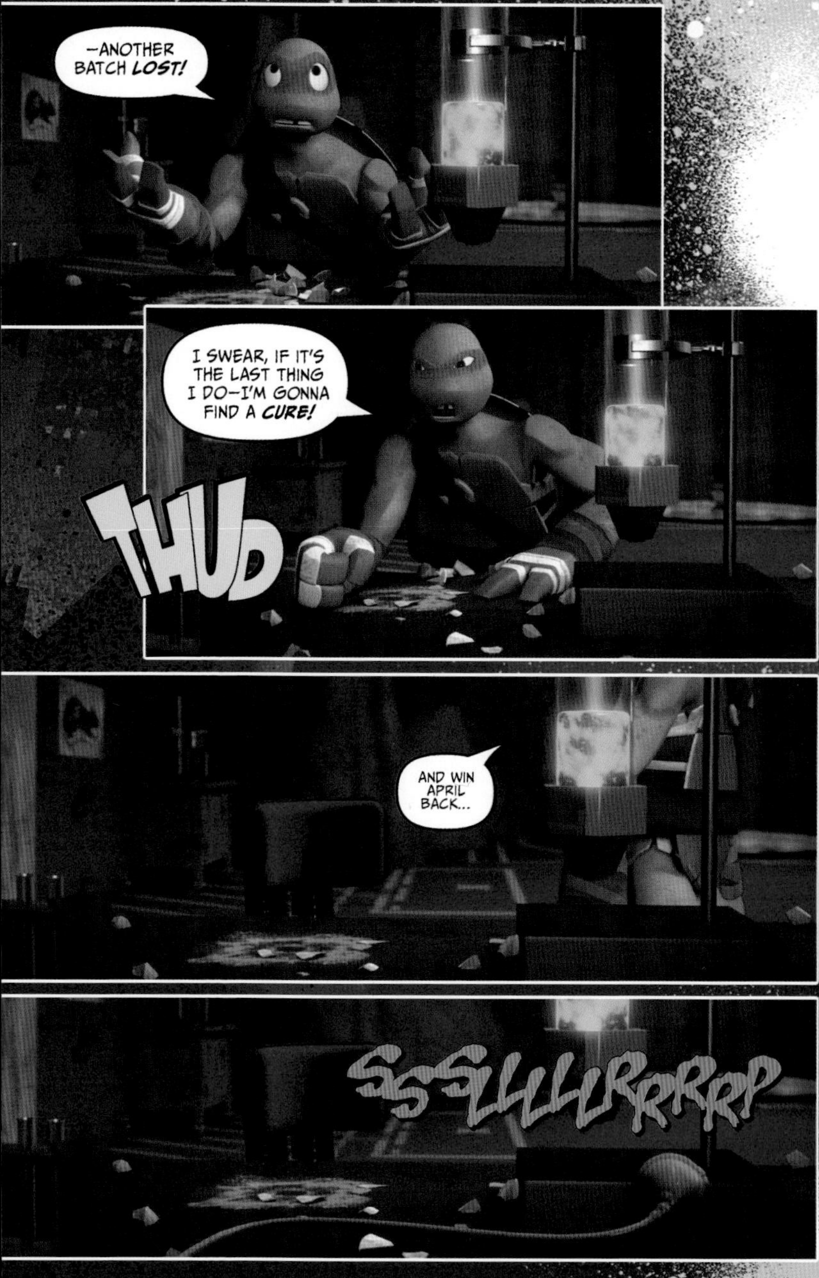
—ANOTHER BATCH LOST!
I SWEAR, IF IT'S THE LAST THING I DO—I'M GONNA FIND A CURE!
THUD
AND WIN APRIL BACK...
SSSLLLLRRRRP

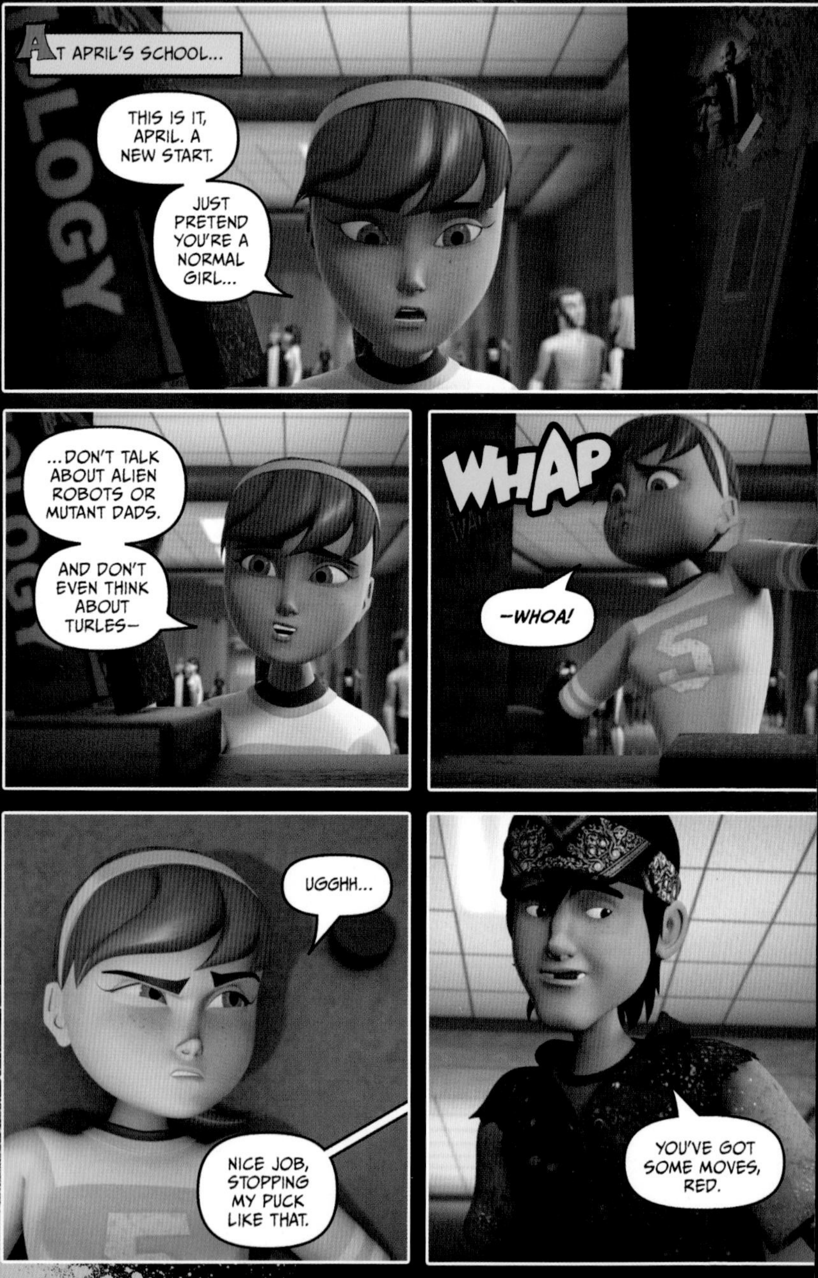
AT APRIL'S SCHOOL...
THIS IS IT, APRIL. A NEW START.
JUST PRETEND YOU'RE A NORMAL GIRL...
...DON'T TALK ABOUT ALIEN ROBOTS OR MUTANT DADS.
AND DON'T EVEN THINK ABOUT TURLES—
WHAP
—WHOA!
UGGHH...
NICE JOB, STOPPING MY PUCK LIKE THAT.
YOU'VE GOT SOME MOVES, RED.

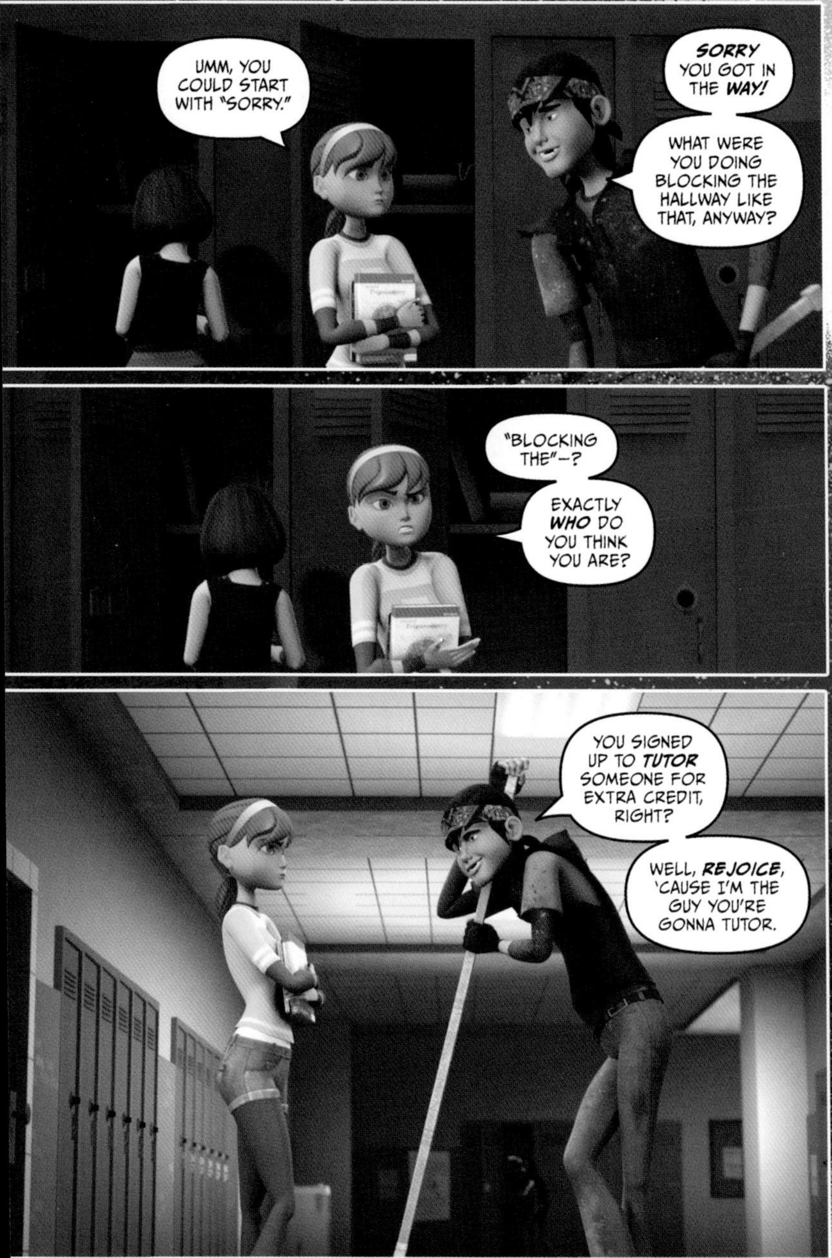
UMM, YOU COULD START WITH "SORRY."
SORRY YOU GOT IN THE WAY!
WHAT WERE YOU DOING BLOCKING THE HALLWAY LIKE THAT, ANYWAY?
"BLOCKING THE"–?
EXACTLY WHO DO YOU THINK YOU ARE?
YOU SIGNED UP TO TUTOR SOMEONE FOR EXTRA CREDIT, RIGHT?
WELL, REJOICE, 'CAUSE I'M THE GUY YOU'RE GONNA TUTOR.

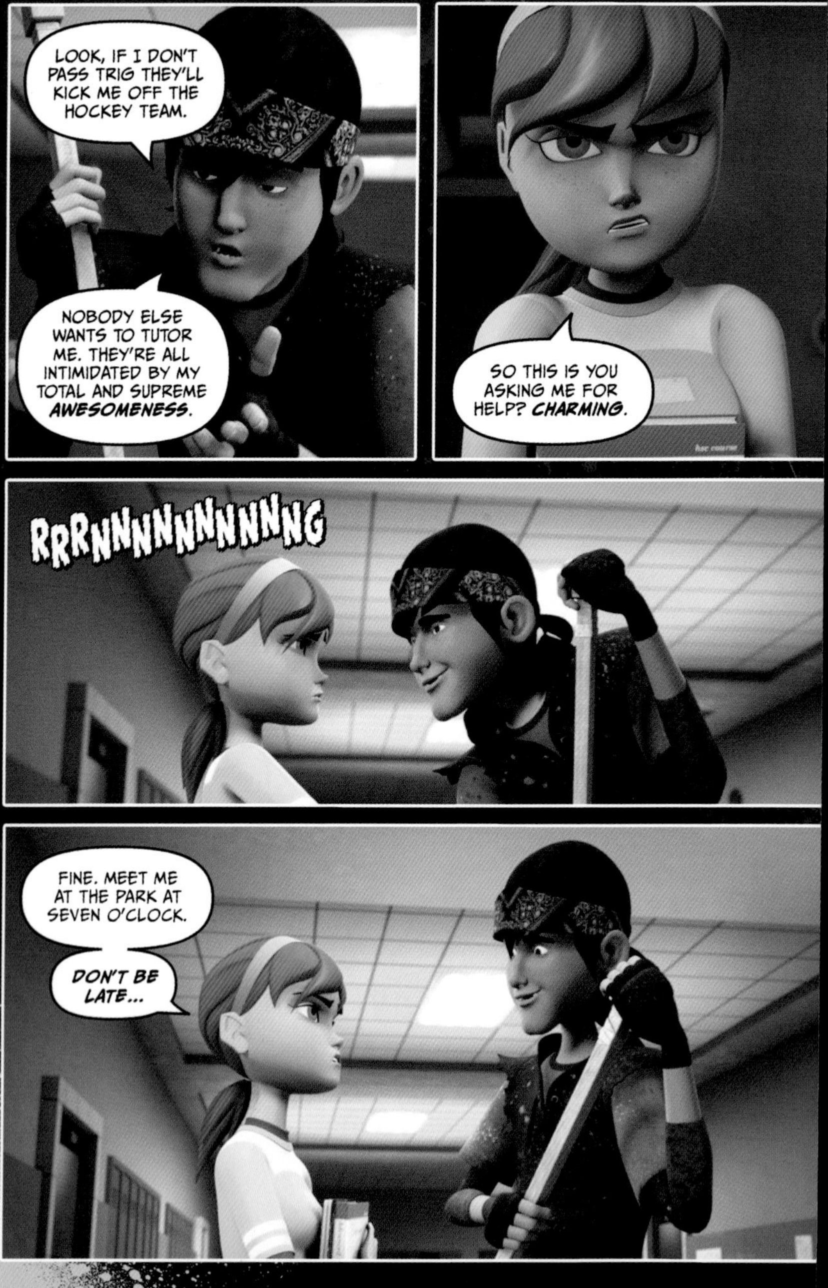
LOOK, IF I DON'T PASS TRIG THEY'LL KICK ME OFF THE HOCKEY TEAM.
NOBODY ELSE WANTS TO TUTOR ME. THEY'RE ALL INTIMIDATED BY MY TOTAL AND SUPREME AWESOMENESS.
SO THIS IS YOU ASKING ME FOR HELP? CHARMING.
RRRNNNNNNNNNNG
FINE. MEET ME AT THE PARK AT SEVEN O'CLOCK.
DON'T BE LATE...

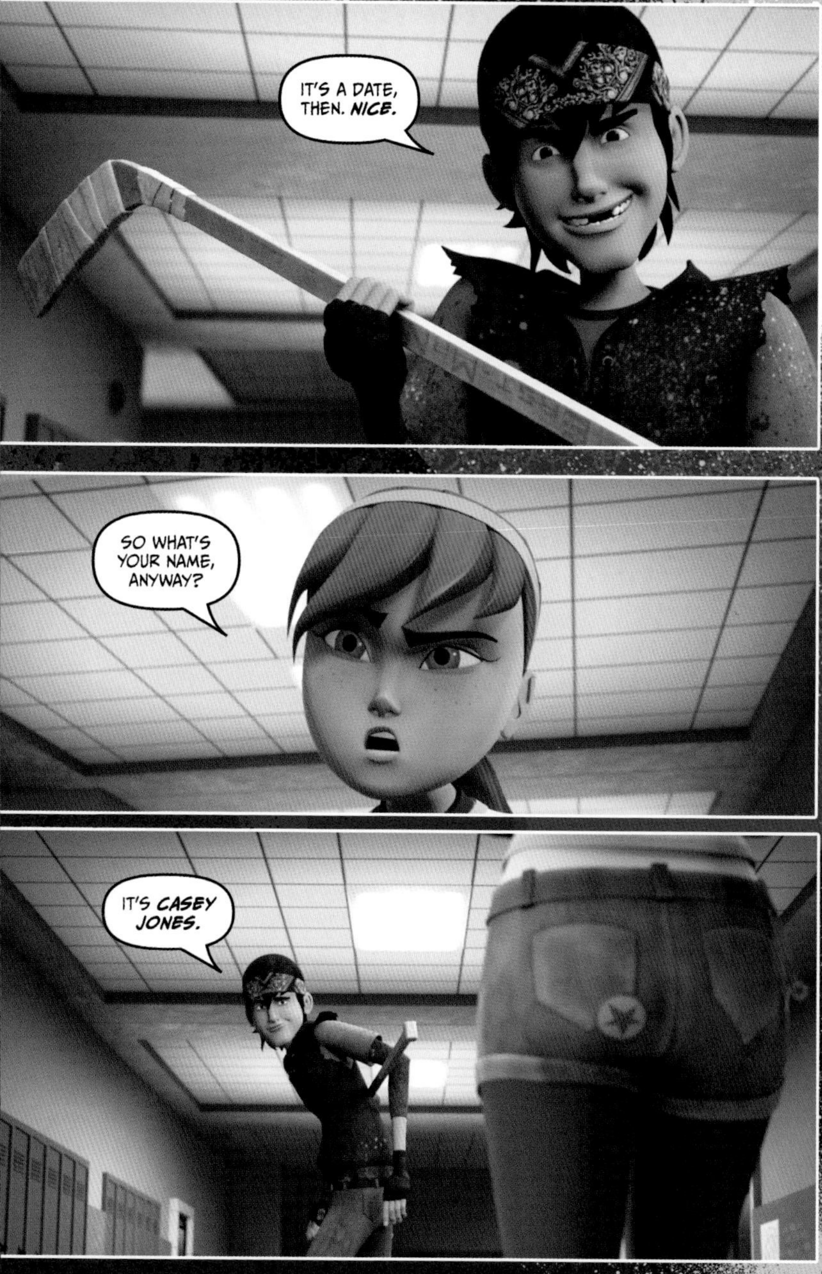
IT'S A DATE, THEN. *NICE.*
SO WHAT'S YOUR NAME, ANYWAY?
IT'S *CASEY JONES.*

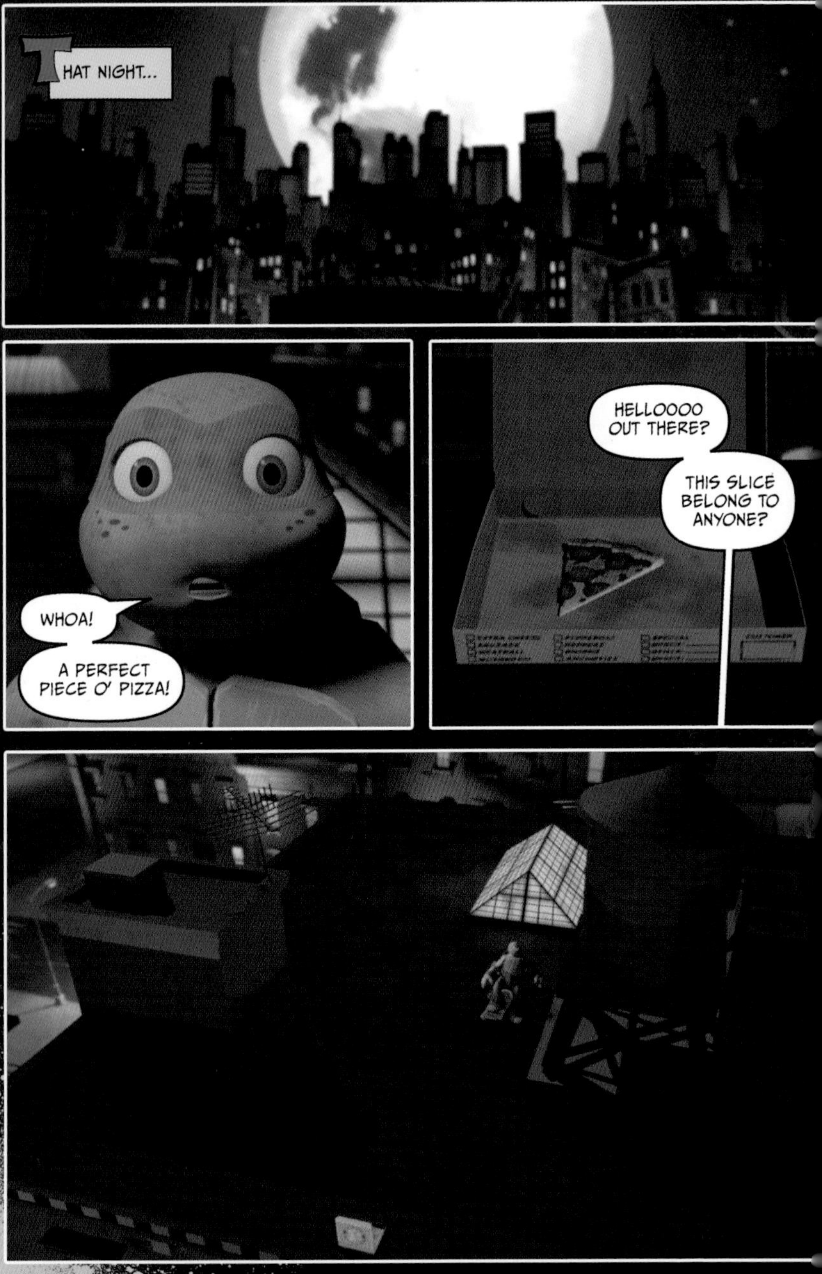
THAT NIGHT...
WHOA!
A PERFECT PIECE O' PIZZA!
HELLOOOO OUT THERE?
THIS SLICE BELONG TO ANYONE?

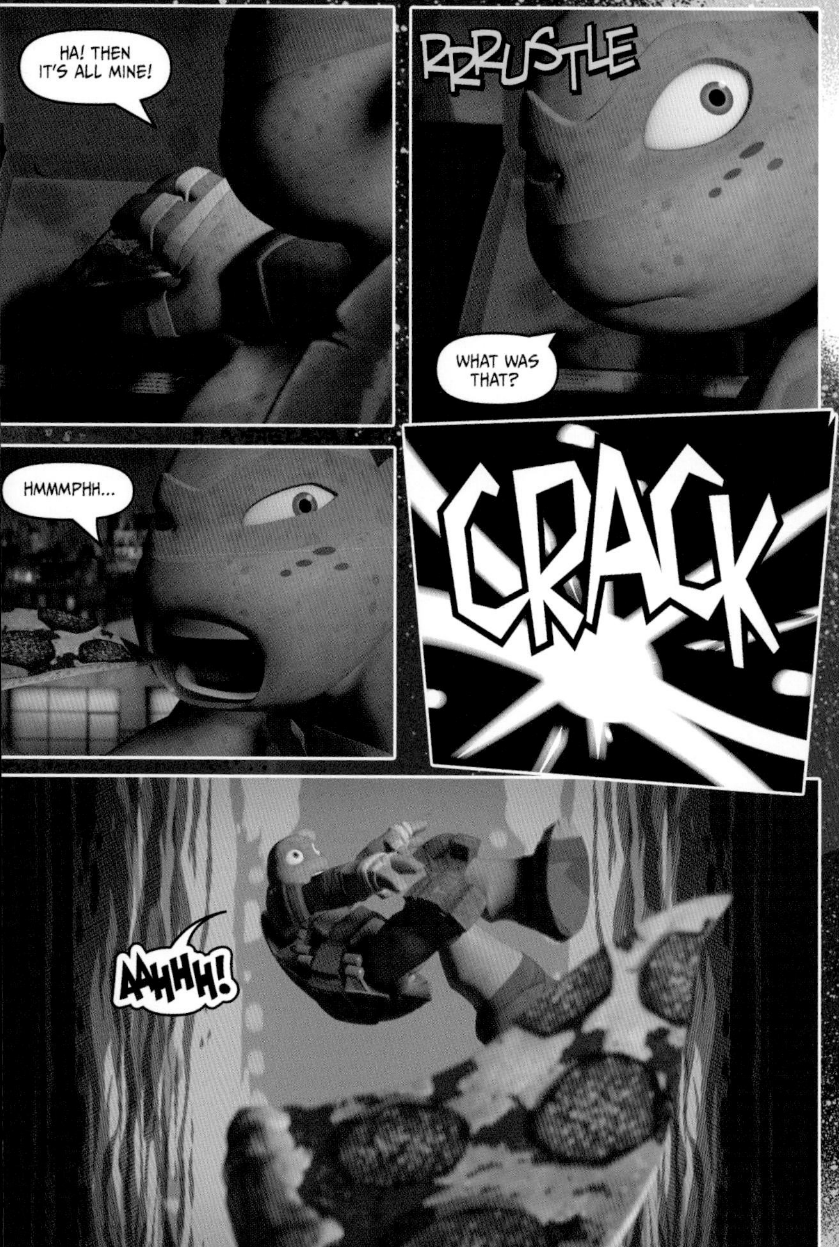

HA! THEN IT'S ALL MINE!
RRRUSTLE
WHAT WAS THAT?
HMMMPHH...
CRACK
AAHHH!

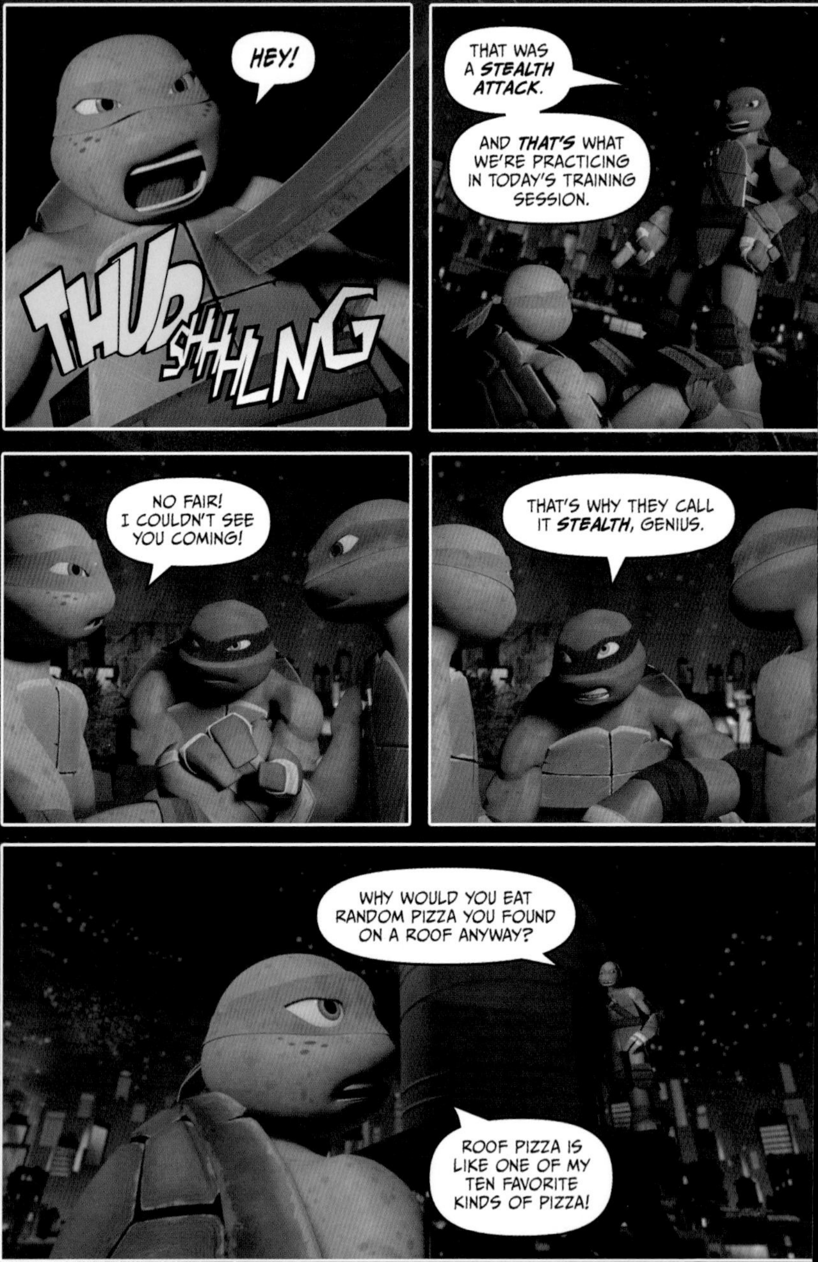
HEY!
THUDSHHHLNG
THAT WAS A STEALTH ATTACK.
AND THAT'S WHAT WE'RE PRACTICING IN TODAY'S TRAINING SESSION.
NO FAIR! I COULDN'T SEE YOU COMING!
THAT'S WHY THEY CALL IT STEALTH, GENIUS.
WHY WOULD YOU EAT RANDOM PIZZA YOU FOUND ON A ROOF ANYWAY?
ROOF PIZZA IS LIKE ONE OF MY TEN FAVORITE KINDS OF PIZZA!

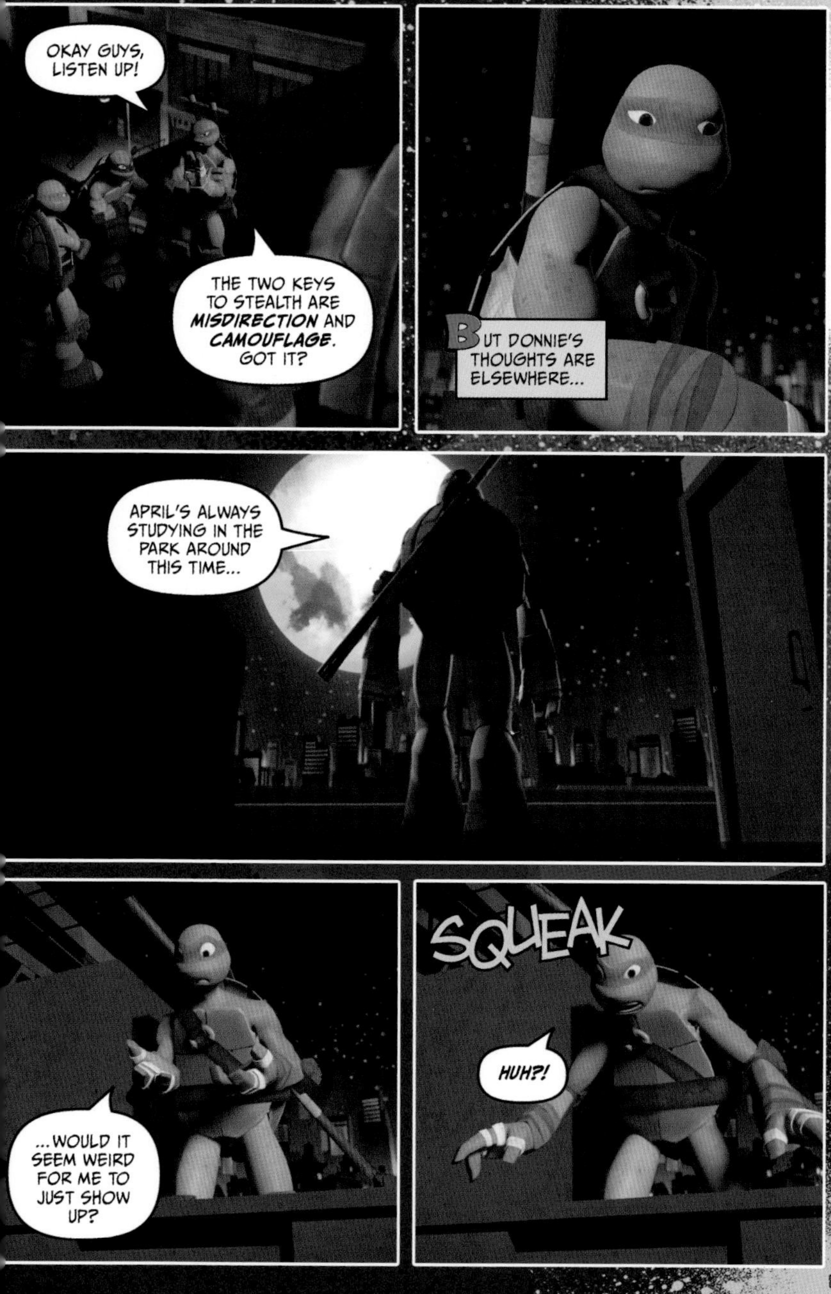
OKAY GUYS, LISTEN UP!
THE TWO KEYS TO STEALTH ARE MISDIRECTION AND CAMOUFLAGE. GOT IT?
BUT DONNIE'S THOUGHTS ARE ELSEWHERE...
APRIL'S ALWAYS STUDYING IN THE PARK AROUND THIS TIME...
...WOULD IT SEEM WEIRD FOR ME TO JUST SHOW UP?
SQUEAK
HUH?!

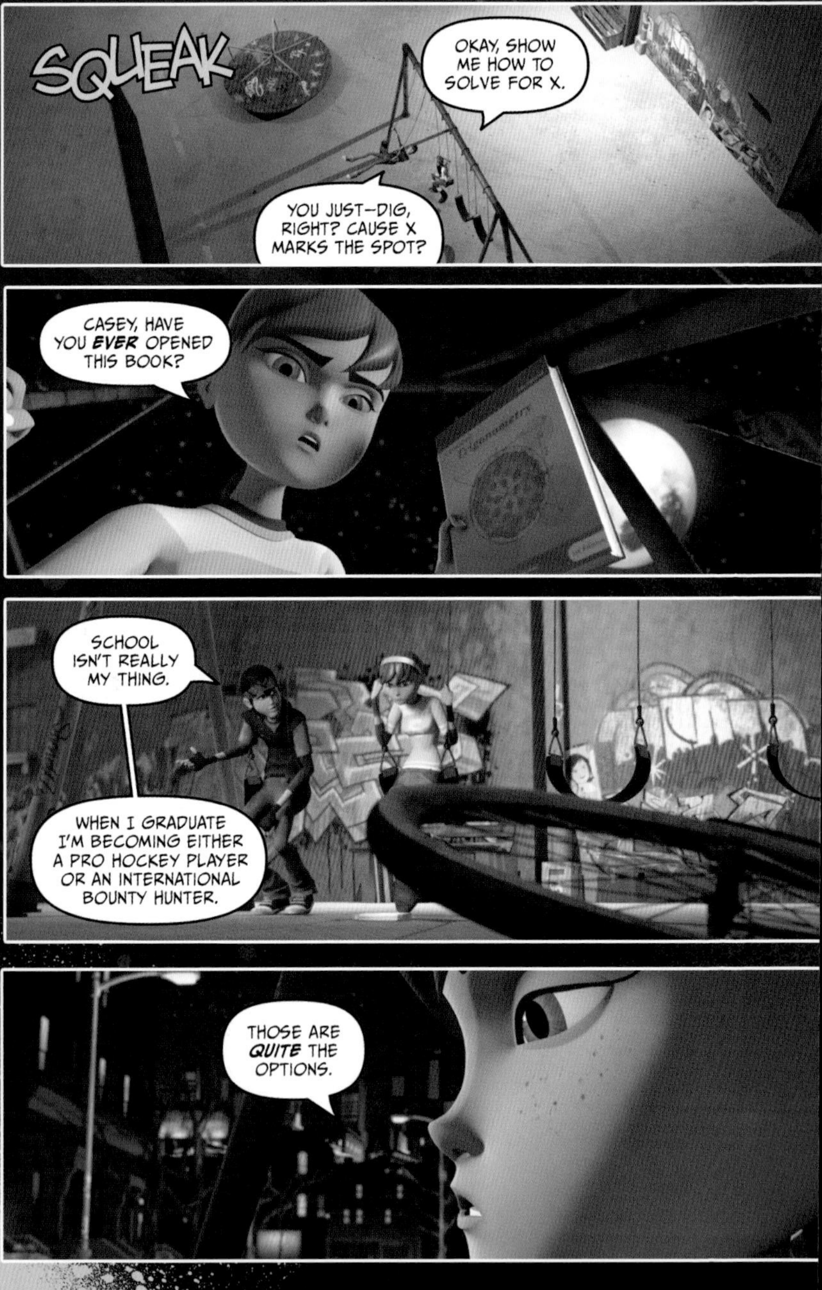
SQUEAK
OKAY, SHOW ME HOW TO SOLVE FOR X.
YOU JUST--DIG, RIGHT? CAUSE X MARKS THE SPOT?
CASEY, HAVE YOU EVER OPENED THIS BOOK?
SCHOOL ISN'T REALLY MY THING.
WHEN I GRADUATE I'M BECOMING EITHER A PRO HOCKEY PLAYER OR AN INTERNATIONAL BOUNTY HUNTER.
THOSE ARE QUITE THE OPTIONS.

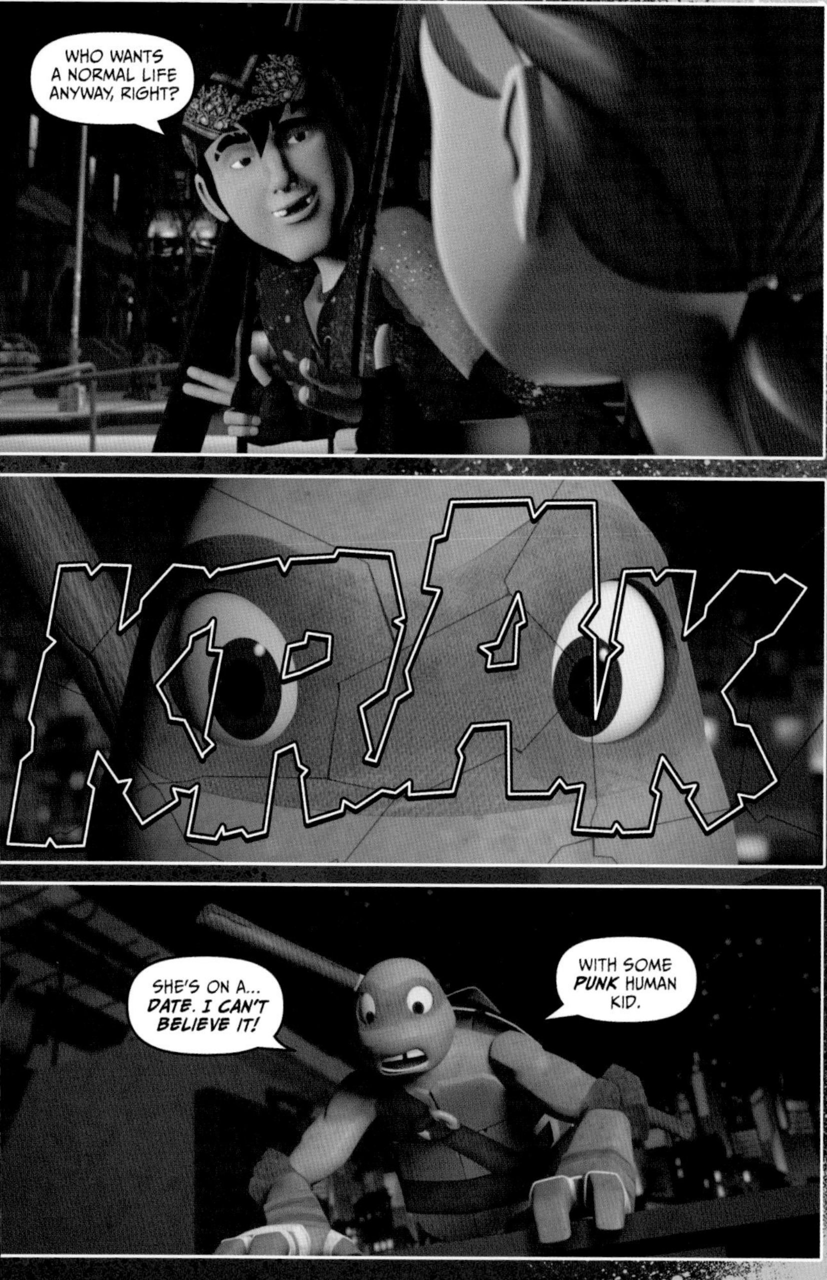
WHO WANTS A NORMAL LIFE ANYWAY, RIGHT?
KRAK
SHE'S ON A... *DATE*. I CAN'T BELIEVE IT!
WITH SOME *PUNK* HUMAN KID.

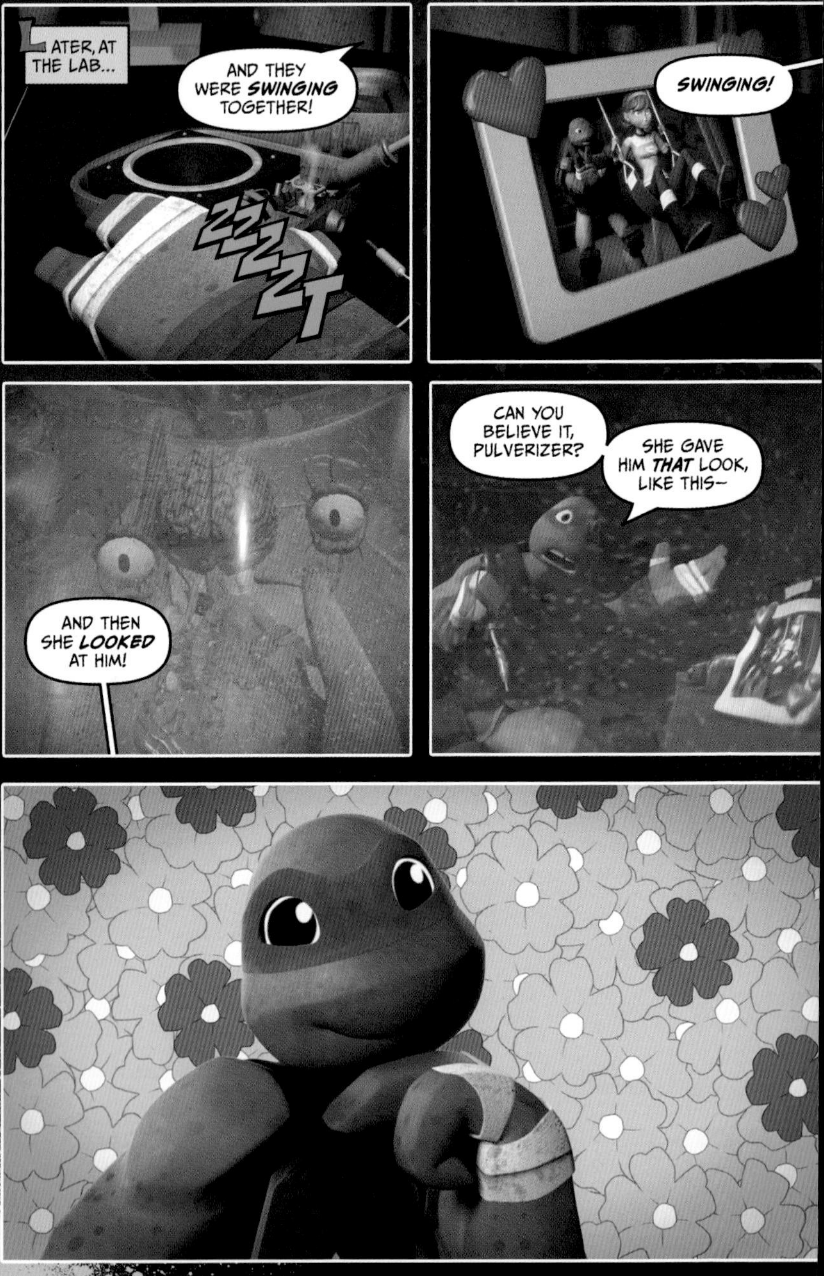
LATER, AT THE LAB...
AND THEY WERE SWINGING TOGETHER!
ZZZZT
SWINGING!
AND THEN SHE LOOKED AT HIM!
CAN YOU BELIEVE IT, PULVERIZER?
SHE GAVE HIM THAT LOOK, LIKE THIS–

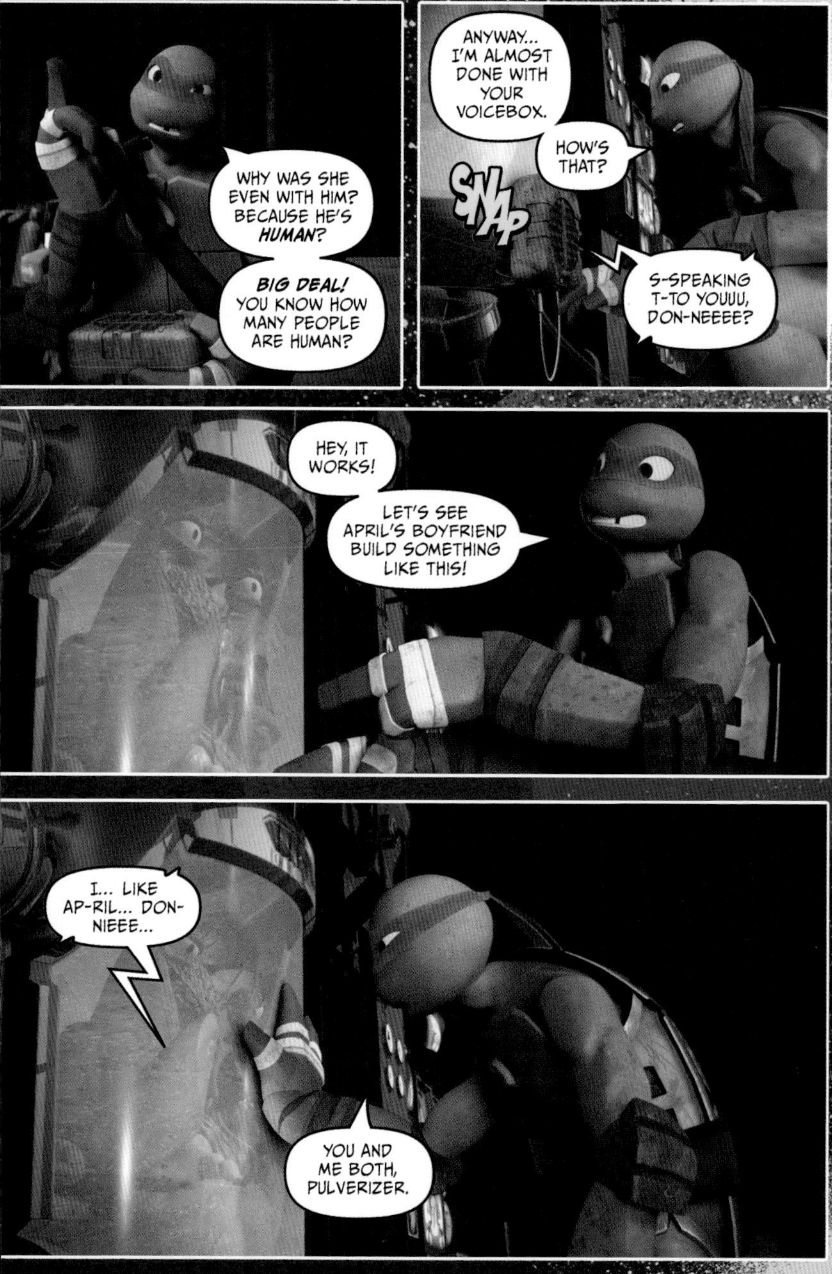
WHY WAS SHE EVEN WITH HIM? BECAUSE HE'S *HUMAN*?
BIG DEAL! YOU KNOW HOW MANY PEOPLE ARE HUMAN?
ANYWAY... I'M ALMOST DONE WITH YOUR VOICEBOX.
HOW'S THAT?
SNAP
S-SPEAKING T-TO YOUUU, DON-NEEEE?
HEY, IT WORKS!
LET'S SEE APRIL'S BOYFRIEND BUILD SOMETHING LIKE THIS!
I... LIKE AP-RIL... DON-NIEEE...
YOU AND ME BOTH, PULVERIZER.

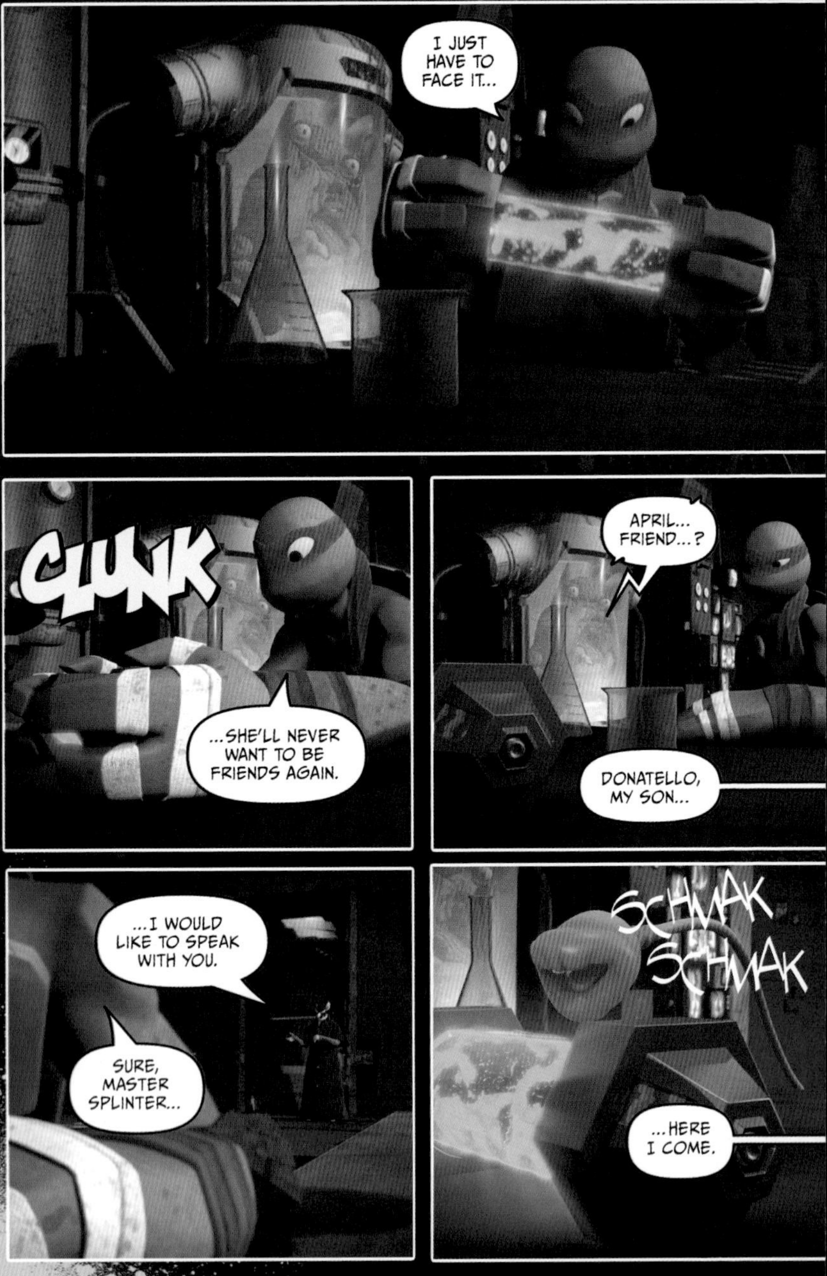
I JUST HAVE TO FACE IT...
CLUNK
...SHE'LL NEVER WANT TO BE FRIENDS AGAIN.
APRIL... FRIEND...?
DONATELLO, MY SON...
...I WOULD LIKE TO SPEAK WITH YOU.
SURE, MASTER SPLINTER...
SCHMAK
SCHMAK
...HERE I COME.

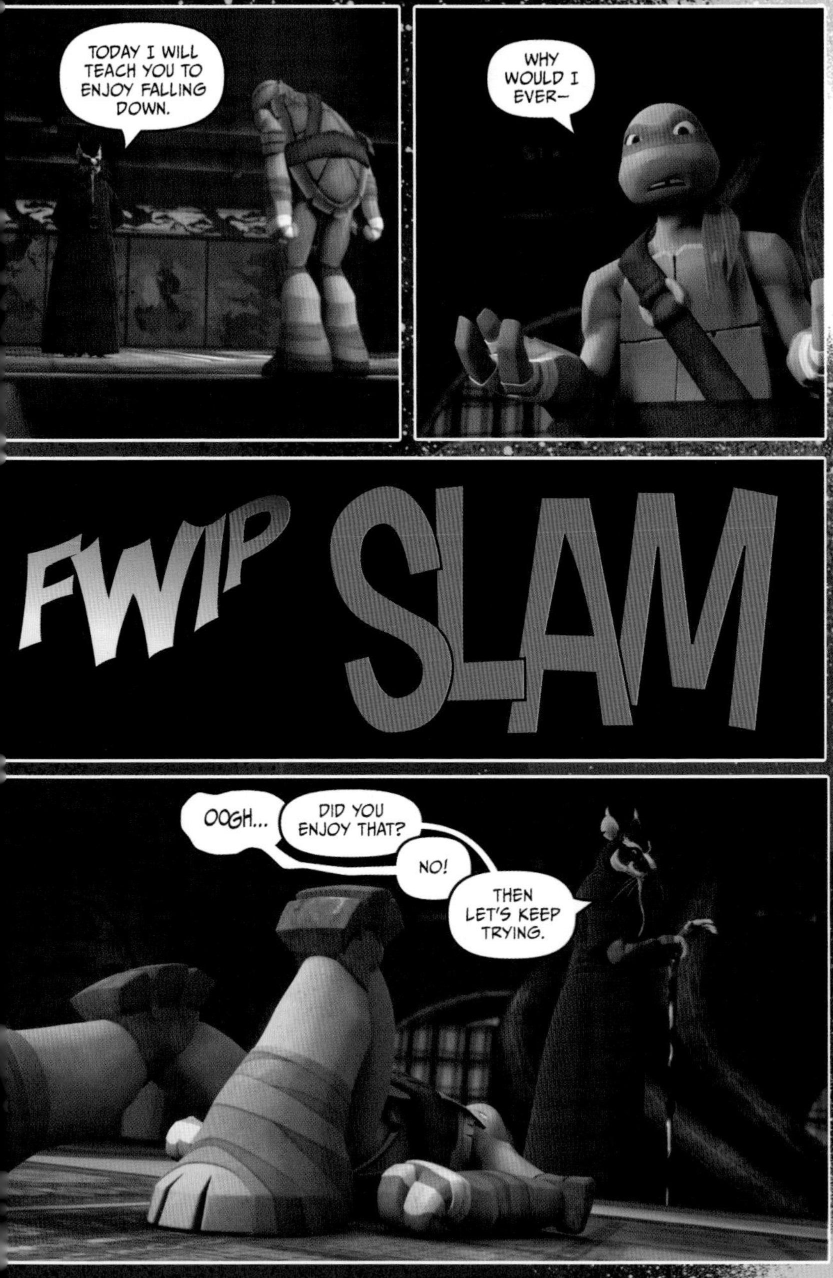
TODAY I WILL TEACH YOU TO ENJOY FALLING DOWN.
WHY WOULD I EVER–
FWIP
SLAM
OOGH...
DID YOU ENJOY THAT?
NO!
THEN LET'S KEEP TRYING.

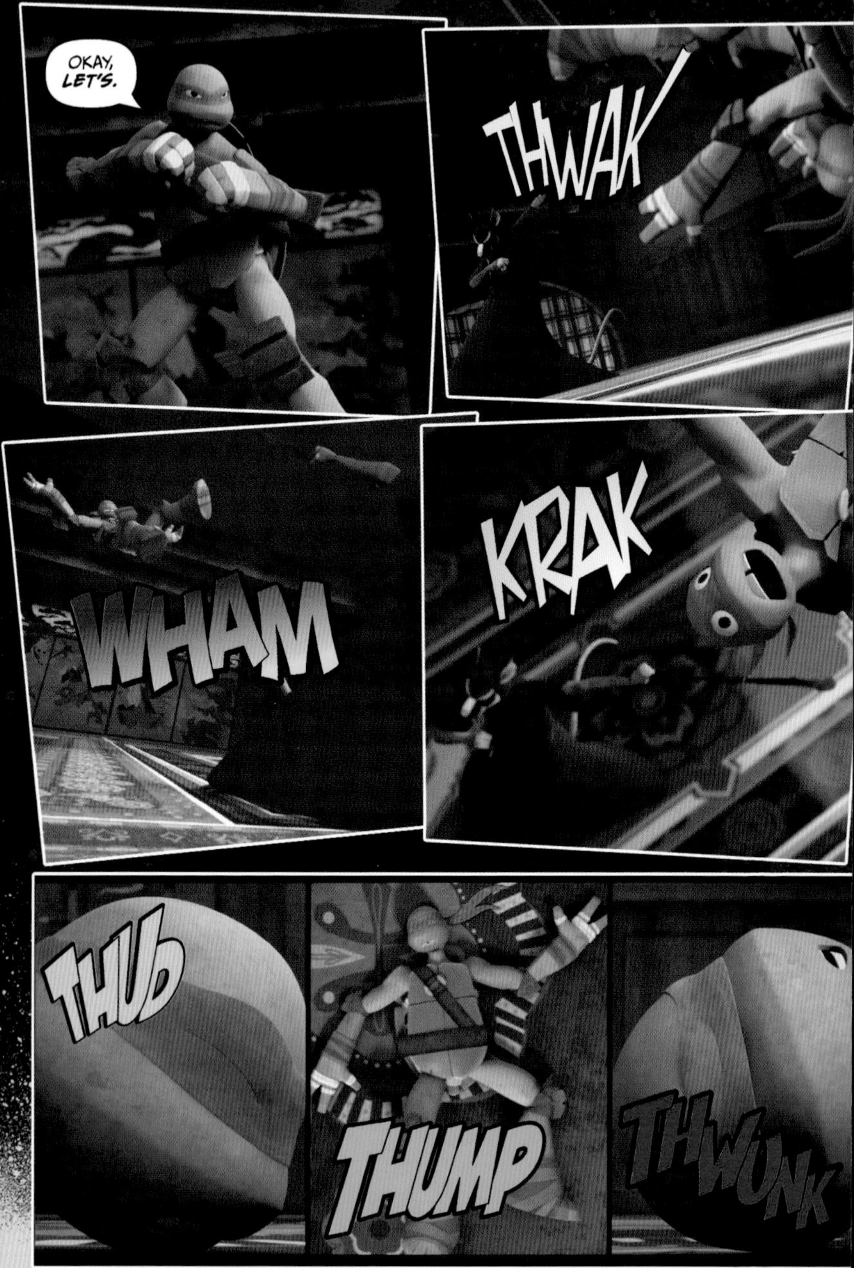
OKAY, LET'S.
THWAK
WHAM
KRAK
THUD
THUMP
THWONK

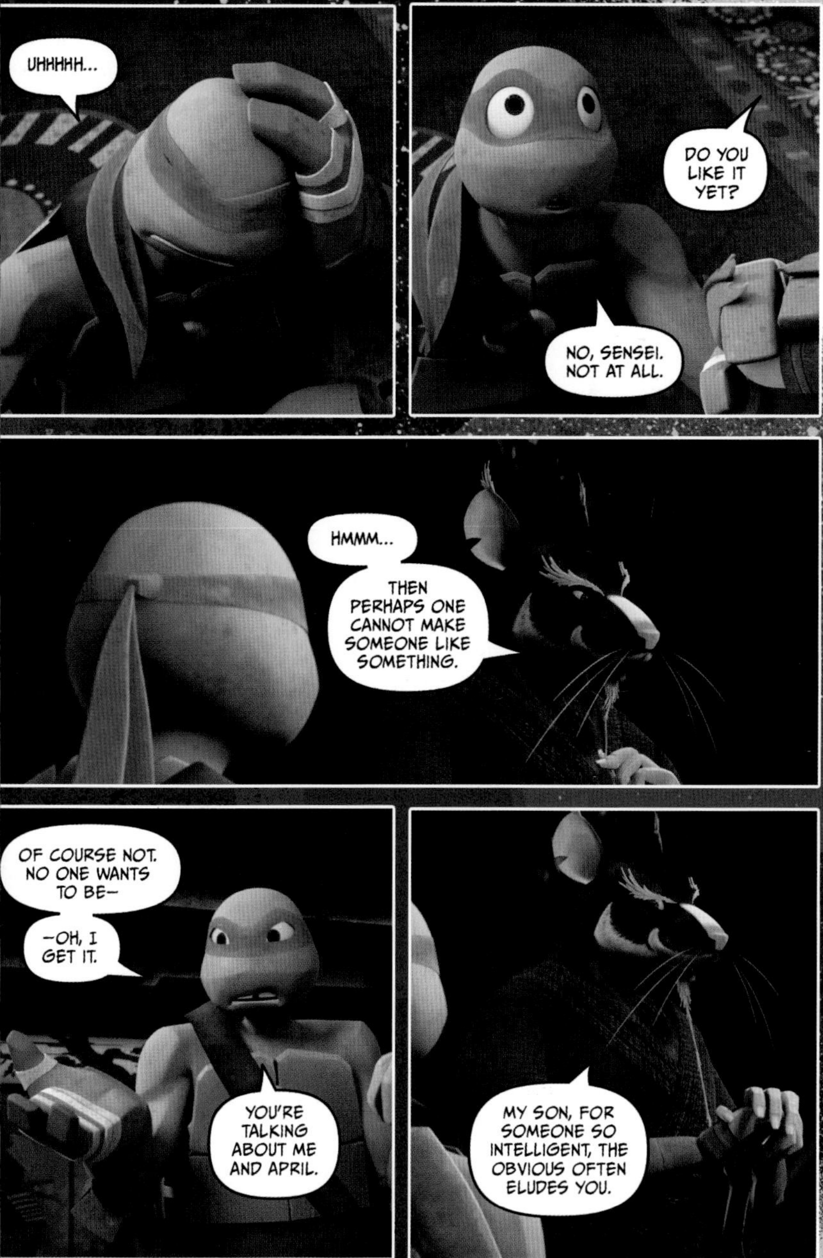
UHHHHH...
DO YOU LIKE IT YET?
NO, SENSEI. NOT AT ALL.
HMMM...
THEN PERHAPS ONE CANNOT MAKE SOMEONE LIKE SOMETHING.
OF COURSE NOT. NO ONE WANTS TO BE—
—OH, I GET IT.
YOU'RE TALKING ABOUT ME AND APRIL.
MY SON, FOR SOMEONE SO INTELLIGENT, THE OBVIOUS OFTEN ELUDES YOU.

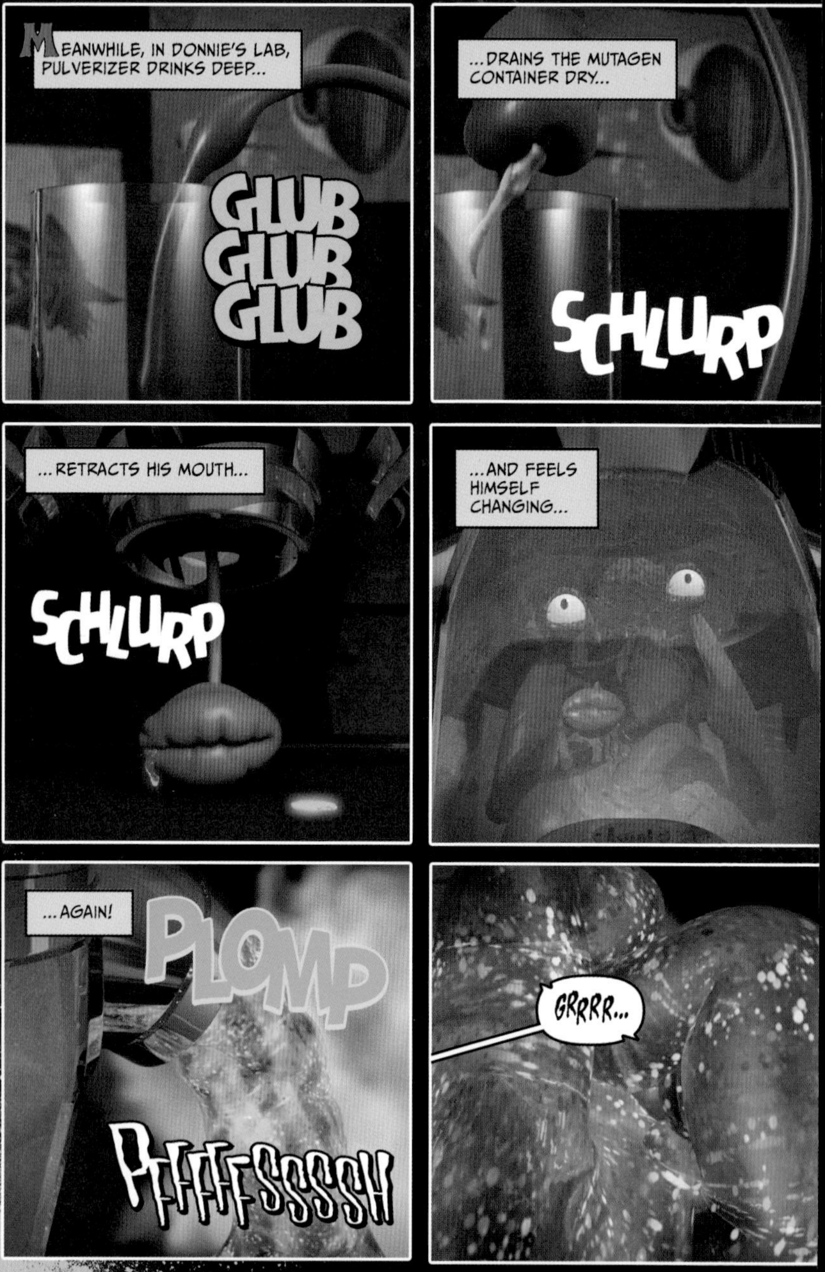
MEANWHILE, IN DONNIE'S LAB, PULVERIZER DRINKS DEEP...
GLUB GLUB GLUB
...DRAINS THE MUTAGEN CONTAINER DRY...
SCHLURP
...RETRACTS HIS MOUTH...
SCHLURP
...AND FEELS HIMSELF CHANGING...
...AGAIN!
PLOMP
PFFFFFSSSSSH
GRRRR...

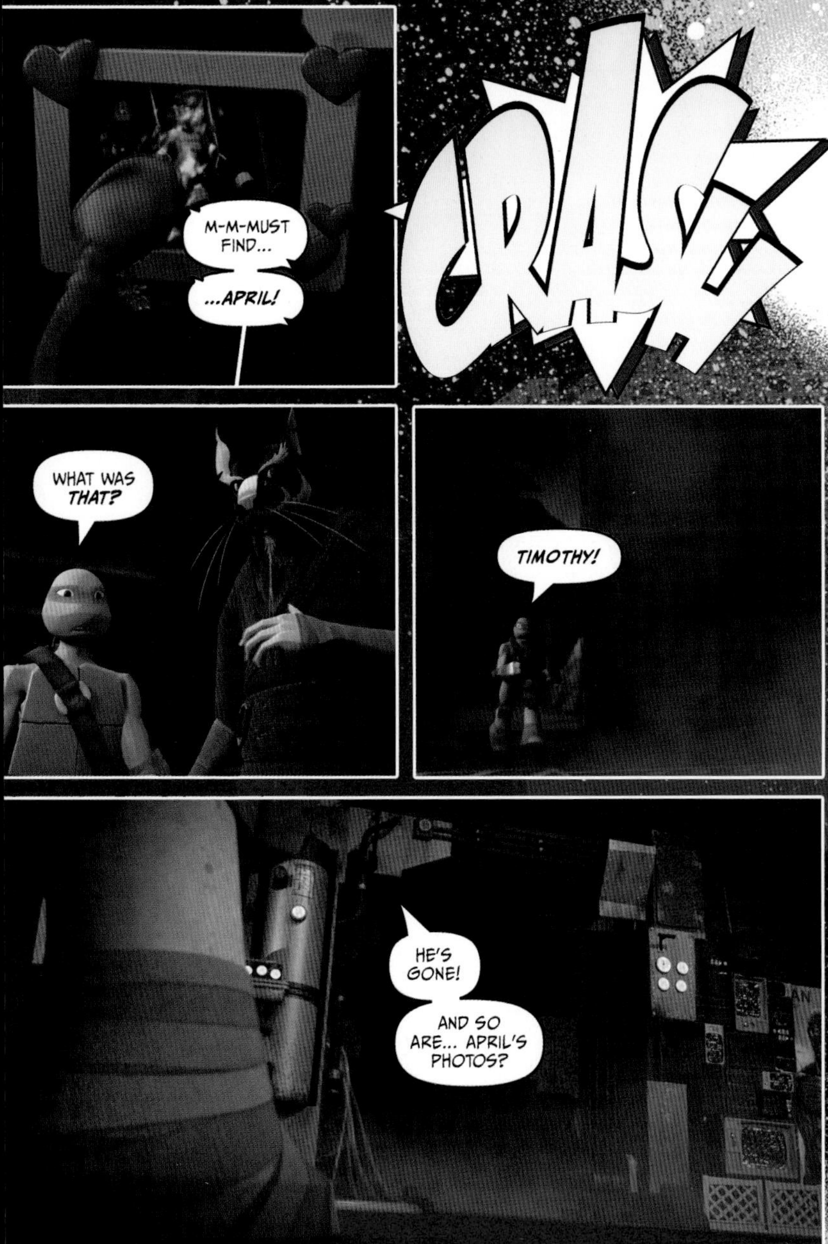
M-M-MUST FIND...
...APRIL!
CRASH!
WHAT WAS THAT?
TIMOTHY!
HE'S GONE!
AND SO ARE... APRIL'S PHOTOS?

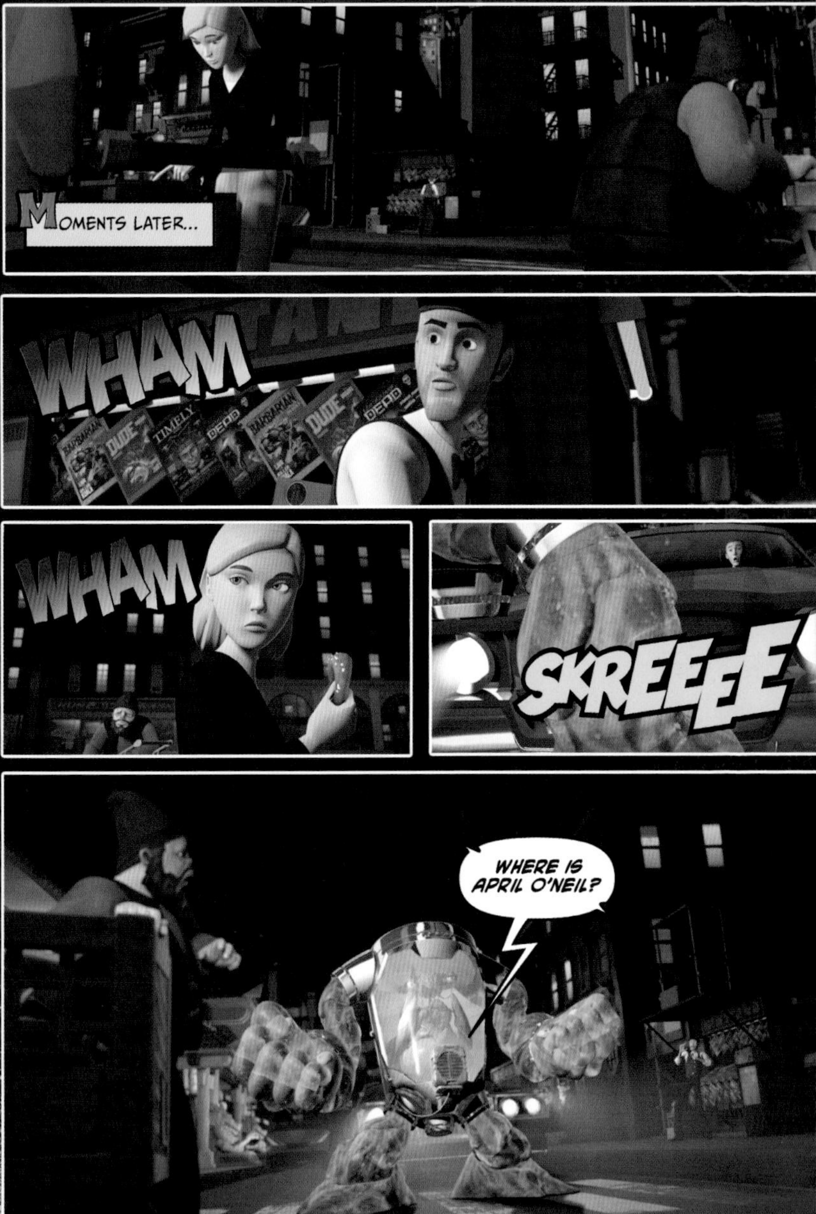
MOMENTS LATER...
WHAM
WHAM
SKREEEE
WHERE IS APRIL O'NEIL?

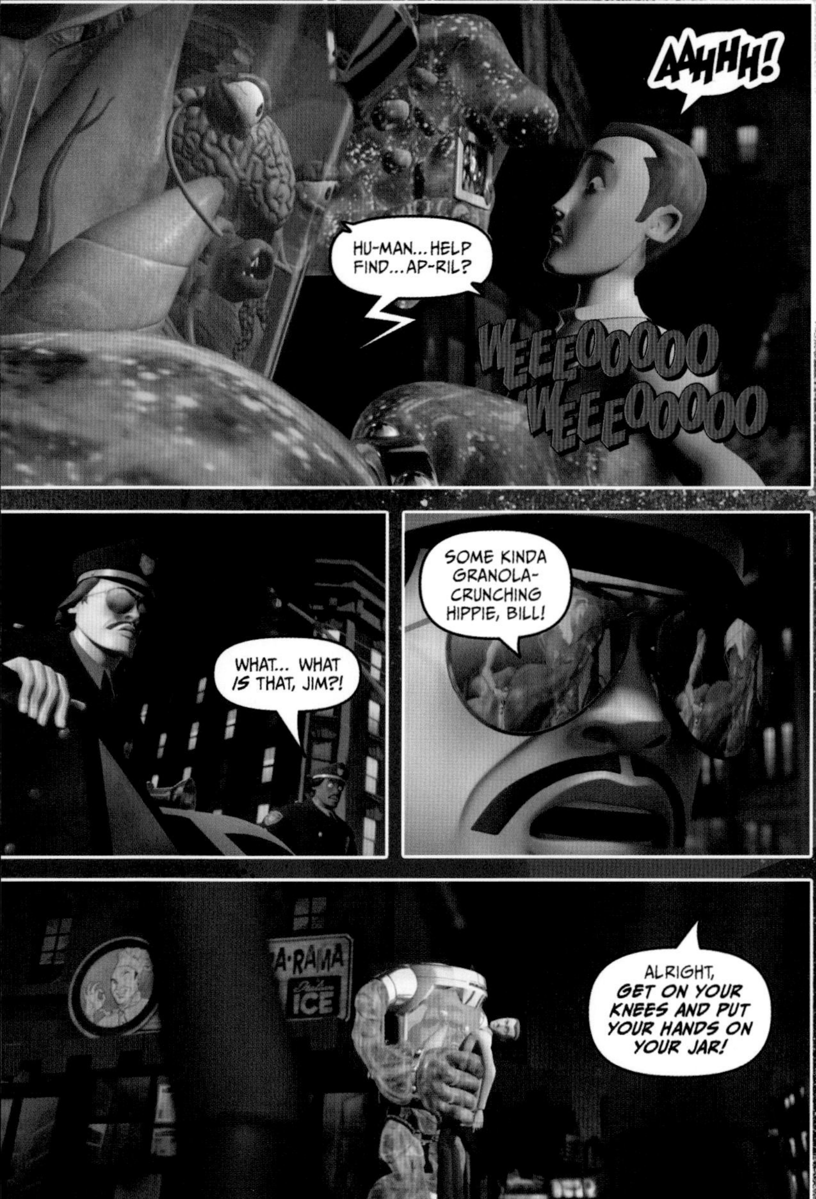
AAHHH!
HU-MAN... HELP FIND... AP-RIL?
WEEEOOOOO WEEEOOOOO
WHAT... WHAT IS THAT, JIM?!
SOME KINDA GRANOLA-CRUNCHING HIPPIE, BILL!
ICE
ALRIGHT, GET ON YOUR KNEES AND PUT YOUR HANDS ON YOUR JAR!

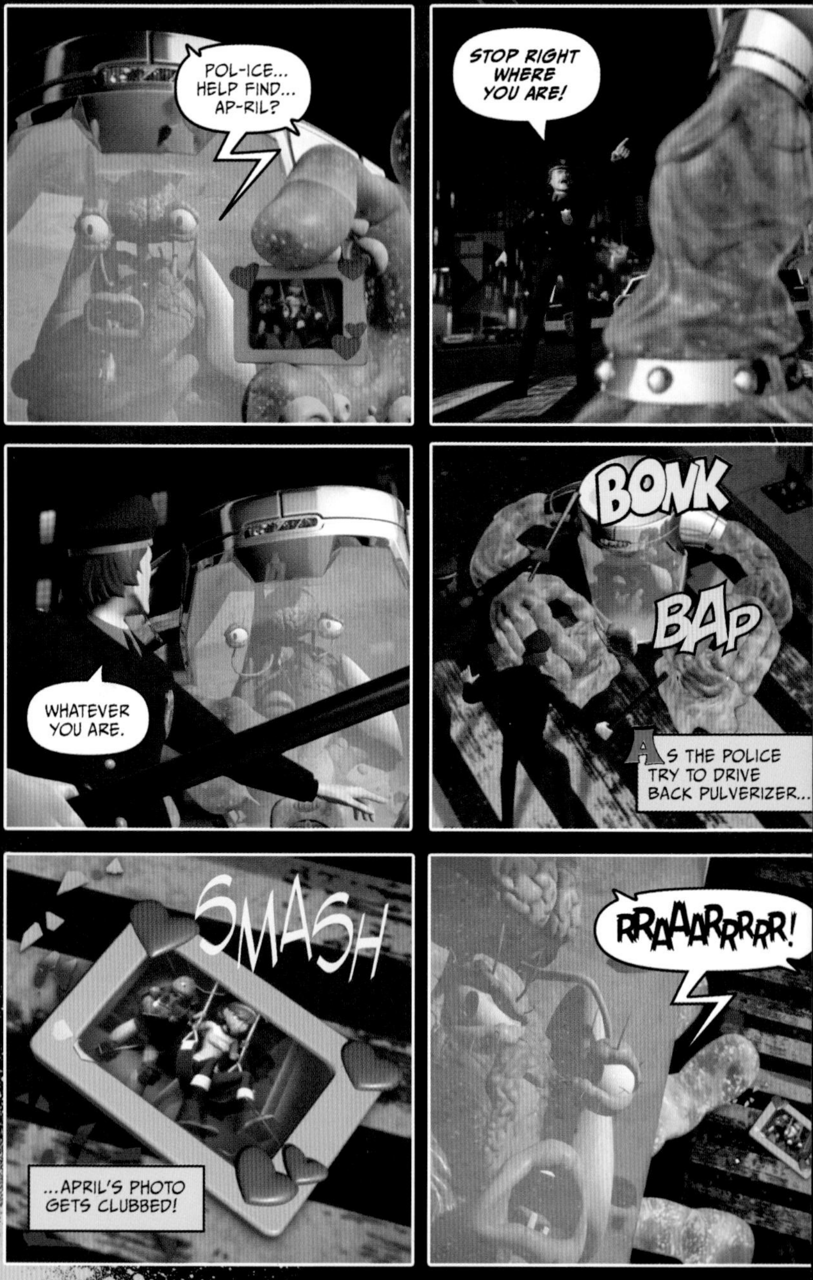
POL-ICE... HELP FIND... AP-RIL?
STOP RIGHT WHERE YOU ARE!
WHATEVER YOU ARE.
BONK
BAP
AS THE POLICE TRY TO DRIVE BACK PULVERIZER...
SMASH
...APRIL'S PHOTO GETS CLUBBED!
RRAAARRRRR!

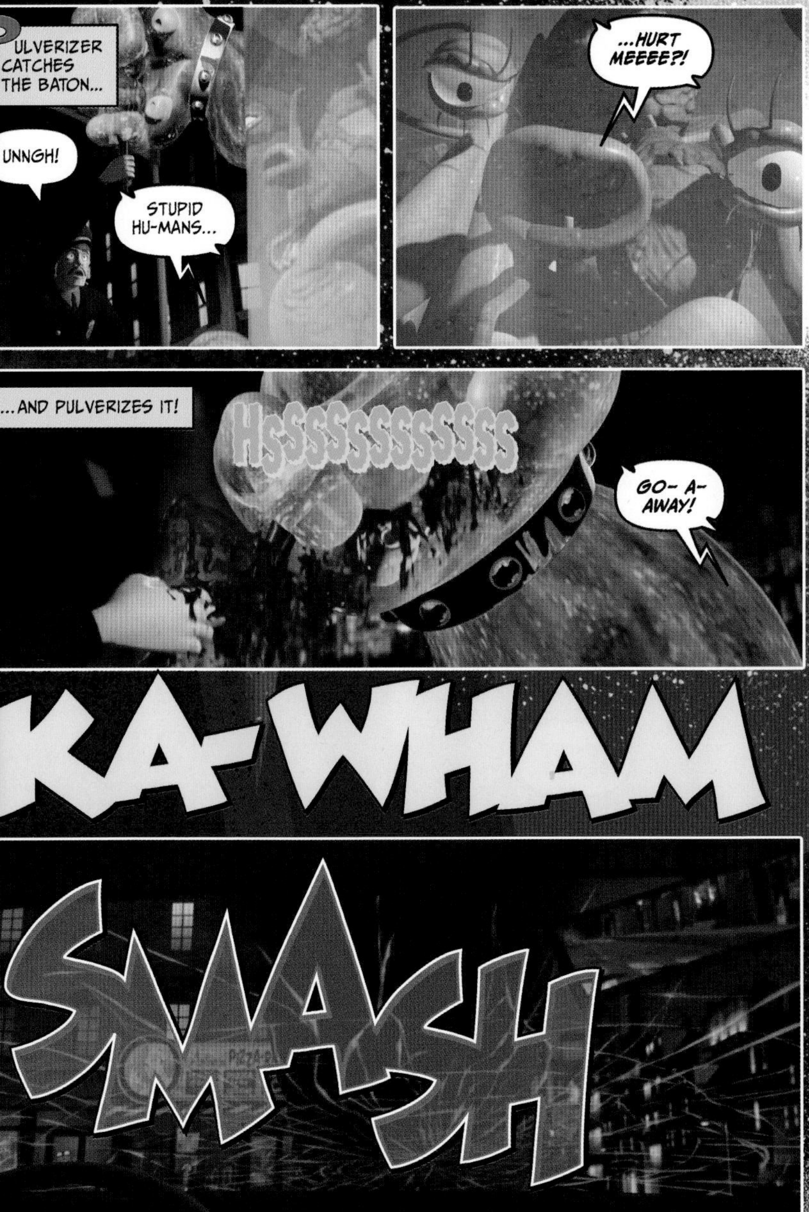
ULVERIZER CATCHES THE BATON...
UNNGH!
STUPID HU-MANS...
...HURT MEEEE?!
...AND PULVERIZES IT!
HSSSSSSSSSSS
GO- A- AWAY!
KA-WHAM
SMASH

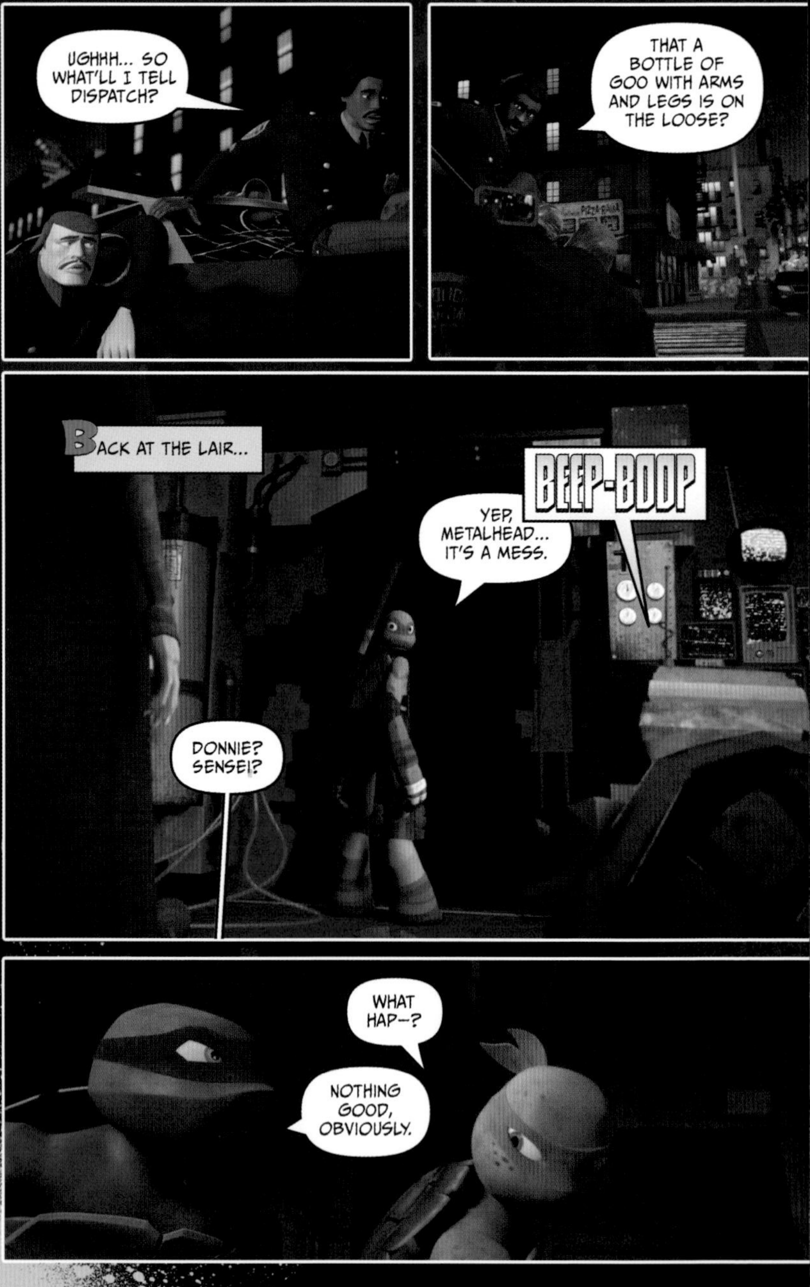
UGHHH... SO WHAT'LL I TELL DISPATCH?
THAT A BOTTLE OF GOO WITH ARMS AND LEGS IS ON THE LOOSE?
BACK AT THE LAIR...
BEEP-BOOP
YEP, METALHEAD... IT'S A MESS.
DONNIE? SENSEI?
WHAT HAP--?
NOTHING GOOD, OBVIOUSLY.

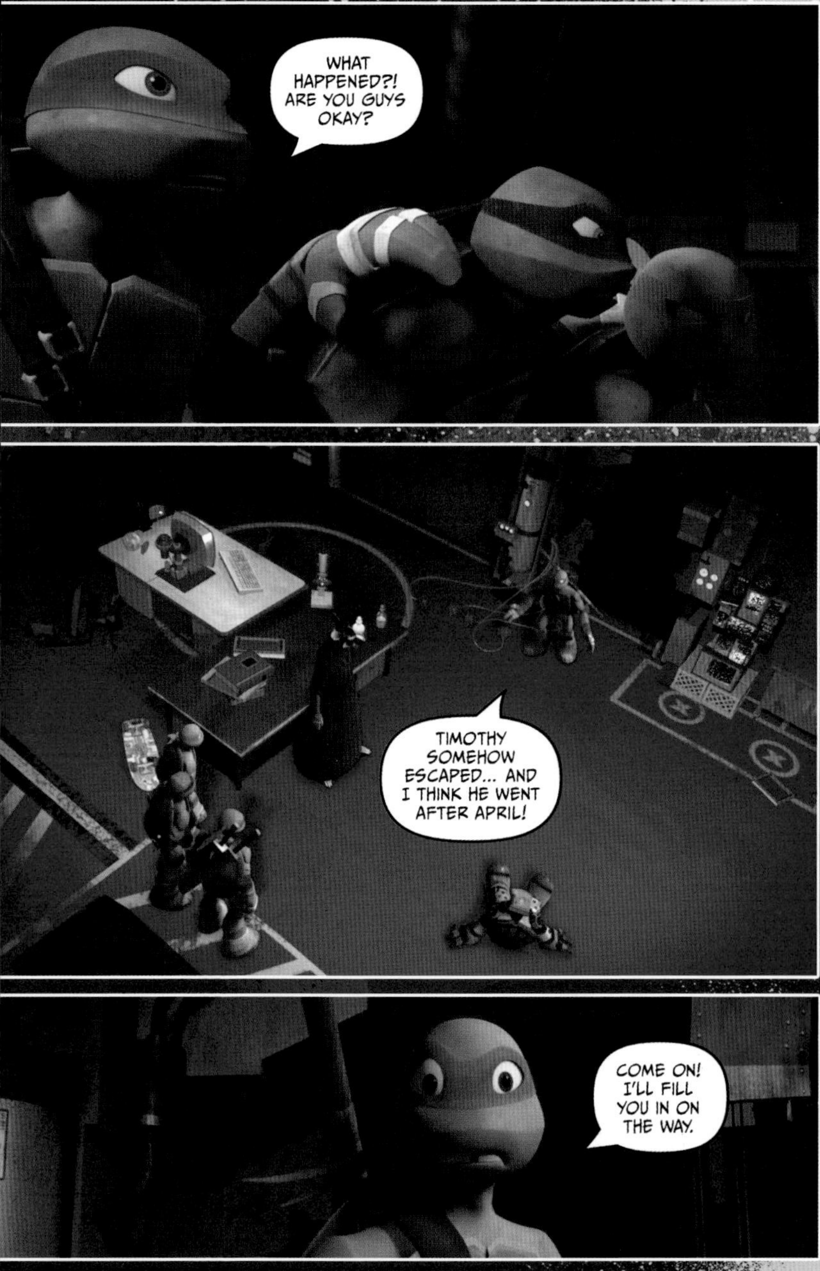

WHAT HAPPENED?! ARE YOU GUYS OKAY?
TIMOTHY SOMEHOW ESCAPED... AND I THINK HE WENT AFTER APRIL!
COME ON! I'LL FILL YOU IN ON THE WAY.

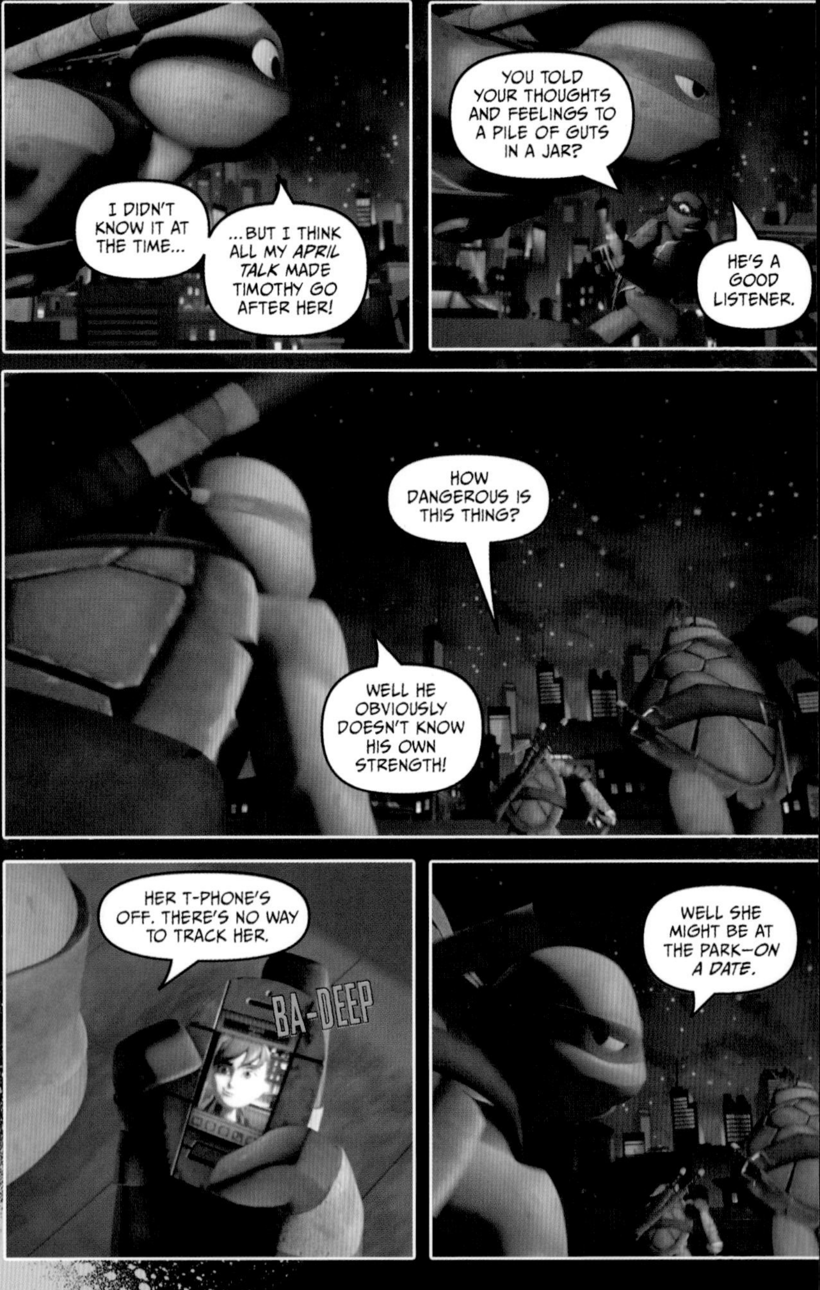
I DIDN'T KNOW IT AT THE TIME...
...BUT I THINK ALL MY *APRIL TALK* MADE TIMOTHY GO AFTER HER!
YOU TOLD YOUR THOUGHTS AND FEELINGS TO A PILE OF GUTS IN A JAR?
HE'S A GOOD LISTENER.
HOW DANGEROUS IS THIS THING?
WELL HE OBVIOUSLY DOESN'T KNOW HIS OWN STRENGTH!
HER T-PHONE'S OFF. THERE'S NO WAY TO TRACK HER.
BA-DEEP
WELL SHE MIGHT BE AT THE PARK—*ON A DATE.*

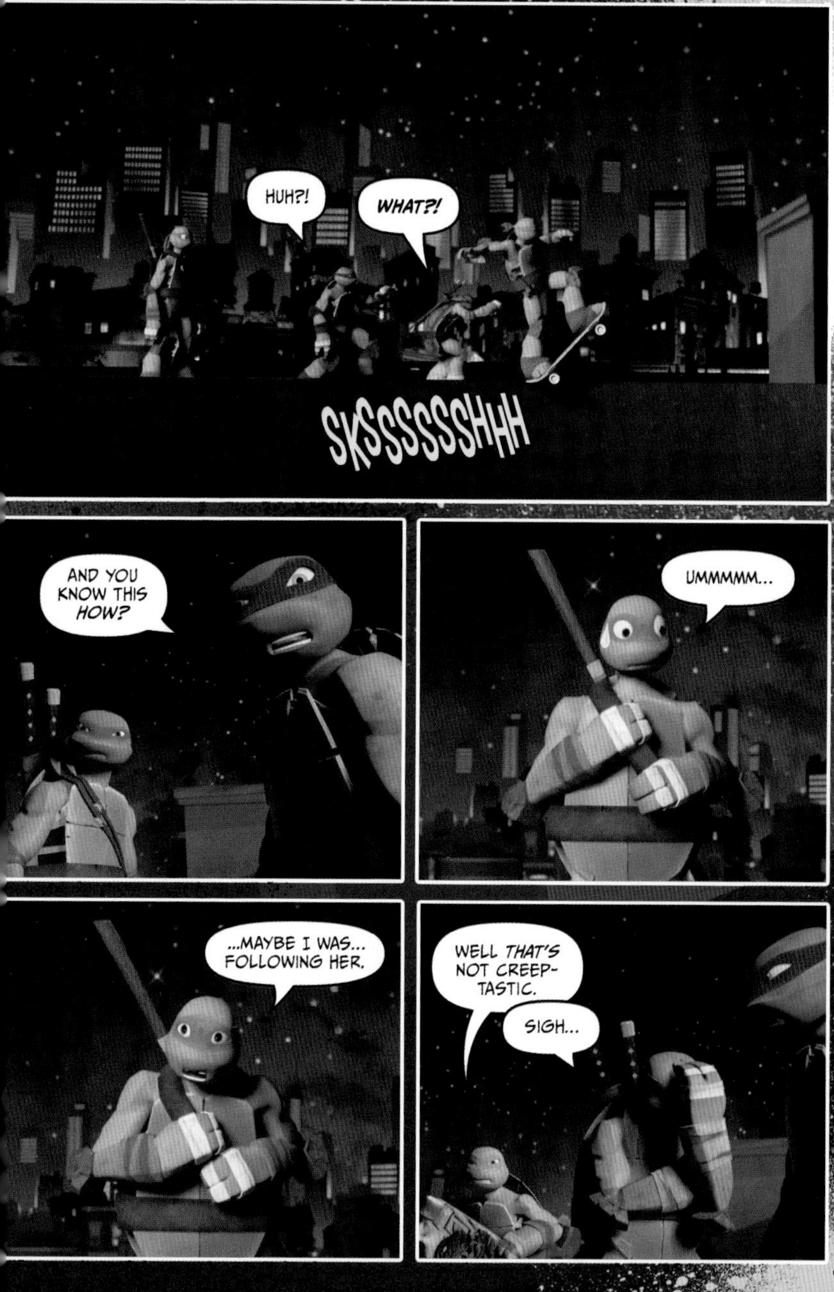
HUH?!
WHAT?!
SKSSSSSSHHH
AND YOU KNOW THIS HOW?
UMMMMM...
...MAYBE I WAS... FOLLOWING HER.
WELL THAT'S NOT CREEP-TASTIC.
SIGH...

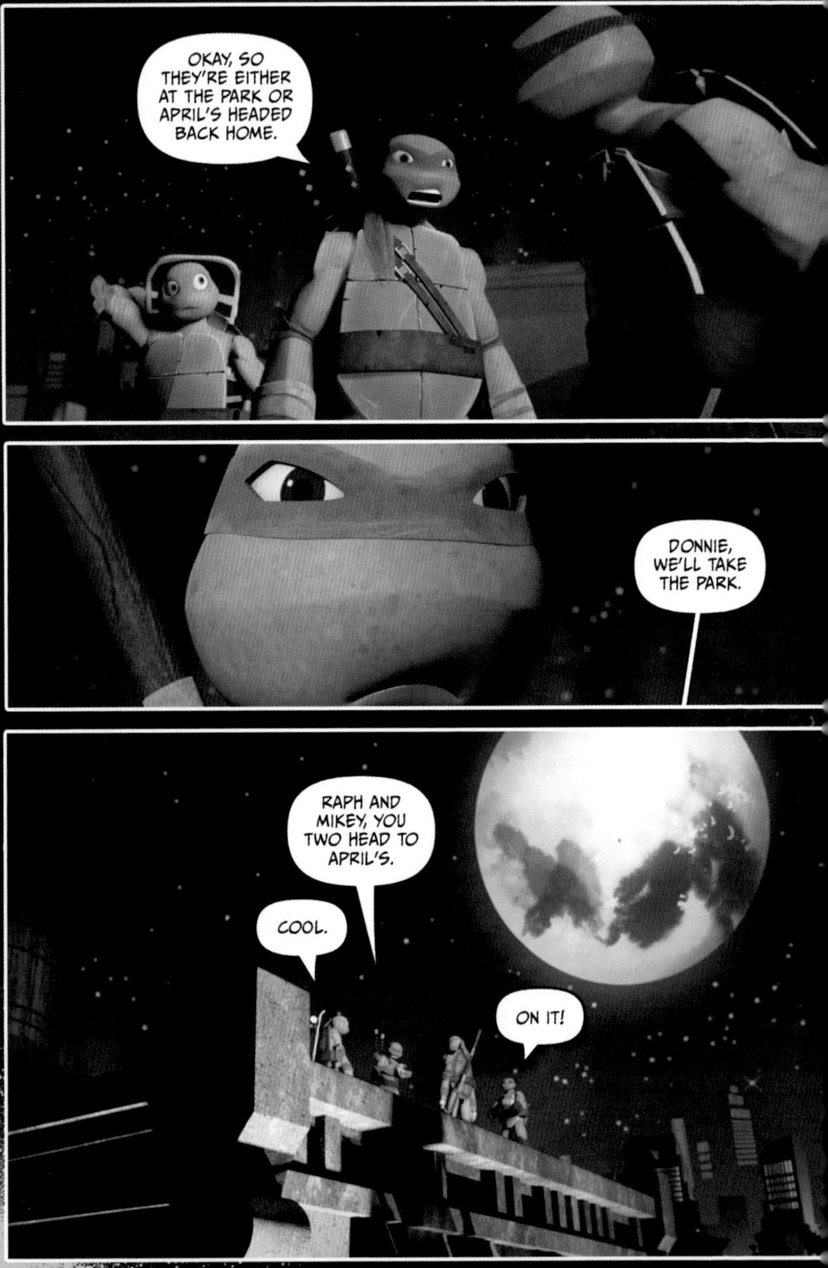
OKAY, SO THEY'RE EITHER AT THE PARK OR APRIL'S HEADED BACK HOME.
DONNIE, WE'LL TAKE THE PARK.
RAPH AND MIKEY, YOU TWO HEAD TO APRIL'S.
COOL.
ON IT!

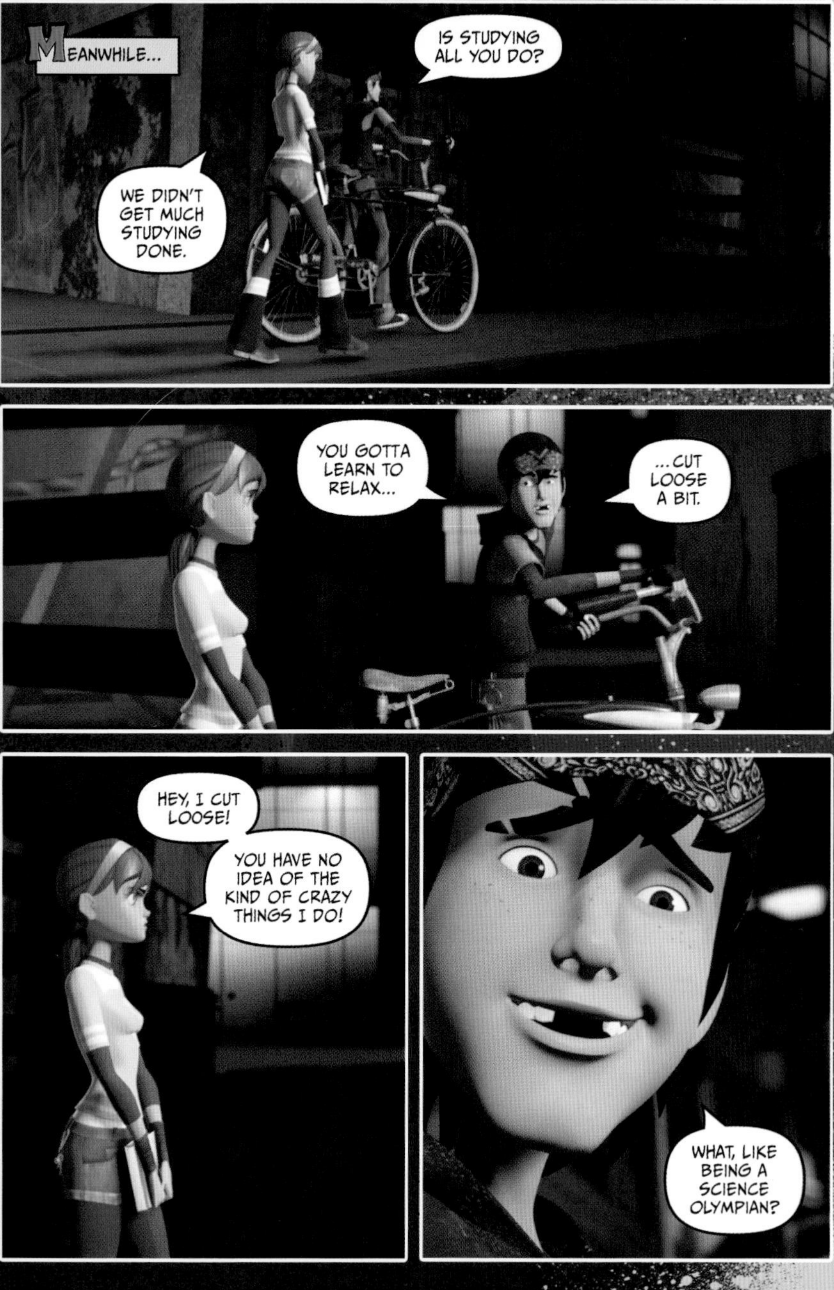
MEANWHILE...
IS STUDYING ALL YOU DO?
WE DIDN'T GET MUCH STUDYING DONE.
YOU GOTTA LEARN TO RELAX...
...CUT LOOSE A BIT.
HEY, I CUT LOOSE!
YOU HAVE NO IDEA OF THE KIND OF CRAZY THINGS I DO!
WHAT, LIKE BEING A SCIENCE OLYMPIAN?

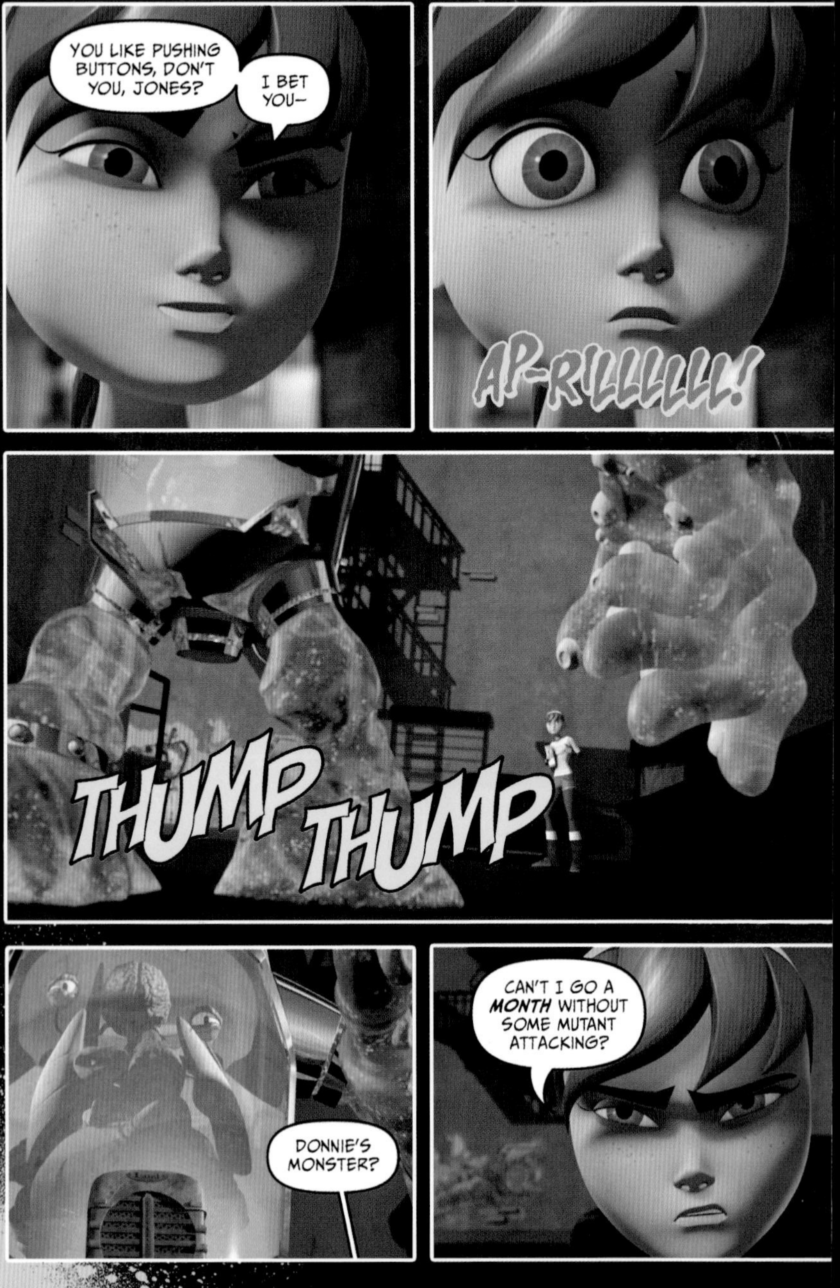
YOU LIKE PUSHING BUTTONS, DON'T YOU, JONES?
I BET YOU–
AP-RILLLLLL!
THUMP THUMP
DONNIE'S MONSTER?
CAN'T I GO A *MONTH* WITHOUT SOME MUTANT ATTACKING?

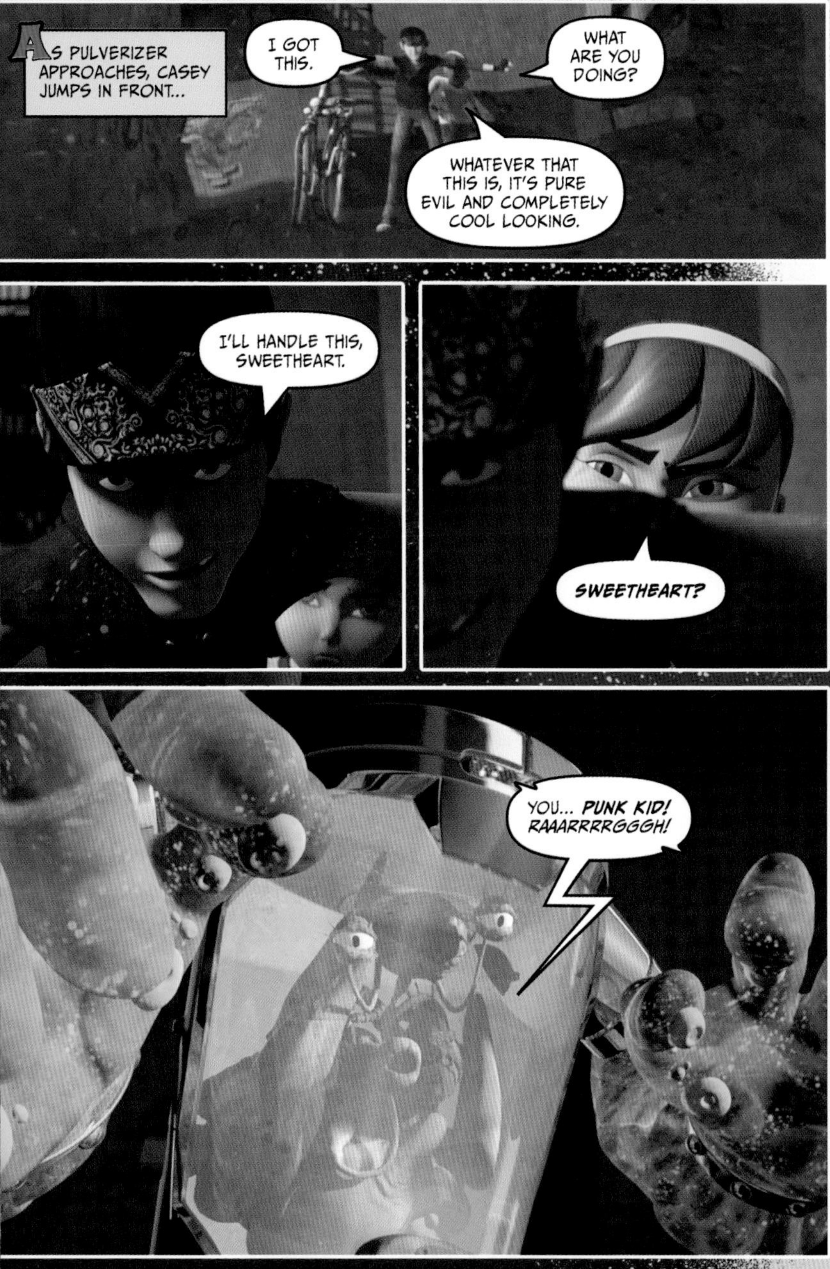
AS PULVERIZER APPROACHES, CASEY JUMPS IN FRONT...
I GOT THIS.
WHAT ARE YOU DOING?
WHATEVER THAT THIS IS, IT'S PURE EVIL AND COMPLETELY COOL LOOKING.
I'LL HANDLE THIS, SWEETHEART.
SWEETHEART?
YOU... PUNK KID! RAAARRRRGGGH!

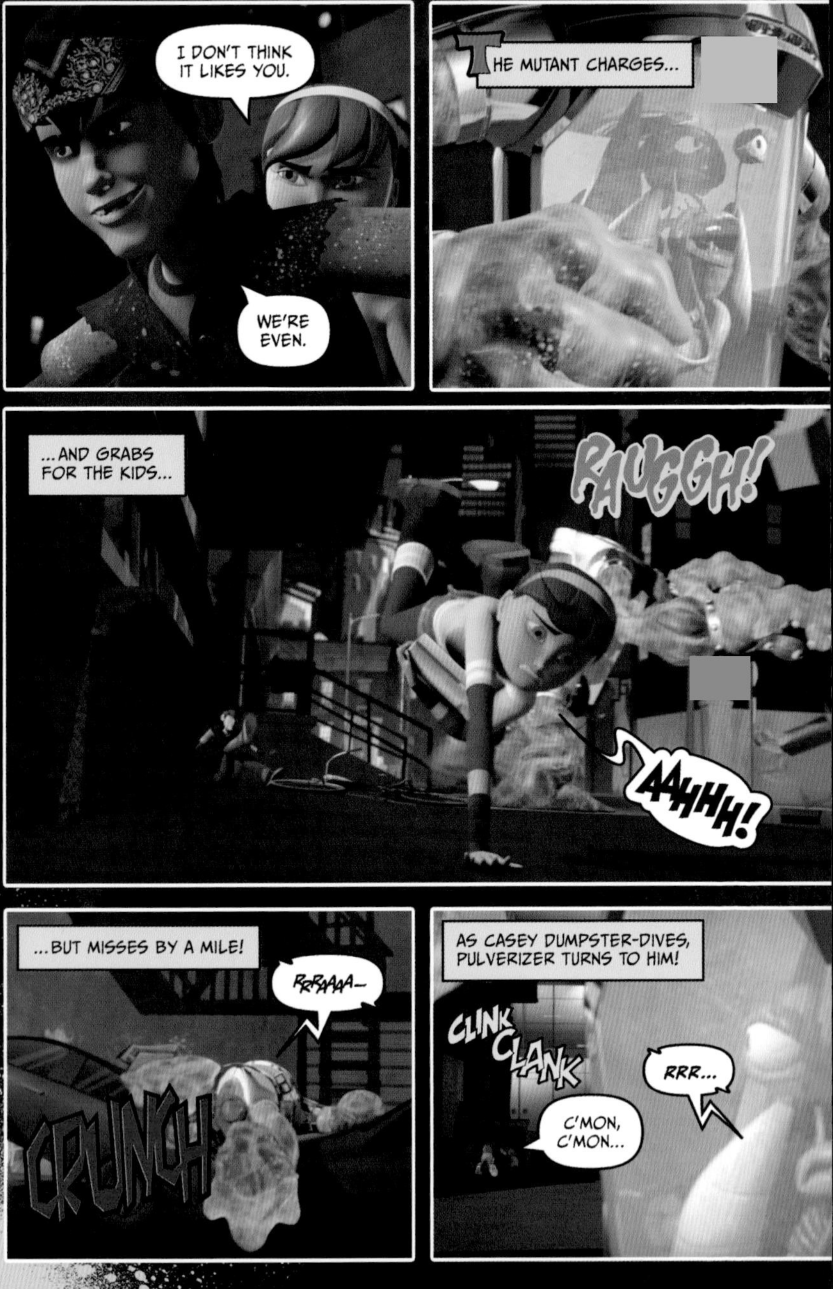

I DON'T THINK IT LIKES YOU.
WE'RE EVEN.
THE MUTANT CHARGES...
...AND GRABS FOR THE KIDS...
RAUGGH!
AAHHH!
...BUT MISSES BY A MILE!
RRRAAAA—
CRUNCH
AS CASEY DUMPSTER-DIVES, PULVERIZER TURNS TO HIM!
CLINK
CLANK
RRR...
C'MON, C'MON...

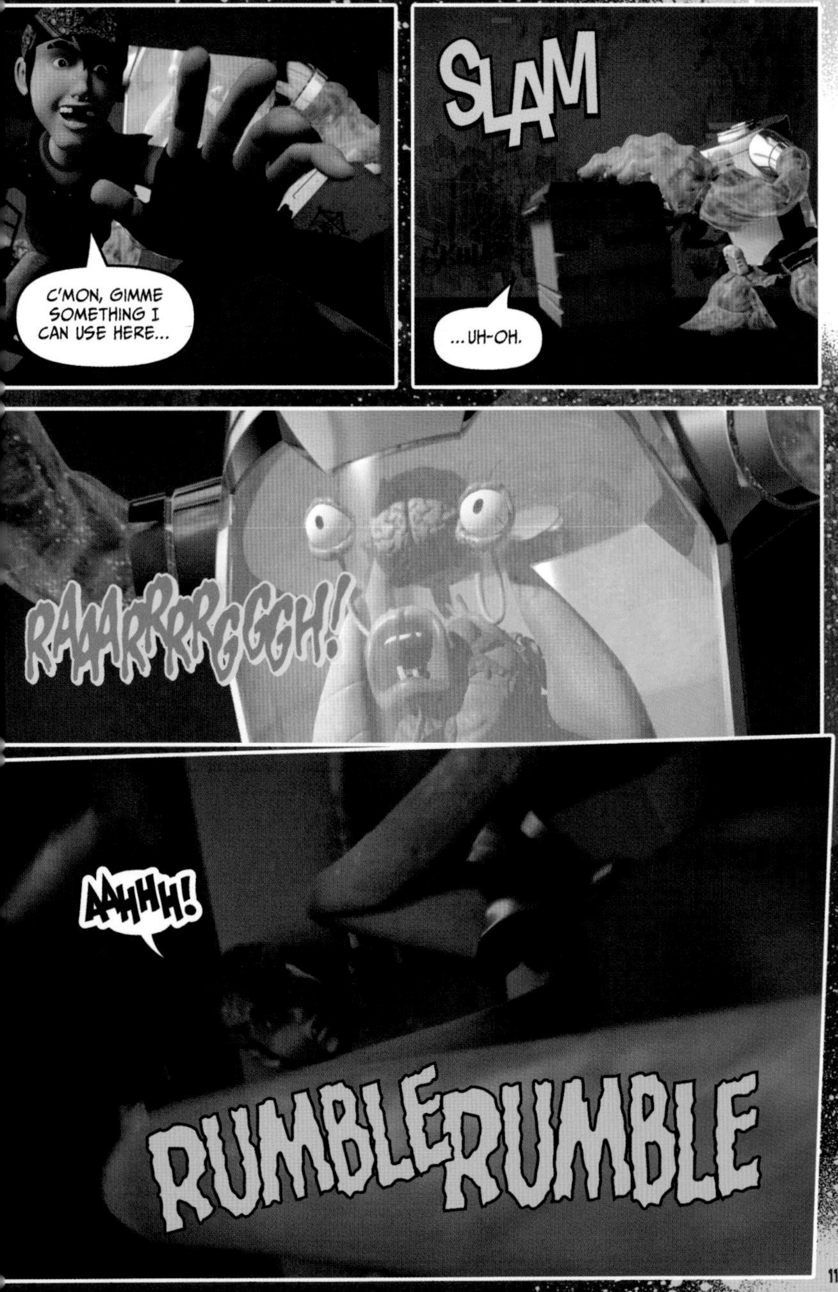
C'MON, GIMME SOMETHING I CAN USE HERE...
SLAM
...UH-OH.
RAAARRRRGGGH!
AAHHH!
RUMBLERUMBLE

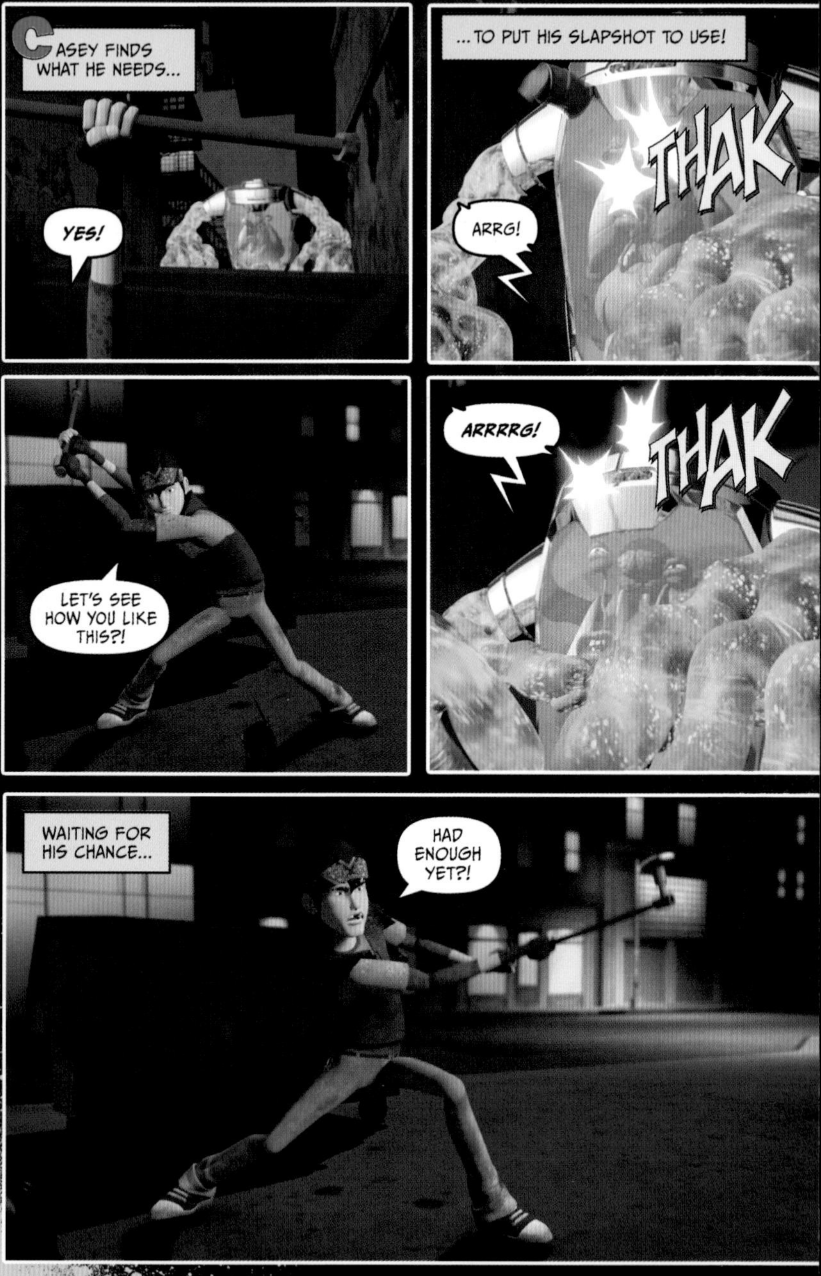
CASEY FINDS WHAT HE NEEDS...
YES!
...TO PUT HIS SLAPSHOT TO USE!
THAK
ARRG!
LET'S SEE HOW YOU LIKE THIS?!
ARRRRG!
THAK
WAITING FOR HIS CHANCE...
HAD ENOUGH YET?!

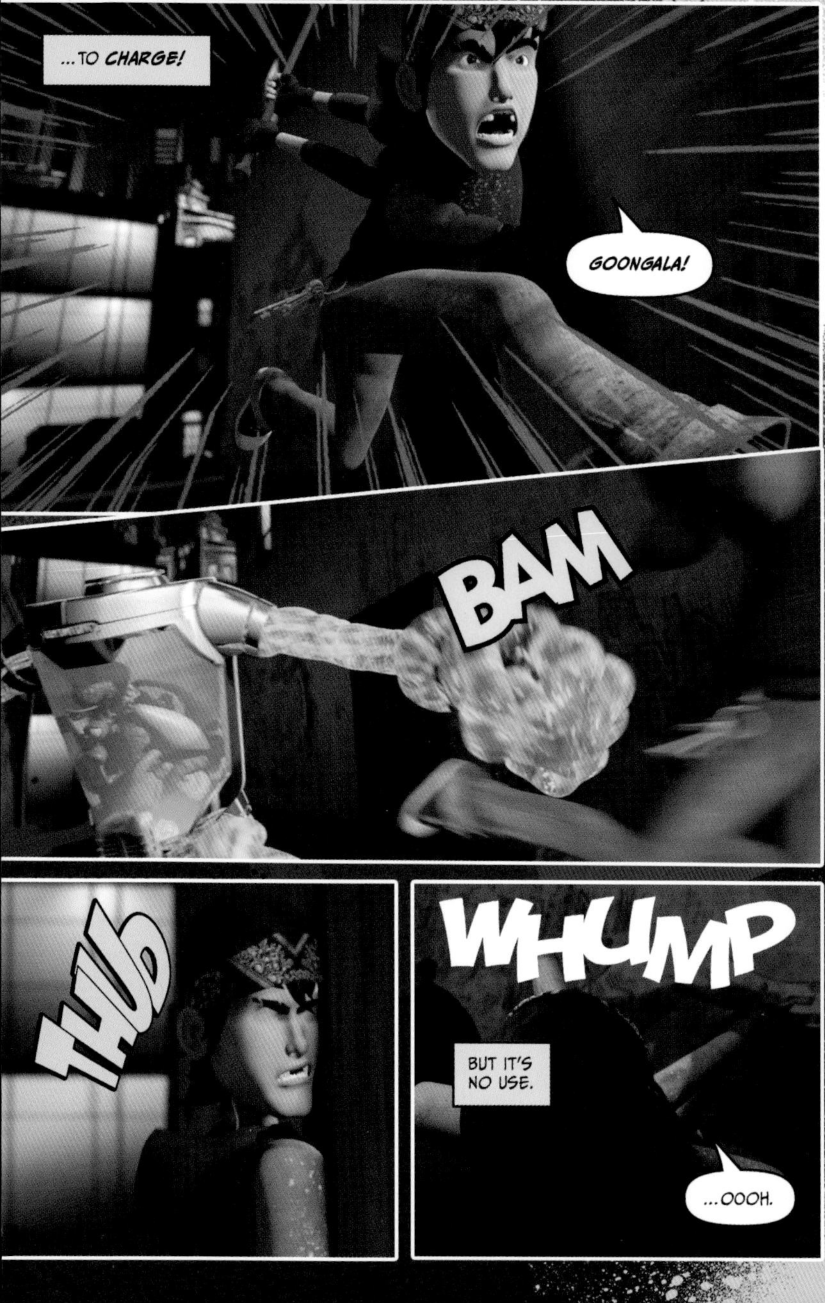
...TO CHARGE!
GOONGALA!
BAM
THUD
WHUMP
BUT IT'S NO USE.
...OOOH.

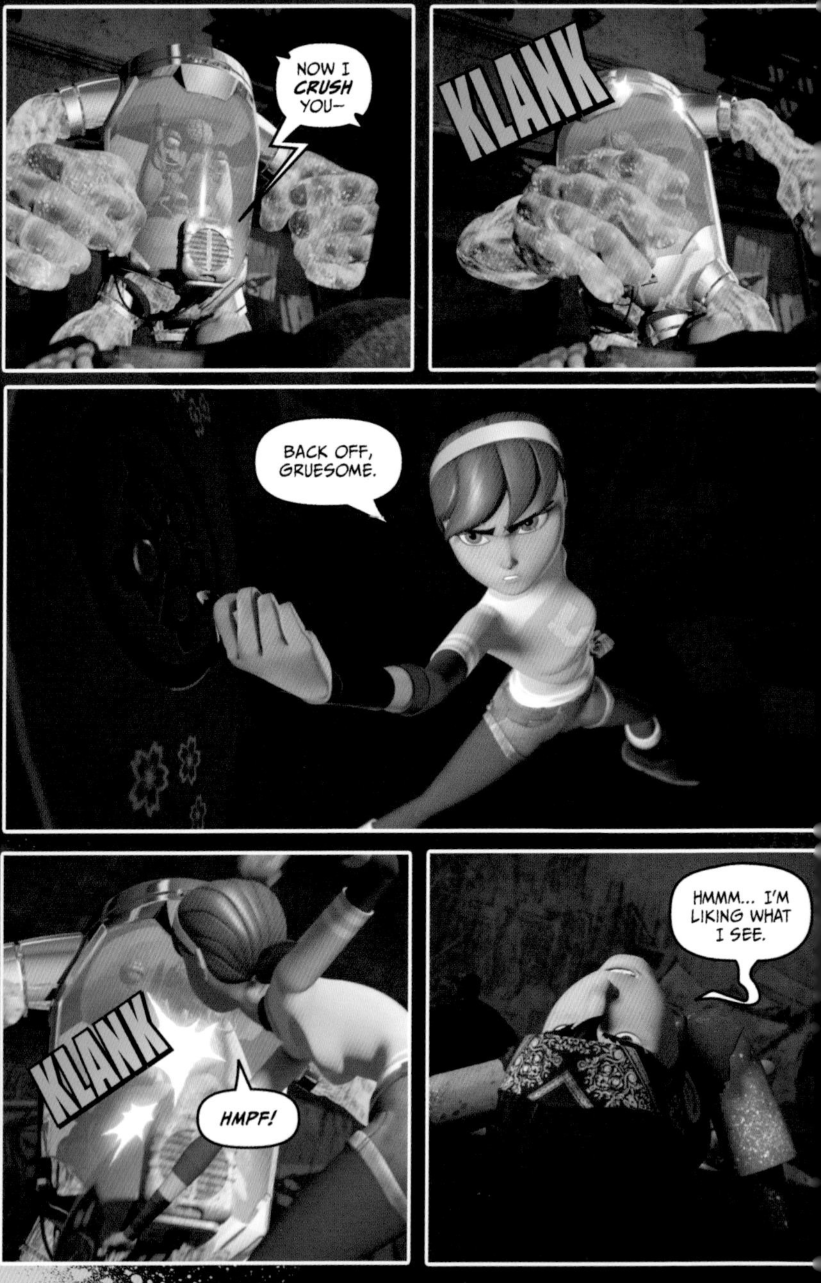
NOW I *CRUSH* YOU—
KLANK
BACK OFF, GRUESOME.
KLANK
HMPF!
HMMM... I'M LIKING WHAT I SEE.

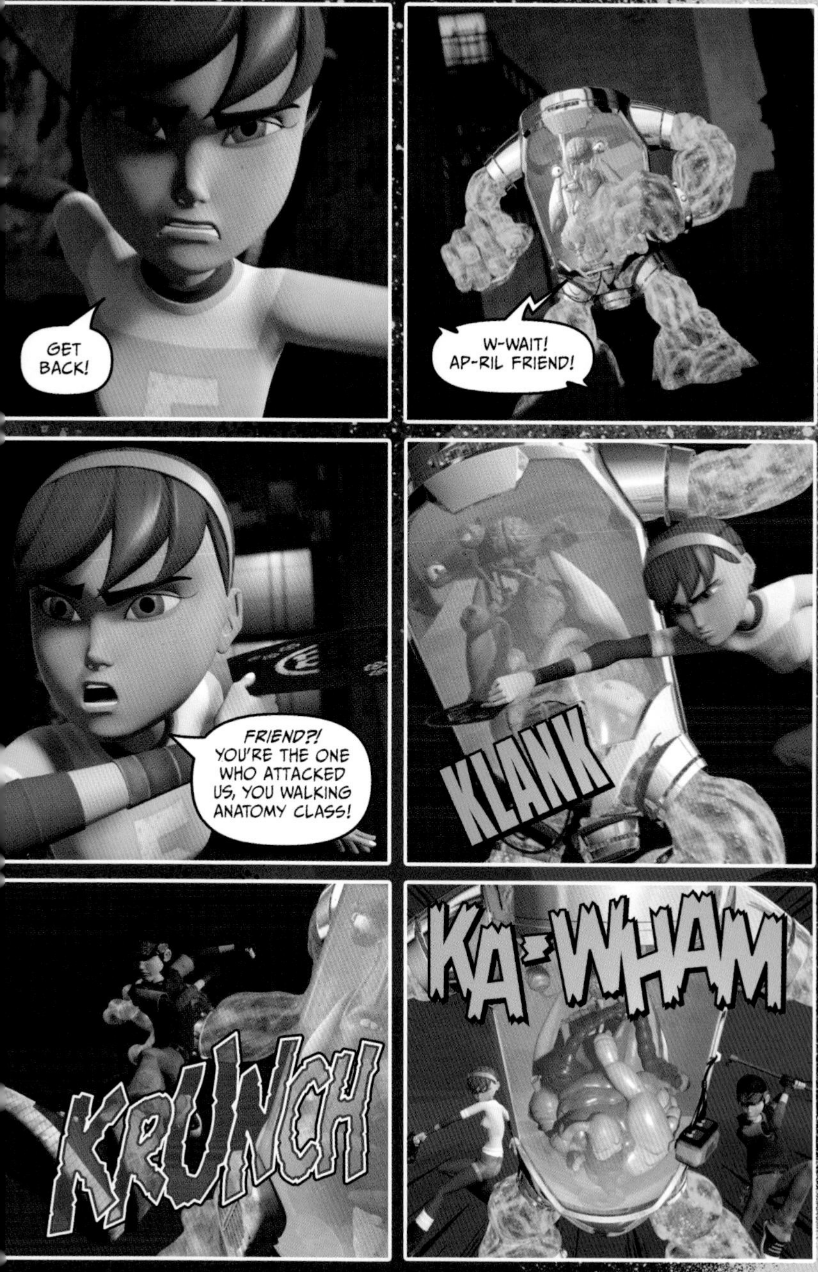
GET BACK!
W-WAIT! AP-RIL FRIEND!
FRIEND?! YOU'RE THE ONE WHO ATTACKED US, YOU WALKING ANATOMY CLASS!
KLANK
KRUNCH
KA-WHAM

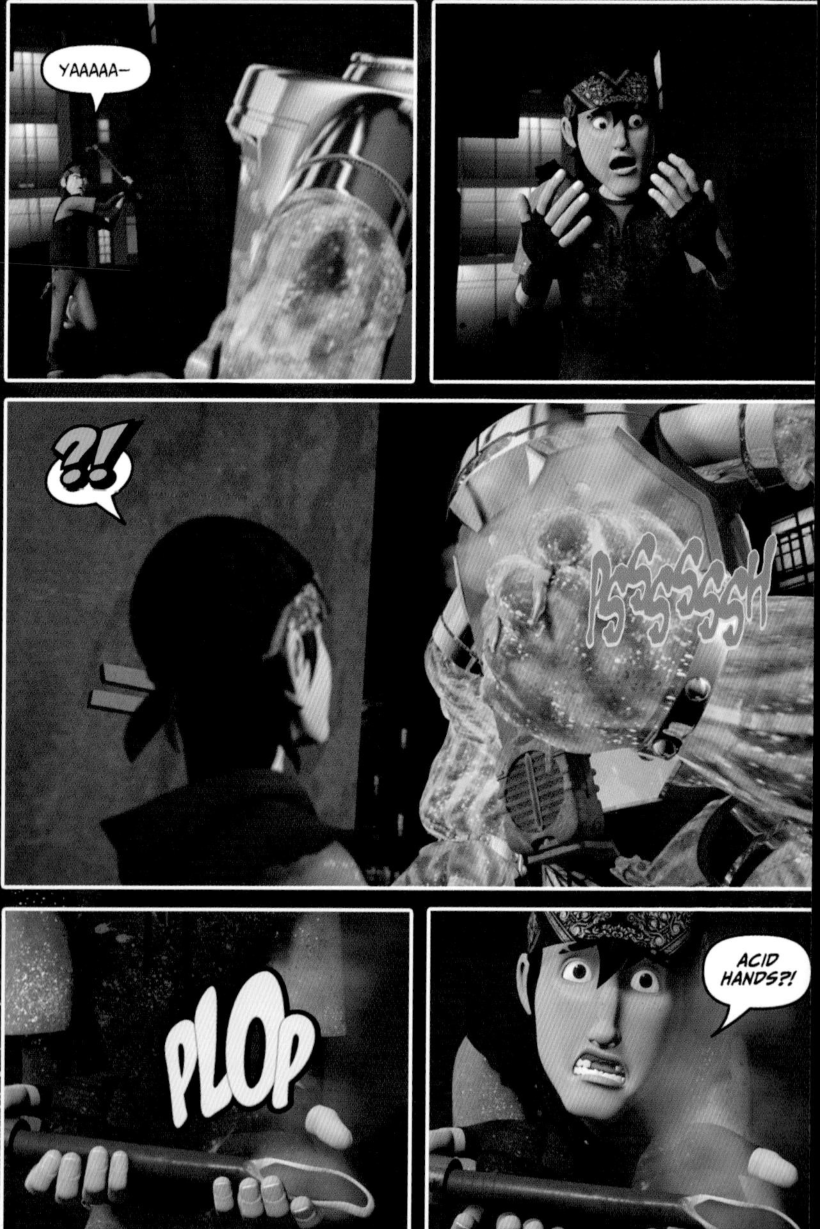
YAAAAA—
?!
PSSSSSSH
PLOP
ACID HANDS?!

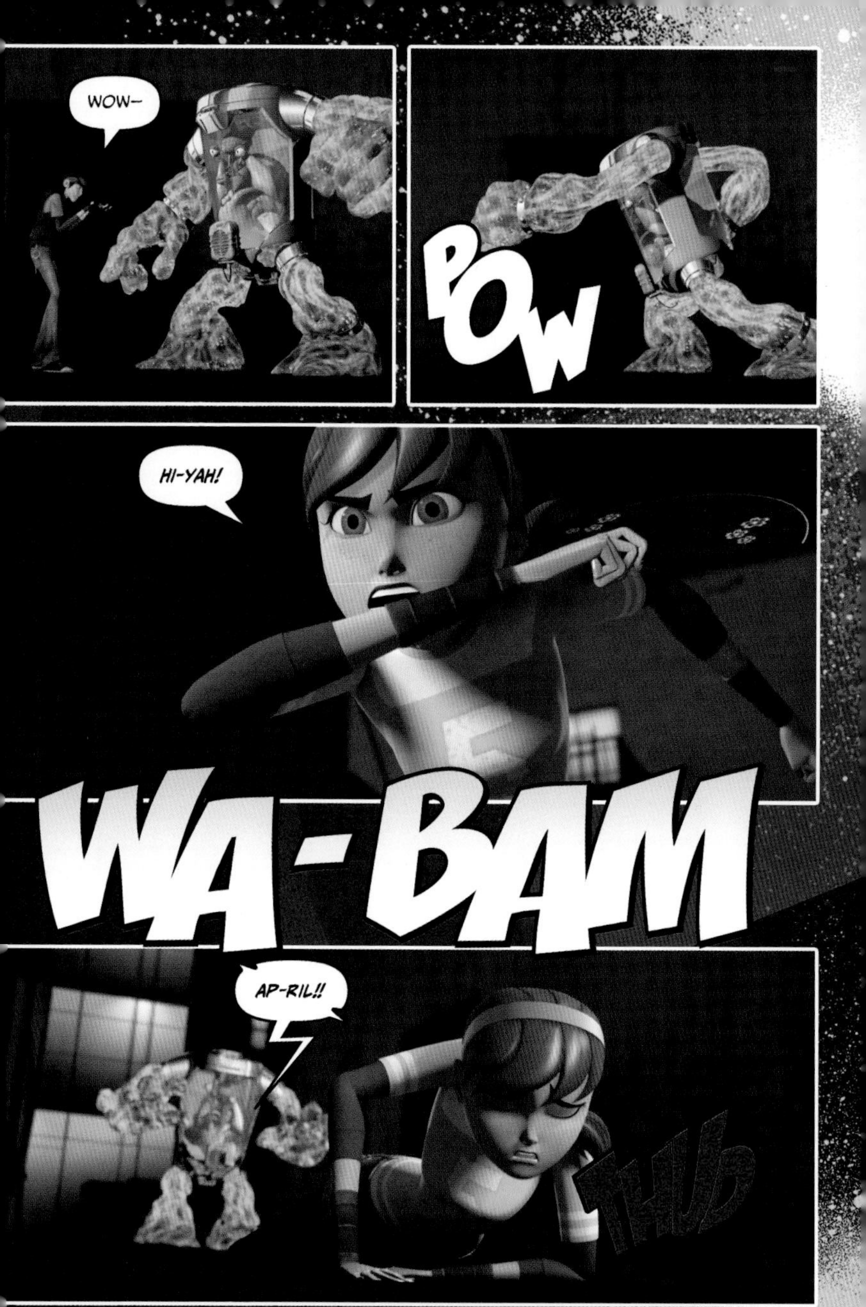
WOW—
POW
HI-YAH!
WA-BAM
AP-RIL!!
THUD

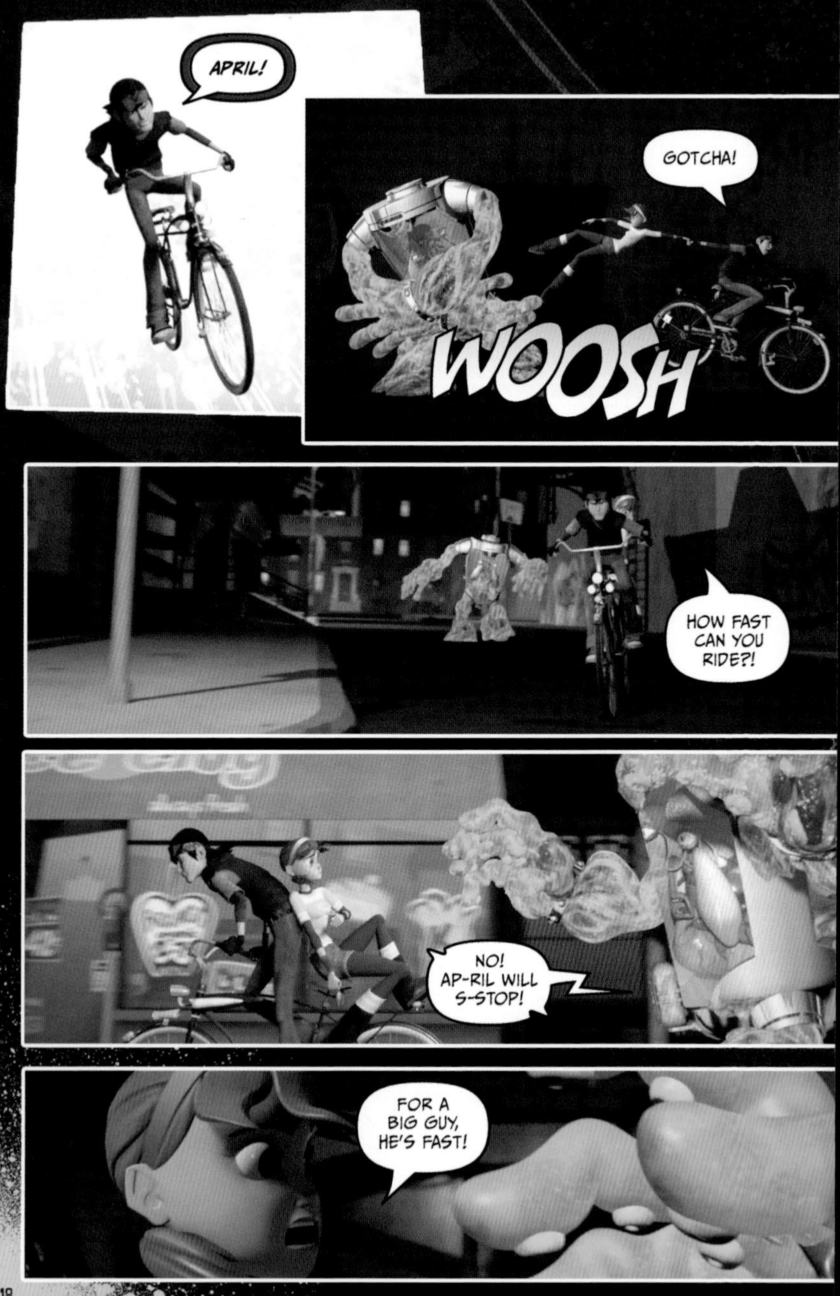
APRIL!
GOTCHA!
WOOSH
HOW FAST CAN YOU RIDE?!
NO! AP-RIL WILL S-STOP!
FOR A BIG GUY, HE'S FAST!

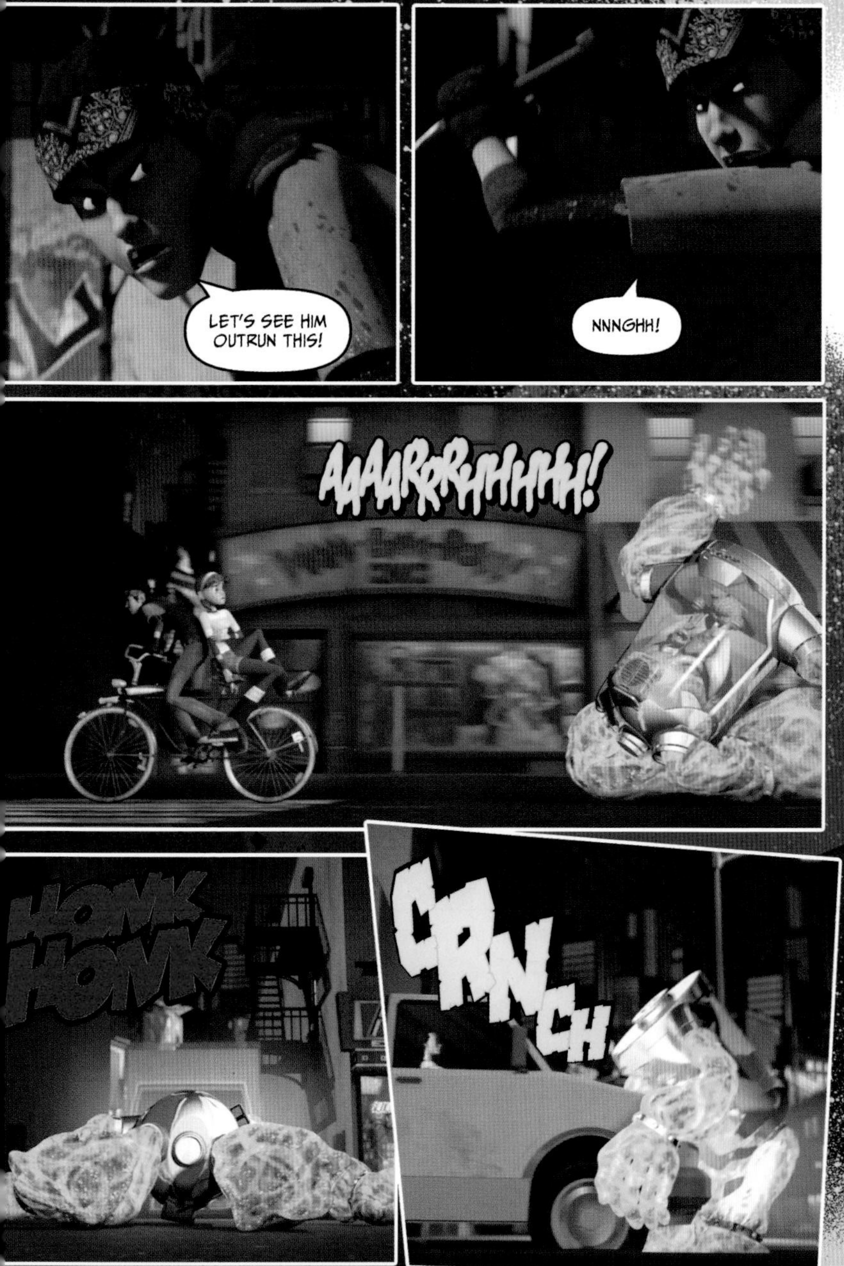
LET'S SEE HIM OUTRUN THIS!
NNNGHH!
AAAARRRHHHHH!
HONK HONK
CRNCH

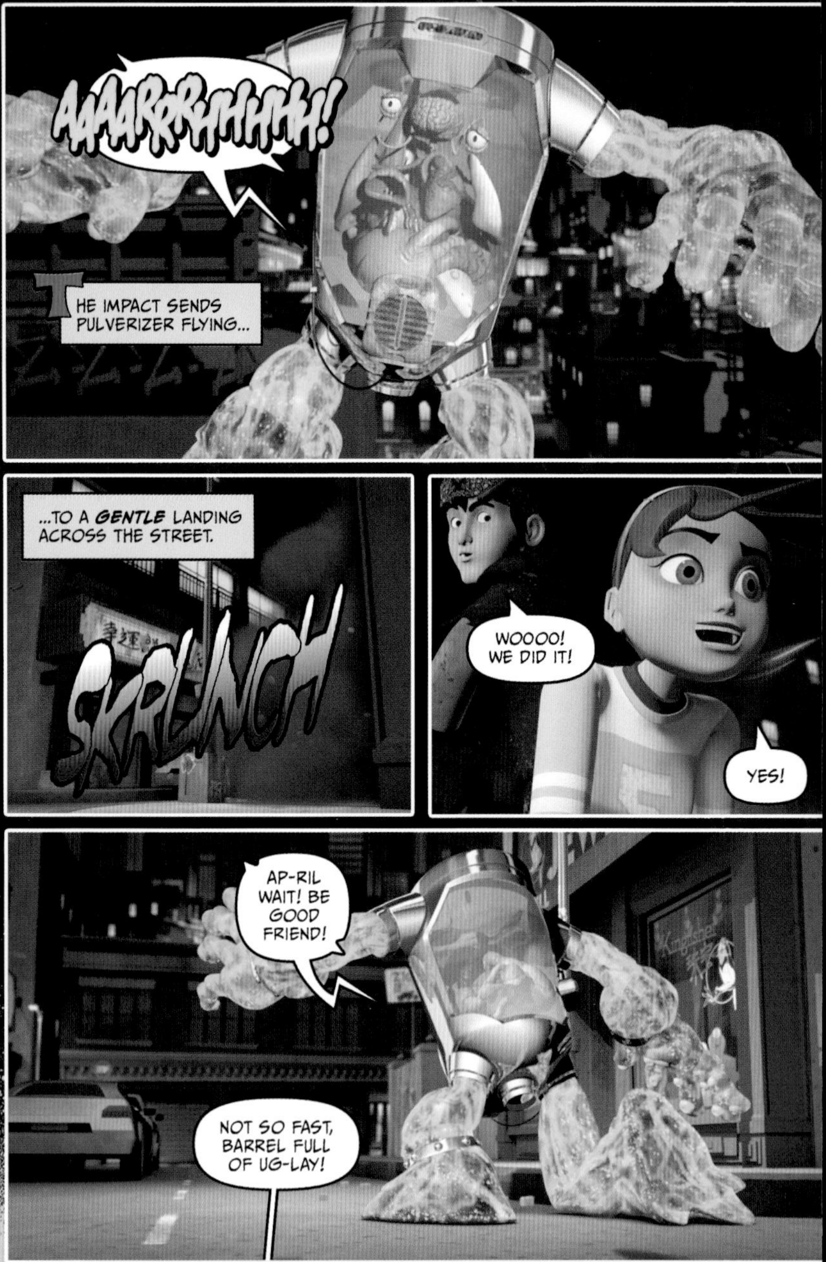
AAAARRRHHHHH!
THE IMPACT SENDS PULVERIZER FLYING...
...TO A GENTLE LANDING ACROSS THE STREET.
SKRRUNCH
WOOOO! WE DID IT!
YES!
AP-RIL WAIT! BE GOOD FRIEND!
NOT SO FAST, BARREL FULL OF UG-LAY!

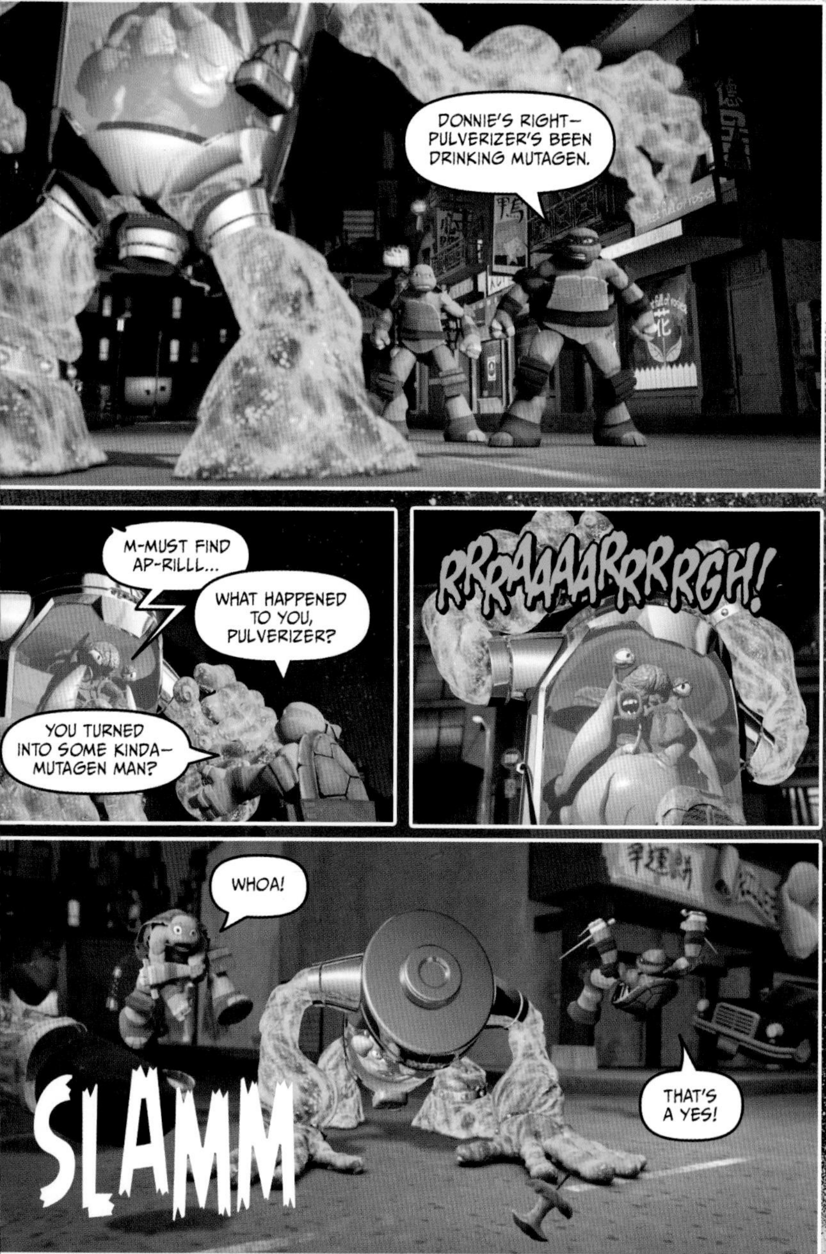
DONNIE'S RIGHT—PULVERIZER'S BEEN DRINKING MUTAGEN.
M-MUST FIND AP-RILLL...
WHAT HAPPENED TO YOU, PULVERIZER?
YOU TURNED INTO SOME KINDA—MUTAGEN MAN?
RRRAAAAARRRRGH!
WHOA!
SLAMM
THAT'S A YES!

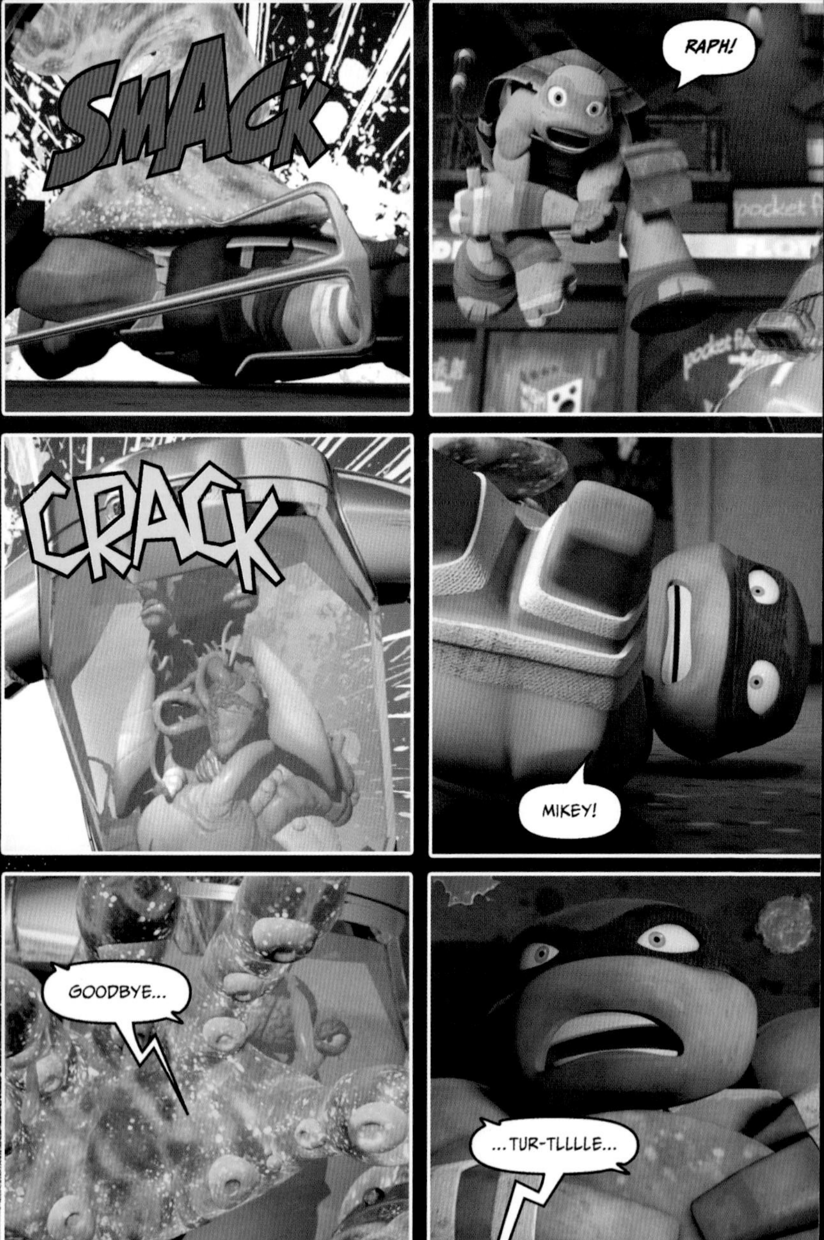
SMACK
RAPH!
CRACK
MIKEY!
GOODBYE...
...TUR-TLLLLE...

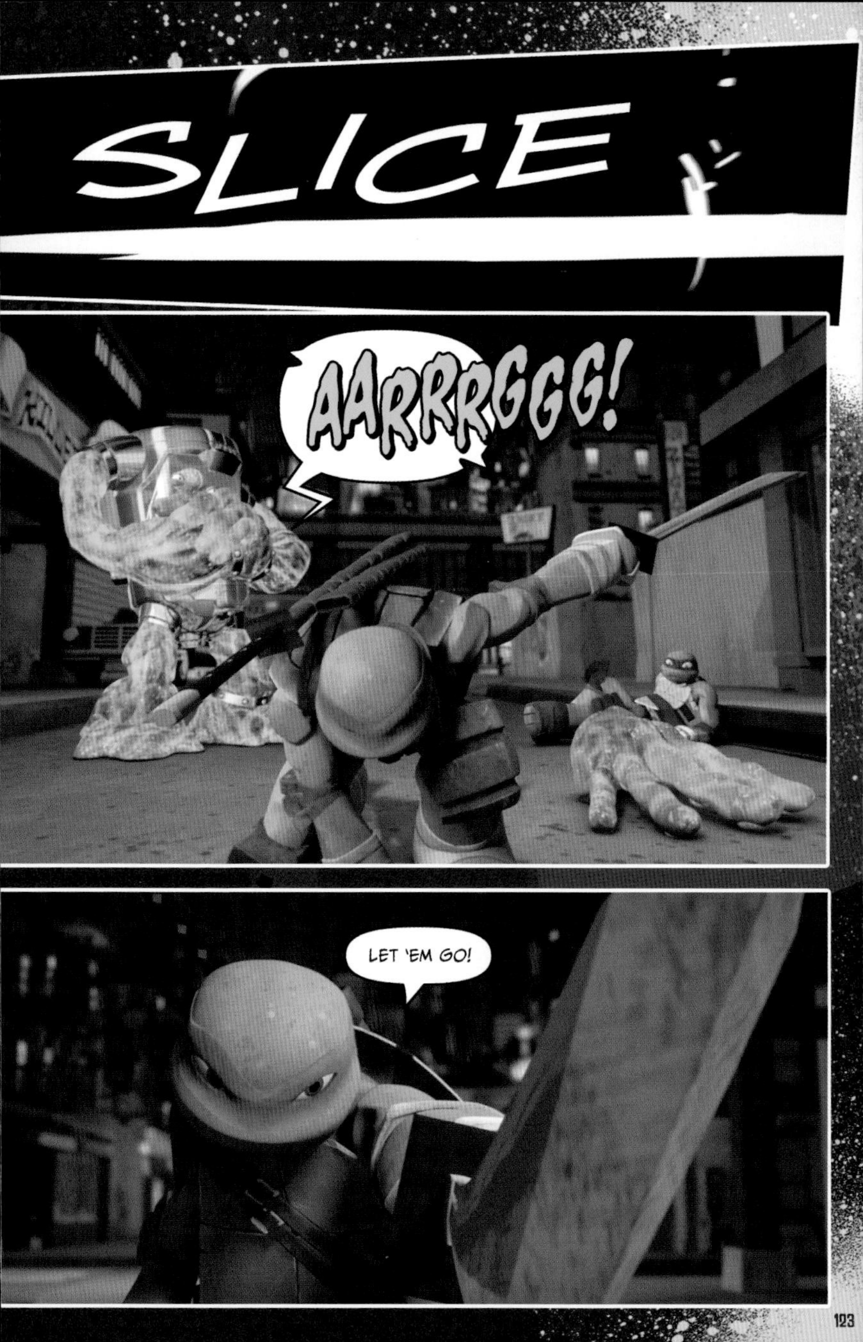
SLICE
AARRRGGG!
LET 'EM GO!

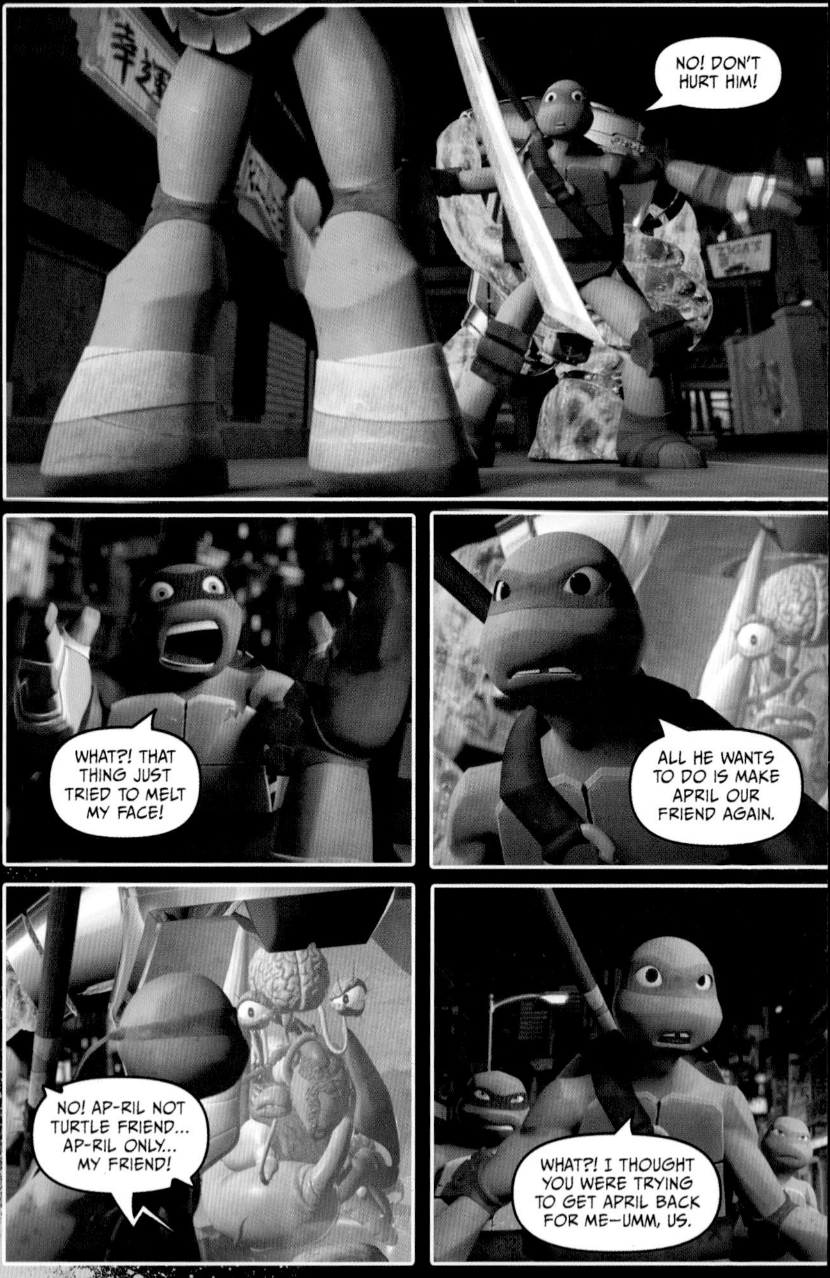
NO! DON'T HURT HIM!
WHAT?! THAT THING JUST TRIED TO MELT MY FACE!
ALL HE WANTS TO DO IS MAKE APRIL OUR FRIEND AGAIN.
NO! AP-RIL NOT TURTLE FRIEND... AP-RIL ONLY... MY FRIEND!
WHAT?! I THOUGHT YOU WERE TRYING TO GET APRIL BACK FOR ME—UMM, US.

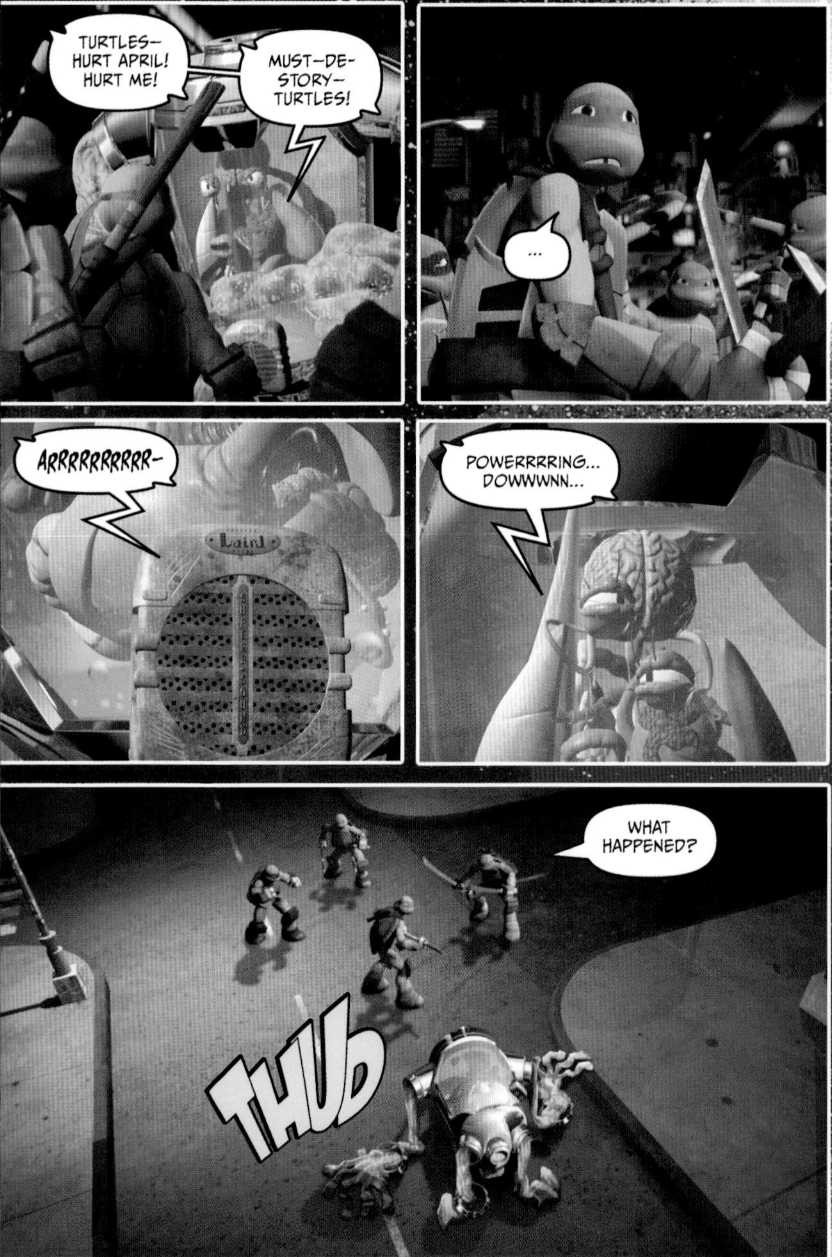
TURTLES— HURT APRIL! HURT ME!
MUST—DE-STORY— TURTLES!
...
ARRRRRRRRR-
POWERRRRING... DOWWWNN...
WHAT HAPPENED?
THUD

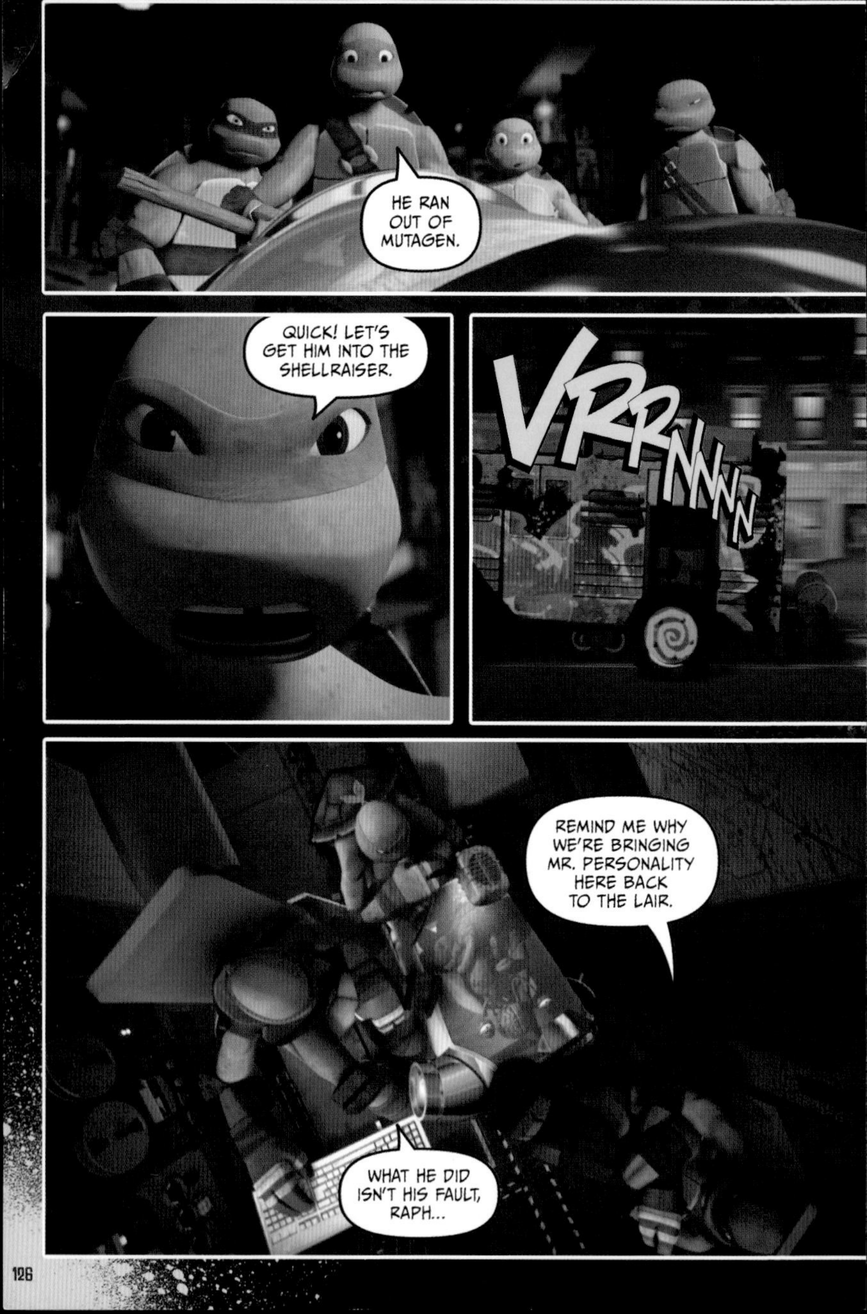
HE RAN OUT OF MUTAGEN.
QUICK! LET'S GET HIM INTO THE SHELLRAISER.
VRRNNNNN
REMIND ME WHY WE'RE BRINGING MR. PERSONALITY HERE BACK TO THE LAIR.
WHAT HE DID ISN'T HIS FAULT, RAPH...

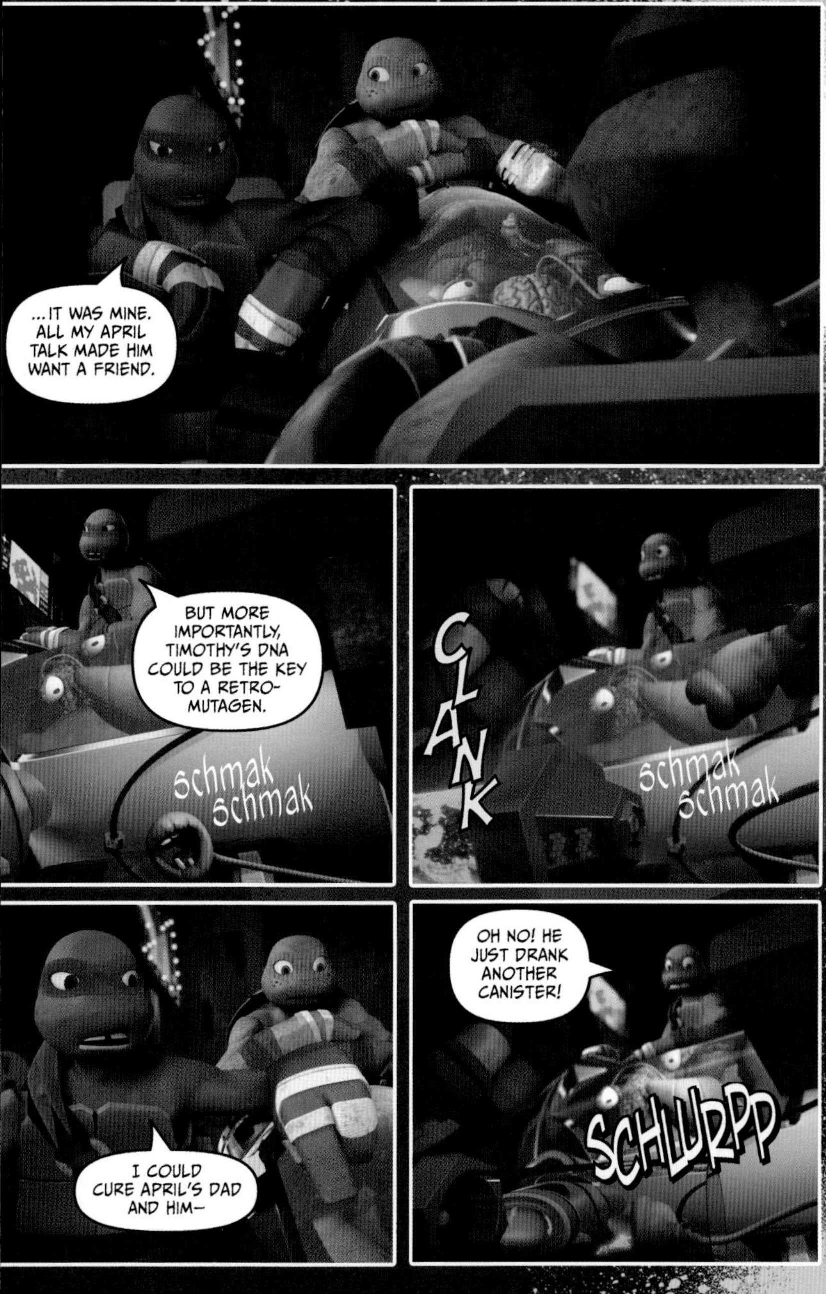
...IT WAS MINE. ALL MY APRIL TALK MADE HIM WANT A FRIEND.
BUT MORE IMPORTANTLY, TIMOTHY'S DNA COULD BE THE KEY TO A RETRO-MUTAGEN.
schmak schmak
CLANK
schmak schmak
I COULD CURE APRIL'S DAD AND HIM—
OH NO! HE JUST DRANK ANOTHER CANISTER!
SCHLURPP

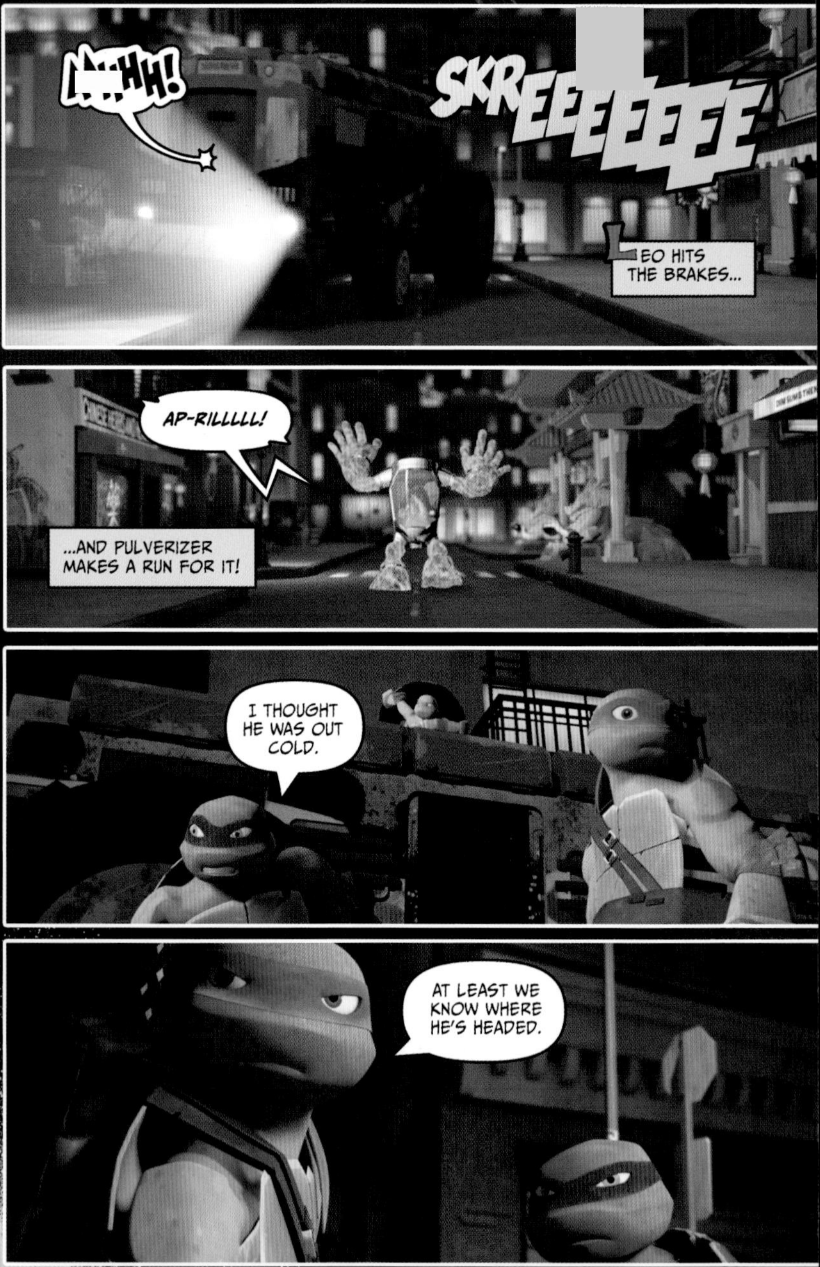
[redacted]HH!
SKREEEEEEEE
LEO HITS THE BRAKES...
AP-RILLLLL!
...AND PULVERIZER MAKES A RUN FOR IT!
I THOUGHT HE WAS OUT COLD.
AT LEAST WE KNOW WHERE HE'S HEADED.

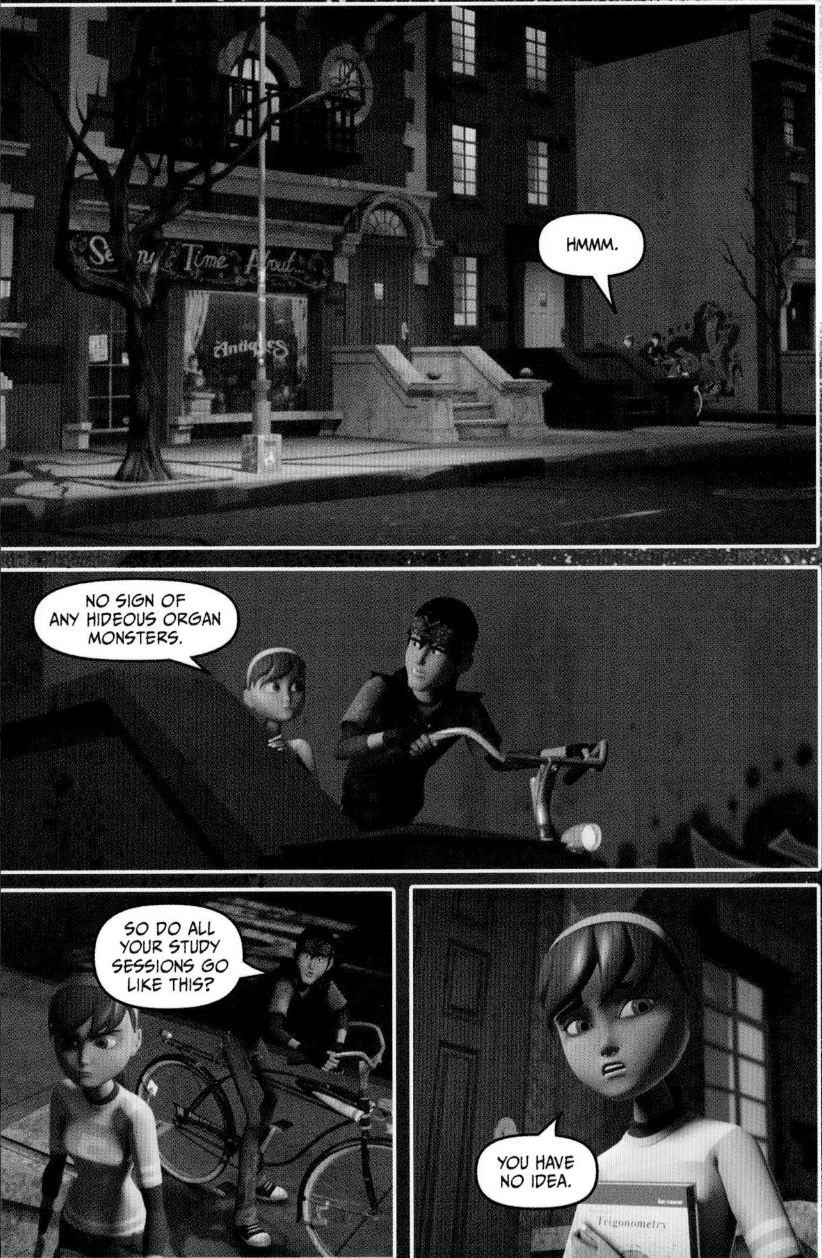
Second Time Around...
Antiques
HMMM.
NO SIGN OF ANY HIDEOUS ORGAN MONSTERS.
SO DO ALL YOUR STUDY SESSIONS GO LIKE THIS?
YOU HAVE NO IDEA.
Trigonometry

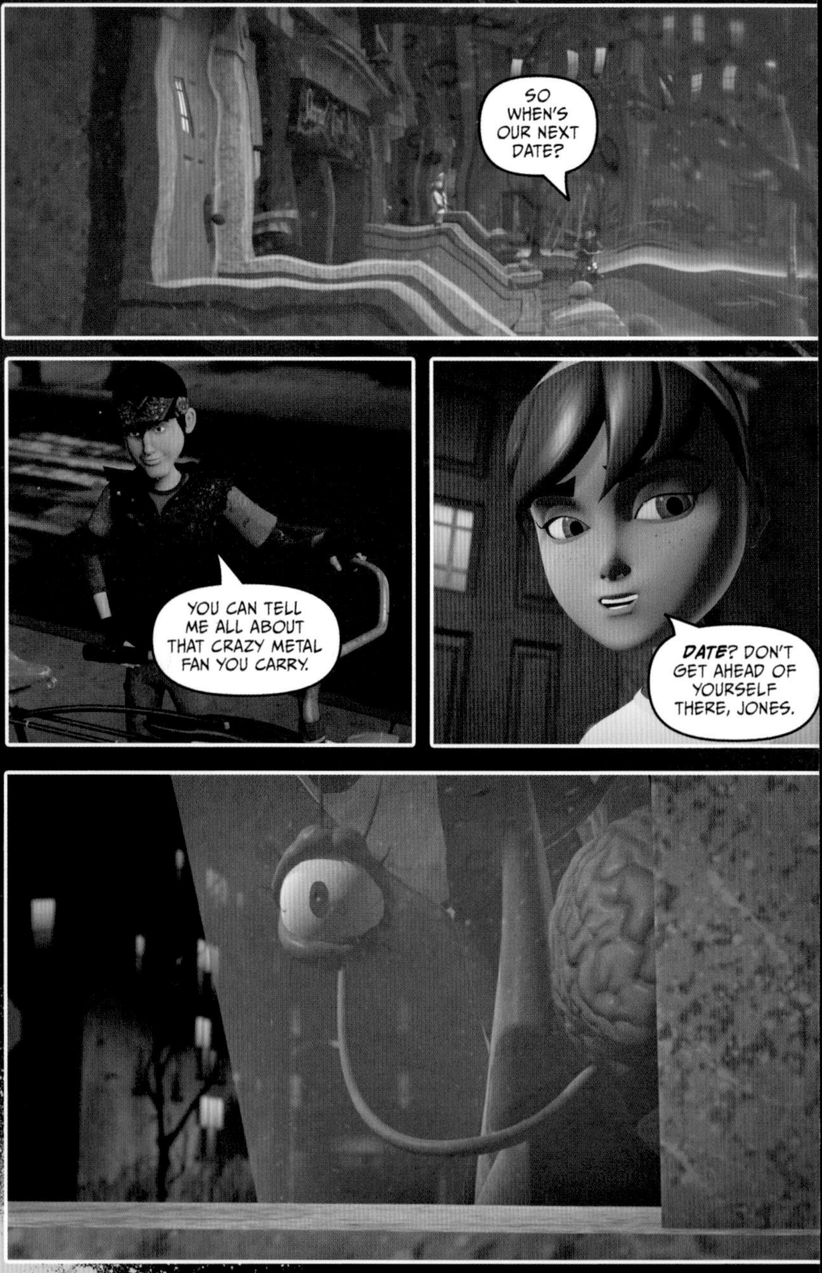
SO WHEN'S OUR NEXT DATE?
YOU CAN TELL ME ALL ABOUT THAT CRAZY METAL FAN YOU CARRY.
DATE? DON'T GET AHEAD OF YOURSELF THERE, JONES.

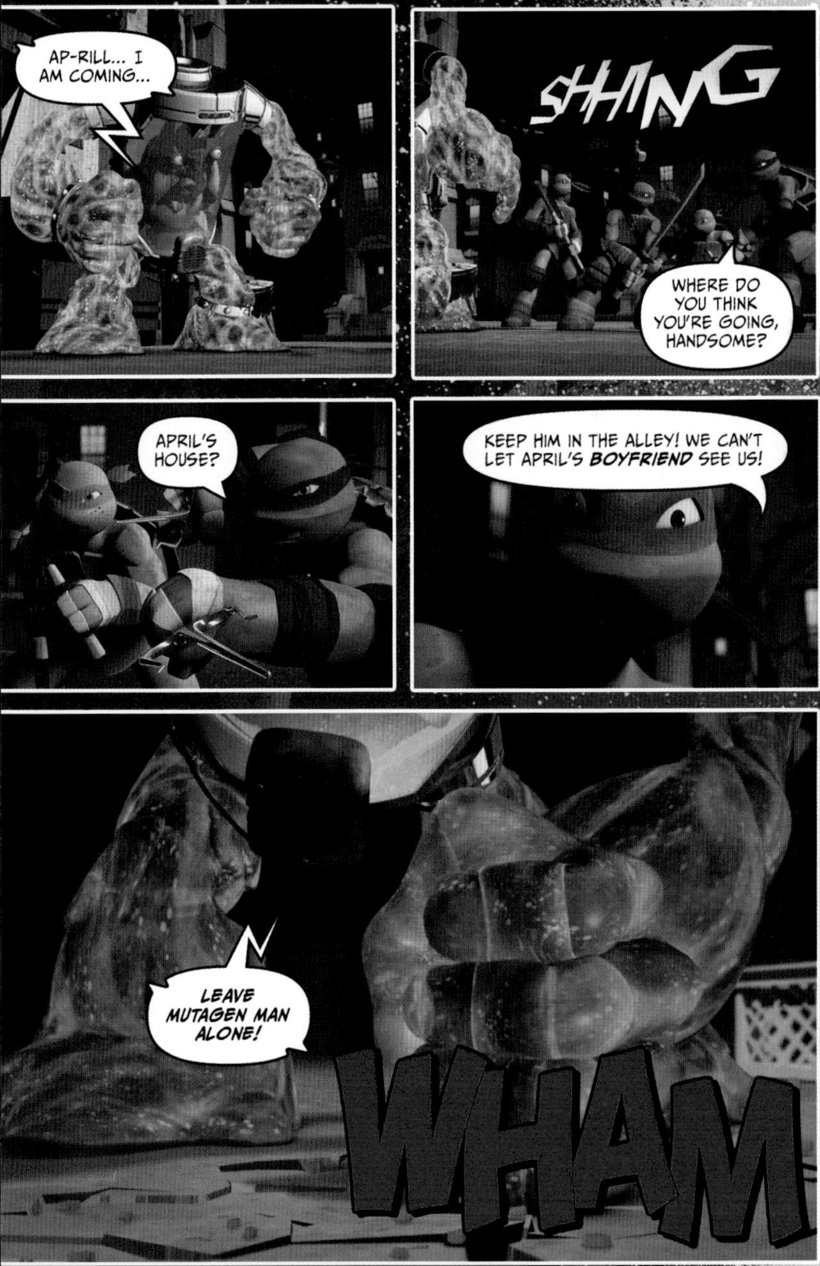
AP-RILL... I AM COMING...
SHHING
WHERE DO YOU THINK YOU'RE GOING, HANDSOME?
APRIL'S HOUSE?
KEEP HIM IN THE ALLEY! WE CAN'T LET APRIL'S BOYFRIEND SEE US!
LEAVE MUTAGEN MAN ALONE!
WHAM

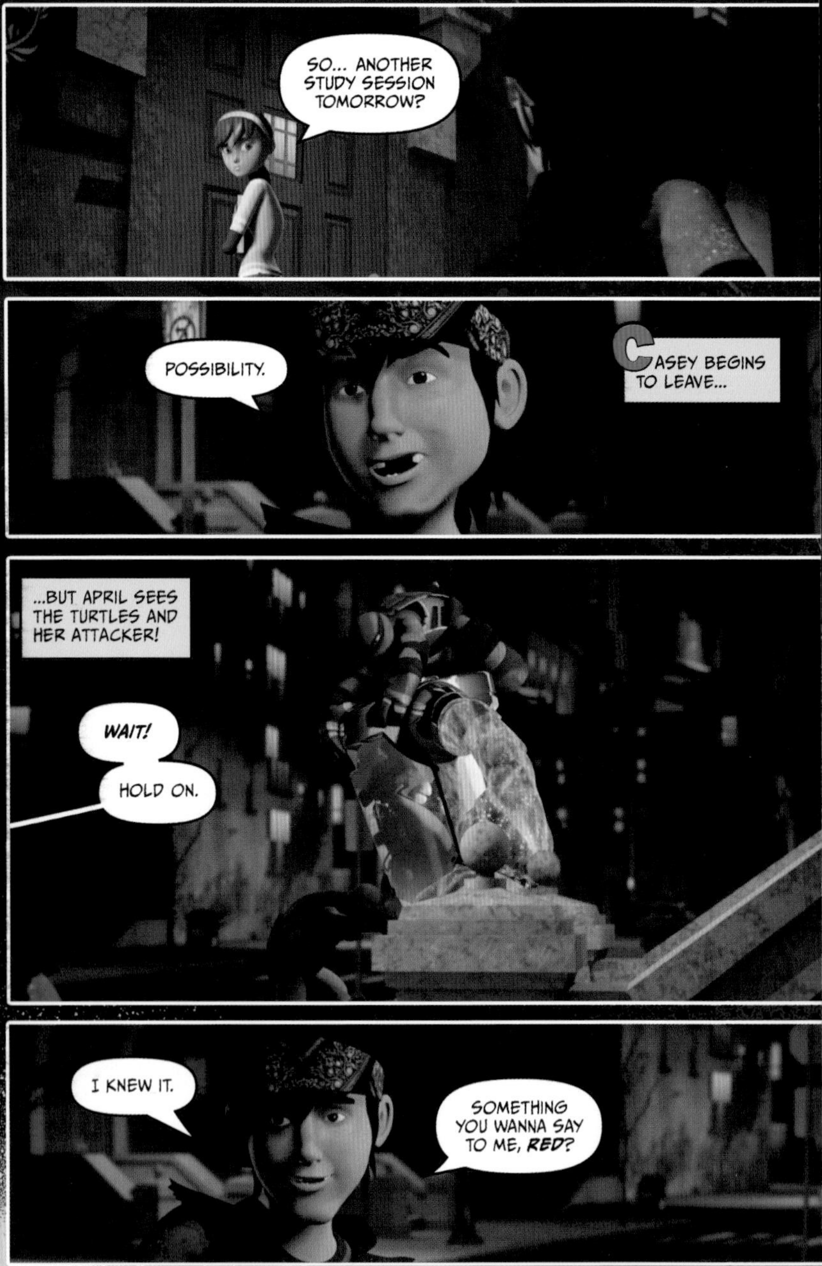
SO... ANOTHER STUDY SESSION TOMORROW?
POSSIBILITY.
CASEY BEGINS TO LEAVE...
...BUT APRIL SEES THE TURTLES AND HER ATTACKER!
WAIT!
HOLD ON.
I KNEW IT.
SOMETHING YOU WANNA SAY TO ME, RED?

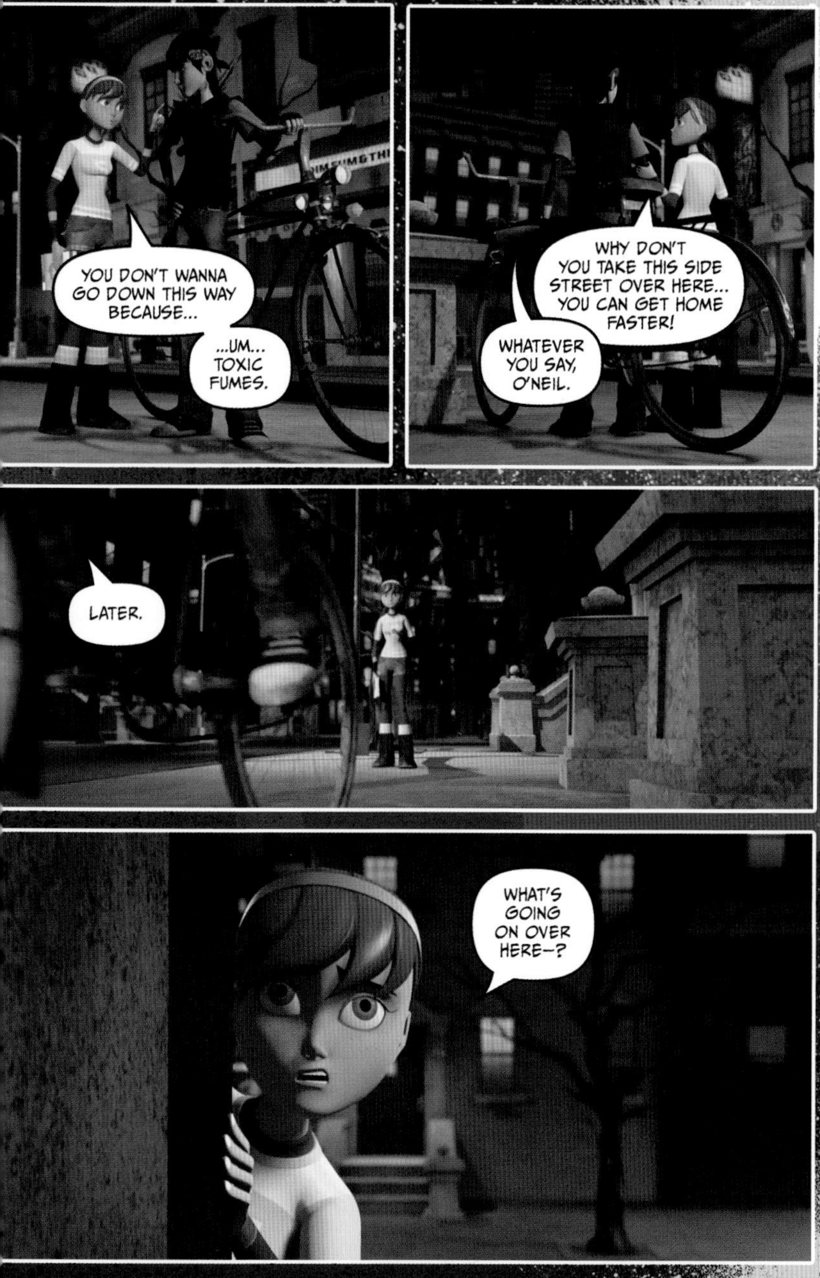
YOU DON'T WANNA GO DOWN THIS WAY BECAUSE...
...UM... TOXIC FUMES.
WHY DON'T YOU TAKE THIS SIDE STREET OVER HERE... YOU CAN GET HOME FASTER!
WHATEVER YOU SAY, O'NEIL.
LATER.
WHAT'S GOING ON OVER HERE–?

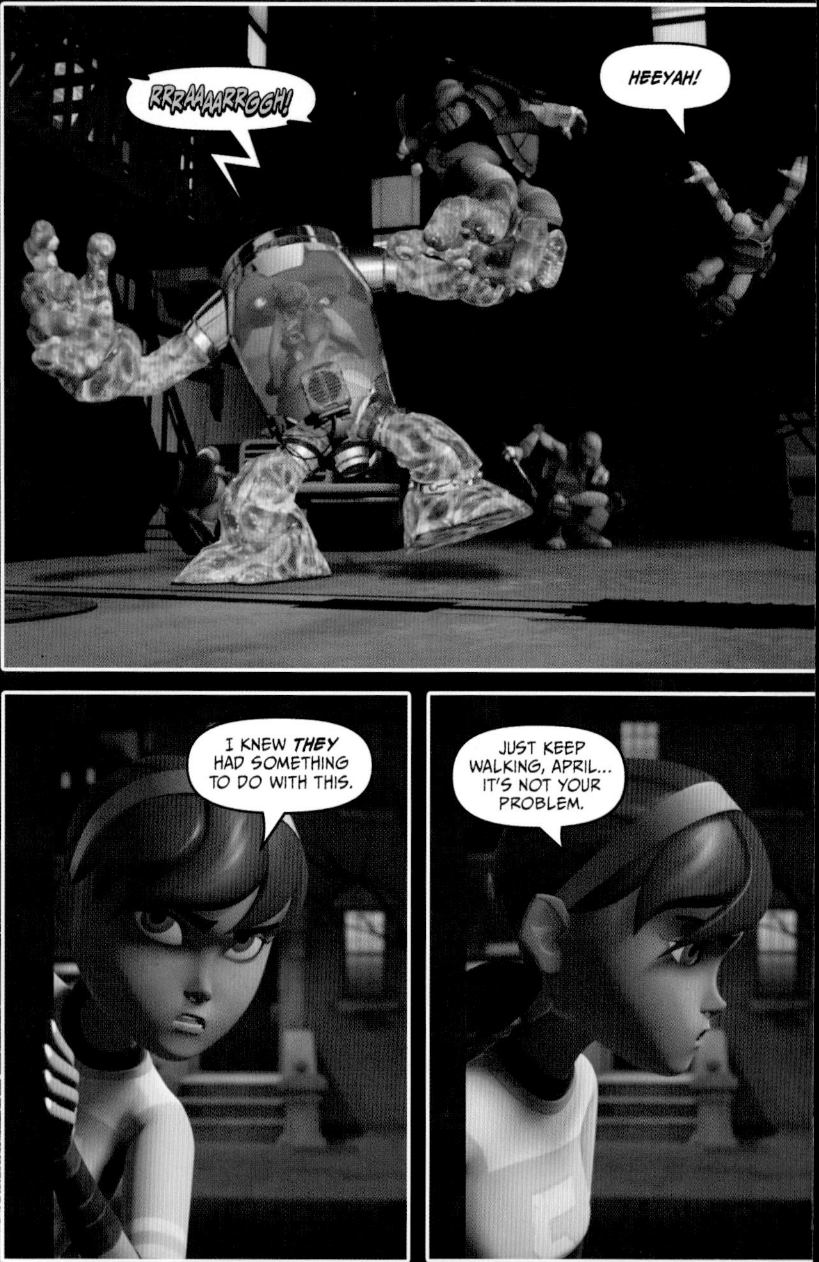
RRRAAAARRGGH!
HEEYAH!
I KNEW *THEY* HAD SOMETHING TO DO WITH THIS.
JUST KEEP WALKING, APRIL... IT'S NOT YOUR PROBLEM.

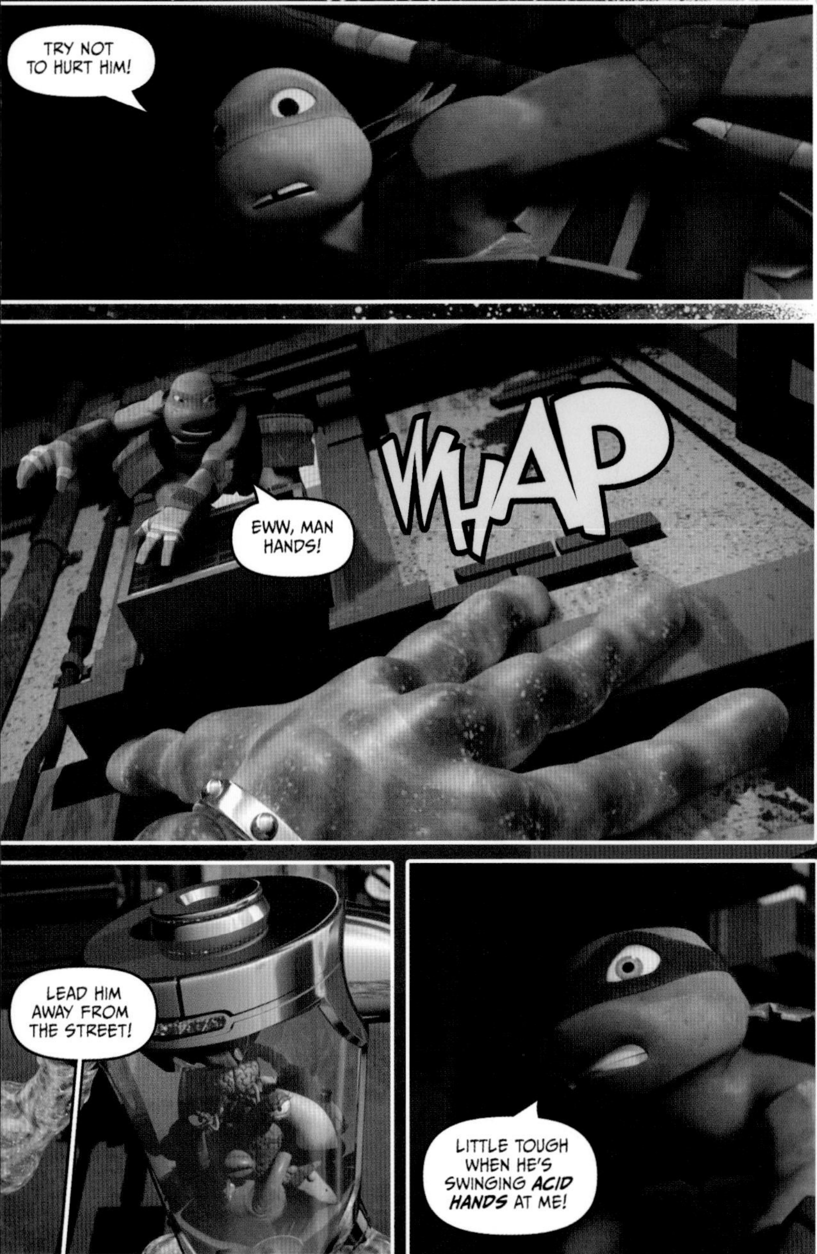
TRY NOT
TO HURT HIM!
WHAP
EWW, MAN
HANDS!
LEAD HIM
AWAY FROM
THE STREET!
LITTLE TOUGH
WHEN HE'S
SWINGING *ACID*
HANDS AT ME!

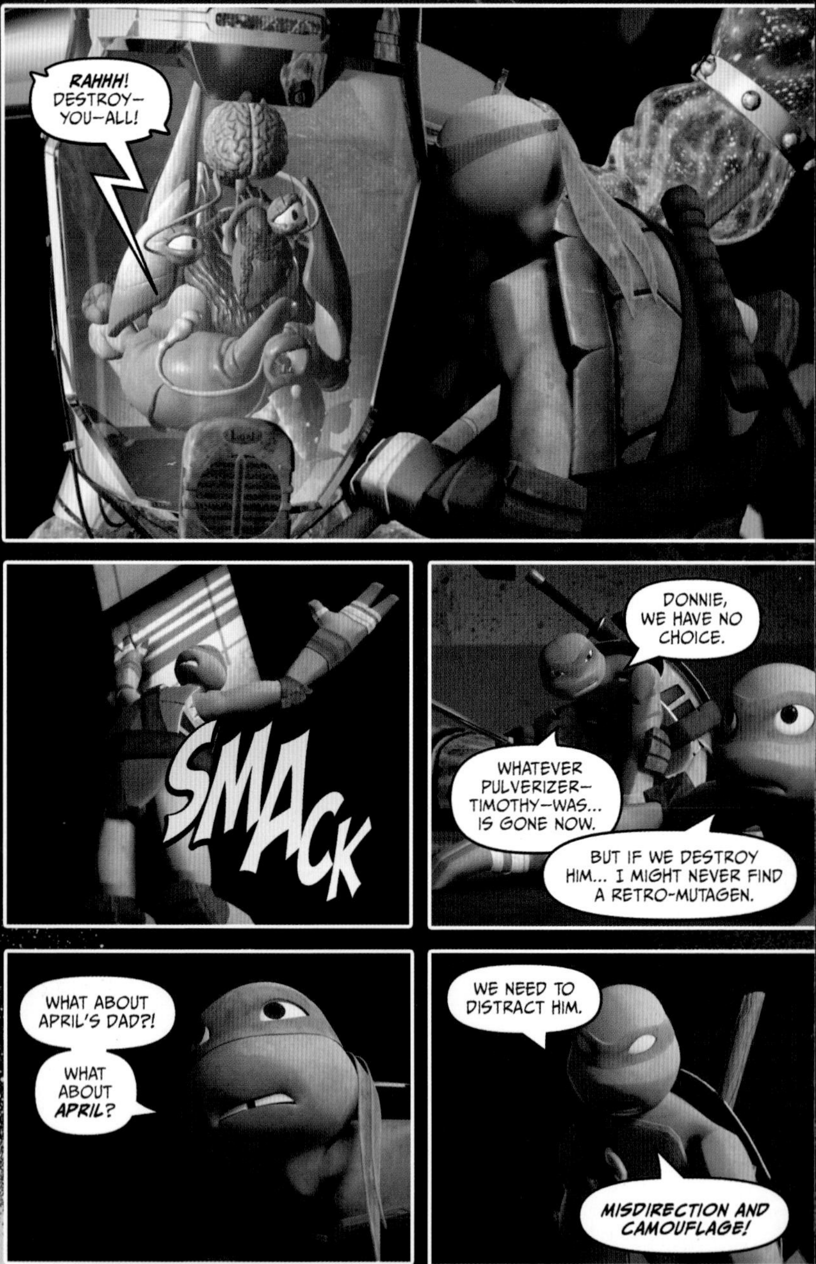
RAHHH! DESTROY—YOU—ALL!
SMACK
DONNIE, WE HAVE NO CHOICE.
WHATEVER PULVERIZER—TIMOTHY—WAS... IS GONE NOW.
BUT IF WE DESTROY HIM... I MIGHT NEVER FIND A RETRO-MUTAGEN.
WHAT ABOUT APRIL'S DAD?!
WHAT ABOUT APRIL?
WE NEED TO DISTRACT HIM.
MISDIRECTION AND CAMOUFLAGE!

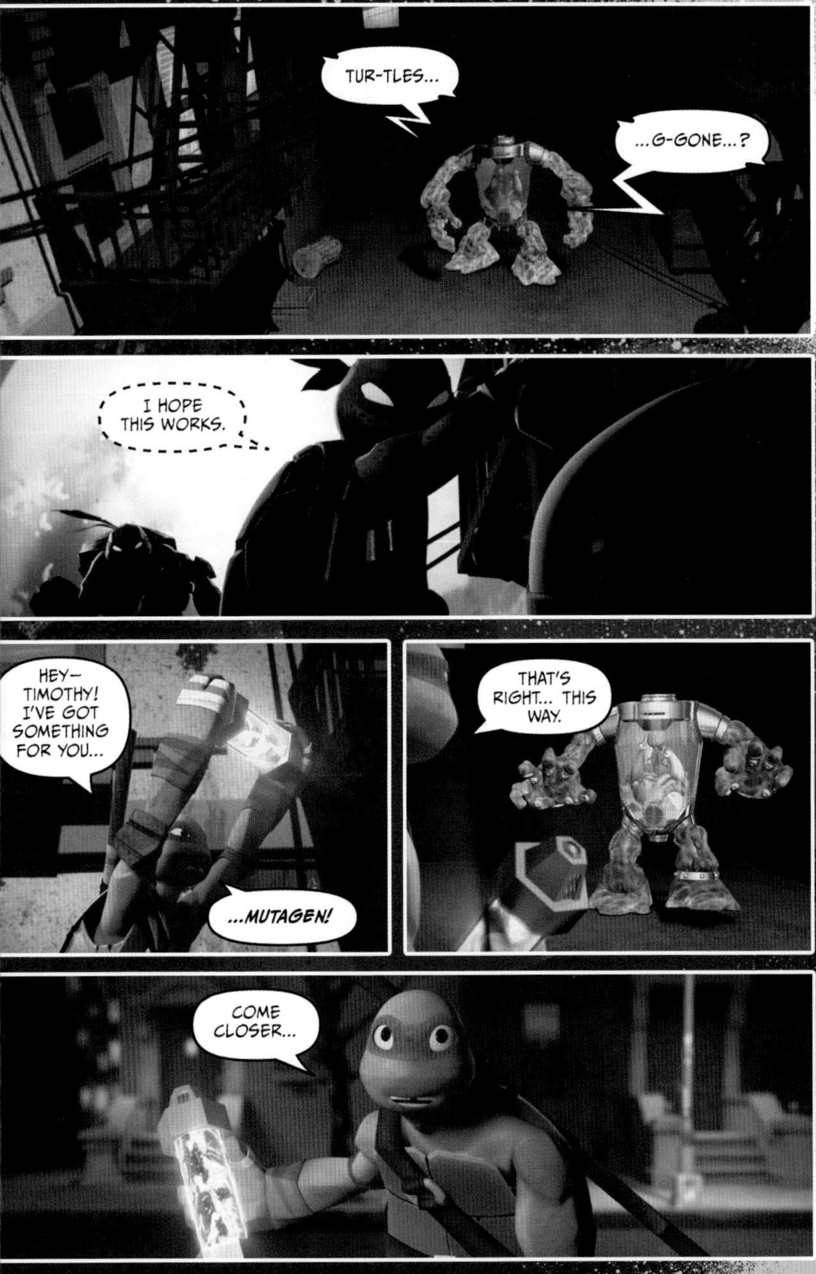
TUR-TLES...
...G-GONE...?
I HOPE THIS WORKS.
HEY— TIMOTHY! I'VE GOT SOMETHING FOR YOU...
...MUTAGEN!
THAT'S RIGHT... THIS WAY.
COME CLOSER...

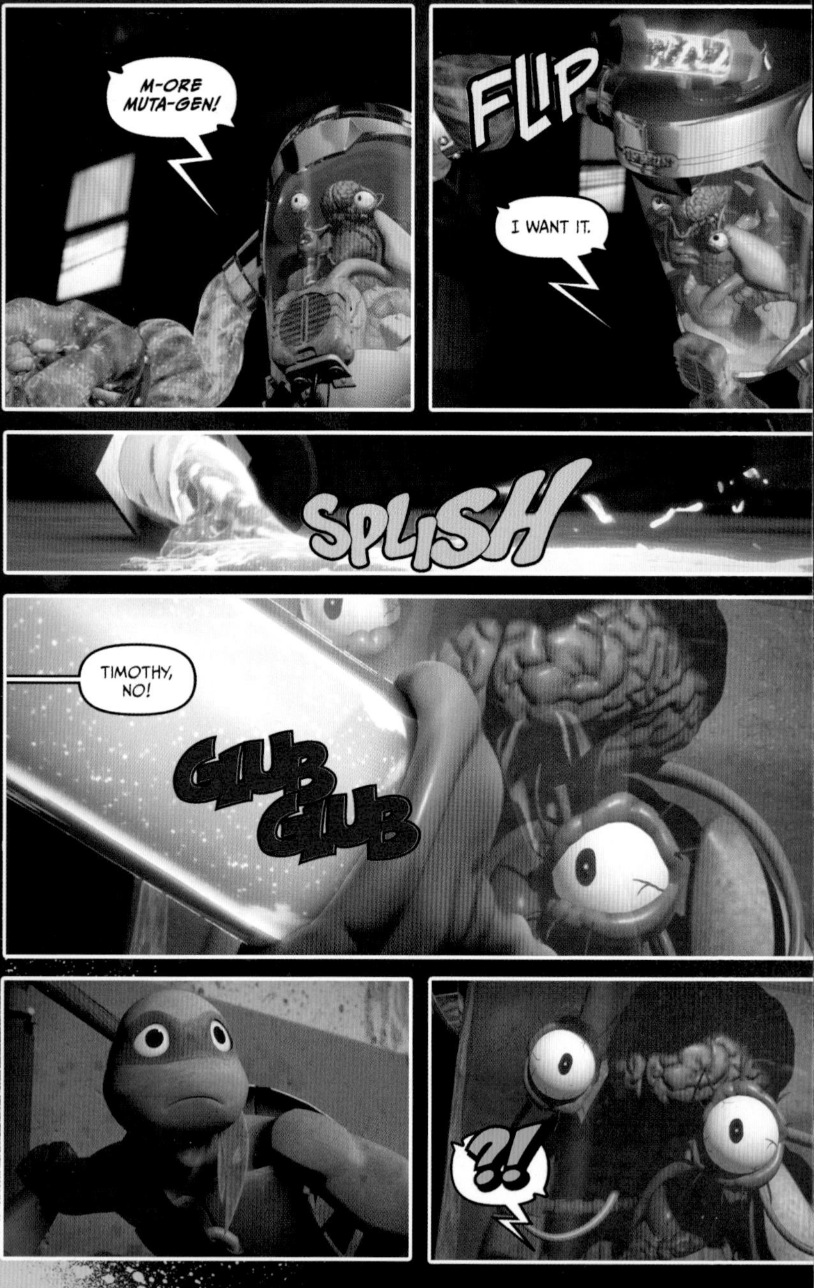
M-ORE MUTA-GEN!
FLIP
I WANT IT.
SPLISH
TIMOTHY, NO!
GLUB GLUB
?!

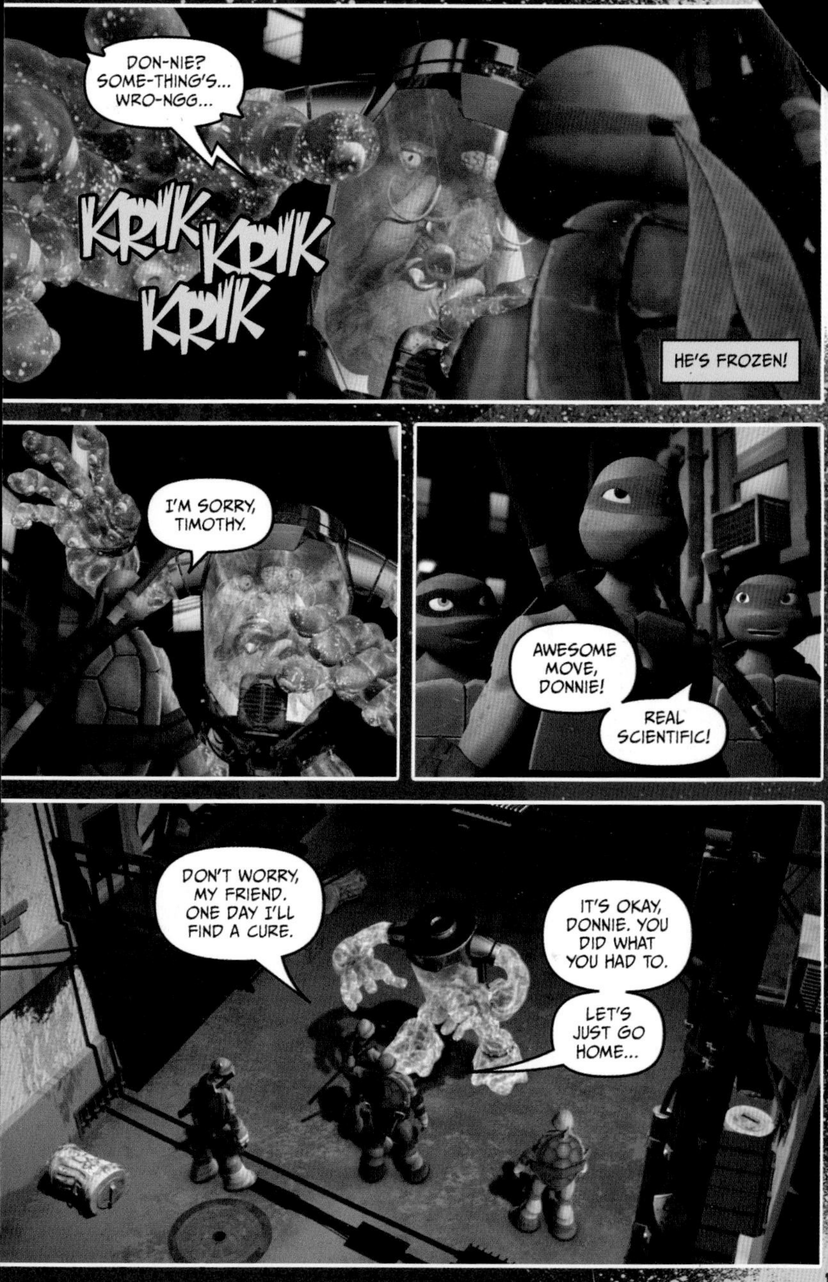
DON-NIE? SOME-THING'S... WRO-NGG...
KRIK KRIK KRIK
HE'S FROZEN!
I'M SORRY, TIMOTHY.
AWESOME MOVE, DONNIE!
REAL SCIENTIFIC!
DON'T WORRY, MY FRIEND. ONE DAY I'LL FIND A CURE.
IT'S OKAY, DONNIE. YOU DID WHAT YOU HAD TO.
LET'S JUST GO HOME...

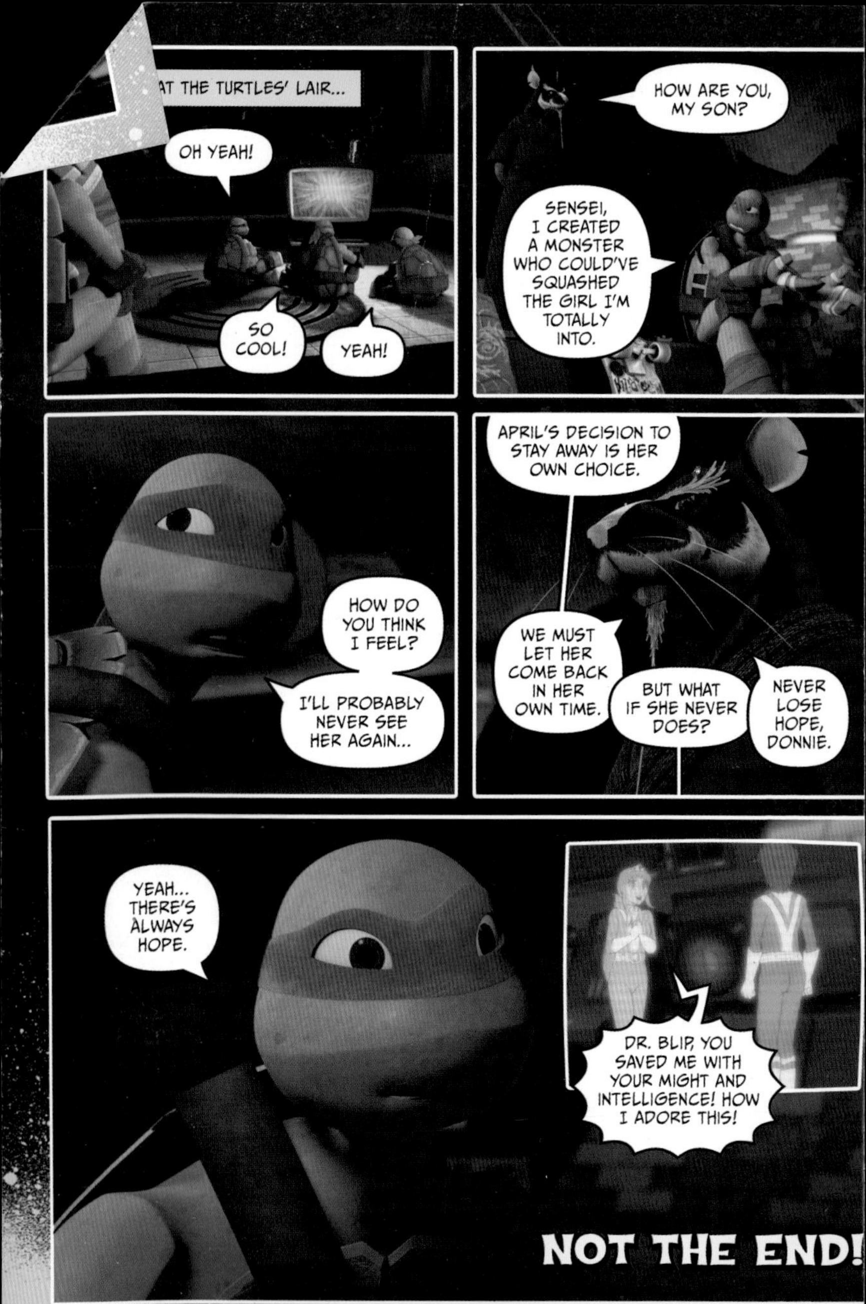
AT THE TURTLES' LAIR...
OH YEAH!
SO COOL!
YEAH!
HOW ARE YOU, MY SON?
SENSEI, I CREATED A MONSTER WHO COULD'VE SQUASHED THE GIRL I'M TOTALLY INTO.
HOW DO YOU THINK I FEEL?
I'LL PROBABLY NEVER SEE HER AGAIN...
APRIL'S DECISION TO STAY AWAY IS HER OWN CHOICE.
WE MUST LET HER COME BACK IN HER OWN TIME.
BUT WHAT IF SHE NEVER DOES?
NEVER LOSE HOPE, DONNIE.
YEAH... THERE'S ALWAYS HOPE.
DR. BLIP, YOU SAVED ME WITH YOUR MIGHT AND INTELLIGENCE! HOW I ADORE THIS!
NOT THE END!